BEAUTIFUL
GHOSTS

Also by Eliot Pattison

Skull Mantra

Water Touching Stone

Bone Mountain

BEAUTIFUL
GHOSTS

Eliot
Pattison

St. Martin's Minotaur
New York

www.minotaurbooks.com

Library of Congress Cataloging-in-Publication Data

Pattison, Eliot.
    Beautiful ghosts / Eliot Pattison.
        p. cm.
    ISBN 0-312-27759-8 (hc)
    ISBN 0-312-33509-1 (pbk)
    EAN 978-0312-33509-0
    1. Shan, Tao Yun (Fictitious character)—Fiction. 2. Monasteries,
Buddhist—Fiction. 3. Ex-police officers—Fiction. 4. Tibet (China)—Fiction.
I. Title.

PS3566.A82497B43 2004
813'.54—dc22   2003062543

10 9 8 7

This book is dedicated to the memory of
Patrick J. Head, lama lawyer.

Acknowledgments

Special thanks to Natasha Kern, Keith Kahla, Catherine Pattison, and Lesley Kellas Payne.

PART ONE

CHAPTER ONE

There are sounds in Tibet heard nowhere else in the world. Hollow moans inexplicably roll down the slopes of snowcapped peaks. Rumbles like thunder course through valleys under cloudless skies. On moonlit nights in the mountain wilderness Shan Tao Yun had heard tiny ringing tones floating down from the stars.

At first, lying on his gulag prison bunk, Shan had felt fear at hearing such eerie sounds. Later he had decided they had to be the workings of the thin, high altitude atmosphere and the wind, of shifting ice formations and temperature changes between summits and valleys, had concluded there were scientific explanations. But after five years Shan was no longer certain. After so long in Tibet, he had abandoned most of his prior beliefs about the workings of the world.

Certainly the wrenching sound that now rose across the bowl in the mountains could have no explanation in the physical world. A young woman standing near Shan groaned, clapped her hands to her ears, and ran away. The first time he had heard the sound that came from the red-robed man sitting thirty feet away, Shan, too, had shuddered and wanted to flee. Throat chanting, the monks called the strange grinding moan, but Shan preferred the description used by his old friend and former cellmate Lokesh. Soul rattling, Lokesh called what Surya, the old monk, was doing, explaining that in the world below, souls were often so undeveloped that the only time the sound was heard was in those near death as the soul struggled for release. But in Tibet no one spoke in fearful tones of the death rattle. Here the sound was for the living. Here the devout had learned to make souls speak without tongues.

Shan watched the woman retreat with a pang of sorrow. It was a day of great joy, but one of even greater danger. The outlaw monks Shan lived with, who for decades had remained hidden in their secret hermitage, had decided not only to reveal themselves to the hill people but to lead the strangers in illegal rituals. This would be a day of wonderful surprises, Gendun, their senior lama, had declared, one of the days when the world was changed.

Shan had warned the monks about the danger of bringing these particular Tibetans to the ruined monastery. Gendun had replied by dropping onto one knee and turning over a pebble, invoking a teaching the monks sometimes used. The world could be changed by the subtlest of actions, so long as it was pure, and even the smallest of actions was pure so long as it was free of fear and anger. But these herders had been conditioned by fear all their lives.

Beijing had dealt harshly with the people of the rugged lands of southern Lhadrung County, who had stubbornly resisted the Chinese occupation long after Beijing's army had seized Lhasa. The ruins they now stood among were all that remained of Zhoka *gompa,* the monastery that for centuries had served the people living south of the county's central valley. Forty years earlier it had been attacked from the air by the People's Liberation Army, one of the thousands of gompas annihilated by Beijing. The brave, devout people who had futilely tried to defend Zhoka and the way of life it represented had been dispersed, destroyed, or simply hollowed out.

"We'll be arrested!" a woman in a tattered red vest had warned when Shan and Lokesh had met them on the grassy ridge above and motioned them to descend toward the half-mile-wide tract of ruined buildings.

"It's haunted!" another herder had protested as Lokesh had stepped into the maze of crumbling stone walls. "Even the living become like ghosts here!"

But when Lokesh kept walking, singing an old pilgrim's song, the man fell in behind his companions to enter the ruins. They had followed in an uneasy silence until they had emerged in what had been the gompa's central courtyard.

"A miracle!" the woman in the red vest had gasped as she clutched at an old woman beside her and gazed at the ten-foot-high shrine, obviously newly constructed, which stood in the center of the yard. The two women advanced hesitantly, watching Surya, who sat in front of the shrine. They touched the brilliant white structure, skeptical at first, as if not believing their eyes, then reverently sat before the monk. Others had slowly followed, some touching strings of beads that hung from their belts.

But now, as Surya's throat chant began, several of the hill people retreated toward the shadows. Those who remained seemed paralyzed by the sound, staring wide-eyed as Surya joyfully threw his head back, still chanting.

"Godkiller!" The shout came from nowhere and everywhere, echoing off the ruined walls. A stone flew past Shan's shoulder and bounced off Surya's knee. "Murderer!" the same fearful voice cried. The monk's chant faltered, then stopped as he stared at the stone that had been aimed at him.

"Godkiller!" As the word was repeated Shan spun about to see a short, leathery-faced man in the tattered clothes of a herder, pointing at Surya with rage in his eyes.

By the time the herder raised another stone Shan was at his side, clamping a hand around the man's wrist. The man resisted, twisting his hand, pushing Shan. "Flee for your lives! The murderers!" the herder cried out to the others who lingered in the yard.

A tall, lean Tibetan, a stubble of white hair on his scalp and jaw, appeared at the man's other side and the herder, studying him uncertainly, stopped moving. Lokesh pried open the herder's fingers, letting fall the pebbles they held. "Surya is a monk," he said quietly. "He is the opposite of a godkiller."

"No," the herder growled as Surya's chant started anew. It was not anger, but despair that now filled the man's eyes. "The government puts men in robes to trick us, to get us to act out the old ways, then they arrest us, or worse."

"Not here," Lokesh said. "Not today."

The man shook his head then, as though to refute the old Tibetan, gestured into the shadows between the crumbling stone walls behind him.

A woman appeared, her hands behind her, gripping two corners of a rolled blanket. Two boys, the oldest no more than ten, walked behind her, solemnly carrying the other end of the long burden inside the blanket, their eyes gaunt and weary. As the three reached the herder they lowered their heavy load, the boys darting to the woman, burying their heads in her heavy felt skirt, the youngest releasing a long, silent sob.

As Lokesh knelt and slowly pulled back an edge of the blanket, a hoarse groan escaped his throat.

It was an old man with a thin, wispy beard. His left ear hung loose where it had been nearly ripped away, the left side of his face was caked with blood and sagging where his cheek and jawbones had been ravaged. His lifeless eyes seemed to look up at the sky in question.

"They beat him to death," the herder declared in a low whisper, still eyeing Shan and Lokesh warily. "Just beat him and left him like that."

Shan bent and pulled the blanket down. Both the man's legs appeared to be broken, one turned at an unnatural angle, the other bloody at a tear in his trousers that exposed a piece of bone. "Who would do such a thing?" he asked, looking at the empty brown eyes.

"His name was Atso," the herder said. "Over eighty years old. He lived alone in a hut at the base of a cliff two miles to the east, toward the valley." The herder's eyes filled with pain and he paused for a moment, as if struggling to control his emotions. "Of all the people in the hills he was the one who knew most about the old ways."

"Someone killed him for following the old ways?" Shan asked.

The herder shrugged. "They kill for a word in these hills," he said in a hollow, matter-of-fact tone that sent a chill down Shan's spine. The man extracted a knife from his belt and with the blade pushed a twig of heather from Atso's hair. The Tibetans were loath to touch the dead. "The only way he would let strangers near him would be if one wore a robe," he said in an accusing tone, casting a worried glance toward the woman and boys, who moved toward the throat chanting. "Murderers are among us," he whispered.

The words caused Shan to look toward the ridge above the ruined gompa. In a patch of summer flowers sat a solitary figure, a slender woman in black, scanning the landscape with binoculars. Liya, one of the few hill people who secretly helped the monks, was keeping watch.

"Prayers must be spoken," Lokesh declared.

"No," the herder shot back. "We have no rites in these hills. That's how people get arrested."

"But you came today," Lokesh pointed out.

"That woman up there," the herder said, gesturing toward Liya, "she rode a horse from camp to camp, saying in front of my family that a miracle was going to happen here today. How could I say no to Liya with the children listening? They were even singing on the way this morning. They never sing. Then we found Atso lying like that near his hut."

It wasn't the herder's description of events that pained him the most, Shan realized, but the way his despair was somehow devoid of emotion, as if all his grief had long ago been used up.

"And now a man in a robe waits to trap us," the herder added. "The way of godkillers."

The expression tore at something inside Shan each time it was spoken. "Why would you use such a terrible word?" he asked.

With his blade the herder lifted a small sack from the side of the corpse. As Shan took it and upended its contents onto the blanket another mournful cry left Lokesh's lips. It was a small, delicate silver statue of Tara, the protective goddess, perfect in every respect except that her head had been flattened, destroyed by a violent blow. The herder prodded the statue over with the blade. The goddess's back had been split open, as if she had been stabbed from behind.

The devastated statue seemed to upset Lokesh even more than the dead man. The old Tibetan picked up the broken goddess, cradling her in his arms a moment, his eyes glistening with moisture, before laying her back beside the battered corpse, whispering to her all the while. Shan could not hear the words, but the sorrow in his friend's voice was unmistakable.

When Lokesh looked up again he gazed at the herder with an unexpected determination. He slowly rose and took the herder's arm, leading him a few steps to where they could see Surya again. Lokesh would not let the herder's fears destroy the festival.

"Listen to that sound he makes. Look at that *chorten*," the herder said, referring to the shrine. "If he's not from the government he is a sorcerer. I bring my sheep to these hills every spring. It was never there before. Built by ghosts."

Built by ghosts. Shan and Lokesh exchanged a glance. In a way the man was right. For the monks of Yerpa, the hidden hermitage where Shan and Lokesh lived, had built the small elegant structure by moonlight, with one monk always praying as the others constructed the tiered foundation and its bell-shaped spire. It was to be a monument to the ruined gompa, a sign that the deities had not entirely forgotten the local people.

"Ghosts and murderers, and Liya makes me bring my family here."

"I'll tell you a secret," Lokesh whispered, an unusual edge of emotion in his voice. Shan knew how it pained his old friend to see the people of the hills react to them with such suspicion and distrust. Lokesh closed his eyes a moment as if to calm himself. They were on the brink of disaster, Shan realized. A few more words from the herder to the other Tibetans and they would all flee, some perhaps spreading word of killers, but others of illegal monks, which would bring soldiers into the mountains.

Lokesh pulled out the silver amulet box, the *gau*, he wore around his neck and carefully opened it. It was an extraordinary thing to do with a stranger, and the action quieted the man. Inside the gau, under several small folded pieces of paper which Lokesh emptied into his hand, was a tiny photograph of a bald monk wearing spectacles, his face serene but laughter in his eyes. "That monk who chants," Lokesh explained, "his name is Surya. He comes from high in the mountains, not the world below. And inside his gau he also carries a picture of the Dalai Lama." He pointed with a gnarled finger to the photograph. "Have you truly forgotten what today is?"

The man's brow furrowed and he pressed his palm tightly against his temple, as if in sudden pain. He stared at Lokesh, then Surya, and the fear in his eyes slowly waned, replaced by a sad confusion. He reached into his shirt and extracted a prayer box that hung around his own neck. "I have one of those. My father wore it, and his father." He stared at his small, elegant silver gau. "But it's empty," he added in a haunting tone. "When I was a boy my teacher burned what was inside." The words seemed to remind him of the dangers in the hills, and he glanced back at Atso's body. "His murderer is out there, stalking old Tibetans. You must flee, too. In town they say there's a bounty on someone's head. Soldiers are searching. We have to..." His voice faded as his gaze returned to Lokesh.

"What old Tibetans?" Shan asked in alarm. "Who has a bounty..." His own words drifted away as he glanced back at Lokesh.

With a fingernail the old Tibetan was slowly prying the photograph from his gau. As the herder watched in disbelief Lokesh placed the photo in the man's own prayer box. "We will ask Surya to write a prayer for it, to keep by your heart," he said.

The herder's jaw opened and shut several times as if was struggling to find words. "You truly mean it, that he is a real monk?" Emotion flooded the man's face. Confusion, but also gratitude, then awe and pain. "My name is Jara," the man whispered, not taking his eyes off Surya now. "In all my life I have never seen a monk, except the ones who visit from Lhasa once a year with the Bureau of Religious Affairs. They make speeches, not prayers. The children never..." The words choked in his throat.

"It's too dangerous for a real monk," he continued in an urgent voice. "If he's a real monk, here, then he's an outlaw. Those soldiers will take him to that prison in the valley. He must cover his robe. Please, for all of us, cover his robe. You have no idea how terrible that prison is."

Lokesh grinned and rolled up his sleeve. The herder stared in confusion, until his gaze fell upon the long line of numbers tattooed on the old Tibetan's forearm.

"You were there?" the herder asked with an anguished groan. "You were a prisoner and still you risk doing this?"

Lokesh pointed to an old cracked metal brazier by the chorten, a ceremonial *samkang,* where a small juniper fire burned. "The fragrant smoke attracts the deities. They will protect us. You'll see."

Shan glanced back toward Liya, still perched high on the hill. Not everyone relied on the deities for protection. She was watching the west, toward the garrison at Lhadrung Valley, and surely would have called out if she had seen soldiers.

"That song he makes," Jara said, gesturing to Surya. "Is that what monks do?"

Lokesh shrugged. "It's part of the celebration. He has found his serenity and is rejoicing," he added as he exchanged an uncertain glance with Shan. The day before at Yerpa they had found Surya destroying a painting of a god he had worked on for weeks. He had not acknowledged them when they had asked why, only silently slashed at the cloth, had not spoken to anyone since. But now the chanting appeared to have brought back the joyful Surya they both knew.

The words seemed to heighten Jara's anxiety. He nervously looked back toward the slopes. "Tibetans don't celebrate in Lhadrung, unless it is a Chinese holiday. This is Colonel Tan's county," he added with a shudder, referring to the iron-fisted officer who ran the county, one of the few still under military rule.

"No. You are at Zhoka now," Lokesh said, as if the windswept bowl constituted a different place, a sanctuary not part of Tan's county. "There is so much to be thankful for."

Jara surveyed the ruined gompa, without a single building left intact, and the frightened, impoverished group of Tibetans in the courtyard, then looked at Lokesh as if the old man were crazy. "I know what day it is," he said, whispering again. "A man with a tea shop in town was arrested for marking this day on the calendar in his window."

"Then call it something else. A festival, because the monks have returned."

Jara swept his arm toward the ruins that filled the barren landscape. "From where? From the dead? In the country I live in monks don't return unless the Bureau of Religious Affairs says so."

"Then call it a festival for the choice."

"Choice?"

Lokesh gazed somberly at Jara, then at his gau. "From this day forward you can choose the place you live in."

The herder gave a dry, bitter laugh. As he looked at the old Tibetan, Lokesh's features became distant, as if looking past Jara's eyes, into another part of him. The herder soberly returned the stare then tentatively raised his hand as though to touch the taller Tibetan's white stubbled jaw, the way the others, disbelieving, had first touched the chorten.

"You will change forever the country you live in," Lokesh said softly, "by taking back a prayer in your gau." As he spoke another figure in a robe appeared, a tall, graceful man with a face worn smooth as a cobblestone. Gendun, the head of Yerpa, the hidden hermitage that was home to Surya and Shan and Lokesh, looked serenely at Jara, then gazed with a sad smile at Atso's body. *"Lha gyal lo,"* he said in a quiet, reverent tone toward the dead man. Victory to the gods.

A strange excitement seemed to flash in Jara's eyes at the sight of the lama. No one could look into Gendun's open, serene face, and suspect subterfuge. As the lama stepped back toward the courtyard Jara slowly followed, gesturing toward the body again. "There is a still a killer out there," he said in a tentative voice, as if arguing with himself.

"Not here. Not today," Lokesh said for the second time that hour.

To Shan's surprise, Lokesh did not follow as Jara joined his wife and children in the courtyard, but motioned Shan back toward the shadows. When they stopped a few feet from Atso's body Lokesh turned toward the courtyard and planted his feet apart like a sentry. Shan studied him in momentary confusion, then realized that none of the other Tibetans could see Shan or Atso.

He pushed back the broad-brimmed hat he wore then knelt by the dead man, working quickly, compiling a mental list of his discoveries. One of Atso's hands was wrapped around a gau that hung on a worn silver chain, the fingers of the other hand entwined about a *mala,* a strand of prayer beads. The back of the hand with the prayer box was split open, a jagged wound that could have come from fending off a club or a rifle butt. The palms of both hands were scratched and abraided, the ends of his fingernails split and broken. At his waist a small plastic bottle half filled with water hung from a piece of rope. Pulling back the blanket, Shan exposed the left foot, revealing a tattered leather boot with a two-inch-wide band of heavy jute cord wrapped around the sole.

In his trouser pockets Atso carried two small pouches, one of freshly picked flower heads, the other of chips of juniper wood. A small pocket sewn inside his felt vest held a tightly folded paper, a printed announcement about a free children's health exam in the valley. On the back of the paper was inscribed the *mani* mantra, the prayer for compassion, in tiny cramped writing, row after row of miniscule Tibetan figures. Shan stared at the old man's face then looked back at the paper. The mantra had been written at least a thousand times, then the paper rolled and folded as if Atso had intended to leave it somewhere very small.

He lifted the ruined statue, the little silver Tara. It had a patina of great age, except for a patch of bright metal at one shoulder where the devout had rubbed it for good luck. Shan held it close, studying the dented, imploded head, holding it at various angles, examining the long gash along the goddess's spine, Jara's haunting declaration echoing in his head. *They kill for a word in these hills.* The goddess was hollow, and empty inside. Often the Tibetans inserted small rolled-up prayers inside such statues.

Shan looked back at Lokesh. Instead of beginning the death rites his old friend had invited him to study Atso's body—even though the hill people would not be happy that Shan had touched the body, even though they both knew the monks would resist any effort by Shan to investigate the murder for, to them, the only investigations that mattered were those of the spirit. He lowered the goddess to the blanket then stepped to Lokesh's side. "What is it you know?" he asked. "What is it you're not telling me?" He extended the paper. "What had so worried Atso he would labor for a thousand mantras?"

Lokesh studied the paper forlornly, as if reading every mantra. "I met him only once, when I was gathering berries in the mountains above here two weeks ago," he said, nodding toward the snowcapped peaks to the east. "He asked what it was we were doing at Zhoka. When I told him it was a secret, that he should come today to find out, he grew angry, then sad. He said we didn't understand, that Zhoka is a place of strange and powerful things that must be left alone. He said that the most dangerous thing about Zhoka is not understanding what it does to people."

"Are you saying he died because of something here?" Shan asked.

Lokesh turned back to look at the corpse. "Somewhere gone is what he seeks," he said quietly.

Shan studied his friend. The old Tibetans had a way of mixing tenses, of slipping over time, ignoring spans of decades, even centuries, when speaking, in order to express essential truths. As he was about to press him, a figure appeared in the shadows behind Atso. A young woman, dressed in black, her hair in a long braid down her back, knelt beside the body. She returned the broken statue to its bag without examining it, then pulled at the blanket, straightening it, patting it around his body, as if putting a loved one to bed. As she did so Shan glimpsed Atso's right boot. It, too, had a wrapping of jute, identical to that of the left boot. But the boot was not so tattered as the other, did not need the jute to bind it together.

"Liya," Shan said, "where have you seen the statue before?"

When she looked up Liya's eyes were full of tears. "When I was a little girl Atso carried me on his shoulders so the sheep would not run over me. I haven't seen him for ten years, not since his wife died and he moved into that hut."

"Where were they taking him?" Shan asked, not understanding why the Tibetans seemed to be avoiding his questions.

"There were strangers in the mountains last night when I was riding, between here and the valley." Anguish rose in Liya's eyes. "I dismounted, thinking I could hide. But suddenly they aimed lights at me and began shouting. They said I was not allowed to go to the east, as if they owned the land around Zhoka. I thought they were herders passing through, worried about pasturelands. I thought the monks would be happy to have as many as possible here today. When I said there was to be festival here, with monks, two people began speaking in English, very excited. A man and a woman. A man put a light on my face, then he apologized in Chinese and they all backed away. It made no sense. What would a Westerner know about Zhoka? What Chinese even would remember the place?" Liya scrubbed at one of her eyes. "I should have known better. I should have warned people."

"The work they did here was famous all over Tibet, famous even with the gods," a deep soft voice suddenly interjected. Surya was a few steps behind Shan, standing at what had been the entrance to a small building. He was intensely studying a piece of rock in his hand. Not a rock, Shan saw, but a piece of plaster, part of a painting. The front half of a deer was plainly visible, a familiar image from a scene of Buddha's first sermon. "Here," the tall, thin monk said, speaking to the deer in a voice that was strangely apologetic, "here you must be nailed to the earth."

As Shan approached him Surya stepped into the ruined building, still seeming unaware of any of them, like the day before.

In the silence that followed the monk's odd words Shan surveyed the rubble in which Surya stood, a sudden, terrible sense of premonition making him desperate to understand. Part of one wall remained erect, the rest was nothing but stones, shards of plaster, and charred debris. Surya took another step, then seemed to weaken, falling to his knees. Lokesh rushed to his side then froze as Surya extended his long fingers toward the sky, opening and closing them repeatedly, as if trying to gesture something down from the heavens.

After a moment the monk reached toward a pile of rubble a few feet away. Shan stepped uncertainly toward the pile, a heap of burnt timbers and broken roof tiles. Liya stepped forward to help and in less than a minute they had uncovered a small cracked, wooden chest with two drawers, eight inches high, nearly twice as long. Surya's eyes gleamed with excitement as Shan handed it to him, as if the monk, who like the rest of them was a stranger to the ruins, knew the chest. The brittle wooden front broke as the monk pulled the bottom drawer. Surya reached inside and extracted a handful of long graceful paintbrushes, gripping them tightly, holding them toward the sky. He closed his eyes as if praying a moment, then began passing out the brushes, one to each of those present. "Today will be the end of all things," he declared in a dry, strangely joyful whisper, then smiled as he handed the last brush to Shan. "Blessed Atso. Blessed protector!" he cried.

Shan stared at the monk, his confusion greater than ever. Surya knew about the dead man. Had Surya somehow been trying to explain what had happened to Atso?

"Listen to that little girl," Surya blurted out. "She is understanding." The monk abruptly stood and stepped back toward the courtyard. Shan and Lokesh exchanged a confused glance. There was no little girl. The only children they had seen had been Jara's sons.

Today will be the end of all things. Surya's words echoed in Shan's mind as he stepped back into the courtyard with Lokesh, the long narrow brush in his pocket. It would indeed be the end for Gendun and the monks if soldiers came.

He forced himself to focus on the chant and the reverent Tibetans in the courtyard. Jara stood with his wife ten feet from the chorten, watching the young monk who had taken up the chant, nodding as Surya settled beside the monk and joined the chant. Lokesh nudged Shan's arm. Jara's wife had one arm around a young girl, no more than eight or nine years, who huddled between Jara and the woman.

"She is my sister's daughter," Jara explained as Shan approached with his gaze on the girl. "From a city in Szechuan Province, hundreds of miles to the east, come to us to learn about life in Tibet. Her parents were from these mountains, but they were sent to work in a Chinese factory before she was born. She has never been here, never even been with Tibetans except her parents."

"That statue," Shan said. "Do you know where it came from?" As he watched, one of the old Tibetan women, then a second, rose and walked back into the shadows, toward where Atso's body lay.

"There are many like it, if you know where to look," the herder replied. "That one found the first god that was slaughtered, the big man," he said, nodding toward a huge ox-like herder in a dirty fleece vest standing thirty feet away. "He said godkillers are the worse kind of demons. He brought one of the dead ones to us, in case someone in my family could heal it."

"Are the godkillers the ones you meant," Shan asked, "the ones who kill for a word? What word?"

The question seemed to hit Jara like a physical blow. He recoiled, then pressed a fist against his mouth, as if he feared what might escape, and stepped away.

"What is it?" the girl blurted out, her eyes locked on Surya, who sat only a few feet away. "What is wrong with these poor men?"

"It's just a sound that souls make," Lokesh explained with a satisfied grin. The words sent the girl deeper into her aunt's apron.

"They don't teach how souls speak in those factory towns," Jara's wife said, warning in her voice.

"But something in her is trying to listen," Lokesh observed as the girl straightened, her head slightly cocked, her fear seemingly replaced with wonder as she gazed at Surya. One of the old Tibetans reappeared, her face clouded with worry, but she did not spread alarm. She was trying to control her fear, Shan saw. Despite Atso's death she did not wish to disturb their first festival in many years.

"It scares me," Jara's wife confided in a nervous voice. "All these monks. If anyone from town . . ."

"My mother said each year this day is full of miracles," Lokesh said, rubbing his grizzled white jaw thoughtfully. "Saints could appear from some *bayal,* she told me," he said with a twinkle in his eye, referring to the traditional hidden lands inhabited by deities and saints. "It is a time for joy, not fear. When is the last time you celebrated this day?"

The woman turned her head away, but Shan could not tell if she was embarrassed or just trying to ignore Lokesh. After a moment her head slowly turned back toward Surya. "I was just a girl," she said with a tiny, distant smile.

Lokesh turned toward a clay jar on a flat stone behind them, one of several scattered around the old courtyard, dipped his hand inside, then extended it toward her. She pulled her hands behind her back as though afraid, then, hesitantly, brought one hand forward and let Lokesh pour some of the white flour from the jar onto her palm. The woman stared uncertainly at her hand.

Lokesh grinned and made several small, upward motions with his open hand.

"I have a cousin who is in prison for doing what you ask," the woman said, gazing solemnly at the flour Lokesh had placed in her palm. She sighed, then abruptly threw the contents of her hand into the air, a gleeful cry escaping her husband's lips as she did so. In the next moment Lokesh did likewise, so that they were enveloped in a small cloud of barley flour.

The woman's tense face cracked with a smile as Lokesh danced a little jig, his arms outstretched at his sides, looking so light it seemed he might float away. She flung more flour into the air, then clapped her hands as she raised her face to let the flour drift onto her skin. "He is alive for another year!" she called out. The cry was taken up by several of the older Tibetans, who began reaching into the jars themselves.

Throwing barley flour into the air was a traditional act of celebration, but the government had made it a crime for Tibetans to do so on this particular day. For today was the birthday of the exiled Dalai Lama.

"Lha gyal lo!" Lokesh called toward the sky. "Victory to the gods!"

The woman paused, looking over Shan's shoulder and he turned to see the girl standing behind them, worry back on her face. Her aunt threw a handful of flour over the girl, who backed away from the cloud as if frightened of it.

As the woman studied the girl, her glee disappeared. She motioned the girl back toward Surya and the younger chanter.

But as Shan retreated several steps, the girl followed him. He lowered himself onto a rock and after a moment's hesitation the girl sat beside him.

"Is it all right?" she asked him in a timid voice. She had switched to Chinese.

"All right?" Shan replied in Tibetan.

"May they do this?"

Suddenly Shan could not bear to look into the girl's face. When he did not answer the girl began to nervously wipe the flour dust from her cheeks.

He reached out and gently pushed her arm down. "They did not have to ask me."

"You're Chinese."

He recalled a day five years earlier when soldiers had heaved him from a truck into the gulag compound near Lhadrung. He had lain facedown in the cold mud, semiconscious, not knowing where he was, bleeding from one ear, pain spiking from his arms and belly where electroshock clips had been fastened, his eyes and mind struggling to focus because of the interrogation drugs still in his system. "From this day forward, your pain will subside," a quiet voice had suddenly whispered, and Shan had forced his eyes open to gaze into the serene face of an old Tibetan who, Shan soon learned, was a lama in his fourth decade of imprisonment. "In all your life it will not be so bad again," the lama explained as he had helped Shan to his feet. But during the year since his release Shan had discovered a new pain that not even the lamas could cure, an agony of guilt that could be triggered by the innocent question of a young girl.

He put his hand on the girl's arm to stop her. "I wish the Dalai Lama was with his people," Shan said in a near whisper. "I wish him a long life."

"You mean you're Buddhist?"

A bowl of buttered tea was thrust over Shan's shoulder.

"Something like that." Lokesh chuckled and squatted before them, sipping a second bowl. "When I was young," he continued, gazing solemnly at the girl, "my mother would take me deep into the mountains to see old suspension bridges over bottomless chasms. The bridges connected us to the outside world. No one knew how they were made or what held them up. They seemed impossible to build. When I asked, my mother said they were just there, because we needed them. That is our Shan."

"But is it all right?" the girl asked Shan again in her meek, earnest tone.

"What is your name?" Shan asked.

"Dawa. My father is a model worker in a Chinese factory," she added quickly. "He saved all year to be able to send me here. He could afford only the bus fare for me. I have never been out of the city." Shan glanced at Lokesh. Listen to the little girl, Surya had said as if in warning. But Dawa did not even know Tibet.

"Dawa, I want it to be all right. Do you want it to be?" Was that Surya's point, Shan wondered, that they could only understand the day's strange events by looking on them as an outsider?

The girl shyly nodded, searching Shan's face. "How can a Chinese do such things?" she asked. "Be a bridge. Does he mean you are part Tibetan?"

"Other Chinese put me in prison, not because I committed a crime but because they feared I would tell the truth. I wanted to die then. I was going to die. But Lokesh and others like him taught me how to live again."

The girl seemed unconvinced. Shan lifted a jar of flour and extended it toward her. She slowly shifted her gaze to the jar and then, her fingers trembling, she pulled some flour from it. A shiver of excitement seemed to course through her, then she threw the flour over their heads and solemnly studied it as it drifted downward. "I saw where they go. I think I know the way to the hidden land," she declared uncertainly, looking at Surya, who had risen from his seat beside the younger chanter and was now moving across the yard in a slow, graceful gait.

Shan looked at her, not understanding, then watched as the girl followed the monk into the ruins. A sudden unfamiliar sound caused him to turn toward the chorten. Laughter. Several of the older Tibetans were laughing, throwing flour over each other's heads. The festival was truly under way.

But then a hand closed around his arm. Liya was at his side, her face pale. She gestured with her head toward the old stone tower on the ridge above the ruins, nearly a mile away.

At first Shan saw nothing but then something green at the base of the tower moved and his heart leapt into his throat. There were soldiers at the tower, at least a dozen. He quickly surveyed the yard. No one else had noticed that the army was watching. If the Tibetans were warned they would panic and try to flee, though most lived to the west, above the valley, and their path home was now blocked.

"You have to tell him," Liya said. "You have to try," she added in a forlorn tone.

Shan slowly nodded, watched as Liya disappeared into the nearest alleyway, then gazed upon the joyful Tibetans. They may have finally forgotten the hard existence they eked out of the rocky slopes, forgotten the fears that always shadowed them, but their jubilation would be short lived. He began searching for Gendun.

He found the lama five minutes later, sitting in a small clearing at the northern edge of the grounds, looking into the five-hundred-foot-deep chasm that abutted the northern edge of the ruins. Strangely, Gendun sat with his legs casually extended over the edge of the chasm. He was watching a hawk soar in the updrafts above the gorge, his eyes shining with pleasure. He did not turn but patted the rock beside him, inviting Shan to sit. "I have not known such a day since I was a boy," the lama said. "We would erect a white tent by the monastery in the mountains where I was born. We sang all day. The monks would fasten a secret blessing to the top of a high pole and we would take turns climbing, trying to retrieve it."

"There are soldiers," Shan said quietly, studying the tattered lines of ropes and splintered wood that hung from the edge of the opposite side of the chasm, the remains of the old bridge that had once connected to the clearing, the northern foregate yard of the old gompa.

As though in reproach, Gendun turned his head to gaze toward a long stone atop a low mound of rubble, a lintel stone from over a collapsed doorway. Someone had cleared the rubble from it, exposing words that had been painted across it, faded but still legible. STUDY ONLY THE ABSOLUTE. On the lintel stood a framed portrait of the Dalai Lama and a fragment of a life-sized bronze statue, a graceful, upcurved hand.

"Once this would have been a festival day for all the people," Gendun said. His voice was like dry grass rustling in the breeze. "We are making it so again. This is the beginning."

For Gendun it was the beginning, but Surya said it was the end. Shan looked back at the legend on the stone, then searched Gendun's face carefully. The old lama's countenance could be as complex as the sky. His eyes had grown more sober. He would not abide talk of dangers to the monks, or of murderers or foreigners stalking the hills. Shan replayed in his mind's eye the scene of Gendun looking at Atso. The lama had not been surprised, had not expressed remorse, but offered words of rejoicing on seeing the old man's body.

"Rinpoche, I do not understand what is happening," he said at last, using the form of address for a revered teacher.

"We do not just dedicate the shrine today," Gendun declared. "We are rededicating the gompa. Zhoka is going to live again. Surya is going to reside here."

Something icy gripped Shan's belly. Surya and Gendun did not understand the tyrannical, often vengeful nature of the Bureau of Religious Affairs, to whom an unlicensed monk was a criminal. They did not know Colonel Tan, who had the authority to condemn the monks to labor camp without a trial.

As Shan looked at Gendun again he felt a sudden, deep sadness. It was the way the Tibetans defended themselves, taking virtuous positions against impossible odds. In the original war against the Chinese invaders thousands of Tibetans had charged machine guns with muskets and swords, or holding only prayers in their hands. Coming to Zhoka was Surya's way of doing the same thing. "Lha gyal lo," Shan said at last in a tight voice.

The old lama nodded somberly.

"Why now?" Shan asked.

Gendun waved his hand toward the ruins. "Zhoka was a very important place once, a place of great miracles. There are many things to learn here, things that must be revived."

Shan surveyed the abandoned gompa. The deep bowl in which the monastery had been built was over five hundred yards across at its base, and the ruins spilled up the slopes. Many of the rock walls that had defined courtyards and gardens had survived, even a number of the building walls stood, though none could be called intact. One huge wall, the end of what must have been an assembly hall, towered nearly twenty feet high, with a jagged six-foot hole in its center. Charred floor and roof timbers jutted from walls that leaned precariously. Shan knew little about Zhoka, except that it had been famed for its artists. Many of Zhoka's remaining walls bore fragments of paintings like the broken image of a deer Surya had held. Surya was Yerpa's most accomplished artist, the creator of magnificent *thangkas,* traditional Tibetan cloth paintings, and murals that graced the walls of the hermitage. For Surya, Lokesh had once said, his art was the way he prayed. But Gendun was sending him to live in a place where all the art had died.

They sat in silence and listened to the distant throat chant.

"What can be said to all these people, who have never been inside a temple?" Shan asked at last. "To those whose fear has been so great they have never even spoken with a monk?" There was to be a meal at noon, when Gendun meant to address the gathering.

Gendun smiled. "We will teach them to begin falling with their eyes open." It was one of the old teaching riddles, one Gendun had used with Shan in Shan's first days at Yerpa. What is the way of human life, the student asked. An open-eyed man falling down a well, the master replied. As jarring as the words seemed at first, Shan had come to recognize them as the perfect caption for the lives of those who lived at Yerpa. The spirit was jostled through many life forms in its development, Surya had told Shan during his early days at Yerpa, and could expect to live a brief human incarnation only after a thousand other incarnations. Life was so short, and the human incarnation so precious, that the hermits of Yerpa devoted every moment to enriching it, not only through their religious teachings but by creating wondrous works of art, illuminating manuscripts, writing histories, composing poetry and creating beauty in the ways that translated the teachings of compassion into the smallest of actions. Once you recognized the well you were tumbling into, Gendun was fond of saying, what else could you do?

Gendun knew as well as Shan that one informant, one errant patrol on this day, could mean the end of Yerpa, which had sheltered monks, scholars, and hermits for nearly five hundred years. The end of a place Shan had come to view as one of the great treasures of the planet, a brilliant gem on the crust of a drab world.

"I have brought what you will need, Shan," Gendun said, gesturing toward a tattered canvas drawstring bag with faded, once elegant Tibetan script depicting the mani mantra, the traditional invocation of compassion. "Lokesh can show you the way this evening. There is a full moon."

Gendun and Shan had solemnly packed the bag the day before as Gendun spoke of ancient hermits and recited poems the hermits had written. In the excitement of the day Shan had forgotten that he was about to leave on a solitary month-long hermitage in a cave deep in the mountains.

The sight of the bag released a new flood of emotion. Not long after he had returned to Yerpa from the north the month before, Shan had fallen gravely ill, burning with fever, lapsing in and out of consciousness for three days. When he recovered, Gendun had been very quiet around Shan, as if troubled. Something had happened that no one would speak of. Fearful that a new danger had arisen for the monks, Shan had pressed Lokesh until the old Tibetan had explained that in his fever one night Shan had called for Gendun like a frightened child, crying, saying he had to go home, saying he had to be free now.

The words from Shan's sickness had strangely shaken Gendun and Lokesh. It was why Shan's fever had lasted so long, Lokesh had explained, leaving him so weak he could barely sit up, because his spirit had become so imbalanced, because he had what the Tibetan doctors called heart wind.

Shan had no home beyond Yerpa, no real family but the monks and Lokesh. But Lokesh explained that the fever had burned away into a dark place inside Shan, a desperate place that had not been touched by the Tibetans' healing, a place the Tibetans did not know how to reach. It had hurt Shan beyond words to see the self-doubt on the countenances of Gendun and Lokesh, and it had been days before he could bring himself to speak about it, to try to explain it away, as a dream perhaps, one of the recurring dreams of himself as a boy looking for his father. Don't believe that voice, he had wanted to tell them, don't believe that part of me doesn't want to stay with you, don't believe that you are incomplete as teachers.

"You must journey inside," Gendun had finally told him, using one of his phrases for a long-term meditation. "You must find a way to stop imprisoning yourself. I know a cave," he had announced, and they had spent more than a week preparing, meditating together, selecting the items to accompany Shan. A few butter lamps. Two blankets. A pouch of barley, a small pot, a pouch of yak dung for fuel. And his old heirloom throwing sticks, used by Shan and several generations of his family before him to contemplate the Tao te Ching, the ancient Chinese book of wisdom.

"How could I leave now?" Shan asked in a whisper, not even sure Gendun could hear, but knowing what the answer would be. "The soldiers will tell Colonel Tan about the festival now. There will be danger for the monks of Yerpa, danger like never before."

"For us there is nothing more important than meeting these people, for whom the Buddha has been but a shadow all these years. For you there is nothing more important than reaching that cave."

There was movement behind them. They rose and discovered Liya, gazing at them hesitantly. The shy young woman seemed somehow stricken. Lokesh appeared behind her, glancing with a worried expression toward Shan, trying to calm Liya with a hand on her shoulder.

The big ox-like herder emerged from the shadows, leading Jara and most of the other hill people.

"Soldiers!" he barked, pointing to the old stone tower. "Between us and our homes!" The Tibetans were murmuring excitedly, fear back in their eyes. "The whole world knows of your secret festival!" the big herder snapped at Liya in an accusing tone. "You may as well have sent a personal invitation to that damned colonel."

Liya turned toward Gendun, and her eyes grew wide in surprise. Shan followed her gaze to discover that Gendun had settled onto the long lintel stone. He was in the lotus position, feet folded under him, his right hand open, fingers pointing downward, in the earth witness *mudra,* one of the ritual hand gestures. He was facing the western ridge, in the direction of the soldiers. One of the old women who had been sitting at the chorten pushed forward and settled to the ground in front of the lama. "If soldiers are coming today," she declared, "here is where they will find me."

Liya stepped to the woman's side. "We can hide and be safe," she said. "Shan and his friends will help us."

Strangely, the words silenced the crowd. Liya gasped, her hand shooting to her mouth, then exchanged an alarmed glance with Lokesh.

"Shan?" the big herder shouted at her, then stepped to Shan and knocked off the wide-brimmed hat that had been obscuring his features. "Damn me!" he spat, then turned to those behind him. "This is the one? The Chinese who always intrudes in Tibetan things? She's right, Shan will help us get out of this," he said with a cruel grin, his scarred face looking wild and hungry.

"Shan is going on retreat," Lokesh declared in a plaintive tone and stepped between Shan and the herder.

"Right," the man growled. "With a chain and a pickax." He turned to address the Tibetans gathered behind him. "He's the one they're looking for. There's cash money on his head," he declared, raising his voice. "One hundred American dollars. Enough to keep all of us fed for months."

Gendun began a mantra.

Shan stared, his throat suddenly bone dry, looking from his friends to the fiery herder. "Who is paying?" he heard himself ask. Bounties were not uncommon in modern Tibet, whose communist masters had developed their own peculiar twists on market economies.

"Only a rumor," Liya said in a tight voice. "It's Tan. People say you're to be taken to Colonel Tan." She looked up into Shan's eyes. "You never go to town. Even if it were true we thought you would be safe staying up here. These people don't know you. Didn't know you," she corrected herself, pain in her eyes.

"It's no rumor," the herder snapped. "There're papers in shop windows now."

"I'm sorry," Liya said to Shan. "Tan must want you back. You just have to go deeper into the mountains. Your retreat. Go now," she said, gesturing toward the bag.

Shan's release from prison had never been official. Liya meant back in hard labor prison, back to the 404th People's Construction Brigade.

Shan's gaze drifted toward the bag bearing the mani mantra. He knew his friends had not been trying to deceive him by not revealing the bounty, nor trying to protect him. Bombs fell, bullets were fired, bounties were levied. To Shan, like his Tibetan friends, such things had become little different from hailstorms and winds, part of the harsh environment that had evolved in the world they inhabited. They might pull their hats down and quicken their pace, but they would not step off their path. The bounty would have as little significance to Lokesh or Gendun. What mattered to them was that Shan completed his month's retreat.

"Soldiers like that, if they get angry they'll burn our houses, kill our herds," the huge herder growled.

Liya stepped beside Lokesh, in front of Shan. "We would not give up Shan any more than we would give up one of these monks," she declared sternly.

"You understand nothing!" the scar-faced herder shouted, glaring at Liya. "You never told us about what you planned here. It is the wrong time for monks and festivals. So naive!" he spat. "You brought this on by luring everyone here with false hope! The only chance to keep the soldiers away now is to give up Shan."

Jara's wife appeared, holding the hands of their two sons, looking at her husband with an intense, searching expression. Jara took a step toward his wife, then looked down at his chest, seeming surprised to find one hand closed tightly around his gau. His head slowly rose as he looked at Lokesh and his sons, then he turned and sat cross-legged in front of Gendun. Two more herders, tough middle-aged men with bone-hard faces, pushed past Jara's wife to join the big herder, eyeing Shan with hungry expressions. But the woman seemed not to notice them. She stared in wonder at her husband, still clasping his gau, and the joy slowly returned to her face.

"A hundred American!" the scar-faced herder spat. "They want him in prison!" The man turned to those behind him. "When did we ever have a chance to put a Chinese in prison?" he asked with a laughing snort. "We can make this a day for celebration after all!"

"No!" Liya barked. "He is one of us! He is protected by our clan!"

"You just run and hide in the south when danger comes," the herder shouted at her. "It's easy for you to appear for a day, then leave. We cannot hide. We have to live here. Atso was murdered. Isn't that warning enough? We must be rid of the Chinese and their godkillers," he growled, pointing at the monks.

Shan did not move. He sensed Liya tense as if she were about to spring on the man, but instead she closed her hand around his arm, as though to keep them from dragging Shan away.

"Not murdered," Shan said. "It was an accident."

"You don't know that," the herder spat.

"I do. Atso has told us."

The herder's face darkened. "We don't make light of the dead."

"But you would make light of the truth?" Shan asked soberly, surveying the Tibetans. "Why was Atso at the foot of that cliff?"

"That's where the godkillers found him, that's where they beat him, a hundred feet from his hut."

"His boots were wrapped in jute but they were not falling apart. His hands were scratched and gouged."

"He fought back," the herder snapped. "They probably beat that little Tara in front of him, to torture him."

"No," Shan said. "She was attacked elsewhere." He glanced at Liya, who nodded then darted out of the yard. "What did Atso do, all these years since his wife died?"

The Tibetans glanced uneasily at each other, the oldest keeping their eyes from Shan.

"There were no strands of wool on his clothes, none of the lanolin in his hands that he would have if he worked with sheep. I'll tell you what I think," Shan said. "He tended the old shrines, the hidden ones. He had a prayer box, he had beads. He had a pouch of flowers in his pocket, another of wood chips. And water. It's what you put on altars in the old days. He still believed. He was going to an altar."

Liya reappeared, holding the little silver statue. Shan set it on a flat rock in the bright sun. "I think I know that high valley where Atso lived," he continued. "It is very dry, all rocks and heather. Why was the hut there? Who would build in such a place?" When no one answered he pointed to the gash in the back of the goddess. "If you look carefully you will see something trapped in a fold in the metal, because whoever did this cut the statue open first then turned it over and smashed the head. A piece of grass was trapped in the folded metal. There is no grass where he lived."

Liya extracted a folding knife from her pocket and pried back the fold in the metal. She reached into it and pulled away a green blade, holding it up for all to see.

"It proves nothing," the herder growled.

"Why was the hut there?" Shan demanded again, very slowly.

"The cliff above faced south with a small spring below," Lokesh offered in a contemplative tone, referring to two of the attributes of a traditional place of spiritual power. The old Tibetan turned toward the others and repeated Shan's question.

"A cave," the old woman by Gendun said, nearly in a whisper. Someone near her cursed, another shouted for her to be silent. Instead she spoke more loudly, turning to speak to Gendun, as if he had asked the question. "High up on the cliff," she cried out, "an ancient place where gods dwell. The hut was built for those who protect the cave, who serve the gods."

Shan looked at Gendun, and realized that the lama's glance at Atso's body and brief words should have told Shan everything he needed to know about the dead man. The lama had known that Atso was engaged in sacred work. "When he found the goddess somewhere else, on a grassy slope, he decided he had to protect it," Shan said, "maybe heal it, by taking it to the holy cave."

"It's what he would do!" the old woman gasped in sudden realization.

"He wrote a mantra a thousand times for protection, then wrapped his boots in jute for better traction and climbed the cliff," Shan said. "But he fell, breaking his legs, ripping his ear, breaking the bones on one side of his face where he hit the rocks. There is no murderer," Shan declared in a loud, slow voice. "There are no monks who kill."

As he spoke Liya pointed excitedly toward the old tower. "The soldiers are gone!"

The Tibetans followed Liya's gaze, then looked back at Shan, wide-eyed, as if he had performed some sort of sorcery. One by one, they left the big herder's side, several joining Gendun in a mantra. The scar-faced man sighed. "Lha gyal lo," he offered in a tone of resignation, but kicked Shan's hat as he walked away.

The chanting started again. The celebration began anew. As he retrieved his hat Shan heard snatches of prayers, then watched several of the Tibetans embrace each other. Several stepped forward and shook his hand, one gave him a small prayer scarf. Some of the children brought jars from the courtyard and began tossing flour into the air, laughing again. The sounds of joy grew louder, more heartfelt, than before, as if by eliminating both the soldiers and the spectre of a murderer in the hills Shan had confirmed that it was indeed a day of miracles. Gendun, who stayed on the fallen lintel, smiled. They would still have their festival, Gendun would still address the people of the hills. Lokesh began teaching some of the herders another pilgrim's song.

As Shan began helping Liya distribute flour she cocked her head toward the courtyard. "Listen—"

"There's nothing—" he began, then remembered the throat chant, which was supposed to continue without stopping until Gendun's teaching.

As Shan turned in the direction of the central courtyard, a scream pierced the stillness. He ran.

The terrified, quivering howl kept repeating itself, the scream of an hysterical child. He was still in the foregate when Dawa emerged from the courtyard. The front of her shirt was soaked in blood. As she frantically waved her hands over her head, still screaming, Shan saw that her palms, too, were stained crimson, fresh blood trickling down her forearms.

The girl was inconsolable. Jara approached, reaching out for her, but the girl seemed not to notice, instead darting away, grabbing the nearest pot of flour, which she flung into the gorge, then another and another, the flour drifting out of the pots in long white plumes as they sank. She seemed to mindlessly reach for anything that lay on the ground and then pitch it into the chasm. Not mindlessly, Shan realized after a moment. The girl was destroying anything that hinted of Buddhism, any sign of the clandestine celebration. The photo of the Dalai Lama. The graceful bronze hand. Suddenly her hands were on Shan's hermitage bag with the mani mantra. Too late Shan ran forward. The bag, with his supplies for the next month and his precious heirloom prayer sticks, tumbled over the edge, into the deep ravine.

There were more sounds now, frantic shouts as people began fleeing up the slope. Shan darted into the central courtyard. Lokesh stood by the chorten, staring in horror toward the stone where the throat chanters sat. Surya, whom they had not seen for an hour, sat clad only in the rough grey muslin garment worn under his robe. His robe lay on his lap, or what was left of it. With a glazed expression he was ripping the maroon cloth into shreds and feeding it to the fire in the brazier. Lokesh stepped forward, one hand raised as if to prevent Surya's hand from reaching for the fire again. But Surya pushed him away. Lokesh resisted for a moment then froze, staring at the wet stain left from Surya's touch. It was blood.

"I am a monk no more," Surya moaned as the flames consumed the last of his robe. "I have killed a man," he said in a wrenching, hollow voice. "No more a monk. No more a human."

Chapter Two

Dawa ran into the courtyard, still screaming, beating her fists against her uncle's chest as Jara caught up and wrapped his arms around the girl. Lokesh reached into the flames, futilely trying to retrieve the burning cloth, then looked up at Shan with a desolate gaze. Someone else had died. The hill people were fleeing in terror and Surya was abandoning his vows. They were falling down the well, eyes open.

Lokesh pulled something from his belt and urgently pressed it into Surya's hand. It was his mala, his rosary. Surya stared numbly at the ashes of his robe as Lokesh lifted the monk's fingers and entwined them around the beads. *"Om mani padme hum,"* Lokesh intoned in a plaintive, whispering voice, as if he had to remind Surya how to invoke the deity of compassion. The old monk's eyes, empty as glass, drifted toward Lokesh, then dropped to gaze absently at the beads in his fingers. He opened his hand, letting the mala fall to the earth. Lokesh grabbed the beads and began a new mantra, an urgent invocation of Tara, protectress of the faithful.

No more flour flew in the air. No more cries of celebration were flung toward the sky. The few hill people remaining in the courtyard with Surya had retreated to the walls, staring at him in fearful confusion. The younger monk who had taken up the throat chant was silent, his eyes on the burning robe, torment clenching his face.

Liya appeared, surveying the chaos with a wild, frightened expression. She leaned on the chorten with one hand, then two, closing her eyes a moment, then she straightened, calmer now, and retrieved a clay pot of water from behind the chorten. As Jara held the sobbing Dawa, Liya silently began washing the blood from the girl's hands.

Helplessness surged through Shan as he approached the once joyful, gentle monk. "Surya," he whispered near the monk's ear. "It's Shan. Tell me what it was, what happened."

Surya gave no sign of hearing. A new sound came from his lips. Not a throat chant, not a mantra, but a low, terrible creaking, the sound of a dying animal. He stared at the ground, his eyes like fading embers.

Shan shuddered, and moved to Dawa. As Liya glanced at Shan he pointed toward the fleeing Tibetans. "Those soldiers could still be in the mountains," he observed in a grim tone. Liya bit her lip, gazing forlornly at Dawa for a moment, then handed the clay pot to him and darted toward the slope.

"What was it, Dawa?" he asked as he knelt at the girl's side. She pressed her head into her uncle's chest. "What did you see when you followed Surya?" Neither the girl nor her uncle seemed to hear. Then with a pang of guilt he recalled she had spoken before, with question in her voice, and he had not responded. I saw the way to the hidden land, she had said. He rose and studied the ruins, trying to recall Surya's movements after his first cycle of chanting.

Between their turns of chanting Surya and the other chanters usually sat in meditation. If Surya was coming to live in the ruins, he no doubt had studied them more closely than the others, had perhaps found his own special place for meditation. Shan followed the path Dawa had taken into the shadows and soon found himself facing two pillars of natural rock that had supported one of the ruined structures.

Shan stepped between the two pillars. To his surprise he found no floor in front of him, only a dimly lit flight of stairs hewn out of the rock, cupped by centuries of use, the top steps overtaken by lichen. He had not previously seen the eight-foot-wide stairway that sank into the earth, perhaps because the walls that hid it on either side were leaning so treacherously they had seemed too dangerous to approach. He studied the walls a moment. If either collapsed, he would be trapped in the darkness below. Surely Dawa would not have ventured into such a place, surely Surya would not have considered it a place for mediation. He was about to turn back when he noticed a few moist red drops in a line coming from the shadows below. Shan descended into the darkness.

He counted a hundred and eight of the steep, nearly foot-high steps, before the passageway leveled into a dark corridor. It was a powerful, symbolic number, the number of beads in a Tibetan rosary. The smell of singed butter hung in the air, the acrid, sooty residue of butter lamps. He stood completely still. There were other smells. A faint, musty scent of incense that probably clung to the walls from centuries of smoldering braziers. A vague odor of tea. And something more recent, something alien. Tobacco. Twenty feet down the passage a dim flame burned. It was a butter lamp, tilted on its side, its contents flowing onto the rock floor in a small flickering stream. He pushed the small pot upright and with a chip of stone scooped the butter back inside. Raising the lamp he continued down the chill passage until, half a dozen steps later, two

27

doorways opposite each other came into view. A few steps beyond, the corridor ended abruptly in a wall of solid rock.

The opening to the right led into a small, square room, five feet to the side, that may have been a meditation chamber or a storeroom. Inside it sat a large clay jar filled with water, beside a rough piece of burlap large enough to serve as a blanket or prayer rug. He lifted the burlap. It was a bag, supple, not dried out, with plastic thread in the bottom seam. Large Chinese ideograms stenciled onto the cloth declared its original contents to be rice, produced in Guangdong Province.

The second chamber was larger, its walls each over fifteen feet long, with another, smaller, doorway at the far end of the wall to his right. He took two steps inside and froze, staring at a black glistening patch on the floor of the smaller doorway. Shan closed his eyes, calming himself, then approached the dark patch and squatted, extending a fingertip into it. It was a pool of fresh blood.

He wiped his finger on the stone floor and stood, the light over his head, studying the room. He smelled the damp metallic scent of the blood now, combined with another scent he had come to recognize in the gulag. Not a scent as such, Lokesh would have said, just one of the sensations of the spirit, which perceived things that could not be explained by the physical senses. If you let it, Lokesh insisted, the spirit inside could feel the shadow of recent terror, like a lingering echo, or the disturbance left when another spirit wrestled free of a suddenly broken body. Shan would have been happy not to let his own spirit do so, but he did not know how to stop the sensation. Death had visited the little chamber.

Suddenly he felt empty and cold. Something inside shouted for him to run back to the surface, and he found himself pressed against the rock wall, pushing down, until he was crouching, his arm over his head, fist clenched as though to fend off an attack. What had Atso said about Zhoka? It was a place of strange and powerful things, a place dangerous to misunderstand. No, not exactly. He said it was dangerous not to understand what it did to people. Shan closed his eyes again and calmed himself. As he lowered his arm something frigid touched his hand and he slowly extended his fingers to grasp a long metal cylinder. It was a hand lamp, of sleek heavy metal, the kind the Public Security troops favored, because they could double as batons for crowd control. He pushed the button near the top. Nothing. His fingers were wet again. The light was covered in blood.

Dropping the broken light, Shan stepped along the perimeter of the room. The walls had been expertly plastered once, and covered with painted images. He paused at the pool of blood, holding the butter lamp high again. Above it was the image of a wrathful deity carrying a skull cup of blood, one of the mythical *lokapalas,* guardians of the law. The image had nine angry heads and over a dozen pairs of arms. All the eyes, every eye on every head, had been blinded, some precisely gouged out, others burnt away as though with the end of a cigarette. The powerful deity appeared sad and helpless, its cup tipped as if the blood on the floor had spilled out of the skull. Beneath the painting, in a line where they had rolled against the wall, were dark, worn beads. He lifted one, studying it forlornly. Surya had broken the ancient rosary he carried, passed down through generations of hermit monks, and left the beads as if they meant nothing to him.

A trail of moist crimson smudges led from the pool back to the first door, toward the stair passage. Surya's forearms had been covered in blood, as had Dawa's palms and the front of her dress. Even her shoes had shown smears of blood. He studied the stains on the floor. Dawa had slipped, falling into the grisly pool, pushing up against the floor. But the expensive metal light had not been hers, and she would not have entered the room without light. Surya must have been in the room, with the butter lamp. If she had ventured so far, had stepped in the blood, Surya must have been beyond, on the opposite side of the smaller doorway. Shan stepped over the blood into the shadows, seeing for the first time another trail, not of smudges but large drops of blood, where they had fallen from the one who must have died. The tunnel outside the room widened and sloped gradually downward. In the blackness was a vague rustle of sound, like distant wind. To the right was a small meditation chamber. As he turned to it his foot connected with something on the floor. He bent and recoiled. It was a bone, a human femur bone, dripping fresh blood.

He pressed against the wall again. Someone had died and been stripped of their flesh, a voice gasped from the place of his fear. Impossible, a second, uncertain voice said. Surya would not have had time for such grisly work, Surya was not a killer.

Shan forced himself to gaze at the bloody bone. The blood was fresh, but the bone was not. It was the kind of bone traditionally used by artisans to make *kangling,* the trumpets of Tibetan ceremony. There were three more bones, leaning against the wall. They must have been left there decades earlier, by one of the Zhoka craftsmen. But they had been rearranged. The center bone was vertical, the other two leaning against it, forming an arrow that pointed to a symbol drawn in blood a few inches above. A ten-inch oval had been drawn, its long axis parallel to the floor. In the center of the oval was a square, inside the square was a circle.

He stepped toward the meditation cell and discovered two four-inch-long rectangles cut into the floor, each nearly two inches deep, eighteen inches apart and eighteen inches from the wall. They could have held the legs of an altar or some sort of platform. On the floor of the cell was a pile of debris covered by coarse dust-encrusted sackcloth. Under the cloth, and scattered around it, were shards of pottery. Dried, shriveled kernels of barley, years, probably decades, old. A plank, dried and split, five inches wide and sixteen long. He looked back toward the pool of blood. Someone's life had drained out onto the floor. But where was the body? There was no trail of blood except that left by Surya and Dawa, and if Surya had carried the body somewhere the front of his robe and underrobe would have been soaked with blood. The hysterical girl must have fled after falling into the blood. Surya himself must have dropped the lamp, far from the sunlight above, still burning, not bothering to retrieve it. Because he had been frightened by something he had seen? Or by something he had done? No, Shan told himself again, it was not possible that the gentle Surya, who often blessed Shan's feet so they would not crush insects, could kill another human being.

Shan studied by the debris. The slab of wood was deeply cracked, but it had been carved with an intricate pattern of deer leaping through trees. It was the cover of a *peche,* he realized, one of the unbound books traditionally used in Tibet. He leaned the wooden cover against the wall and lifted the cloth, revealing more shards of pottery and a small unbroken clay image of the compassionate Buddha. Beyond it, lying against the wall, was a long piece of parchment, a leaf from a peche. He gently lifted the long narrow paper and read it, then looked up, staring into the darkness a moment. He read it again, turning it over, examining it with the lamp drawn closer. It was impossible, like so much else that had happened that day. The text was old, though not from a wood block, the traditional method of printing a peche. It was in blue ink, as if from a quill or pen, in a bold ornate hand that at first glance had the appearance of the elegant Tibetan script used for scriptures. But it was not in Tibetan, it was in English. *Death is how deities are renewed,* the parchment said. *Know, then let go. Lift the brush a thousand thousand times then let it sink to the stone. Holy Mother, Holy Buddha, Holy Ghost. Death is how deities are renewed.*

Along the bottom of the leaf were painted more deer in the traditional Tibetan style, as well as small intricate figures of yak. He read it, stared at the bloody bone, and shivered. The peche leaf spoke of death like a poem, or a eulogy. It was decades old, perhaps a century or more. It had been dropped exactly where somebody, this day, had died. A coincidence, he would have said years earlier. But if Lokesh were with him the old Tibetan would have solemnly clapped his hands together and exclaimed how fortunate they were to be present when the movement of two wheels of destiny, however briefly, meshed together.

Shan raised his lamp again. There were no more pages, nothing but more shards of pottery, shreds of sackcloth, and what may have been a shriveled apple. He examined the parchment once more, read its strange, haunting English words again, then rolled the leaf and placed it in his pocket. As he straightened he spied one last object, something small and dark in the corner of the little alcove. He pressed the lamp close to it. A cigar, the end of a narrow cigar. He picked it up with his fingertips and held it under his nostrils. The tobacco had a cloying, sweet odor, unlike any tobacco he had ever known. It was not a Tibetan thing, not even a Chinese thing. He wrapped it in one of the shreds of cloth. As he did so, something cold seemed to breath down his back. He turned and turned again, then quickly stepped back over the pool of blood into the chamber, noticing for the first time a subtle contour in the center of the pool, a small round shape, the relief of a disc perhaps an inch and a half wide, not much thicker than a coin. Using a chip of plaster he pushed it out of the blood, wrapped it in the corner of his handkerchief, and placed it in his pocket.

Suddenly he was trembling. The strange events, and perhaps even stranger words, of the day swirled through his mind. Once—had it been only an hour ago?—Gendun had said the day was one of the most joyful of his long life. Today everything was going to end, Surya had said. Godkillers were in the mountains. This was a day when the world was changed. Zhoka held secrets that were dangerous to misunderstand.

A low hollow moan abruptly rose from the darkness behind him, from the descending tunnel past the blood pool. He told himself it was the wind playing on some rock formation or a hole in the debris, but he found himself against the wall again, his skin crawling. Whoever, or whatever, had taken the body had done so in the last twenty or thirty minutes, and could still be lingering nearby. Shan extended the light toward the sound, but as he did so the lamp began to sputter, its fuel nearly exhausted. He darted through the doorway. By the time he reached the stair passage the flame was out. He climbed toward the daylight above, backwards, watching the darkness.

Outside, the ruins were empty. The only thing that moved in the central courtyard was the thin column of smoke drifting from the old samkang. Shan jogged to the foregate by the gorge and its ruined bridge. There was no sign of the festival except a few white smudges on the rocks underfoot. He stepped to the lip of the gorge. Somewhere, hundreds of feet below, lay his hermitage bag and the bamboo case of lacquered yarrow sticks for practicing the Tao te Ching that had been passed through so many generations of his family. They had survived war and famine, had survived the death of his uncles and father at the hands of Mao's Red Guards, had even survived his own gulag imprisonment. But they had not survived the terror of a ten-year-old girl.

He walked slowly through the ruins, calling for Lokesh and Liya, then found himself facing the chorten shrine. He absently lifted the paintbrush from his pocket, staring at it a moment before he suddenly remembered the soldiers, turned and ran.

In a quarter hour Shan was at the top of the ridge above Zhoka. Half a mile to the northwest over a dozen bent figures moved along the crest. He paused and studied the landscape. The deep chasm cut Zhoka off from the north. The south, where steep, jagged peaks seemed to warn travelers away, was said to be a barren, forbidding land. The soldiers had last been seen to the northwest, between Zhoka and Lhadrung Valley. As he looked in that direction, toward the ruined stone tower that hovered over the northwestern end of the ridge, he thought he saw a flash of maroon, the color of a robe.

In another ten minutes Shan had caught up with the slowest of the fleeing Tibetans, who glanced at him resentfully then looked away. As he passed them he asked each one where the monks had gone. At last one of the old women who had prayed with Surya fixed him with an anguished gaze and pointed forward.

He found Lokesh standing on a ledge near the ruined tower that overlooked the narrow valley beyond. His old friend was staring toward the shadows inside the tower, feverishly working his beads. As Shan reached his side, Lokesh grabbed his arm as if to restrain Shan from venturing closer to the tower.

It was the first time Shan had been at the tower, and he saw now it wasn't totally destroyed. Only one scorched wall remained of the top section, reaching nearly twenty feet from the ground, with pieces of iron still holding fragments of what once had been a ladder secured to the outer wall. But the small chamber beneath, formed of a natural rock formation, was intact, a snug open-fronted alcove where travelers or sentries might have taken shelter from the elements. A solitary figure knelt on the floor of the chamber, facing the rear wall. Surya.

"Why would he come this way?" Shan asked Lokesh. "Toward Lhadrung, the soldiers—he could be arrested. The people are terrified. They will admit he is an unlicensed monk if asked. They are as scared of him now as of the soldiers." He looked into Lokesh's face and saw a deep, painful confusion. "We have to take him back home, to safety, then we can ask him about what happened, then we can help him." If Colonel Tan learned of unregistered monks, or a man professing murder, he would send troops to scour the mountains, and no one arrested could be expected to stay silent. While Yerpa had evaded detection for decades, under the influence of interrogators Surya would eventually divulge the location. If Surya were arrested, Yerpa would be destroyed as thoroughly as Zhoka, and Gendun and all the other monks arrested.

"He's not going to town," Lokesh declared, though his voice was uncertain. "He came here. In the courtyard he would not speak, not to anyone, nothing but those terrible words you heard. Suddenly he just stood, looked toward the tower, and started running. When I reached him he was just cleaning the walls inside, brushing away the old dirt. Then the girl came, with Gendun following," he added, gesturing toward a rock a hundred feet away where the lama sat watching Dawa, who sat at a spring, washing the blood from her dress, her aunt and uncle watching her forlornly fifty paces beyond, sitting with the other children. "She won't let Gendun or anyone get close to her. She says she wants to go home to her Chinese factory town. She says she hates monks. She says she hates all of us for tricking her."

Images of Dawa's day in the ruins flashed through Shan's mind. She had felt confusion and fear at first, then awe and joy, finally horror and grief. "She came to learn about life in Tibet," Shan said in a tight voice.

Lokesh nodded soberly. "We must take Surya back to Yerpa. He wants much healing."

Shan had never heard his friend's voice sound so frail. He watched Lokesh gaze with a strange, sad longing toward Zhoka. "What happened to Surya also happened to the girl. What did we misunderstand?" the old Tibetan asked Shan. Shan could only shake his head slowly.

After a moment Shan approached Dawa and sat on the grass beside her. She did not acknowledge him, just kept washing, pushing at the blood on her dress.

"I know you saw something terrible under the ground," he began. "I went down there. I saw the blood, and the bones. It was so dark. There were sounds. I was frightened, too. But there was no body. Did you see a body?"

The girl made a sound like a whimper. Not a whimper, he realized. She was humming. With a chill he recognized the song. "The East Is Red," one of the standard hymns of political officers, a favorite anthem for the public address systems in Chinese schools. Shan sat in silence, looking back at Lokesh and Gendun, trying to understand why they would not approach Surya. "Dawa," he pressed. "I need to know what you saw. I will help."

The girl stopped her frantic washing, catching the bloody water that dripped from her dress in one hand, staring at it with a terrible fascination. Just as he was about to rise she looked up. "He had an eye in his hand," she said in a tiny voice. "And a nail through his body." She began her chilling song again.

As he rose and moved back toward the tower a figure rushed past, stopping so abruptly at the entrance to the tower that she almost stumbled inside. It was Liya, panting, steadying herself with a hand on the rocks. "Quickly!" she called to Surya, then stepped into the shadows. "He has to leave," she gasped as Shan joined her. "We must carry him if there is no other way." Her voice drifted away as she stared at the monk.

Surya was urgently working at the wall at the rear of the little chamber, rubbing it with a strip of cloth torn from his grey underrobe, muttering something under his breath. It was a painting. Surya was frantically cleaning a painting, a mural that could have been painted a century or more earlier. To the left of the old painting were the characters of the mani mantra, invoking compassion, each faded letter ten inches high. On the wall to the right was a recent work, a complex painting of deities that would have taken many days to complete. Shan studied the rich, vibrant style of the second painting then turned to see Lokesh beside him, his eyes reflecting Shan's own surprise. The style of the painting was unmistakable, familiar to them. It was Surya's work.

But Surya was ignoring his own painting.

"Which is it?" Liya asked in a whisper as she stared at the image on the back wall that Surya was cleaning. Shan, too, was not certain of the central deity. It was Tara, the protectress, in one of the fierce emanations meant to combat specific demons and fears, but each major deity had multiple forms and he did not recognize this one.

Shan turned, as had Liya, to Lokesh, but his old friend just stared at the painting, his mouth open. "A terrible thing," Lokesh whispered and gazed back toward Zhoka with a worried expression. He did not mean the art, Shan knew, but the evil it was meant to protect against. Shan recognized the words Surya was now speaking in his low, desperate tone. It was a mantra: *Om Ah Hum,* a special empowering mantra, the last of a series of prayers used to animate deities.

"There is no time for this," Liya said to Surya. "You must flee." She stepped to his side and made a pulling motion with her arms, though her hands were empty, as though she were frightened of touching the monk, his arms still streaked with dried blood. "No time," she repeated, despair in her voice now.

But Shan sensed that for Surya there was time only for this, that despite their own fears, the monk had seen much more to fear, seemed alone to understand the true depths of their desperation, had decided their only possible defense lay with the deity in the painting. For the first time Shan saw that something had been painted below the old painting: a mantra perhaps. The words were obliterated with dark red streaks. Something inscribed there had just been obscured by red pigment, one of the colors Surya carried in little wooden tubes that hung on a leather strap around his neck, inside his under-robe. He saw that the monk's hands held fresh red stains over the drying blood. Surya had fled to the little shelter not only to clean the old painting but to also rub pigment over what had been written below it.

"*Om hum tram huih ah,*" Surya cried out in a strangely fierce voice. It was a mantra to bind guardians. Surya said no more but stared into the eyes of the deity. It was as if he had just concluded a pact with Tara.

Liya stopped her strange pantomime of struggle to stare at the monk, then pushed past Shan, her eyes full of tears. He watched as she searched the landscape beyond Zhoka, as though looking for someone in particular, then began urging the fleeing Tibetans toward the trail below the crest, down the steep switchback beyond the outcropping, toward their camps and houses in the hills above the valley. She ran back fifty yards along the crest and swept a stumbling child onto her back, forcing a lighthearted air as she carried the boy past the outcropping, handing him to his weary parents at the edge of the ledge, calling out a blessing as they disappeared over the crest. Shan stepped a few feet down the grassy slope, calling Jara, gesturing for the herder to bring his family.

Only half a dozen Tibetans remained in sight when Liya halted, looking back with a puzzled expression. Shan followed her gaze to see Surya, out on the ledge now, facing the steep valley beyond, his arms stretched outward at his side. Lokesh took a step toward the monk then halted, cocking one ear upward. Shan heard it, too, as he stepped closer, a deep thunder that came from the cloudless sky. Suddenly, running, stumbling figures appeared at the crest, crying out, racing back up the trail they had just descended, discarding the baskets and packs they carried.

Too late Shan recognized the metallic rumble. As he grabbed Lokesh's arm the thunder roared to a crescendo and a huge whirling blade appeared beyond the ledge, slowly rising to reveal the sleek dark grey body of one of the helicopters used by the army. Everyone seemed to be screaming, scattering in every direction but that of the machine. Jara stumbled through the stream below and began racing toward his niece as his wife gathered the other children. Dawa herself leapt up and frantically ran, not toward her uncle, but along the slope in the opposite direction.

Shan pushed Lokesh back toward the ruins and ran to Gendun's side as the machine paused, hovering a few feet above the ground. As he grabbed the lama and pulled him to his feet half a dozen troops in combat gear dropped out of the helicopter.

Shan and his friends ran, stumbling, tripping over rocks, Shan repeatedly stopping to help Gendun, pulling him forward, struggling because Gendun seemed unwilling to hurry, seemed not frightened but curious about the troops. Suddenly Lokesh, three steps in front of them, halted and stared back at the old stone tower.

Shan turned too, confused. The troops were not chasing anyone, not even Gendun, who wore a robe. Surya was standing on the open ledge, facing the helicopter, arms still raised, palms open, as if in greeting. The soldiers surrounded him, rifles at the ready, pausing as one soldier pressed his hand to his ear. Then, as Shan watched in horror, the soldiers closed about Surya, breaking off the leather neck strap that held his paints, pulling him from the rock and shoving him toward the helicopter, lifting him roughly into its bay. A moment later the soldiers had followed Surya inside the machine. It ascended, veering northward.

The panic did not depart with the soldiers. No one stopped running. The cries of fear did not cease. Some figures resumed their flight down the slope to the west, others retreated toward Zhoka. Dawa was alone, high on the opposite slope now, not bothering to stop to look for her family, running frantically toward the snowcapped mountains on the southern horizon, her uncle now sitting on the ground far behind her, holding his ankle as if he had injured it.

Shan walked in a daze toward the rock where Surya had stood, staring numbly at the heavy bootprints in the soil around the rock and the pigment vials that had been crushed by the boots, stepping past them to gaze over the dropoff. The helicopter was out of sight. The army had struck like lightning, then vanished into the sky.

"No one will ever see him again," a thin voice said over Shan's shoulder. Liya turned, dropped to one knee, and began scanning the southern landscape with her battered binoculars, as if looking for someone who would be climbing the slope above Zhoka. After a moment she rose and sighed. "Two months ago in Lhasa a man unfurled a Tibetan flag outside the military headquarters," Liya said. "A Public Security helicopter took him over the mountains and when it landed he was not inside. It's a way they have for dealing with political embarrassments. They don't bother with trials for people like Surya. He is a . . ." Her voice drifted away.

He is a what? Shan wondered. Shan had known Surya as a monk artist, an old Tibetan with a joyful, serene smile like that often worn by Gendun. But Surya had called himself a killer.

"It was as if he were waiting for them," Shan said. "As if he expected soldiers." Surya had run to the tower, obliterated something written under the old

36

painting, and waited for the troops. Yet even if a murder had occurred, the soldiers could not possibly have known.

Liya wiped a tear from her cheek. "It's my fault. I told those strangers about the festival and the army came searching. They found one of our illegal monks."

But Shan wasn't so certain. Troops had come, but they had ignored Gendun, had ignored the illegal festival, the fleeing Tibetans. Surya had indeed seemed to have expected them, and they him. The hermit artist who knew nothing about the outside world, who had spent all the years since his boyhood inside Yerpa, without seeing modern machines or soldiers or guns, or even a Chinese until Shan had arrived a year earlier, had let Chinese soldiers take him into a helicopter. "They didn't take him because he was a monk," Shan said. "He had no robe on."

Liya looked at Shan with pain in her eyes, as if his words only added to her despair. Shan studied her a moment. "When that herder wanted to take me for the bounty what did you mean when you said I had the protection of your clan?" He knew nothing of her family.

"The people of these hills share many things," Liya said in a tight voice.

Shan recalled how Liya sometimes stared at the distant mountains with a haunted, lonely expression and realized how little he knew about her. "Have you been inside, in the tunnels of Zhoka?" he asked.

But Liya stepped away, back toward the old tower.

When he caught up with her she was beside Lokesh, staring at the paintings.

"I tried to speak with Surya when he was running here," Liya said. "He had said something to Gendun, had given him something, but wouldn't speak with me. I kept asking him to turn back, reminding him of all the people who need him now." Her voice was low and quivering, and she seemed to be struggling to hold back more tears. They followed Lokesh's gaze into the shadows, where Gendun now knelt, studying the painting. "But finally he stopped and put a hand on my shoulder and shook me, saying if we are to save Zhoka we must go to refuge."

Shan looked at Liya again. She acted as if she and Surya were close, as if there where others, outside the hermitage, who needed Surya. He gazed back at the remains of the old gompa. "There are only ruins at Zhoka."

Liya followed his gaze. "Not for him."

"Not for those in refuge." Lokesh spoke from behind Shan's back. As he turned toward his old friend, Shan grasped the words. Surya had not been saying they must hide, he had been referring to the sacred refuge of Buddhist ritual, the place of enlightenment.

"Surya spoke to me of a place of power he had found, on a ridge, used by

Zhoka," Lokesh said suddenly. "This must be the place." He was touching the stone by the low entryway, intensely studying the pattern of lichen that grew on it, looking, Shan knew, for the religious symbols that sometimes could be discerned in the patterns of nature. "Surya told me he always looked for those that had been neglected, as if it were his job to restore them."

Shan surveyed the landscape again and realized that Lokesh was right. The lower alcove of the tower, formed of the natural rock formation, was sheltered from the north and opened to sweeping vistas to the south, toward the snow-capped peaks of the horizon. A ragged but sturdy juniper tree stood a hundred feet down the slope by the spring that bubbled out of the mountain. Lokesh looked at the lichen again, running a finger over a pattern like a wheel. "He said there were deities to be raised."

"Someone died in a chamber under the ruins." Shan explained what he had found beneath the surface of Zhoka.

"The little fresco room," Liya said in a whisper.

"You know it?" Shan asked.

Liya closed her eyes as if in silent grief. "Someone died," she said, eyes still shut, "Surya thought he was responsible. He burned his robe." She spoke slowly, as if to be very careful to recite the correct sequence. "Then he came here, to the old painting."

"Because," Shan said, just as slowly, "he had given up on saving himself. He was interested only in saving Zhoka."

Lokesh gazed into the shadowed rocks. "This is the kind of place where messages are sent to deities. I think the Surya who wore a robe may have come here if he thought his friends were in jeopardy," he said with an uncertain voice. None of them knew the Surya who had shed his robe.

Shan stepped beside Gendun, who was examining the old painting, running his palm across it, an inch above the surface, as though he were reading it through his hand.

"I don't recognize the image," Shan said. "It is Tara, but I have never seen this form."

"Even in the old days it was uncommon," Gendun explained. "It is one of the eight forms of the Holy Mother who protect against fears and demons. This is Kudri Padra. Surya was trying to awaken her."

Shan looked at him with a blank expression.

Lokesh stepped from one side of the painting to the other, staring at it as if he had not truly seen it before, then nodded. "It is the Thief Catcher Tara," he said with surprise in his voice.

Gendun, still gazing at the painting, nodded his head slowly.

"It's all so wrong," Liya interjected in a bitter voice. "A disaster. It will be years before we can try again."

"There was a little girl," Shan reminded her, still watching Gendun. The lama had withdrawn into himself, the way he acted when meditating, but Shan knew it was not a place of serenity he had gone to this time. "She learned how to celebrate with flour. She learned how to listen to the throat chanting."

Liya winced. "She learned how to run from soldiers," she added in a hollow voice. "And now one of our throat chanters is lost. You know how few are left, trained in the old ways of the chanting, who learned directly from the lamas who lived a hundred years ago? They're nearly extinct. There's more snow leopards in Tibet than such men. They will all be gone when the soldiers finish."

"The girl asked about souls and was answered by fear," Lokesh said. "She fled like a frightened antelope." He gazed southward, toward the endless mountains, range after trackless range rolling to the horizon, then turned back toward Shan. "He didn't just speak to Tara. For a moment I heard a prayer, asking the guardians for forgiveness." Shan suddenly recalled the nine-headed deity in the room with the blood, whose eyes had been put out. Surya had asked for forgiveness, as if he had been responsible for the blinding.

"Surya couldn't kill," Liya said in a voice like a whimper. "I spoke with him, two nights ago. He gave me prayers to keep me safe when riding my horse at night. He could have gone into the tunnels and hit his head. He could have imagined . . . but the blood, all the blood. It can't be, he is our monk."

Her strange soliloquy had broken Gendun out of his contemplation. He was looking at Liya with an expression Shan had never before seen on the lama's face. A sad, tormented confusion. Before Shan could react, Gendun stepped away to stand on a ledge that overlooked Zhoka.

He looked back at Liya. None of them could explain the blood. And Dawa had seen a man with a nail through his body, an hour after Surya's strange words. *Here you must be nailed to the earth,* the monk had proclaimed.

"Two nights ago Surya did not come to the chorten," Shan said. "Where did you see him?" Liya turned away, toward Gendun. "Who else was in the hills?" Shan pressed. "You saw foreigners last night. Who did you see the night before?" Shan stepped close to her back. "Jara said there are people who will kill for a word. He would not speak it. What word?"

Liya spun about to face him, her jaw clenched, as if afraid to speak, and backed away.

As Gendun settled onto the ledge Shan approached him, sitting three feet away. He watched the clouds scud westward. He found himself looking not at

Zhoka but beyond it, toward Yerpa. There was a small cell in the old hermitage where he had been made comfortable, given cushions and blankets from the ancient storerooms, where he had spent the most peaceful months of his entire life. He wondered if he would ever see it again.

They sat in silence for a quarter hour as Liya and Lokesh gathered some of the belongings the hill people had left scattered across the slope. Gendun did not move, did not offer a mantra, did not touch his mala, his prayer beads, only folded his hands together, palms down, middle fingers raised against each other. It was the diamond of the mind mudra, for focus, for trying to find the center of things. A small blue butterfly landed on the rock between them. Shan watched as Gendun's eyelids fluttered. His eyes found the butterfly, then Shan.

"You are going to ask what he gave me," the lama said in a near whisper, then handed Shan a crumbled strip of cloth, torn from the grey muslin of an underrobe. "He told me to repeat it ten thousand times, to keep him from coming back."

Shan read the words scrawled on the cloth. *Om Amrta Hum Phat*. It was a mantra for expelling what the Tibetans called hindering demons.

"Keep who from coming back?" he asked.

"Himself," Gendun sighed. "Surya." The lama searched Shan's face, his eyes filled with a mournful confusion. "I can find no balance in what happened today," he said. "Something crushed Surya's deity."

Shan remembered the little statue Atso had with him. The butterfly walked to the edge of the rock and appeared to be staring at the ruins below.

Gendun seemed to follow the gaze of the butterfly. "It is one of the oldest temples in all of Tibet. Before it was built demons roamed freely across the earth. People forget that. People forget the important things."

"I thought it was known for its artists."

"What is the work of artists? To invoke deities. It takes a deity to fight a demon. It is how our artists are made."

Shan gazed at the ruins. It was the way of most of his conversations with the lama, who used short sentences to punctuate long silences, which with Gendun were always more important than words. "You mean if Surya killed something it was a demon."

Gendun looked back at the butterfly, and when at last he spoke it was toward the fragile little creature. "The demon was in the killing," he said. "A killing is the same act, on the killer and the killed. It just affects them in different ways."

"Did you always know about Zhoka, Rinpoche?" Shan asked.

"No," Gendun admitted, offering a small nod to Shan, as if conceding a point. For decades the monks of Yerpa had been wary of venturing more than a mile from their hermitage. "Once there were many gompas in Lhadrung, now many ruins. We did not know how different Zhoka was from the other ruins. It had been kept secret from the rest of the world, for good reason. But Surya found an old book in a cave high in the mountains, wrapped in fur as if it were hibernating. He was so excited. It explained the things that had happened here." He bent low to the butterfly. "Zhoka made the earth quake," he whispered to the fragile creature.

Shan resisted the urge to stare at the old lama, to study his face. Gendun had little trust in words, thought they as often detracted from the truth as led to it. He would never try to reduce to words the complete essence of a thought, a person, a place, because words were incapable of expressing the ultimate truth. But he had begun to express something Shan had not understood before, that the hermits had not come to Zhoka simply because it was a convenient place to reach the hill people, or even because it was a ruined gompa.

Gendun extended his finger in front of the rock and the butterfly climbed onto it. "The child Dawa threw your bag over the edge," the lama said with a sigh. "I am sorry about your throwing sticks. Your father's sticks."

"I strive not to be attached to physical possessions," Shan said in a tight voice.

Gendun offered a sad smile. "They weren't physical to you. They were the spark of your father, and grandfather, and fathers before them. They raised the spirits of your ancestors within you."

For a moment something tightened around Shan's heart. More than once Shan had explained to Gendun and Lokesh how sometimes, using the old lacquered yarrow sticks, he could sense the presence of his father, even smell the ginger he had often carried in his pocket. "Just some old sticks," Shan said in a weak voice.

Gendun whispered to the butterfly and it flew away toward Zhoka, as if on an errand. They watched until it disappeared in the distance, then Shan stood and offered a hand to Gendun. "A sky machine," the lama said as he rose. "One of those sky machines seized him." His hand rose and his fingers extended then slowly closed as if reaching for something invisible to the rest of them. "Last spring, in the north, I spoke to a shepherd woman who had lost her husband that way. She went out every day and sat on a hill with her beads, searching the sky because she said he could return out of a cloud at any time." Shan stared at the lama, for a moment paralyzed by what he saw. A tear rolled down Gendun's cheek. "Surya." He said the name like a prayer.

Shan heard a tiny gasp and turned to see Lokesh was sitting behind them. He had never seen his old friend so pale. The old Tibetan had seen the tear too, and was watching it with a strange despairing awe as it reached Gendun's jaw and hung there.

"For over forty years Surya and I prayed together," Gendun said. "When we were novices our task was to rise together two hours before dawn and light lamps throughout the hermitage, and all these years we never stopped doing it, never asked the new novices to take over. Now I am to pray to keep him away from us. Before him I had never known someone who could take a piece of cloth and pigment and . . ." Gendun looked back toward the tower, with its vibrant paintings and closed his eyes for a moment. "In one writing Surya found, a lama of three hundred years ago said that the artists of Zhoka spread spirit fire."

"They could come back," a worried voice interjected from behind them. Liya was standing at their backs, scanning the hills with her binoculars again. "The soldiers know of this place now."

But the soldiers had not just learned of the place, Shan knew. They had come here, to the stone tower, not to Zhoka, not to the illegal birthday festival. They had behaved as though the tower were their destination. As if someone had ordered the troops in the hills away so they could come to the tower. And if they knew of it already why hadn't they destroyed it? Patrols in the area often carried black spray paint to eradicate any such painted artifacts they discovered, or explosives to collapse such structures. Shan remembered the way the lead soldier from the helicopter squad had hesitated, hand to his ear, just before they had closed around Surya. The soldier had been taking instructions by radio, probably from someone in the cockpit of the helicopter, someone, impossibly, looking for the monk.

"We must go deep into the mountains," Liya said. "Zhoka is too dangerous now. And you can't go to town, Shan. The valley is too dangerous."

In the valley, Shan knew, patrols would be aggressively checking identity papers. Shan had no papers, had no right to be anywhere but in a gulag prison, had a bounty on his head. Lokesh stood and looked toward the sun, an hour above the horizon, then toward the southern mountains. Jara was on the next ridge, limping on his injured foot. Lokesh glanced at Shan, who nodded, struggling to keep the worry from his face.

"The girl," Lokesh said. Without another word he set off along the southern trail, in the direction Dawa had last been seen.

Gendun looked at Liya. "Would it be possible to get two blankets? And a little food and water?"

"We will take you to where there are supplies. Close by," Liya said. "You can sleep there."

"Not for me. They are for Shan. He is going on retreat."

Liya offered a forced smile, as if Gendun had told a bad joke.

"Rinpoche," Shan said in a plaintive tone.

There was never tension, never a wall between Shan and Gendun except the one that was there now. He had experienced it many times, each time more painful than the one before. To Gendun nothing should interfere with Shan's planned retreat, nothing was worth Shan neglecting his deity. But for Shan there was something vastly more important, no matter how adamantly Gendun rejected the notion. No matter how endangered the health of Shan's own deity might be, for Shan, protecting the old lamas would always be more important.

"Do not let this thing separate you, Shan," Gendun said. He was not referring to the day's events, Shan knew, but to the thing that separated Shan from his deity. To Gendun the shadow of Shan's prior incarnation as a senior Beijing investigator hung about him like a jealous ghost, encouraging him to become involved in unimportant events, drawn to the workings of logic and cause and effect that Gendun considered traps for the spiritually aware.

"Rinpoche, Liya must take you to the trail to the hermitage in the morning," Shan said. He regretted the words even as they left his tongue. They sounded too much like a demand.

"At dawn I will be at the new chorten," Gendun said. "And the next dawn after that. There are words to be spoken. All these years no one has paid the reverence that is owed."

"I don't understand," Shan said, gazing into the old face, weathered as a river stone.

"Surya was to stay. Now I will."

"In the ruins?"

"In the gompa," Gendun said, as if the monastery still existed.

"Someone died there."

"Hundreds died there."

"Surely it can wait."

"It cannot. Nor can your retreat."

Shan looked in the direction of Zhoka. Miracles were going to happen there, Lokesh had said. But all Shan knew for certain was that death had happened there, that death lingered there, and the dark secrets that had caused the death.

"Promise me, Shan," the lama said, and there it was again, stabbing Shan like a blade, the torment in Gendun's eyes.

"If I could have seen all this," Shan said with a wrench in his heart, "if I had only known, I would have stayed in prison." He felt responsible. When he closed his eyes he saw a fateful path, a door that had been locked until Shan had arrived at Yerpa. He was the one who had introduced Gendun to the outside world, who had helped Gendun travel into modern Tibet, who had introduced him, and through him Surya, to the gulag camps and the soldiers.

Gendun began tightening the laces of the tattered workboots he wore under his robes. "If I had known all this," the lama said with a calm smile, "I would have come years ago." He straightened and began walking toward Zhoka.

"Please, Shan, they'll arrest you," Liya said in a knowing voice. "Don't do it. If you go to town we'll never see you again, I know it." When Shan returned her steady stare without speaking, she sighed, then fell in behind the lama.

As he stood alone on the windswept crest, desperately trying to grasp the events of the day, Shan's fingers suddenly closed around the bloodstained disc he had found in the tunnel. He pulled it from his pocket, wiped it with grass, and held it up in the last light of the day. It was heavy, as if made of metal, though coated with red vinyl, with bands of green spaced evenly along its raised outer rim. In its center was the image of a savage yellow eye. He stared at it a long time before he could make sense of the English words around the eye. Lone Wolf Casino. Reno, Nevada.

CHAPTER THREE

Nights in Tibet were battlefields for the soul. Shan had seen brave young men stare into the dark endless sky and burst into tears. Lamas tested novices by having them sit for hours under the stars, often by the charnel grounds where the dead lay offered for sky burial. Of all the lands on earth only here, the highest of all, were the skies so black, the stars so dense, the frailty of the human so apparent each night.

In prison, his cellmates had pried up a piece of the tin roof over their barracks. They had moved a bunk under the hole and taken turns lying under the hole, staring out at the stars. A bitter young Tibetan, a drug dealer from Lhasa, had mocked the old men for doing so, saying he understood risking beating and extended sentences for trying to escape past the wire but not just for an escape to the stars. After a few months he had begun waiting his turn for the bunk. Even now Shan associated the stars with freedom and when troubled he would sit, sometimes for hours, watching them, sometimes speaking to them, sometimes watching for the souls of his dead parents perhaps flickering among them.

But tonight the sky tore at him. More than once he thought he heard screams coming from the sky, and every few minutes a shiver ran down his spine. There seemed to be something new about the dark this night, as if the terrible blackness of the tunnels had slipped the bounds of earth and was stalking him.

By midnight clouds filled the sky. It grew so dim he dared not continue down the treacherous slopes. He sat against a rock and fell into a fitful sleep, woke cold and shaking after a nightmare vision of Gendun lying bleeding and broken in the tunnels of Zhoka.

By the time the sky cleared, a half moon had risen and he quickly found his way over the steep ridges, reaching the crest of the final ridge that sloped down into the valley just as the eastern sky began to glow with a hint of dawn. In the distance, still miles away, was the orange shimmer of the streetlights of Lhadrung. He was about to begin the final descent when he halted. A faint scent of wood smoke wafted along the ridge.

Shan ventured warily along the crest for a hundred yards, then heard a lamb bleat. Below him in a gentle swale was the dim outline of a house and two small structures, one with a mound of hay stacked against one wall. He stepped closer and was a hundred feet away when a dog began barking. No one came out, though he saw a dim light, probably from a single butter lamp, past the door of the house, which stood ajar. The lamb bleated again, then another. The dog, invisible in the darkness, snarled now, but did not show itself. Shan backed slowly away, over the ridge, on to Lhadrung.

He approached the town quickly, jogging through the long dawn shadows along the dirt road that led from the mountains, stopping every few minutes in the cover of thickets to survey the valley. There was no sign of helicopters overhead, nor of the dust plumes raised by troop trucks when they patrolled the valley. At the edge of town he mingled with Tibetans arriving with produce for the market, entering the market square with them, then dropping into the shadows of the maze of alleys surrounding it.

Shan had heard descriptions of the Lhadrung that had existed fifty years earlier, a thriving Tibetan community of simple, small houses, each with its own courtyard, each with its own little shrine, arrayed around a small gompa that served the people of the central valley. By the time the People's Liberation Army arrived in the valley, scarred and vengeful from months of guerrilla fighting, the residents expected the gompa to be leveled, as others throughout Tibet had been. The army leveled not just the gompa but nearly the entire town, first with aerial bombs, then with bulldozers. The Chinese town that had grown in its place was a grid of lifeless grey buildings over which towered the four-story structure that served as headquarters for the county administration.

Since leaving prison Shan had carefully avoided the government center, had confined his few town visits to the market on the east side of the town. Much had changed at the building since he had walked out of it, unexpectedly freed, the year before. The front of the structure, but only the front, had been painted bright white, which seemed only to highlight the dirty grey of the other sides. No one had bothered to remove the splatters of paint from the windows. The first-floor windows surrounding the metal entry doors, however, had all been covered with posters fastened inside the glass, filled with images that were familiar fixtures of public places throughout China. On one poster smiling Chinese girls with ribbons in their hair drove tractors past rows of cotton, the red flag of the People's Republic flying from each tractor. On another an old woman looked out over a mountain range, a rifle on her shoulder, a commemoration of past heroes. On a new concrete pedestal beside the entrance was a statue cast of marble chips, the head and shoulders of Mao, in the young, cheerful aspect that had become popular in Party circles. Two trees with the shape of gingkos had been placed on either side of the doors. They were already dead, a stark reminder about Beijing's efforts to transplant things Chinese into a world where they could find no roots. Incredibly, beside one of the dead trees three beggars sat against the wall of the building. Shan slipped along the perimeter of the small square in front of the building, studying the three figures. There should be no beggars. Colonel Tan did not tolerate beggars, certainly would not permit them in front of the seat of county government.

He stepped into the shadowed doorway of a closed restaurant and studied the scene warily. Two cars were parked in the alley at the side of the building. One, a black Red Flag limousine at least twenty years old, appeared to be the vehicle used by Colonel Tan. In front of the Red Flag was a silver sedan, a recent model of Japanese manufacture. He looked back at the beggars. Two of them, a figure whose face was obscured with burlap sacking and the man beside him, draped in a tattered blanket, sat with heads tilted toward the dry cracked earth in front of them. The third, an old woman whose left eye was milky white, tapped a stick against a traditional metal alms bowl. Near the edge of the square, a small knot of Tibetans stood at the rear of a truck, watching the three uneasily. They were not accustomed to seeing beggars. Buddhist teaching would tell them to offer alms. Government teaching insisted they did not.

Shan watched the scene with growing unease. It was still early. The government building was quiet, appearing almost unoccupied. He studied the windows of the top floor, where the senior officers worked. Drapes were drawn in several of the offices. He could discern no movement.

Two men in grey uniforms appeared a block away, semiautomatic weapons slung from their shoulders. Another new feature of life in Lhadrung. He pushed deeper into the shadows and watched, futilely twisting the doorknob of the restaurant, looking for a hiding place should the soldiers approach. They turned at the corner before the square and disappeared down a side street. A moment later one of the Tibetans at the truck advanced hesitantly to the old woman, knelt beside her, and began speaking in low, urgent tones, gesturing toward the street in the opposite direction of the patrol, trying to pull her up.

Suddenly two men burst out of the front doors of the government center. The man kneeling by the woman froze, the color draining from his face, then he stood, turned his back to the doors, and stiffly walked away.

The men on the steps were both Han Chinese, with the air of senior officials. One, a tall sleek man in his thirties wearing neatly pressed black trousers, blue dress shirt, and red tie, extracted a wide roll of paper from what appeared to be a map case and began speaking rapidly, unrolling it in a pool of sunlight on the low wall beneath the Mao bust. The shorter man, perhaps ten years older than his companion, was clad in a brown sweater vest over a white shirt, without a tie. His uncombed hair, showing signs of grey, was long, hanging over his ears, and as Shan watched he used a silver pen to point at the map, a question in his eyes as he spoke. Not a map, Shan saw in surprise as the younger man lifted it from the wall. It was a thangka, a traditional Tibetan cloth painting, an old one judging by its faded colors.

The older man seemed to listen to his companion with thin tolerance, and appeared about to interrupt, when a Western woman with curly russet colored hair stepped outside to join them. She made repeated, vigorous gestures toward the thangka, as if emphatically explaining something about it, then took it and reversed it, pointing to something on the back. Her action quieted the men, both of whom offered her reluctant nods. Shan took a step forward to see the woman better. She was in her thirties, dressed in blue denim jeans with a short, stylish brown jacket over a white blouse. Something hung from her neck on a black cord. A magnifying lens.

The tall man uttered a few syllables, shrugged, rolled up the painting, packed it back in its case, and stepped back inside, followed a moment later by his older companion. The woman lingered, moving to the edge of the steps, putting her hand on Mao's shoulder to lean over, studying the beggars. Worry seemed to cross her face. She rolled a finger in a lock of hair that dangled at her shoulder and spoke. Shan could not hear the words, but the man in the center, wrapped in the blanket, looked up, seeming to understand. Had she spoken Tibetan? The man's face was in shadow, but he seemed to shake his head as though in answer. The woman glanced toward the door then darted down the stairs, reaching into her jacket pocket as she ran. She produced an apple, dropped it onto the lap of the beggar closest to the door, the one draped in burlap, then ran back inside.

As she disappeared, a helicopter burst into sight, flying low and fast over the town center toward the north, in the direction of the prison camp. It was gone in an instant, leaving a cold, fearful silence in the square. When Shan looked back the apple was in the hands of the second beggar, the one draped with the blanket.

Shan stared at the empty doorway, then the beggars. He was certain the two Han men had been government officials, senior officials. They had seen the beggars and done nothing. They had been discussing a Tibetan painting, perhaps arguing over it. Then the woman had appeared and seemed to settle the argument. Had they not acted against the beggars because of the Westerner? He waited another ten minutes, then approached the beggars, walking along the perimeter of the square. He dropped his only coin in the bowl of the old woman, who offered a grateful nod. The other two figures, their faces still obscured, seemed not to notice him, but then the man with the blanket over his head pushed his leg out as Shan approached, as if to trip him. Shan carefully stepped over the leg, squatted by the man who wore the burlap hood, and looked into the shadowed face.

"Surya!" he gasped.

The monk stared at him with glazed eyes, showing no sign of recognition. The side of his face was heavily bruised. His right hand was covered with a bloody cloth. Shan touched the monk's cheek. Surya moaned and pulled away.

"We thought . . . What happened?" Shan blurted out. "They took you into that helicopter. . . ."

Surya stared dumbly at his bandaged hand. Under the burlap he still wore his grey muslin underrobe, torn in several places.

Shan pulled on Surya's arm. "Please. Gendun thinks—" Surya resisted.

Shan stood, examining the square, wondering where the foot patrol had gone, then bent and tried to pull Surya again. "They think you are dead."

"Surya *is* dead," the monk said. "He was killed, too."

Shan glanced back at the doors and the street beyond. If a bounty was posted for him, anyone in the street, not just the soldiers, was a possible threat. "You can't leave them. You are part of them."

A stray dog, skin hanging loose over its ribs, appeared and settled beside Surya. "The only honor he had left to give them was to leave," the old man said. "Even the low creature he has become knows that." His voice had changed. It was cracked and dry and hollow, not the voice of the serene throat chanter Shan had heard the day before. Surya's head lowered and his jaw dropped open. His gaunt, absent expression matched that of the dog.

"I looked inside the lower gompa," Shan whispered. "There was no body. There was only blood. Help me understand what happened."

Surya's mouth turned into a twisted grin, his upper lip stuck on one of his front teeth. "He knew what he did. He saw the black thing in his heart afterwards. If you try to change that, Chinese, that would be dishonor as well."

Chinese. The word wrenched something inside Shan. He and Surya had been friends, had shared many stories of their lives while sharing tasks at Yerpa, had often laughed together. But now Shan was simply another Chinese. "The soldiers will take you if you stay here. Take you again," he added, still perplexed over why Surya had been released. "What did they ask when they interrogated you? Who is the woman with red hair?"

"Soon they will accept the truth," Surya said in his jarring new voice. A string of saliva dangled from his mouth. "They will do to him what killers and eaters of vows deserve. Meanwhile he will pretend to be alive."

Shan suppressed a shudder. He touched Surya's bandaged hand. "Let me clean your wound."

But Surya pushed him away and scuttled crablike past the dead tree, into the shadow cast by the steps of the building.

Shan backed away, across the square. As he paused in the shadows of the restaurant doorway again, a wave of emotion surged through him. Twenty-four hours earlier Surya had been about to embark on a new life at Zhoka, about to change the world. Now the world had caught up and changed him, and Shan felt guilt and confusion, even a fleeting revulsion, at the twisted, hollow thing Surya had become.

Shan waited until morning traffic began moving down the street, battered trucks with broken mufflers, carts drawn by small, aged horses, an old man with a wispy beard pushing a hand barrow full of greens. The wind from the mountains mixed the scents of onions and manure, roasted barley, and diesel. When Shan finally stepped into the street he kept in the shadows, circling the block to reach the rear of the government center. He circled the building once, stealing furtive glances toward the upper windows, and found himself by the automobiles parked in the side alley. The tires of the silver car had red gravel in the treads, gravel that had not been picked up on the streets of Lhadrung. He bent closer to the treads, vaguely recalling he had seen the little red chips before.

Suddenly a strong hand seized his upper arm and dragged him backward, into a doorway on the opposite side of the alley. He was unable to wrench free before a door slammed behind him and he was released. He was in total darkness. He squatted, hands over his head to shield him. A single naked lightbulb flickered on, revealing a small storeroom, its shelves stacked with tins of cooking oil, baskets of vegetables, and sacks of rice and barley. A man with close-cropped grey hair and a face like a hatchet pulled out a chair from the crude plank table in the center of the room, resting his well-polished black boot on it.

"I thought you were dead," the man growled. "At least gone down some hole in the mountains, and smart enough to stay there." He wore the plain, sharply pressed uniform of an army officer, without adornment, without any indication of rank other than the pockets on his tunic.

Shan breathed in deeply and returned the man's steady stare. "I prefer to be gone, Colonel," he said in a brittle voice. "But here we are."

Colonel Tan had been administrator of the county for years—for so long, Shan knew, he had lost all hope of advancement, all hope of transfer out of the remote, impoverished county, which only added to his capacity for fury and brutality. He clenched his jaw, surprised at the anger Tan's sudden appearance had released, but acutely aware that with a single command Tan could send him back to the gulag.

"You have new deputies," Shan observed after he calmed himself. A year ago Tan had unofficially released him after Shan had proven that the murder of the local prosecutor had been committed not by the monk held for the crime but by a ring of local officials.

"Just visitors. I get many offers of assistance these days. Nobody ever heard of Lhadrung until I made the mistake of asking for your help," Tan said acidly.

"You mean no one knew that three of your most important offices were run by drug runners and killers."

Half of Tan's mouth curled upward. It was one of the colonel's distinctive expressions, a half grin that felt like a snarl. "I was reminded that someone of lesser reputation would have been dismissed in disgrace."

"Congratulations." Shan knew Tan expected gratitude but in all his years in Lhadrung Tan had never lifted a finger to stop the brutality at his former labor camp.

Tan looked as if he were about to leap across the table to take a bite out of Shan. "You don't exist," he hissed.

In the harsh silence left by the words Shan lowered himself into one of the chairs at the table, all the while keeping his gaze on Tan, the way one watches a coiled snake. The colonel meant the words as a threat, as a reminder of how easily Shan could be made to disappear.

Shan broke away from Tan's cool glare and conspicuously studied the storeroom. Why hadn't Tan taken him into his administration building? Was he hiding Shan, or was it the fact that he knew Shan? "There are beggars out front," Shan ventured. "You don't permit beggars."

Tan extracted an unfiltered cigarette from his uniform pocket, lit it, and blew a stream of smoke toward Shan. "I'm not asking for your help this time. I am telling you to stay away."

Shan stared at Tan again, trying to hide his confusion. "One of them was brought by helicopter from the mountains. His name is Surya. He was arrested and released. Why?"

"The use of government resources in this county is for me to decide, not for some senile Tibetan ranting about imaginary crimes."

"You mean it is inconvenient to have another murder in Lhadrung."

"He was never officially detained. There was no murder. There is just another pathetic Tibetan who needs help." Tan inhaled deeply on his cigarette, examining Shan. "Why are you so interested? Perhaps I should call one of the social intervention agencies."

Shan fought a shudder. It was an idiom of senior officials. The agencies Tan referred to were government facilities for medical experimentation or special mental health clinics run by Public Security. Lokesh, like Shan, had spent time at one of the institutes for the criminally insane. He said it was where chemicals were used to drive out a man's deity, where a simple injection could turn a man into a lower life form. Shan stared at the floor a moment then forced himself to look back into Tan's eyes. "The Western woman. Who is she?"

"A visitor named McDowell. An art historian."

"We're hiding from an art historian?"

"We hide from no one." Tan watched the smoke drift from his mouth, following it to the ceiling, then sat, interlocking his fingers on the table with the smoldering cigarette jutting from the top. Shan had seen the gesture before. Tan had his own mudras. "If I had to do it over, I would not change anything I did a year ago," Tan said slowly. He seemed to struggle to get the words out.

Shan could not understand the strange pain that rose in his heart. What did he mean? Was it Tan's strange way of trying to shame Shan? A terrifying thought occurred to Shan. Tan could order him to find evidence against Surya, could threaten Shan with imprisonment if he did not cooperate. "I am sorry if you were punished for it," he said after a long moment, looking at the tabletop.

"Don't flatter yourself," Tan snapped. "It wasn't about you, it was about having all those criminals operating under my nose."

"I didn't come looking for you, Colonel. I, too, had decided it would be easier if our paths didn't cross again."

"Then why come to my office? Because of that beggar? I would prefer he go. Take him away."

"He won't go. He acts as if he is chained to the building." Shan understood much about Tan. He had worked for people like Tan in Beijing for years, only they had used larger limousines and smoked more elegant cigarettes. But he did not understand the strange game they were playing now.

Tan stood and pointed toward the door. "Then go. Slip down your hole again. In a few more years I'll retire and you can try the world once more."

"If you don't want me in Lhadrung, why offer a bounty?"

Tan took two steps toward Shan and snapped his arm as though holding a whip, pointing toward the door again.

Shan silently rose, walked past Tan, and stepped back into the alley. He had already taken ten paces when he heard Tan mutter a low curse behind him. Two men were climbing into the silver car, pausing as they saw Tan in the doorway. Shan recognized them as the two he had seen on the front steps. The shorter man with the unkempt hair, a suit coat now over his vest, waved stiffly and called out a greeting to the colonel. The taller man offered an icy grin and stepped into the center of the alley, blocking Shan's path. He did not look at Shan, however, but stared over Shan's shoulder toward Tan with an expression of curiosity. The shorter man studied Shan warily, then offered a disappointed sigh and turned to Tan. "This is the man I told you about, who was watching us from the shadows in front of the building," he announced. "You know him?"

Shan clenched his jaw and stared at the man with new interest. He had thought he had been well hidden, had not even seen the man look in his direction. Another figure was in the car, the Western woman who had appeared on the steps, the art historian named McDowell.

"One of the reformed prisoners," Tan replied without hesitation. "Sometimes they wander aimlessly around the district. They hate us when they are behind wire but can't bear to leave us when we free them. Public Security doctors classify it as a psychological disorder," he added with studied disinterest.

"Sometimes old criminals commit new crimes," the stranger observed. "It is often productive to question them. There is no better informant than a former prisoner."

Tan nodded slowly. "Of course. But not those from our camp in the valley. They have been well conditioned by the time they are permitted to leave. Most have little left to contribute. They just wander into town sometimes, looking for a job, or a meal. Pitiful creatures. This one, his family is destroyed, his reputation ruined, he lives from one meal to the next. I gave him the address for the Tibetan Relief Association. He knows he could be arrested again on my command," Tan added pointedly.

"But he's Han."

"Not any more," Tan snapped impatiently, pushing Shan toward the shadows as he stepped past.

Shan turned back to face the man in the vest, who for the moment appeared more curious about the colonel than him. Then the stranger slowly turned to examine Shan, gazing at his scuffed tattered work boots, the threadbare pants that were two sizes too big, the brown quilted jacket with frayed sleeves, the small red embroidered vase on its shoulder, the symbolic depository of wisdom, placed there by a woman whose herding camp Lokesh and Shan had shared during a winter storm.

The man reached into his pocket and produced a few coins which he pushed into Shan's hand, then frowned and stepped down the alley as the tall polished man opened the driver's door of the silver car and settled behind the wheel, speaking to the woman who sat beside him. Shan turned to see the short man gaze into the darkened doorway where Tan had taken Shan. The man at the wheel tapped the horn and his companion jogged to the car. A moment later they sped away.

When Shan turned Tan was still staring after the car. The strange ambivalence he had shown in the storeroom was gone, replaced by the cold fury that was never totally absent from his face. "It won't be the same this time," the colonel snapped. "If you give me reason to put you back behind the wire, any reason," he said, his eyes still on the street, "you'll never see daylight again."

Shan sat with Surya another quarter hour after Tan disappeared into the government center, but the monk still did not acknowledge him, only stared forlornly into the dirt at his feet, wringing his fingers, sometimes gasping and fighting for breath. Surya had gone to some cold dismal place inside himself, from which no one else could hope to extract him.

"What words has he spoken here?" Shan asked the man wrapped in the blanket, the one who had tried to trip him previously. The man pushed his open palm toward Shan. As Shan dropped into it the coins the stranger in the alley had given him he asked himself again why Tan would permit begging. I would prefer Surya to go, Tan had said. As if someone other than Tan wanted him to stay. And if they let Surya beg in the central square, they could not stop the others. But why Surya? Not because of the killing at Zhoka. He recalled the three strangers and the way they had examined the thangka on the steps. Because he was an artist?

The man pushed back the blanket from his head, as if Shan had now bought the right to see his face. "He sang some songs, in a whisper," the second beggar said in a nervous voice. His cheeks were disfigured with jagged scars, the kind raised by beatings with truncheons. He repeatedly glanced toward the steps. "Some old children's songs, like my mother used to sing to me. He asked me about Chinese magic."

"Magic?"

"He had never seen trucks or cars. He called them Chinese carts. He asked how they could move without horses or yaks." The beggar looked at the coins in his hand with a reluctant, frustrated expression, as if they obliged him to answer Shan's questions. "He asked if the great abbot could make them fly in the air, too." The man glanced up at Shan. His nose had a jagged angle to it, the look of having been broken.

"Abbot? What abbot?"

"That's what I asked him. He said he met a powerful abbot in the mountains, who could make great magic." The man glanced warily at Shan. "Is it true?" he asked in a more urgent, lower voice. "Has an abbot come for the people?"

Shan looked in confusion toward the distant peaks. "I don't know what is happening in the mountains." He studied Surya again. "Did he say what they asked him?"

The man shrugged. "They always ask the same things, don't they?"

"You took his apple," Shan observed.

The man shrugged again. "Look at him. He no longer wants anything of this world. I've seen it before, I saw the way they threw him out the door, the way he cried when they left, because they wouldn't listen anymore. He said he had to go to the place with the wire, where old lamas are kept until they die." The beggar stuffed the coins into his pocket and pushed the blanket back over his head.

Shan shifted through his pockets and found a small *tsa-tsa,* a clay tablet shaped in the image of a saint. He dropped the tsa-tsa into the man's lap. "You didn't say what Surya told them." While the monk had not seemed interested in Shan's questions, and may have ignored those of interrogators, he still seemed to believe there were things that had to be said.

The beggar pushed the blanket from his head with a frown, then slowly cupped his hands around the clay image. A strange mix of resentment and gratitude filled his eyes when he replied. "They asked about caves, about shrines, about symbols in paintings. They showed him some old thangkas. He kept saying he was a murderer. He kept saying he didn't know where any more paintings were."

"He told you this?"

"I heard."

Shan grimaced, chiding himself for not seeing the obvious. "You're an informer."

"Sure. You think I would sit in Tan's square if they didn't tell me to?"

"Why would they ask about paintings?"

Again the man shrugged. "Must be a new campaign," he said, meaning a political initiative. "That was all the old man said, except a warning as they tossed him outside. He said earth taming temples are too dangerous for people like them. As if they would care." The beggar stuffed the tsa-tsa inside his blanket and covered his head again.

As if they would care. But the old Tibetans would care very much about an earth temple. The beggar's words echoed in Shan's mind as he walked through the alleyways. It did not seem possible, but yet it could explain much. Shan had not heard Tibetans speak of the earth taming temples since prison, where they had been woven into the tales told by the oldest lamas on winter nights. Centuries earlier, the construction of Tibet's monasteries, once numbering in the thousands, had begun with the building of a series of temples in far-reaching concentric rings centered on the country's most sacred temple, the Jokhang, in Lhasa, over a hundred miles to the northwest. The Jokhang has been built to anchor the heart of the supreme land demon, which had first resisted the introduction of Buddhism. Each of the outlying temples had been constructed on the appendages of the vast demon, some located hundreds of miles from Lhasa. The network kept the land and its people in harmony. Surya had spoken about being nailed to the earth. Shan had not connected the words to the old tales. It was part of the tradition, that the earth temples kept evil demons at bay by pinning them to the earth with sacred nails or daggers.

Though once considered the most important places of spiritual power in Tibet, earth taming temples were a thing of ancient history to most. But they would not be to Gendun, or Surya, or Lokesh. Though some of the locations were still known, most were lost, although he now recalled debate in prison about the old legend that one was located in the region of Lhadrung. Why would Surya suddenly speak of Zhoka as an earth taming temple, Shan wondered. Because, he suddenly recalled, Surya had found an old book in a cave.

Ten minutes later Shan was walking at the edge of town, watching for a truck that might be heading toward the mountains, when a sudden clamor rose from past the market. He heard applause, and a voice speaking from a public address system. It took him only five minutes to reach the crowd assembled on the athletic field used by the local school. A podium had been erected in front of the small cinder block bleachers, by another bust of Mao on a cement pillar, and a man in a suit was introducing a special guest from Beijing, a renowned scientist, the youngest director ever of his famed institution. A banner ran from the flagpole by the podium to the bleachers, announcing a tribute for Director Ming of the Museum of Antiquities in Beijing, presented by the Chinese Tibetan Friendship Society.

As the assembly of perhaps a hundred people, nearly all Han Chinese, applauded, a man in a blue suit climbed to the podium, his back to Shan. He accepted the microphone from his host. "It is I who applaud you," he said in a polished voice, once in Mandarin and again in Tibetan. "You are the true heroes of the great reform, you are the ones who have learned how to blend the strengths of all our great cultures."

Shan stared in disbelief as the man turned and showed his face. It was the tall, well-groomed man from the steps, one of those Tan had tried to avoid. He was the head of the most prestigious museum in Beijing, perhaps in all of China. What was he doing in Lhadrung? Shan listened for several minutes as Director Ming spoke in an earnest voice about the need to meld the great cultures of China, of how the effort was no less a challenge for those in Beijing than for those in Lhadrung. He spoke of how he had decided to locate his summer workshop in Lhadrung due to the fertile ground it represented for that effort, because it was a county where so few Chinese to date had come to live, and which still had much history to share. To emphasize his point he produced a white silk cloth, a khata, a ceremonial Tibetan scarf, raised it with both hands, and with a dramatic air tied it around the neck of the Mao bust. The assembly broke into another round of applause.

Shan retreated, wary of the soldiers who always watched over public assemblies, but as he stepped away from the field he saw the auburn-haired woman sitting in the driver's seat of the silver car, leaning back, reading a book. He looked to make certain no patrols were near, and approached the open window of the car.

"You gave an apple to a friend of mine," he said quietly, in English. "Thank you."

The woman looked up with a thin smile. "I tried to give it to him. I'm not sure he even saw it." Her voice was sad but her grin remained. "Can you speak with Surya? Maybe he needs to speak with someone he knows better." A small Tibetan boy appeared, squeezing around Shan, handing the woman a bottle of orange drink.

"Thuchechey," the woman said, thanking the boy in Tibetan as she handed him a coin worth four times the cost of the drink. The boy grabbed it and darted away with a cry of glee.

"He can't be reached right now," Shan said.

"Sounds like you were trying to phone him up," the woman said. He could not place her accent. She did not sound American.

"I mean—"

"I know what you mean. It's bloody awful. Please, do you really know him?" She gestured to the seat beside her. "Get in. Please. If you care for him we should speak."

Shan looked about, half suspecting to see soldiers closing in. The crowd was applauding again, and a woman was on the stage, presenting something to their visiting celebrity.

He studied the woman a moment. She knew Surya. But that was impossible. "Did you meet with him in the mountains?" Shan asked as he slipped in beside her.

"Once. I wasn't on every visit," she said. Her voice was soft and refined, well-educated. "My name is McDowell. Elizabeth McDowell. My friends call me Punji, like the sharp bamboo stick."

Shan did not offer his own name. "What visits? Why go to the ruins?"

"It's Director Ming's annual summer seminar. His workshop for graduate students. He's doing an inventory of ancient sites. Students are helping for the summer, and some of his assistant curators." On the seat beside McDowell were several papers, including some oversized envelopes, all with the return address of the Tibetan Children's Relief Fund, at a street in London.

"Surya needs to go back into the mountains," Shan said, "to be with his friends."

"He denies his name is Surya," McDowell reminded Shan. "He says Surya died."

As Shan tried to inconspicuously study the loose papers under the envelopes, the door behind him opened and someone climbed inside. McDowell dropped her book on the envelopes, switched on the engine and eased the car into the street.

"He's had a terrible shock," Shan said. "Someone died. He is . . . inexperienced. His whole life has been his art."

"Study only the absolute," a smooth voice interjected from the rear seat. Shan turned to see Director Ming smiling at him.

"He knows our friend Surya," McDowell announced to Ming, keeping her eyes on the road.

"I didn't mean to interfere," Shan said, and began looking for a safe place to leap from the car.

"Where can I take you?" McDowell asked with an oddly mischievous tone.

"Nowhere. I'll get out here," Shan said, his hand on the door handle. "Please."

"Nonsense. How do you know Surya? Is he really a monk? And if you don't tell me where you are going you'll wind up at the old brick factory south of town."

Shan settled back in his seat. "The brick factory will be fine," he said uneasily. The dilapidated building was less than two miles from the foot of the mountains.

Ming leaned forward, suddenly interested. "You know how to make the old monk talk?" He spoke as if he wanted Surya to confess something, something other than murder. He studied Shan a moment. "You were the one with Tan this morning."

"Surya has sometimes gone a month without speaking," Shan said truthfully.

"But he knows so much that needs telling," Ming said in a disappointed voice. "It could be worth a lot to get him to speak with us again."

Shan could not make up his mind about the earnest young Han. He would not have become the youngest director of one of the country's premier museums based on his scientific skills alone. "Did you visit him at the ruins?"

"Three times," Ming readily admitted. "He explained to me what he was painting, at that old tower. I asked about old shrines. It is quite valuable for my research."

"Were the two of you in the mountains two nights ago?" Shan asked abruptly.

Ming fixed him with a hard, almost threatening stare for a moment, then shrugged. "He has suffered a mental collapse. I thought it was a stroke. But an army doctor was called in and said he was fine, in extraordinary shape, actually. Except he forgets who he is or anything about the art. He moans about death and killing."

"It was you who arranged for the army to pick him up?"

A smug smile crossed Ming's face. "A number of government resources have been made available for our project." Shan would have thought it impossible without having heard it from Ming himself. The museum director had borrowed troops from Tan so he could interrogate Surya about his historic research.

McDowell gave an exasperated sigh. "Comrade Ming fantasizes that he's some kind of party boss," she said, grinning at Shan. She slowed and pointed to a yak pulling a plow in a field. "I keep telling him he just runs a museum. Billionaires aren't interested in him, they're interested in his art."

"Billionaires?" Shan asked, looking at the woman. He realized his hand was creeping toward the old gau he wore under his shirt, reacting the way Lokesh did when the old Tibetan sensed demons.

She continued to look at the yak, smiling, as if the scene gave her pleasure. "You know," she said at last. "Patrons. Customers. The ones who pay for new museum wings. The shareholders in Director Ming's business."

When they pulled into the old factory site it appeared still abandoned. But as McDowell drove around the front of the building a line of Tibetans came into view, mostly women with small children, and beyond them a small red minibus with a Lhasa registration plate. Over a door in a corner of the crumbling brick building was a hand-lettered sign. Free Children's Health Exam, it said, in

Tibetan only. Several of the Tibetans began waving at McDowell. As she waved back and switched off the ignition she noticed the question in Shan's eyes. "The relief group only has money enough for the medicine and travel expenses of the nurses. I help where I can. Get in line and we'll find you some vitamins." She opened the door and climbed out to a chorus of greetings.

"Twenty minutes, no more," Ming called to her, then climbed out himself and lit a cigarette. Shan grabbed one of the loose papers on the seat, stuffed it inside his shirt, and opened his door. He was nearly out of the compound when Ming spoke to his back.

"Who else was in the ruins with the old monk?"

Shan turned. "There were outsiders."

Ming's eyes narrowed. "How do you know this?"

Shan pulled the little cigar stub from his pocket and held it up. "This came from no Tibetan. Is it yours?"

Ming's gaze grew suddenly intense as he saw the cigar. "Let me have that."

Shan set the stub on the trunk of the car and backed away. Ming slowly lifted it, holding it to his nose, then dropping it and crushing it with his shoe. "Not me. It's nothing."

"Nothing," Shan repeated.

But it was not nothing. Ming stared at the shreds of tobacco at his feet, then gazed angrily toward the mountains. "If you truly know Surya," the museum director said in a voice gone suddenly cold. "If you know his friends who hide in the mountains, the hermits, tell them time is short. If it's not going to be Surya, who will it be? We won't settle for half of death," he declared to Shan, staring as if watching for a reaction. "The emperor has waited far too long already."

"The emperor?" Shan asked, certain he had not heard correctly. "Half of death?" Shan was no longer looking at the affable scientist he had heard at the school yard. Ming's eyes were small and hard. "What do you want in the mountains?"

Ming frowned and glanced back at the shredded cigar. "I want another monk. One of those old ones from the high mountains."

Shan's mouth was suddenly bone dry. "Why?"

"Bring me a monk and I'll pay you."

"There are no monks in—"

Ming cut him off with a raised hand. "There are bombs, you know, made for terrorists in caves. They don't destroy the cave, just take all the oxygen out so everyone inside suffocates." A young boy ran by the car, chasing a ball. Ming smiled and waved at him, then turned back to Shan. "Tell them soon the whole world will know who died. It will be too late for them then."

"You know who died?"

"For now," Ming sighed, motioning him away with his fingers, "that remains a state secret. Bring me a monk. Or I will inform Colonel Tan that Surya did kill someone."

Chapter Four

It was early afternoon before Shan reached the hills above the valley. Surya's desolate face, and the strange words of Ming and the second beggar, haunted Shan as he climbed the slopes. He had gone to the town to try to find answers, but had come away more confused, more filled with dread, than ever. A murderer roamed the hills, godkillers stalked the mountains. But if Zhoka was indeed an earth taming temple there would be nothing more important to the old Tibetans than protecting it. Shan would never give Ming the second monk he demanded, but Gendun would willingly go if he thought it would help Surya, or protect Zhoka.

Something new began to gnaw at him as he climbed, Tan's strange way of describing Shan. In trying to dismiss Shan as a pitiable former prisoner Tan had said Shan's family was destroyed. A year earlier Tan had taken pleasure in reporting to Shan that his wife had divorced him during his imprisonment and remarried. His wife had considered Shan a political embarrassment even before his imprisonment, had doubtlessly convinced their son that Shan was dead. But Tan had not said Shan had lost his family, or that his family had abandoned him. He had said his family was destroyed. It was Tan's way of expression, Shan kept telling himself. Probably Tan did not even recall Shan's personal history and had used the words just to complete Tan's portrait of one of the wretched ex-convicts who wandered the county.

When he reached the crest of the first ridge he lowered himself onto a rock, trying to push his mind into a place as quiet as the mountain meadow he sat in so he might make sense of what he had heard. His brief moments with Ming felt like a waking nightmare. Surely he had misunderstood, surely the urbane museum director had not been casually threatening the lives of the monks. No one in Lhadrung knew of the secret hermitage. No one, he realized with a pang, except Surya.

He had to find the monks, had to convince them to flee from the outsiders who had come to Lhadrung. But even as he looked toward the eastern peaks that surrounded Yerpa he knew they would never flee.

As he replayed the scene with McDowell and Ming he remembered the paper he had taken from McDowell's car. It was in a Chinese font, printed from a computer, but it was a Tibetan document, filled with Tibetan place names and instructions for prayer. A *neyig,* he realized after reading it twice. The British woman was reading a pilgrim's guide, one of the ancient books written to help pilgrims find important shrines and sites of spiritual power. Someone had gone to a great deal of work to translate one of the old books word for word. It was numbered at the bottom, Volume fourteen, page fifty-six. He read it once more, recognizing some of the names now. Kumbum. Sangke. They were hundreds of miles to the north. But this was volume fourteen, meaning someone had put huge effort into compiling and translating many of the old guides. If Ming was seeking old shrines in the mountains, the old pilgrim books would tell him how to find them, at least most of them. They would be in caves, in old Tibetan houses, in sheltered sites considered power places. Shan was not familiar with this part of the mountains, did not know many of the sacred places. But he did know one structure that had looked very old when he had found it in the night.

Half an hour later he was gazing down at the house whose outline he had seen in the darkness, a small stone structure with a grey tile roof, built into the side of the hill. Additions had been built into the ends of the house, one of pressed earth, one of plywood and timbers salvaged from a bigger building. Shan approached the house warily, remembering the dog he had heard in the night. Beyond the house was a small field of barley, outlined with rows of stones. A structure with hay beside it was clearly a stable, but a second structure was not for storing fodder as he would have expected. The small sturdy building was constructed entirely of stone, its roof consisting of thin stone slabs, its small chimney constructed of dry laid stone. He stepped toward the building, which looked even older than the house. There was no door, only an opening framed in aged timbers through which Shan saw a domed stone shape like an oven. In front of it was a device with a foot pedal, leather belts that drove a large, horizontal wooden wheel on top. It was a potting wheel and a kiln that had probably been used for centuries.

Sheep dung lay scattered across the small enclosure made of earthen walls in front of the stable, though there were no sheep to be seen. In the sheltered area between the stable and the house the earth had been compacted and a frame of timbers supported a tattered felt blanket, creating a makeshift porch. In the shade of the blanket was a line of clay jars, each covered with a cloth top tied with twine. It was the way Tibetans often stored butter and milk. Beyond the jars, on a square of homespun woolen, lay a mound of coarse salt. Near the doorway sat three small *dronma,* churns used to make buttered tea, and five feet beyond an iron cooking tripod held a kettle over a smoldering fire. Under the edge of the blanket awning thin clay tablets were lined up, perhaps a hundred of them, tsa-tsa, stamped with the images of saints, in the process of being painted.

The weathered plank door still hung ajar. Shan knocked on it once, called out, then stepped inside. The house's single window illuminated a tidy central room, swept clean, the faint scent of incense lingering in the air. It was as if a gathering had been planned, then abandoned by the inhabitants. The pressed earth walls created an alcove that served as a shrine, holding an old cloth thankga and an altar on which were arrayed a painted ceramic statue of the Historical Buddha and the seven offering bowls of Tibetan tradition. He bent to study the thangka and statue. They were old, both extraordinary in their detail, the work of accomplished artists.

Opposite the altar, in the wing made of plywood and cardboard nailed onto timber posts, lay several sleeping pallets tied in rolls and more than a dozen heavy blankets. Only one pallet and one blanket lay open, recently used. He paced slowly along the walls, uneasy with his intrusion but unable to stop wondering about those who lived there and what had happened to them. Suspended on a pole over the rear wall of the main chamber was a large cloth, thin as a sheet, adorned with painted flowers which were all faded to shades of grey and brown. He paced along the wood planks of the floor, studying a small chest in one corner on which cooking implements were stacked, then stepped back to the flowered cloth and pulled it aside, exposing half a dozen deep shelves. The bottom shelves held household items, crockery and pots, long wooden spoons, a bowl of buttons.

On the shelf just below the top were several peche, traditional Tibetan books, their long loose leaves tied between two wooden end pieces with silk cords. Beside the peche were half a dozen other books bound in Western fashion, all in English. *The Works of William Shakespeare. Great Poems of Britain.* A novel by Graham Greene. *Ivanhoe* by Walter Scott. A surge of emotion washed through Shan as he ran a finger down the spine of the *Ivanhoe*. His father had read the book to Shan in secret, in a closet with his mother keeping watch, before the Red Guards had burned his father's books. The novel, like all the other books, was many decades old. It was, he became certain as he examined the frontispiece depicting a straw-haired groom helping a knight with his armor, the same edition his father had read to him.

The only objects on the top shelf were a ceramic bust of a rosy-cheeked, plump Western woman wearing a crown and a large wooden case with a leather handle and brass latches. He looked back across the empty room toward the open door, then pulled the case down. Twenty inches wide and nearly ten inches deep, its brass fittings were as well polished as the walnut case itself. He set the case on the rough little table and stepped to the door. There was still no sign of anyone. He paced uneasily about the room, then returned to the table and quickly opened the case.

It was a porcelain tea set, packed in matted packing fibers, painted with patterns of blue and golden flowers. He lifted the delicate pot, studying it in confusion. Its long spout was painted with blooming vines, and a rosebud finial adorned the top of the lid. It was not Tibetan, nor Chinese. *Staffordshire,* it said on the bottom. Arrayed around the pot had been six matching cups and saucers. One cup, but not its saucer, was missing, leaving its shape in the packing material. He fingered the fibers and suddenly remembered the English word, because in the lessons his father had given him inside their locked closet they had laughed over the way it rolled off the tongue, and because his father had declared Shan a top pupil for mastering the difficult pronunciation. *Excelsior.*

He gently returned the pot to the case, closed it, and replaced it on its shelf. Stealing a glance at the doorway, he lifted the Walter Scott novel from its resting place again and leafed through its heavy white pages, pausing at its color plates of knights in armor and damsels with sad, distant expressions. The borders of the plates, but not the other pages, were stained with many fingerprints. Near the front was a small printed legend. Published in London, it said, 1886. Looking guiltily toward the door but unable to fight the emotions the book had triggered, he turned to the opening page. With an unexpected rush of excitement he read out loud, in a hesitant whisper at first, then louder, pausing to step to the door so he could read toward the sky.

In that pleasant district of merry England which is watered by the river Don, it began, *there extended in ancient times a large forest, covering the greater part of the beautiful hills and valleys which lie between Sheffield and the pleasant town of Doncaster.*

Suddenly he realized his hand was trembling, his heart racing. The names floated on a flood of memory and, for a fleeting instant, he thought he smelled ginger. He read on, in a slow, sometimes quivering voice. His father and he had sat together by candlelight, wondering about the faraway, exotic places described in the novel.

Here haunted of yore the fabulous Dragon of Wantley, he read on, *here also flourished in ancient times those bands of gallant outlaws, whose deeds have been rendered so popular.*

After another five minutes he closed the book, clutched it to his chest a moment, then reverently returned it to its shelf, pulled the flowered cloth back over the shelves, and stepped outside, leaving the door as he had found it.

He walked along the outside walls of the house, circled the stable once more, then ventured down a path that wound through large rock outcroppings toward the northeast. After less than two hundred feet he froze. A Tibetan woman in a black dress sat on a large flat rock, facing the mountains, her back to him, a large brown dog at her feet. Kicking a stone in the path to warn of his approach, Shan slowly advanced. The dog did not move, did not bark, only silently bared its teeth.

When the woman finally spoke, it was in a casual tone, as if she had known he was there. "Do you celebrate the birthday?" she asked, turning, calming the dog with a hand on its head. Perhaps sixty years of age, she wore half a dozen necklaces of elaborately worked silver, lapis, and turquoise, the kind of finery reserved for special occasions.

"Yes," Shan replied hesitantly, pulling his hat low. "Lha gyal lo."

She offered a melancholy smile, rose with what seemed to be a great effort, and walked back toward the house, Shan a few steps behind her. Directing Shan to sit on a small plank stool she rekindled the fire under the kettle and began singing, an old song Shan had heard at the festival. She swayed back and forth as the water heated, clutching the rosary at her belt, her eyes avoiding him but drifting often toward the eastern horizon, toward Zhoka. After several minutes she disappeared inside and returned with a small copper bowl of flour, extending it toward Shan. He took a pinch then waited as she did likewise.

"Lha gyal lo," he said again in a wistful tone and flung the flour into the air.

"May he live forever," the woman said, and tossed her flour over her head.

She silently poured the hot water into the smallest of the churns, mixed in salt and butter, and began churning. Shan searched for words, wary of her seemingly fragile state. When she had poured the buttered tea she stepped back inside and reappeared with a wooden serving board covered with shelled walnuts and small white kernels of dried cheese.

"You think I am crazy," she said, then looked again toward the east and sighed. "I know the festival was to have been yesterday. But everyone in the hills left, taken by a black horse that came in the night. My nephew had promised to visit in the afternoon, so we could have our own little festival." She abruptly pressed a hand to her mouth to stifle a sob. "I think someone may have died. I know them. Only death would have kept them away." She bent and thrust her palms to her eyes, which had welled with moisture.

"You sat out there all night?" Shan asked.

"The clouds kept hiding the moon. I didn't want them to miss the house in the dark." She pulled a little black box out of her sleeve. "I used this."

Shan extended his palm and she set the box in his hand. Shan had seen such devices used by the army. It was a global positioning indicator, with a small screen for displaying latitude and longitude. Its red diode blinked to indicate it was active. It cost more money than half a dozen Tibetans earned in a year.

"One of my nephews gave it to me," she said as Shan returned the device to her. "He says it helps people find their way. But it is so dim. I held it over my head in the night, to help them see it."

"I was there," Shan said. "At Zhoka."

"You saw him, you saw my Jara and his children? He had gone to the bus in town and back to his herd. I should have gone to Zhoka with them but my legs are too worn." She paused, worry in her eyes. "He was supposed to bring a little girl back from the bus. But there were soldiers in town."

"Dawa?" Shan asked. "Dawa was there."

The woman beamed and clutched at the rosary on her belt. "I have never seen her. When her mother was young, she used to help me at the kiln."

"Jara's family should return soon. Jara hurt his leg. Some soldiers frightened everyone. Dawa ran toward the south."

A small moan escaped the woman's lips. "Not the south. She cannot be ready for the south," she whispered into her hands.

Shan looked back at the costly navigation device. "Where is your other nephew, the one who gave you the black box?"

The woman glanced up with worry in her eyes, then looked into the fire. "He lives in faraway places." She looked back at Shan and shifted as though to stand. "If Jara hurt his leg, who will bring Dawa away from that place? I will go, if I have to crawl I will go."

"What place?" Shan asked, but she did not answer. "A friend of mine has gone for Dawa," he said. "She will be safe," he added, hoping his uncertainty did not come through in his words.

They drank the strong, salty tea in silence, the woman gazing into the fire.

"When you said someone had died it was almost as if you expected it," Shan said quietly.

"All who arise will go up," she whispered. It was part of an old prayer, about the certainty of death.

"There was an old man, Atso. He fell climbing to a sacred cave."

The woman was silent for more than a minute, then sighed. "He insisted on climbing up to the deity at least once a year. It was always the way he would die."

For the first time Shan saw a charred strip of paper, at the edge of the fire. The last word written on the strip was still visible. *Phat*. It was the emphatic closing of a mantra to invoke deities. "Someone burned a prayer," he observed.

"I should not have done so." The woman plucked the paper from the ash and straightened it on her knee. "The black horse brought them, one for every family. Recite it a thousand times, she said. But she did not say why we were supposed to burn it after."

"Liya?"

The woman nodded. "Our Liya."

"For what deities?"

She leaned forward, fixing him with a somber stare. "Protectors. The wrathful ones."

"Why?" Shan asked.

The woman said nothing but rose and led him to the stable. Inside, on a beam along the back wall, hung a line of old thangka paintings. They had all been mutilated, one cut in half and sewn back together, others riddled with holes. Underneath were half a dozen painted ceramic statues, some cracked, some with pieces missing.

"Godkillers." The word rushed out of Shan's mouth as if on its own accord, leaving them staring at each other. "They came here?"

"No. What would I have to interest such demons? People in the hills remember that artists once lived here, and bring things hoping they can be repaired." She stepped outside with a quick step, as if the sight of the ruined art caused her pain, and poured them both more tea, motioning for Shan to sit again.

They drank in silence.

"Would you do that once more?" the woman suddenly asked with an awkward smile. "You can bring it outside where the light is better."

Shan looked at her a long time as he tried to understand her words, then set his tea down, stepped inside, and retrieved the novel. She offered a satisfied nod, filled their bowls again, then settled onto a wooden bench by the fire, the dog at her feet.

Shan read for a quarter hour, the woman smiling, sometimes looking dreamily into the fire, stroking the dog's head. He began to sense she was reacting not so much to the words but to the general tones and cadences, the sound of someone reading in English.

When he paused to drink more tea she reached out and stroked the book. "You have a voice like a lama," she said.

"I have to go up into the mountains now," Shan ventured in English.

She flushed. "I not . . . understand good," she said in the same language, apology in her voice. "It just reminds me of old things," she added in Tibetan. "Good years, when I was a girl."

When she looked up into Shan's face he knew his own eyes were full of wonder. The quiet gentle woman had spent good years with someone who read English to her, probably more than fifty years ago. In the mountains of southern Lhadrung.

"I will look for Jara and your other nephew," Shan offered.

She smiled but did not say yes. "The other one does not like people looking for him. He will just hide. I have lots of family," she said with mischief in her eyes now. "But some of them are phantoms. Kind to me with everything but their presence." She sighed. "It is better to forget about that one, about anything I said of him."

Shan rose, handing her the book.

"If you come this way again please stop to read," she said, pressing a handful of walnuts into his palm. "I will fix you a good meal." She darted inside and returned a moment later still holding the book but handing him another object, a small painted tsa-tsa of Buddha.

"Why are there foreigners in the mountains?" he asked as he readied himself for the trail.

"Someone broke their vow," she said in sudden despair, then she seemed to catch herself, and smiled. "Travel safe."

"I am called Shan. I don't know your name," he said.

"My name is Dolma," she said, and clutched the book to her breast. "But you may call me Fiona."

Three hours later Shan was back at the old stone tower above Zhoka. There was no sign of life anywhere, on the slopes or in Zhoka itself. He stared at the paintings inside the tower base once more, then slowly circled the tower, pausing several times to study the ruins. It felt as though the ruins themselves were watching him, as if the old gompa were alive somehow, a living thing, long slumbering but now awake and watching. It was dangerous to misunderstand the secrets of Zhoka, Atso had warned Lokesh. But more than ever Shan was certain he had to understand those secrets.

There were new prints in the soil around the tower, prints of boots with light treads, not army boots, nor the kind usually worn by Tibetans. Someone else had visited the tower. Inside, he knelt in front of the old painting, and lit a match in front of the words obscured by Surya. Someone had made new words with a pencil. No, he realized as he studied the pattern, seeing that in spots the pencil lead followed a few dark lines that had not been obliterated. Someone had traced the old words, as if they had magically perceived them, or had known them before. It was in the old script, the scripture writing, and Shan struggled to make sense of all the words. *Om Sarvavidya Svaha,* it began. Hail Universal Knowledge. After the mantra were more words. Become pure for the earth palace, become fearful of the *Nyen Puk.* He stared at the last words. Nyen Puk. It meant cave of the Mountain God.

Along the cliff between the tower and the gompa was a long shallow swale in the earth he had not noticed before, the vestiges of what long ago was a well-used trail descending along the edge of the abyss that formed the northern boundary of Zhoka. He followed the path a hundred feet, squinting in the brilliant sunlight, then kneeling, studying for the first time the faint line of shadow along the cliff that indicated its route, imagining the cliff with monks walking along it. Returning to the crest he surveyed the landscape again. The cliff trail joined the main trail to the ruins at the tower, and a quarter mile away another, less used trail, continued along the crest after the main trail veered toward the gompa. He studied the crest trail, seeing new shadows now, discovering that it circled the gompa above the bowl in which it sat. The trail had been a *kora,* one of the paths that circled old gompas and shrines, walked by pilgrims to gain merit. It meant the tower had been a station on the kora, the first station encountered by anyone coming from the west, the direction most travelers would have come from. The beautiful painting in the base of the tower, the elegant mantra, and the passage under the painting Surya had erased, had been for pilgrims, to teach them about Zhoka.

He followed the overgrown path along the edge of the chasm, pausing several times to gaze over the edge, remembering his lost throwing sticks. As he entered the ruins he stayed in the shadows, walking along the edge of the courtyard with the new chorten, into the empty foregate yard. There was no sign of Gendun, no sign of the Tibetans who had fled. There was just the lintel and its message, as appropriate for investigators as for pilgrims and monks. Study Only the Absolute. Director Ming had used the words, had visited the ruins and spoken with Surya. Could Surya have destroyed the words at the tower because he knew of Ming's interest? But Ming had been with Surya at the tower before. Surya, Shan suddenly realized, had destroyed the words because he had learned of something just the day before, in the tunnels, that would suddenly make them of interest to Ming and his colleagues, that would, if read, result in damage to Zhoka.

In the central yard, he found a butter lamp, left at the wall behind the chorten from their nighttime work there, lit it, and cautiously moved down the stairs. The pool of blood was still on the floor of the chamber with the paintings, dried a dark brown. He paced along the walls of the room. The terrible haunting air of the chamber seemed to have dissipated, the scent of death gone. For the first time since pocketing it he touched the strange peche leaf written in English, then examined the walls again. He explored the walls with his fingertips, reaching into the small cracks and ridges of each wall, examining every corner, gazing at the one wall of exposed rock and the image of the blinded deity on the adjoining wall. Surya and Gendun had acted as if the ruins on the surface were unimportant, as if the gompa had never been destroyed. Was it because the important features of Zhoka were all underground? If Zhoka had indeed been an earth taming temple its ancient builders may have started inside the earth.

Suddenly the sound of footsteps echoed from the tunnel beyond. Shan blew out his lamp. The steps stopped, low voices spoke, and beyond the entrance the strobe of a camera flashed, twice. The white shaft of an electric lamp pierced the darkness of the tunnel beyond, then into the entry that led toward Shan. Shan darted to the nearest corner and crouched. He waited thirty seconds, a minute, then just as he stood again a figure emerged through the door, fixing him in the beam of light.

"You!" a voice cried out in surprise.

Shan threw his hand up to shield his eyes and began slowly stepping sideways along the wall toward the door he had entered.

The intruder walked slowly toward Shan, keeping the beam fixed on his face. "What are you doing? How did you find this place?" The man stepped between Shan and the stairs.

As the beam was lowered toward the floor Shan was able to discern the features of the short Han from the government center, still wearing his white shirt and brown sweater vest.

"Are you lost?" Shan asked slowly, as his mind raced. "It is dangerous here."

"Do you have any idea of the penalties for looting?" the man demanded.

"Looting? I thought everything was destroyed." The man must have come in a helicopter, and it was not likely that such an official came without an escort of soldiers. Troops probably waited somewhere on the surface, perhaps in hiding. He edged toward the door.

The man raised his lamp as if he might use it as a weapon. "What are you doing here?" he demanded in a slow, authoritative voice. "Who do you work for? Who brought you here?" Despite the man's disheveled appearance Shan saw his eyes burned with a sharp, intense intelligence.

"I live in these mountains." Shan studied the pad the man had been writing on and realized the stranger, too, had been looking. But for what? "This is a dangerous place for tourists."

The man gazed at him with a hard, impatient expression. "Neither of us are tourists, comrade. What were you doing in these ruins? Why this room?"

"Something happened here."

"What do you mean?" The stranger swept the walls with the beam of light.

"First, someone stole something from here."

The man froze for a moment, then turned back to Shan. "Why," he asked with sudden interest, "would you think that?"

"There were plaster frescoes on three of these walls. One survives," Shan said, pointing to the faded painting. "One crumbled away," he said, pointing to the adjacent wall, to the left of the dim fresco. "You can see the plaster dust," he added, pointing to the long low mound of crumbled plaster at the base of the wall. "But the third was strong and solid."

He extended his hand toward the man's light, which he released to Shan. Shan stepped to the right corner of the empty wall and lit a tiny crusted edge that ran parallel to the edge. He then lit the hidden crack at the top of the empty wall which he had previously explored with his fingers. "Whoever did this was careful to remove the traces of the old plaster. But not every trace. They would tape it or paste cloth or paper over it, then cut and break it off at the top, in this crack." In the light, the edge of the plaster inside the crack, the top of the fresco, was visible. "And here," Shan said, pointing to a piece of half-inch wire stuck in a crack. "A remnant of the brush they used to clean the wall afterwards. They tried to hide their crime."

"Do you have any idea how difficult a process is involved in removing such a fresco?" the stranger asked in a skeptical tone. "There's probably only a few dozen people in the world who could do it well." He seemed to pause over his own words, then retrieved his lamp and studied the evidence Shan had pointed out, bending close to the corner, running his finger into the crack at the top just as Shan had. He extracted a six-inch-long brown fiber from the vestige of plaster at the top.

"Horsehair," Shan said. "It was common to mix horsehair in the plaster, to help bind it. Many Tibetans still do so, in their houses." He examined the hair extended by the stranger. "This particular horse probably lived several hundred years ago. It was brown and the hair was probably cut from its mane. Monks would have said prayers to its spirit, to thank it for helping to build the temple."

The stranger cocked his head, staring intensely at the hair now with a strange mixture of fascination and chagrin. And then, as Shan watched with increasing alarm, he produced a small glassine envelope from his pocket and dropped it inside.

Shan inched closer to the door. If he pushed the man off his feet he could make the stairs, take his chances with any soldiers on the surface.

The man stared at Shan again, shining the light in his face once more. "That bastard Tan," he muttered. "Did he really think he was going to hide you so easily? You're the one. The prisoner Shan."

Ice seemed to form around Shan's spine. If he ran now, with the stranger knowing his identity, it would only bring more soldiers, more searchers in the mountains who would likely find and detain Lokesh and Gendun, even little Dawa.

"The Chinese who has gone wild," the man continued, as though deliberately goading Shan, "who knows how to speak with the Tibetans in the mountains."

"I am Shan," he confirmed in a whisper. "Just speaking Tibetan means little," he added. "The people will never speak freely with the government."

"Why?"

Shan clenched his jaw in silence a moment. "You must be new to Tibet."

The man cocked his head at Shan, the way he had at the ancient horsehair. "We want to hire you for a few days, until I go home, to help interview a few Tibetans. You'll be paid well by my colleague. You have no regular job, you're an ex-convict."

"Home to where?"

The stranger made a little rumbling sound in his throat. "I am Inspector Yao Ling of the Council of Ministers in Beijing."

The silence in the room was like a cloud of dust, welling up, almost choking Shan. Not only was Yao from Beijing, he was from the tiny, elite council that served the special, secret needs of top ruling officials. "I never knew the Council had investigators," Shan said in a cracking voice.

"Investigator. Only one. The work I do doesn't lend itself to public attention," Yao said, and aimed the light at Shan's face. "How would you know about the Council?"

"You came here because of the murder?" Shan asked.

"What murder?" Yao asked, drawing closer.

"The theft was only the first crime. Yesterday someone was killed here, in this room. Afterwards the old monk was arrested and interrogated."

Yao frowned. He paced about the room, studying the wall with the missing fresco again. "Not arrested. We had to discuss something with him."

"You and Director Ming?" Shan took a step toward the doorway. "Why would the Council of Ministers be interested in an old monk?"

Yao frowned. "You saw a body here?"

Shan pointed to the stains on the floor. "I saw the fresh blood. Surya . . ." he hesitated, still not knowing what Surya's role had been. "Surya saw the body."

The inspector sighed. "Ming said the old man knew about the old art, knew how to make its symbols speak, maybe about where it used to be hidden. But he had some kind of breakdown. Speaks like a lunatic now. We couldn't make sense of anything he said, couldn't use him at all. Next he will be inviting us to the moon to see all the bodies he left there."

"You couldn't use him," Shan repeated. "But yesterday it was so important to speak with him Ming sent a helicopter?"

"Send it? He guided it."

So it had been Ming giving orders to the soldiers over the radio, Ming who had acted as though he knew who died. "You didn't come from Beijing because of the murder that was commited yesterday. You were already here."

"There was no murder."

"I was upstairs, in the ruins on the surface. I saw Surya's face when he came up to us. He had been here. Someone had been killed."

The inspector did not conceal his impatience. "Murder is a legal term. No one is murdered unless it is established by legal process. Brown stains on the floor of a cave, a raving old Tibetan, these things are of no concern to us."

"But you are here."

Inspector Yao raised his palm and opened his mouth as if to argue, but was cut off by a frantic shout.

"Yao! Jesus! You've got to—" The frantic cry was cut off by a long gasping groan. The speaker seemed to be moving away from them, fast.

As Inspector Yao disappeared through the door he had entered Shan hesitated, realizing it was his chance to escape. Then the cry came again, muffled, desperate, and Shan followed Yao, sprinting into the darkness. He had nearly caught up with the light beam ahead of him before he realized the desperate voice had spoken in English.

When Shan arrived at Yao's side the inspector was standing at the end of the corridor, staring upward at the rock ceiling where a six-foot-wide torrent of water fell from above, into a pool that drained into the darkness to their left.

A short black metal electric hand lamp lay in the swift stream, still illuminated.

Yao searched the darkness with his light. Shan reached into the frigid water and retrieved the small light, which seemed none the worse for its soaking.

"There!" Shan exclaimed a moment later, pointing out a pair of boots on a rock by the pool. They were expensive leather hiking boots, with thick woolen socks stuffed inside them. "The rocks are worn very smooth," Shan said, "very slippery." But Yao was not listening. The inspector was staring at something on the wall beyond the little pool, dim shapes outlined in paint on the black rock.

Shan stepped away, into the darkness, slowly at first, then at a jog, following the path of the water down a series of wide steps that had been cut into the rock along the left edge of the cupped, hollow course etched by the water. It would have been like a chute for anyone who had slipped from above, a treacherous slide, without handholds, without purchase of any kind, any means of stopping. He passed chambers carved into the rock, then a crumbling fresco. After a minute he realized there was light ahead and switched off the little lamp. The passage began to descend more gradually, straightened until it was nearly level. He rounded a bend and was facing sunlight. The path ended with a rock pillar, at the side of a pool, on the far side of which was a rectangular opening perhaps five feet high and eight across, through which the water plunged hundreds of feet into the gorge below. Iron bars had been set into the stone long ago, spaced perhaps twelve inches apart, but most had rusted away, leaving broken rusty spikes hanging from the top of the opening. On the far side of the opening two bars had stayed intact, but were thinned and pitted with corrosion. A large, big-shouldered man, a Westerner, lay with his feet braced against the two remaining bars, raking the rock wall beside him with his right hand, futilely trying to find a grip as he braced himself with his left hand, which was submerged in the shallow, fast moving water.

"Are you all right?" Shan asked in English.

"What do you goddamned think, Yao? As far as I can tell I am about to die. These bars won't last forever." The stranger was older than Shan, his curly brown hair streaked with grey. He wore a vest with multiple pockets. An expensive camera hung from a strap around his neck.

"I am not Yao," Shan said as he searched for something, anything, to extend to the man.

The Westerner glanced sideways toward Shan. "Good!" he shouted. "He's probably not strong enough to do what has to be done. He probably would have run to call Beijing for advice."

"Who are you?" Shan asked as he began pulling his belt from his waist. He could not step into the water to help the man. If he slipped he would either slide out into the gorge or into the Westerner, which would probably dislodge the bars the man was braced against.

"Did you come to help me or write my goddamned obituary?" the man barked angrily. His fingers were leaving traces of blood as they clawed the wall.

But Shan repeated the question as he kept looking for something to use to pull the man to safety.

"Corbett," the stranger yelled. "FBI."

"You must throw me your camera," Shan said.

"Like hell."

"I have no pole, no rope. I am going to tie your camera strap to my ankle, and my belt to your strap. There is a rock pillar here. I am going to tie myself to it with my shirt and stretch out in the water. You'll have to catch the belt so I can pull you over."

The American looked at Shan with a grim, scared expression, then with his bloody hand pulled his camera from around his neck, whirled it over his head, and launched it toward Shan. The camera hit the wall behind Shan, the lens shattering and breaking away from the body of the camera. Shan unfastened the heavy strap, looped it through the buckle to his belt, tied the strap to his ankle, and, a moment later, eased himself into the water, holding one sleeve of his shirt, the other tied to the pillar.

"What did they ask the old monk?" he called as he moved.

The American cursed. "I don't know, dammit. They asked him to draw a picture of death."

Shan braced himself. "You've got to reach out with your left hand when I say," he called.

As the stranger slowly raised his hand from the floor of the stream, putting more of his weight on his legs, the iron bar beneath his right foot snapped loose, broken away at the bottom.

Shan extended his leg, struggling to direct the end of the belt close to the man's hand. "You've got to turn and grab it when I say," he called.

"If I miss it I'm gone." The man groaned.

"I don't know which is going to last longer," Shan said, "my shirt or that last bar." He pushed his leg as far as it would go, lifting it, twisting it, watching the end of the belt as the water carried it closer to the man. "Now!"

In the same instant the man twisted and grabbed the belt, the last bar broke, and Shan's shirt began to rip. The American began to slip out the opening, his legs hanging over the abyss, the heavier man pulling Shan toward him. Then, suddenly, a hand appeared on Shan's arm and began pulling him back. He twisted to see Yao, one arm wrapped around the pillar, pulling Shan, until Shan could grasp the pillar himself, then straddle it as he and Yao together pulled on the strap tied to his ankle.

Suddenly the American was in their grasp, and they hauled him out of the water. Shan collapsed beside the man. Yao sat down heavily, gasping, but not before, with a small sideways motion of his foot, hidden from the American, he had kicked the American's camera into the water, where the current quickly pushed it over the edge.

"Where the hell were you?" the American growled at Yao.

"Don't complain," Yao said as he struggled for breath. "I saved you a hundred dollars."

Shan looked from one man to the other as they lay exhausted on the floor of the tunnel, Yao staring angrily at the American, the American making a low laughing sound. Shan forced himself to his feet, grabbed his shirt, pulled the little electric lamp from his pocket, and ran back up the tunnel.

Chapter Five

Shan kept running when he reached the surface, darting into the shadows of one of the long alleys of the ruins toward the slope, listening for pursuit, watching for signs of soldiers on the surface. Nothing. He jogged, following the mental map he had been making of the ruins, until he arrived at the eastern edge, the side opposite the stone tower. He looked down at his wet legs as he caught his breath. If a man had been murdered in the fresco chamber the day before, then the body had been quickly disposed of. What better way than to throw it into the swift subterranean stream and let it wash out into the gorge, as the American almost had?

Following a foot trail along the top of the curving wall he found a perch that afforded a view into the gorge below the old gompa. The full length of the waterfall that sprouted from the mountainside was visible. The water tumbled into a pool five hundred feet below, from which a stream wound its way out, north and west toward Lhadrung Valley. He knelt and studied the treacherous, nearly vertical walls of the gorge. There would be no access to the pool below without traveling miles east to the valley and miles back up the gorge. There was no sign of a body, but there was no way of knowing how deep the pool was, or if the body had washed away or fallen into the shadows surrounding the pool. He saw bits of color and shapes that seemed not to belong to the rocks of the ravine, and remembered how in her fit of fear Dawa had flung so many things over the edge. Somewhere down there was Gendun's little Buddha, and the bag with Shan's ancient throwing sticks.

He surveyed the landscape, searching futilely for any sign of Lokesh or Gendun. He could travel to the east, beyond the head of the gorge three miles away, across the next ridge, and be at the hidden entrance to Yerpa before the moon set. He looked west. He could return to the strange, comfortable home of the woman called Fiona and pass the night reading English novels to her. Then he looked to the south, toward the rugged treacherous lands between Lhadrung and the border with India, nearly fifty miles away. He had last seen Lokesh hurrying in that direction, looking for the terrified girl.

He was about to rise, to head south, when the faint hint of incense touched his nostrils. Five minutes later he was back in the ruins, and in five more had followed the scent to its source.

The lama sat below the largest of the standing walls, the one with the jagged hole in its center. Shan lowered himself to Gendun's side, struggling to keep his fear for the lama out of his voice. "There are men here like those who took Surya," he said when Gendun acknowledged him with a nod.

"I was just going to go speak with them about how beautiful the sky is today," Gendun said, then seemed to recognize the reaction in Shan's eyes. "A temple is for disseminating truth, Shan. Not hiding it."

"Should we not understand the truth first?" Shan asked. "Have you found the truth of what Surya did, of the prayer he gave you to keep him away?"

"It was a prayer to keep a demon away," Gendun corrected him.

Shan quietly explained what he had learned in town. "What troubled him so, Rinpoche? What happened to him in the tunnel wasn't the beginning of his pain, it was the end. You knew him better than anyone."

Gendun folded his hands into his lap and stared at them. "I had never seen him happier than when he found that old chronicle from Zhoka. It was an old record book, hidden two hundred years ago, but it explained all we needed to know about Zhoka and its founders. He said all his life had been a preparation for this, for living here. He began leaving the hermitage during the day to come here, to learn about it. Then two days ago I found him in his cell shaking, unable to speak. It was the evening after he had slashed his painting. He would not say a word. I stayed with him all night. He recited prayers with me but never spoke to me."

"Did you know he was meeting outsiders here?"

"A week or more ago, he said people from all the world were embracing Zhoka, nothing more. I thought he meant the hill people."

"He said he met a great abbot."

The lama considered Shan's words a long time before replying. "There have been no great abbots in these mountains for decades." He searched Shan's face, as if looking for answers. But Shan had none to give. He knew the conversation was difficult for the lama. It was the most Gendun had ever spoken about a flesh and blood dilemma, about one of the mysteries that Shan tried to resolve. It was because, Shan knew, Gendun, like Shan, could not grasp whether Surya's mystery was one of the flesh and blood or one of the spirit.

"I met policemen in the tunnels," Shan said, glancing in the direction of the stairs that led underground.

Gendun looked into the coil of smoke rising from the incense. "If they are looking for evidence against Surya you should give it to them," he said quietly.

Shan stared at him, dumbfounded.

"It is what Surya would want."

"I cannot, Rinpoche," Shan said. The pain of defying the lama was like a vise on his heart. "I am going to save Surya from himself." He looked and met Gendun's gaze. Words said could not be taken back. He would protect the monks, even if it meant he could never live with them again.

"Save Surya, save the people from the godkillers, save the little girl who ran away, save Yerpa and its monks," Gendun said in a level voice. "Not even you can do all these things."

"No," Shan admitted. "But what would you have me do?"

"The only important thing. Save Zhoka."

They sat in silence as Shan considered the words. "That book about Zhoka," he said. "Where is it?"

"It was too dangerous to keep. Surya took it back where he found it. Only he knows the cave."

As he studied the ruins once more, Shan saw two figures climbing the slope above. Yao and the American were leaving, walking back toward the stone tower.

A dozen new questions leapt to Shan's tongue, but when he looked back, Gendun's eyes were closed. He had begun a meditation. "Lha gyal lo," he said softly, and rose. Perhaps not all his tasks were impossible. He was not sure where to look for demons and sacred books, but Lokesh and Dawa could be found in the south.

A quarter hour later Shan jogged along the southern path, cresting the ridge above Zhoka, when he stumbled, falling hard against a boulder, landing on his belly. As he wiped dirt from his mouth he saw a yak hair rope which had been stretched across the path, and a worn pair of boots. Shan pushed himself up on his hands, and looked into the eyes of the ox-like herder who had tried to seize Shan the day before. As the man's boot swung at him Shan turned, easily evading the blow, then rose slowly, sitting on the boulder, wary of inviting further violence.

"Once I got a bounty for killing a wolf," the big man growled. "The price they're paying in the valley makes you worth fifty wolves."

"I'm sorry your prayers were interrupted yesterday," Shan said in an even tone. "I wanted to ask you about the godkillers."

"I said I'm taking you in," the man said, stepping forward, raising a fist. As he did so Shan saw a piece of knotted twine hanging from a button and a piece of rolled paper tied to a cord around his neck. The man was wearing protective charms.

Shan reached out and grabbed a handful of dirt from where the man had stood, from his bootprint. He spat into his hands and began to roll the earth into a ball. "Did you see them, did you see the godkillers?"

The man glanced uneasily at Shan's hands. "Don't do that," he said, scraping his foot along the ground, obliterating his other bootprints.

"Have you?" Shan opened his palm, began pressing the moistened earth into the shape of a man.

"I've seen strangers, three or four times, these past two weeks. I don't get close enough to see who they are. Expensive clothes. Backpacks. Binoculars. They make a lot of noise. Laugh a lot. You can smell their cigarettes a mile away."

Shan kept working the earth. It was a very old thing from pre-Buddhist Tibet. He was making an effigy of the man, which could be manipulated to cause injury to him. Usually a piece of hair or scrap of clothing would be used, but soil from a footprint would suffice.

"You can't know . . ." the man said uncertainly as he stared at Shan's hands. He took a step back. "Damn you! Don't!"

"Where?" Shan asked.

"The last time, four, maybe five miles from here. Closer to the valley. A pasture past small gullies, rough terrain. No one but herders go there. So when one of my dogs barked I figured it was Jara or one of the others with a herd. But it was a party of ten or twelve, Chinese and Tibetans, with colorful jackets, acting like tourists. I sent my dog back and got closer, thinking I might earn some money guiding them. I got close enough to hear them reading to each other out of a pilgrim book, enough to see they already had a guide, that bastard with the bad hand from town."

"Were they praying?"

"Of course not."

"Then why a pilgrim book?"

"It's how you get to the old pilgrim places, to the things inside the old shrines," the man said. "If you don't come to pray, you come to do the opposite."

"You mean they destroyed the sacred things."

"They moved a flat rock that covered a little stone altar. I used to go there with my father when he prayed to the deity inside the altar. A copper statue of Buddha. It was smashed like that little silver Tara when they left."

"Have there been other statues broken like that?"

"Five that I've seen, all smashed in the head, all cut in the back. All emptied."
The man stared at the mud figure as he spoke.

"Did you see any of the strangers yesterday? Last night?"

"I don't know. Maybe. After dark there were people moving toward the south, carrying things like logs. I didn't go closer."

"Why would the godkillers go out at night?"

"Because that is when the monks come out." The man grimaced and gestured toward the little effigy. "You think you can scare me with a little mud? You have to speak the words. It doesn't work without the words."

"I've had teachers," Shan said. He bent and drew in the dirt with his fingers. *Om ghate jam-mo,* he wrote.

The man grew very quiet, gazing forlornly at the words in the dirt, then at Shan. After a moment he pointed to the inside of Shan's wrist, to the long tattoo of numbers, then sighed and erased the words with his boot. As Shan rolled up his sleeve the scar-faced man grimaced. "Where?" the herder asked.

"The 404th, in the valley."

The man stared at the little mud figure again. "No one said anything about bringing in a convict." He cursed under his breath, then rolled up his own sleeve, revealing a similar line of numbers. "Eight years, in the big prison by Lhasa. Go," he said, but extended his palm.

Shan lowered the figure toward his hand, then paused. "What is the word that people will kill for?"

"You're crazy. Don't!"

"Then tell me about it without saying it."

The herder gave a quiet groan, and looked again at the mud effigy Shan kept in his palm. "He was a protector god of Zhoka, a special form of Yama. There was a festival in his honor, with people from the hills, with costumes and mask dancers. At dusk a great wind came and grabbed the costume of the deity, took it into the sky never to be seen again. The next day the airplanes came." Shan dropped the figure into the man's open hand. The herder would have to hide it now, where no harm would come to it. He pushed Shan roughly down the trail, cursing as if Shan had cheated him. "What do I care?" he called to Shan's back. "Keep going south and you'll have a lot more to fear than the likes of me. Nothing but fleshcutters and bluemen in the south."

By the time he found a goat path that led due south the sun was disappearing in a blaze of purple and gold. A sudden mechanical throbbing sent him behind a rock, and he watched with relief as a helicopter settled onto the ridge above Zhoka, taking off a minute later, no doubt taking Yao and the American back to Lhadrung. Then he remembered the small cigar he had found in the tunnels. Someone else had been at Zhoka, could still be lurking there as Gendun meditated.

He walked slowly, preoccupied with his fears and the confusing events of the past two days, unable to drive Surya's hollow, empty face from his mind, trying to make sense of the big herder's tale. The name the godkillers wanted was a form of Yama. A form of the Lord of Death. The FBI agent had said his interrogators had asked Surya to draw a picture of death. He paused at the screech of a nighthawk, watching its flight against the stars, and as it disappeared he became aware of a new sound, a soft wailing that rose and fell with the wind. Five minutes later he stood over a small hollow on the side of the ridge, staring down at a figure dancing beside a raging fire, watched by a woman and child who sat with their backs toward Shan.

The dancer wore a thatch of long grass tied around his forehead, obscuring most of his face. Only a vest covered his torso, and more grass had been fastened around his waist with a length of twine. Grass was stuffed into his pants legs. He was chanting as he danced, not a mantra but an old song, a gnarled branch in one hand. Suddenly the dancer raised the branch over the head of the child, who emitted a high-pitched sound. Shan had taken a step forward before he realized it was not fear, but laughter he heard.

It was Dawa, he saw with great relief, exclaiming with glee as Lokesh danced around the fire. Beside her sat Liya. Lokesh was telling the girl about Milarepa, the sainted hermit, acting out one of the saint's songs, in which his sister discovers him in his cave, his skin turned green after eating only nettles for years.

With the energy of a much younger man Lokesh leapt off the ground and landed in a crouch in front of Dawa, he and the girl both laughing. He was pulling the grass from his clothes as Shan appeared. "Buddha be praised," the old Tibetan said in greeting, a surprised smile on his face.

"Uncle Lokesh has been teaching me about old things," Dawa announced in a sober tone after greeting Shan.

"There's *tsampa*," Lokesh said, referring to the roasted barley flour that was a staple of the Tibetan diet. "We can reheat some."

"I would like that," Shan said, suddenly realizing he was famished. As Dawa retrieved a small pan from among the rocks he studied the rest of the campsite. A big wooden packframe leaned against a boulder, beside a blanket strewn with objects. He could not see all the blanket's contents in the dim light but noticed a small bronze deity statue, a long narrow metal container that may have held pens or brushes, and a hinged wooden box, open, that held lengths of heavy twine and huge needles, the kind used for sewing tents. Liya followed his gaze. "Just some old things," she said, and kicked the edge of the blanket with her foot, covering its contents.

But not all were old. Shan also had seen a small metal compass, a folding knife, a heavy nylon rope, and metal clips, the kind used by mountain climbers. She had not had them at Zhoka.

Shan accepted a battered metal plate heaped with steaming tsampa and began eating with his fingers. After a few mouthfuls he asked if they had seen any of the hill people.

Lokesh stroked the white stubble on his jaw, looking toward the southern horizon. "I found Dawa last night, at midnight, sitting on a rock gazing at the moon, talking to her mother a thousand miles away. At dawn we found a stream, in the morning searched the slopes for others. Many of the herders were going home this morning, taking other trails to stay far from Zhoka. But Dawa insisted on going further south. This afternoon we met Liya. Dawa says we should go even further south. She keeps asking if I heard the crying."

"Crying?" Shan asked. "You heard it, too?"

Lokesh sighed and looked into the fire. "I don't know if I did. I said maybe it was when Liya was coming up the trail toward us. She had the look of one who had been crying for days when we met her, but Dawa said no."

Shan stood and stepped to the edge of the circle of light cast by the fire, trying to understand what it was about Lokesh's words that confused him. Liya. They had been walking from the north and met Liya coming from the opposite direction. She had been farther south, had returned with a new pack on her back, new supplies that seemed of no use to them. Away from the glare of the flame Shan saw shapes on the horizon, black against the sky. The mountains looked like crouched beasts. Go further and there's fleshcutters and bluemen, the herder had warned.

He quietly began speaking of what he had learned in Lhadrung, studying Liya's face as he spoke, not mentioning the mantras she had secretly delivered to all the hill families. Her eyes were dark and swollen. She had indeed been grieving. "Are you scared to speak the name of a god?" he abruptly asked her.

"Yes," she said readily. "In all my life I have not said it. No one has, since that day."

"But now outsiders come and ask for it. I think they were asking Surya about how it looked, how it was to be painted. Why?"

"You must not speak of those things, not in these hills."

"Not even to help Surya?"

"Not even Surya would—"

Stones rattled on the trail above the camp. Dawa moaned and huddled closer to Lokesh. A figure tumbled into the small circle of light cast by the fire, falling headfirst toward the ground, barely avoiding slamming his skull onto a rock by throwing his hands out.

"Buddha's teeth!" Lokesh muttered, then grabbed a flaming stick and stepped over the fallen man, toward the trail. The sound of gravel being kicked by running feet came down the slope.

Shan darted to the stranger's side, pulling on his shoulder, helping him into a sitting position. The left side of the man's face was heavily bruised. Blood trickled from his mouth and from several small cuts on his cheeks. A rivulet of blood had run down his neck, and now was dried and cracked.

Shan grabbed another burning stick and ran to Lokesh's side. Someone had brought the injured man to them and fled. He remembered the American's handlamp still in his pocket, and pulled it out to illuminate the slope above.

"Oh," the stranger said as he saw the anxiety on their faces, "it's all right. There's no one." His voice was small and quivering, though somehow assured. The man stood and leaned against a boulder, turning his face away from the fire as if shamed by his wounds. He glanced at Shan. "He saw it was you and left."

As Liya threw more wood on the fire, and Lokesh began dabbing at the man's wounds with a cloth, Shan suddenly recognized the man. "Is Surya safe?" he asked quickly. It was the angry beggar from town who had taken Surya's apple. The informer. There was new movement at the edge of the camp. Liya was quickly loading her pack.

"He stopped speaking, except for his mantras." The man pushed Lokesh's hand away. "He keeps getting smaller."

"Smaller?" Shan asked.

"It's what happens when things inside dry up," the man said with a knowing tone. "My mother knew a man who killed his wife. The police didn't do anything, but he kept getting smaller and smaller until one day he just disappeared."

Dawa appeared at Lokesh's side, holding the metal plate, now filled with warm water. Lokesh rinsed the cloth, and the man frowned. "I don't need that. I need food."

As Shan stepped toward the pot with the tsampa, he looked for Liya. She had disappeared.

A minute later, as the man began gulping down tsampa, Shan squatted by his side. "Who did this to you?"

"You're the one called Shan?" the man inquired.

Shan nodded. "Who hurt you?" The man had not been seriously injured. It was more like he had been slapped repeatedly.

"It's okay. Just what herders do when they find me," the man said.

"Someone in town sent you," Shan suggested. "From the government."

The man nodded, then squatted by the fire with his plate, looking into the flames. "I have to help them. My name is Tashi." He spoke as though it was just another job, as if it were his expected role in life to regularly inform for the government, and be regularly beaten for it by other Tibetans.

"Why?" Shan asked. "Why do you have to?"

"My mother is old and sick. I have to stay close to town. I have no other way to make money to help her. Once I worked in a factory. Now this is what I do."

As he set the plate down Shan saw that two fingers were missing from his hand. "You have been guiding the groups into the mountains for Ming," he said.

"Not anymore. They got angry when I couldn't find a cave."

"A pilgrim's cave."

Tashi nodded.

"If you found it, what would they have done?"

"I found others before. They are scientists. They have special procedures. First they call Director Ming. He must be the first inside, because he is the most expert on how to preserve old things."

"What did he do when he went inside?" Shan asked.

"Once he came out with an old book. Another time there was only an old Buddha painted on the wall, and a sacred well. The army came and sealed it with explosives."

Shan cast a worried glance at Lokesh. Ming wasn't seeking shrines for his research. He was searching for something and then preventing others from seeing the shrines he investigated. "Was Ming in the mountains two nights ago?"

"Ming and the beautiful one with red hair. Punji. I help her find the children who need help. I watch her sometimes when she doesn't know." Tashi seemed compelled to tell all his secrets.

"What made it so urgent that he take Surya the next day, why send soldiers to look?"

"Because he didn't find one that night, but he learned that someone else had." Tashi extended his plate for more roasted barley. Shan opened his mouth to press him but suddenly understood. In her sudden, unexpected encounter with them, Liya had told Ming and McDowell that monks would be at Zhoka, and they had assumed that someone else had access to monks, was somehow using Surya or another monk. He recalled Ming's reaction to the cigar stub. Ming seemed to think he had competition in his quest in the mountains. A competition of godkillers.

"You said you came to see me?" Shan asked.

Tashi nodded, but he grew silent and distracted. "I don't like leaving town. I hate those helicopters. First time up, I wet myself. I never would have found you if that herder hadn't ambushed me. And at night, too. So I couldn't see his face. Then he agreed to take me to you for only half the money Ming gave me for the purpose. For me," he declared in an oddly whimsical tone, "it has been a lucky day."

It was Shan's turn to stare into the fire. The man was a self-confessed informer but grateful he could not report on the identities of the hill people. He had arrived in the helicopter Shan had seen, the one that had taken Yao and the American. "Did you tell the message, the one you brought for me. Did you tell the herder?" Shan asked.

Tashi shrugged. "I tell everyone everything if they ask. It's how I stay alive. My mother needs me. He didn't ask."

"And what was so important that they would bring you into the mountains?"

"The helicopter was coming anyway, to pick up those policemen. It goes out every day now, into the mountains in the morning and back to pick up the teams at night."

"What was so important?" Shan asked again.

"I was outside the colonel's office, because they wanted to know if the old beggar had said anything. Colonel Tan was speaking on his radio with that Yao, arguing. Yao was at the ruins and sounded furious about something you did. Director Ming was with him. They don't know I heard. Ming said the reward would mean you were brought back to Lhadrung soon. The colonel said no, that you would know to stay away now, that you had buried yourself deep in the mountains by now. Then Yao said something on the radio I couldn't hear and the colonel got on the phone with someone for a long time. After a while Director Ming appeared and took me to a conference room. He said I had not been helpful enough to him, that to show him I could be helpful I had to get you."

"Why would he think you could do that?"

"Because of the words I was to speak."

"What words?"

Tashi looked up with an uncertain grin. "That if you come back down into the world to help them, they will bring you your son."

For the first quarter hour Shan ran in the darkness toward Lhadrung, slipping, falling on the loose sharp gravel. His pants tore. He felt blood trickling down his shin. Then he halted, catching his breath, trying to calm himself, leaning against a rock as he looked toward the stars, thinking he should say something to his father but not knowing what.

He had sat under the stars before leaving the camp, unable to understand, but unable to control the wild emotions Tashi's message had triggered. After several minutes Lokesh had sat beside him.

"It is some kind of trap," Shan had murmured. "They can't know where my son is. I have to stay. I have to find a way for Surya to come back to us, make sure they take no more monks."

"When I was young," his old friend said, "I heard my mother say to her sister that once you have a child it isn't just your own deity that resides inside you, that there is something new, that your child becomes like an altar. I never understood then. I thought it was strange, that she meant something about worshiping children. I forgot about it until the year I spent in prison with my mother." Lokesh referred not to being with his mother, who had died before the Chinese invasion, but to the year he had dedicated to meditation on his mother, in honor of her, when he had tried to recall every event of their life together, sometimes offering stories to the other inmates, sometimes staying silent for entire days, immersed in memory.

"If I go back to them, to that inspector I met, to the colonel, they will try to force me to help them with whatever they are doing in the mountains. They will demand I help them find another monk from the mountains."

Lokesh gave no sign of hearing him. "I realized one night what she meant," he continued. "She meant that a parent honors his or her deity through their children, that your child is part of the way you worship."

"I'm not sure I understand."

"Don't stay in the mountains because of Gendun or Surya. They will follow the path of their own deities. Go to the valley because your son needs what only you can provide. Hold that in your heart, and no matter what happens, you will have done the right thing."

The memory of those words calmed Shan now. If nothing else the news from the informer had cracked open a door in his mind that had been too long sealed, the entrance to a chamber that held images of a timid little boy walking with Shan in city parks, of a baby cradled in his arms, a baby who, impossibly, was his offspring, even scenes of his son sitting with lamas and other images that existed only in his fantasies. At times in prison such images had helped him stay alive. But when, a year before, Tan had brutally reported that his wife had divorced him and remarried, doubtlessly telling their son Shan was dead, Shan had slammed the door shut, vowing to himself never to enter the place again, for only pain resided there. That pain had flooded out now, but so, too, had a desperate, ridiculous hope.

He stared into the sky until he saw a falling star, then set out once again.

For the second time in two days, Shan entered the town through the market square. He waited at a public water pipe as a woman filled two buckets, then, exhausted from his nighttime trek through the mountains, he opened the faucet and held his face under the stream of cold water. He kept kneeling after he shut the faucet, watching the water drip into a small cement basin at its base, trying again to calm himself. He should turn and run back into the mountains, a voice shouted inside his head. No one in Lhadrung could possibly have information about his son. It was just the kind of cruel trick Tan might use to lure him.

But as he rose and took an uncertain step toward the shadows of the next building a hand clamped around his upper arm. A radio crackled, and someone began speaking excitedly. Shan turned and looked into the eyes of a young soldier with a pockmarked face, a face he had seen previously in Colonel Tan's personal security squad. Another soldier stood at the open door of a small army truck, leaning his head into a handheld radio.

Moments later they were speeding across the valley floor, Shan sitting between the two soldiers in the cab of the truck. They drove in silence for less than ten minutes, entering a thin forest on the western slope, climbing a winding road Shan recognized. He had traveled up the same road over a year earlier, to a small walled compound, a partially destroyed gompa that had been under reconstruction as a private club for officials. Reconstruction seemed to have stopped, Shan saw as they climbed out of the truck. The stucco walls were heavily cracked, weeds still grew in the beds at their base. Only the bilingual sign at the entrance was new, announcing the Lhadrung Guest House.

As they stepped through the gate the soldier in front of him kicked up gravel. It was red. It was the gravel he had seen in the tires of the car driven by McDowell. Inside, canvas hung down from the top of the rear wall of the center courtyard, covering a row of bulky objects, no doubt the same architectural artifacts, dismantled or broken, he had seen arrayed along the wall the year before. A small fountain in the center of the yard wheezed and sputtered, ejecting a feeble spurt of water every few seconds.

His escort pushed him into the entry of the largest building and surrendered Shan to another soldier wearing a tunic with breast pockets, the sign of an officer, who led him toward a door painted with bright red enamel.

The large chamber they entered had been plastered and painted since Shan's last visit, converted to a combination meeting room and lounge. At one end a long sofa sat in deep shadow, flanked by two overstuffed chairs adorned with lace doilies on their backs and arms. Beyond the sofa, in the far corner, were wooden chairs in deeper shadow. To the left of the entrance stood a long wide wooden table with a dozen wooden chairs. On the wall behind the table hung a map of the county and another of the People's Republic of China. The only light in the room came from a fixture suspended over the table, illuminating three sour faces, all staring at Shan.

Colonel Tan sat at the head of the table, holding a cigarette close to his lips, letting the smoke waft around his head. Inspector Yao, wearing a peeved but satisfied expression, like a teacher about to dole out punishment to his least liked student, held a steaming porcelain cup in his hands. Opposite Yao, Director Ming sat with a stack of files in front of him, hands pressed to the table, an expectant look on this face.

The silence seemed as heavy as Tan's cigarette smoke, broken only by a muttered curse from the colonel.

"Some pants. Get him some damned pants," a slow, deep voice said from the shadows, in English.

Shan looked down at his legs. His trousers, already tattered and threadbare, had jagged tears below the knee from his falls the night before. A flap of cloth hung from his left leg, exposing part of a scraped and bleeding shin. Dried blood darkened the fabric in several places.

Tan glared at Yao, as if expecting a translation. But before Yao could speak, Ming stood with a melodramatic air. "There seems to be some mistake," he said, stepping toward Shan. Shan gazed at the floor, at the elegant Tibetan carpet that ran the length of the table. Prisoner reflexes came easy after four years in the gulag. He did not move, did not react as Ming lifted his arm and pushed up his sleeve, then pointed to the tattoo on Shan's forearm. "This man is a convict. A criminal."

Shan sensed movement in the shadow, someone rising from a chair. "This man saved my life," the same deep voice boomed, now in Chinese. "If you do not give him some clean pants I am going to take mine off and give them to him." The words rang like an alarm.

Yao stood up, muttering to Tan, who rose a second later and barked an order. The officer who had escorted Shan reappeared, running to Tan, then out a rear door, returning less than a minute later with a pair of grey pants which he tossed to Yao, who laid them on the sofa in the shadows. When no one spoke Shan stepped to the sofa and changed pants. Near the sofa a large pad of paper was fastened to an easel, its top page bearing a name in large ideograms. Kwan Li. Below it was a description that read like a resume: Age forty-four; Prince; General; Served in Lhasa, Beijing, Xian. Turning, he stepped out of the shadows and found the American he had seen the day before seated at the table.

"Thank you," Shan murmured, in English.

"Introductions were a bit rushed yesterday," the man announced. "I'm Corbett. Federal Bureau of Investigation. Glad you could make it." The American pulled out the empty chair beside him, nodded at Shan, then placed one hand over the other on the table and gazed expectantly at Yao.

Shan stared at the American. Corbett didn't know him but seemed to be welcoming him, almost seemed to be taking Shan's side in some battle that was about to erupt.

"Our messenger found you then," Yao said.

Shan slowly shifted his gaze from the American to Yao and nodded.

"We require your assistance. International criminals are at work in Lhadrung."

Shan did not answer until he had studied the faces of each of the men at the table, settling his gaze on Tan, who was himself staring at the small black portfolio in front of Yao. Tan had asked for Shan's assistance once before. "I am not an investigator," Shan said in a tight voice.

"Of course you're not," Yao shot back. "We need someone who can guide us in the mountains, someone who can explain things there. Reliable Tibetans are difficult to find in this county, it seems." The inspector's casual, almost disheveled appearance was deceiving. His voice was cold and sharp—well practiced, Shan suspected, in giving orders and political criticism.

Shan found himself looking at the black portfolio. "I won't help put Tibetans in jail."

Tan cursed. Director Ming made a high-pitched sound that could have been a laugh.

Yao gave a disappointed sigh. "We have been briefed on your politics." He rose and retrieved something from a chair in the shadows behind the table, shaking the object to make it jingle. Leg manacles. He extended them toward Shan for a moment, then draped them over one of the empty chairs at the table. "You are not officially an ex-convict. You are still a convict. Someone," Yao said pointedly, "chose to grant a parole to you. Paroles may be revoked."

Strangely, Shan realized he no longer felt fear. Like many of the prisoners released from the gulag, he had half expected to return to it one day. He studied each of the men at the table again, then silently stepped to the manacles. He lifted each foot in turn onto the chair, locking the manacles around his ankles.

"Jesus," Corbett muttered.

Tan's lips curled in a thin grin aimed at Yao. Yao replied with a frown, then glared at the chains on Shan's feet. Ming, however, seemed delighted with

Shan's behavior. He rose, sprang to the door, and called out enthusiastically for the soldiers.

Shan retreated to the carpet by the door, staring at the pattern along its edge, facing the door. It was frayed and faded, but he could see its weavers had worked a line of sacred symbols along its edge. A treasure vase, a lotus flower, leaping fish. He kept staring at the carpet as two soldiers came through the door for him, each grabbing an arm. It was another of the prisoner's reflexes that had been ingrained in him. When you're in the outside world, imprint small, colorful pieces of it in your memory, for the dark, grey times to come. His original sentence had been indefinite. Tan had warned him if he went back inside he might never come out again.

"Director Ming was mistaken," Tan said to the soldiers in a low, cool voice. The soldiers retreated, disappeared out the door.

"You came out of the mountains because of your son," Tan said to Shan's back.

As Shan turned back toward the table he recalled Lokesh's words. Maybe in Shan's case this was the way the father's deity was completed, letting them use his son to inflict his final punishment. His gaze settled on the black file again. "I won't put Tibetans in prison," he repeated, his voice nearly a whisper.

Yao reached into the black portfolio and pulled out a yellow folder that held several pages from a facsimile machine. "Shan Ko Mei," Yao said in a slow, sharp voice.

The name caused something to pinch in Shan's heart. He had not heard it spoken by another voice in at least six years. He himself had only whispered it, infrequently, toward the stars, when he tried to find words to ask his father's spirit to watch over the boy. But he had stopped even mouthing the words long ago. Shan was dead to his son. The name was a wound over which thick scar tissue had grown. Now they had jabbed a blade into the old wound and were twisting the steel.

Someone touched his arm and he recoiled with a sound like a sob.

"Sit down." It was the American, Corbett, motioning to the chair beside him. "You should sit."

Shan dropped heavily into the chair. Tan stared at him, clenching his jaw, anger in his eyes, but also wariness, as if Shan were laying a trap for him. Director Ming kept glancing at the others, amusement still in his eyes. Yao was angry, impatience obvious on his face. The American locked his fingers together on the table and stared at Shan, worry in his eyes.

"My son doesn't know who I am," Shan said.

Yao gave a satisfied sigh, as if Shan's words signaled they were commencing with business. He spread the pages from the yellow folder in front of him. "An early opportunist," he began, his eyes on the papers now. "Thief. Vandal. Destroyer of state property."

Shan recognized the folder now. It was a Public Security file, the file of a convict, the record they sometimes dragged out to shame a prisoner in front of those who did not know him. But Yao was mistaken. It wasn't Shan's file. Reading back the file of a particularly hardluck convict for its intimidation value was a crude interrogation tactic. Shan would have expected more from Yao.

The Beijing inspector cast a satisfied glance toward Shan, then raised the front page and continued. "Those were the early years. Later, repeated charges of hooliganism," he reported, using one of Beijing's favored labels for antisocial behavior. "The reluctance to mete out firm discipline and instruction in the socialist imperative early on guaranteed the outcome," he read. "In the end an assault on a Public Security officer. Fifteen years *lao gai,*" he added, referring to a sentence of hard labor. Yao dropped the paper. "One of the coal mine camps," he said, meaning one of the massive open pit mines where malnourished prisoners excavated their own particular hell, digging coal with crude tools all year long, seven days a week, year after year. Half the coal pit inmates died before completing their sentences.

Yao leafed through the papers clipped to the file, pausing at one of the rear pages. "In the beginning it was one of those elite schools for children of party members. When a child gets in trouble they get assigned extra readings about the heroes of the people. He was caught stealing from classmates. They called a doctor. He interviewed the boy. He reported to the Deputy Mayor."

Something icy crept down Shan's spine.

"The doctor reported that the boy was incurably antisocial. He kept boasting his father was a famous criminal, head of a gang that robbed and killed all over China, that even the Chairman feared him."

Shan sensed the blood draining from his face. His wife, who was assigned to a city nearly a thousand miles from Beijing after they were married, had raised their son, sometimes—not often—visiting Shan in Beijing on holidays. His wife, the Deputy Mayor, who had divorced Shan after his imprisonment.

"One night he was caught writing slogans against the party. He was expelled from school. A week later telephone poles began falling down in the night. It took another week before they found him with an ax at a line of fallen poles. He had taken down eighty poles in total. His mother was sent to a special party facility for discipline. He went to a farm labor camp, from which he escaped a month later and surfaced with a gang that sold heroin outside factory gates. He was using a new name. Tiger Ko. When he was caught that time he attacked the arresting officer, sent him to the hospital. His mother left office in disgrace."

Yao seemed to keep talking but Shan could not make out the words. Something like a mist seemed to have settled over Shan. He felt a falling sensation, held onto the table.

"Someone get him some tea," he heard the American say, in Chinese.

When his eyes found their focus again there was a porcelain cup of steaming green tea by his hand. "He's not even twenty," Shan said at last, in a hoarse voice. He lifted the cup and poured the scalding liquid down his throat.

"He needed a father's care," Director Ming said, in a voice heavy with sarcasm. "His mother abandoned him. Remarried, moved to the eastern coast, took a new name. She has had no contact with him for years."

Shan shifted his legs and heard the rattle of the chains on his ankles. "You mean you're sending me to the coal mine," he said, looking absently into his cup. It was a thin, delicate piece, a tiny panda painted near the lip.

Yao closed the folder in front of him and stood, carrying his own cup with a little panda as he stepped toward Shan. "Surely you were not always so dense, comrade. We want to bring your son for a visit. Here in Lhadrung." Yao pulled a small key from his pocket and set it on the table beside Shan.

"Why?" Shan asked, disbelieving.

"As a reward for your undivided attention. An incentive to assure your help. There is an international conspiracy with elements in these mountains. You agree to help us resolve our problem and we will bring your son for a visit."

Shan stared at the little panda, saying nothing.

Yao shrugged. "So you wait until the end of his fifteen years to see him, assuming you yourself are still a free man. But your son . . ." He gave an exaggerated sigh. "Already he has been punished with severe discipline three times for security violations." Shan knew all too well what severe discipline meant in lao gai. Beating, doses of electroshock, the application of pliers to small bones in the hands or feet. "I'm afraid," Yao said in an earnest voice, "your Ko is not going to survive fifteen years."

Chapter Six

There had been a theft in Beijing, Inspector Yao explained as they wandered down the ridge toward the ruins of Zhoka, a theft of vitally important artwork. It was only early afternoon. Tan had wasted no time in arranging for a helicopter to transport them back to the old stone tower. There had been a rushed, silent meal of dumplings and noodle soup, served by Tan's sullen soldiers, then, as the helicopter arrived to take them to the mountains, a momentary argument between Tan and Yao as the colonel tried unsuccessfully to persuade Yao to bring soldiers with them.

"Art?" Shan asked. "An artifact?" Once Shan had stiffly nodded his head, agreeing to help for the chance of seeing his son, Yao had become enthusiastic, almost cheerful, as if Shan's assent were a breakthrough in a particularly difficult case. But Shan still understood little of their investigation or why they were in Lhadrung.

"A plaster painting," Yao said. "A fresco."

"A Chinese fresco that wasn't Chinese," Corbett interjected. His Chinese was fast, almost slurred, as if he learned it in southern China. "It's about art. People are dying for good art all over the world." It had the sound of a worn joke.

Shan studied the American investigator. Corbett was older than he had first thought, though his tall, athletic build blurred signs of aging. He was not many years from sixty, Shan decided, seasoned at his business. Perhaps too seasoned. He seemed to have no interest in hiding his emotions. Impatience was often on his face, sometimes anger. "This isn't the place, Yao. I told you," Corbett complained as Shan watched him. "We've got ten more to check at least. This is just ruins. A deathtrap." During the brief flight into the mountains the American had watched out a window, repeatedly consulting a map in his hand. They had set down briefly at a camp several miles to the north to unload supplies, where a dozen Chinese, young men and women in their twenties, had been working at the mouth of a cave, clearing away rock debris as a woman with short hair paced up and down, reading from a pilgrim guide on a clipboard about the miracles a pilgrim would discover inside. Yao and Corbett seemed to be looking for a den of thieves hiding in the mountains. But that did not explain why Ming was looking for caves. It did not explain the godkillers, or why the Council of Ministers might be interested in Tibetan miracles.

Yao shrugged and kept going toward the tunnels. The case might involve international elements but it was being investigated on Chinese soil, so there would be no question about who was in charge. "It was nearly two months ago," the inspector explained, pausing, studying Shan as if interested in his reaction. "In the Forbidden City."

"But there are guards everywhere," Shan said "It's like a fortress. It is a fortress." The Forbidden City was the centuries-old home of the emperors, a vast compound of temples, residences, and meeting halls. Shan had once known almost every passage, every chamber of the complex, for he had discovered early in his life in Beijing that it offered many calming, quiet refuges from the rest of the city. A high, thick wall surrounded the entire compound. Most public access was through closely watched gates at the northern and southern ends.

"There was a cottage built by the Qian Long Emperor for his retirement, at the northern end of the City." The Qian Long was one of the longest-serving Manchu emperors, revered for his justice and benevolence. He had left the throne at the end of the eighteenth century after a reign of sixty years.

"I know the place," Shan said as he watched for signs of Gendun. "Red enamel pillars supporting the roof in front. At the rear a small courtyard with a fountain, with wisteria growing up the walls. I used to go and sit in that courtyard. But the cottage itself was always locked."

"Locked for decades," Yao confirmed. "In fact, barely touched since the emperor died. But it was decided to restore the interior, to allow tourists inside. Work crews started going in and out. The emperor had commissioned a beautiful fresco, even had a famous artist from Italy come and live in the Forbidden City to paint it. A crew was restoring the cedar beams of the ceiling in the dining chamber. One morning they were called off for an emergency repair on the opposite side of the compound. When they returned the next day the Italian fresco was gone. A piece of the wall over eight feet long and more than three high, cut out, leaving nothing but the bare wall timbers."

Shan gazed toward the shadows that marked the passage to the lower level. Was Yao there because a fresco had been stolen from Zhoka as well? But Shan had just explained that theft to him the day before. "So the Council of Ministers is investigating a missing plaster painting?" he asked in a skeptical voice. The game Yao was playing had a familiar rhythm. Never tell a complete story, not even in the final report, never share a complete fact. It was an instinct bred into senior Beijing investigators. Yao would not be working for such high-level political bosses unless he knew to keep shuffling the available facts until he grasped the political truth of his case.

A sound like an amused snort came from Corbett, who had begun to descend the stairs. He had been staring into the shadows below, where he had almost died on his last visit, but turned when he heard Shan's question. "The Chairman had shown the Qian Long fresco to a delegation from Europe during a state visit," Corbett explained.

Yao cast a peevish glance at the American, then continued the story. "They decided to dedicate the cottage to friendship between the peoples of Europe and China. The Qian Long fresco was going to be its centerpiece, the perfect symbol of the bonds between east and west. The European governments were going to pay for its restoration and the cottage publicly opened in a ceremony during an upcoming state visit." Yao stared at Shan with challenge in his eyes, as if daring Shan to say something.

Shan returned Yao's stare. He had been gone from Beijing five years but nothing had changed about how the assignments of senior investigators were chosen. Yao wasn't involved because of the theft but because of the political embarrassment.

"The Qian Long had a special attachment to Tibet," Shan recalled. "Tibetan lamas were members of his court. The emperor probably had Tibetan art in his cottage," he ventured.

"He did. It was not touched."

"So you're in Tibet because they stole a European painting," Shan goaded.

"The Chairman was furious. He considered the theft a personal affront. He sent very specific instructions to my office."

"And to Director Ming?" Shan asked.

"Ming offered the full resources of his institution. He has much experience with such things, was already involved in the restoration of the cottage and planning of the new hall. He pointed out that the people we are dealing with are no amateurs." Yao directed a sour expression toward Shan. "You have no right to ask questions. You are here to help us with the Tibetans, nothing more."

But Yao had not explained why he thought Tibetans were involved, or why he was in Lhadrung. Shan turned his gaze to the American. "And no doubt the FBI just has an interest in preserving art?"

"You are not here to interrogate us," Yao growled.

Corbett let the inspector step ahead of them then turned to Shan. "There's a new FBI office in the embassy in Beijing. Everyone's looking for opportunities for U.S.–Chinese cooperation in law enforcement. Mostly it's work on investigations of terrorists."

"You're stationed in Beijing?"

"Seattle. In the American northwest. When that fresco was stolen in Beijing there was also a theft in Seattle. At the same time. From a man named Dolan, one of the wealthiest citizens in a city of wealthy citizens. One of those computer billionaires." He reached into his pocket and produced half a dozen small photographs, handing them to Shan. They were all of display cases containing Tibetan artifacts: exquisite, very old pieces, jeweled gaus, an ornate silver butter lamp, ceremonial masks, an elaborate costume, and several delicate deity statues. "Reported to be the best private collection of Tibetan art in the world. Took Dolan fifteen years to collect. Over fifty pieces, the whole collection, was stolen. Insurance value of over ten million." The last photograph was an aerial shot of a sprawling brick building with multiple levels that wandered across a hillside, above what appeared to be the ocean. "Came in the night. Broke through a state-of-the-art security system. Left without a trace. No fingerprints. Video surveillance disrupted. All they left was a dead girl."

Shan paused. "A girl was killed?"

Corbett looked ahead of them, as if making sure Yao was out of earshot. "Twenty-three years old. One of three part-time governesses, an art student hired because she could give the children art lessons." The American's face clouded, though Shan could not be sure if it was because of the dead girl or because of the darkness looming ahead of them.

"Look," Corbett said, stopping, touching Shan's arm. "You need to know the rules. Finding the artifacts, and the girl's killer, that's why I'm here. This is an American investigation. We're doing it American style. You understand?"

"No," Shan admitted.

"I don't pick suspects according to political favorites. I don't devise a theory and select facts to fit it. I build facts by relying on science and sense. I believe only in facts. The evidence is everything. I have no motive but justice, and no one has ever been too big to get in my way."

"Part George Washington, part Sherlock Holmes."

The words clearly startled Corbett. "Who the hell are you, Shan?"

"Someone who also wants justice," he said somberly.

"Fine. I have never not solved a case," Corbett added.

"How many times have you given that speech?" Shan asked as the American continued down the tunnel.

Corbett glanced in Yao's direction. "Just once before," he said with a slow grin.

Yao had brought a duffle bag stuffed with a dozen electric lanterns borrowed from the army. He lit one and laid it at the base of the stairs, then as they reached him opened the bag for the American and Shan each to take a lantern. They soon had the corridor lit with lanterns placed every ten feet. Yao stepped into the room where he had discovered Shan on their prior visit.

As Corbett began to follow, Shan turned to the American. "What did you mean the crimes happened at the same time?"

"It was the middle of the night in Seattle, midday in Beijing. I think the thieves walked out with their artwork in Beijing and Seattle at the same hour."

"Surely a coincidence."

Corbett shrugged. "I don't think so."

"But you haven't explained why you came here. To Lhadrung."

"We searched. God how we searched. Dolan, he was furious. A founder of one of the big software companies. Major political supporter of the president. Head of one of the biggest foundations in America. We had a forensic team there for days. No real clues at the scene. We checked the whereabouts of known art thieves. We put photos of the artifacts at every airport security checkpoint in America, posted them on the Internet. We began checking stores in the region that handled that sort of thing, showed them the photos, asked about anything unusual coming in. After a week of dead ends, most of the team moved on to fresher crimes and I got the file. Because I am the chief investigator for art theft west of the Mississippi."

"But why Lhadrung?"

"There was only me and the two junior agents assigned to me, my boys. We digested every report, studied all the interview notes. We found that four different antique art stores within fifty miles of Seattle reported recent inquiries by young women asking about the value of Tibetan beads. Some fellow had met each of them at a bar, bought each drinks, charmed them with his exotic style, and gave each a rare old bead to bring them good luck. On two different nights." Corbett pulled a familiar-looking bead from his pocket, an inch and a half long, half an inch wide, tapered at the ends. "I bought one." It was agate, in shades of red and green, etched with white stripes.

"It's called a *dzi* bead," Shan explained, "they are thought by Tibetans to attract protector deities." He looked up from the bead. "He was at the bars the night of the theft?"

Corbett nodded. "And the night before."

"We located two of the women, because they had left their beads on consignment for sale. They had never met him before. Spent a couple hours talking and dancing. Innocent fun, they said. Exotic accent, one said. Kind of

British but not exactly. He was thirty, maybe thirty-five. Black hair, moustache, deep blue eyes. They loved his eyes. He traveled a lot, he said, so he couldn't give them a home address, but he took theirs, like he would be back again, said he was leaving for Asia. They had met him at two different bars. Between the bars was a big hotel. We checked their guest records against flights the day after the theft. Twenty-seven men traveling to Asia close enough to the description to check further, six who stayed at the hotel. Took almost a week to get copies of the six passport photos. The two women identified his photo in an instant, no question. British citizen. William Lodi. Flew Seattle to Beijing, then caught the next flight to Lhasa. We called our Beijing office, which asked for assistance from Public Security. Public Security reported that on his landing card he gave his address as a hotel in Beijing, even paid in advance for one night there, but the hotel never saw him. So Public Security did a broader search of records. They discovered he had flown on to Lhasa, that he had an export license for shipments from a craft shop in a little town no one ever heard of. A part owner of the shop, in fact."

"Lhadrung."

"Exactly. But by the time I got here he was gone, into the mountains they say in town. Being hidden by Tibetan friends after committing the biggest theft of Tibetan art ever." Corbett did not wait for Shan to reply, just stepped into the fresco chamber where Yao was already at work.

Yao had illuminated the room with half a dozen lanterns and was busily writing in his notepad. He looked up as Shan entered.

"But there's no market for expensive art in Tibet," Shan said.

Yao ignored the comment. "You were interrupted last time," he said. "You were explaining how this fresco was stolen."

Shan stood silently a moment, watching the frustration build on Yao's face. "First tell me why Ming wanted Surya."

"Ming found him in that tower painting one day and discovered he knew about the old art, about how art gets hidden in the mountains. Ming says we are dealing with thieves with a political agenda. Restoring plundered art to its native land, that sort of thing."

"Ming suspected Surya?"

"Only of knowing secrets that could be useful to us. Surya spoke in riddles about the pictures and what he called power places. It seemed to intrigue Ming. But in the end he was just a crazy old man. He insisted he had never even been to Lhadrung. He acted as if he lived in the rocks, like some burrowing animal. Said he was a monk, then said he wasn't a monk. He kept playing with the light switches in the office, turning them on and off like he had never seen electric lamps before." Shan glanced at Corbett, who had told him Surya had been asked to draw a picture of death. Meaning, he was convinced, a picture of the demon that protected Zhoka, whose name no one could utter.

Yao aimed his hand lamp into the tunnel that led to the underground stream, looking at the darkness with a wary expression.

"Why do you connect the thieves to these ruins?" Shan asked. "You didn't know the fresco was stolen until I showed you."

"We don't," Corbett said. "We just know this William Lodi went straight from Seattle into the mountains above Lhadrung. Experts say these mountains still have old Tibetan artifacts in the ruins, places where artifacts have been kept for centuries, in caves and old shrines, that they were never systematically searched like elsewhere. If Ming is right, Lodi is taking the stolen items to one of them, maybe just to leave them, seal them in a cave perhaps. Maybe return some to the same shrines they were taken from decades ago."

"And to what shrine would he return an eighteenth-century Italian fresco?"

Yao shot him an irate glance. "I said it was one theory."

Corbett advanced a few steps down the tunnel, then stopped. "They're finished here. Took the art and moved on. So should we." He seemed reluctant to continue toward the treacherous water below.

"Perhaps they left something," Yao said. "This is the most evidence we have had yet of their presence."

"Like what?" Corbett asked.

Yao frowned at Shan a moment, then shrugged. "A pool of blood." As he spoke he held up a wooden prayer bead between two fingers.

A chill ran down Shan's spine. If there had been thieves in the tunnels, stealing sacred art, Shan could not predict how Surya would have reacted.

Corbett gave a frustrated sigh, then pulled from his pack a headband apparatus with a light which he arranged over his head, pulled out a lantern with a purple lens, then dropped onto his hands and knees, switching on only the handlight. "Ultraviolet," he explained, and began searching the trail of blood, which now glowed, following the stream of stains that led to the little cell with the indentations in the floor for an altar, where Shan had found the old manuscript leaf written in English.

"In the old tower," Shan ventured, "you used that light to show the old writing."

"A lot of good it did," Corbett grunted. "Since we couldn't—" he looked up. "You could read it?"

Shan looked from the American back to Yao. "Just an old mantra." He still did not understand why Surya had been so desperate to obscure the reference to the mountain palace and the cave of the mountain god, why he wanted to eliminate the signs of the pilgrim trail.

Yao dropped his own small pack, drew out a bottle of water, and drank without offering any to his companions. "I want a tour," he said. "I want to know what you see, Comrade Shan. You can talk like a Tibetan but can you see like one?"

"I don't know these ruins."

"But you know what to expect in a monastery like this."

"It is not helpful to generalize about anything in Tibet," Shan said stiffly.

"If I go back and tell Tan all his warnings about you were correct, that you have failed so quickly at your chance at rehabilitation, where will you expect to find refuge? Do you think you will ever see your son again?"

Shan returned Yao's stare a moment, then gazed down the dark corridor ahead of them. "Below the ground, there would usually be a *gonkang*," he said, "a chapel for demons and other fierce protector deities. Near the gonkang might be where ritual implements were stored."

"Ritual implements?"

"Costumes and masks used on festival days. Special paintings taken out on festival days."

"Treasures."

"In the eyes of the monks, yes."

"Was this chamber with the fresco the gonkang?"

Shan lifted one of the battery lanterns and stood in the doorway again, surveying the walls. There was no sign of an altar, none of the heavy soot that would have risen from butter offerings that he had always seen in gonkang chambers. "No. This is an entryway, a place to prepare for the gonkang. You might linger here to become calm before proceeding."

"I'm calm enough," Yao pressed. "What else?"

"I don't know. There could be storerooms underground, many storerooms for a gompa so big."

"Hiding places, you mean. The kind of places thieves might use."

Yao began to descend the sloping tunnel toward the stream, Shan following, then pausing to examine a four-inch piece of old wood that had been recently splintered away from something. There were no beams, no posts, nothing of wood in sight. In the few patches where dust had accumulated on the floor there were fresh tracks, two narrow parallel lines eighteen inches apart. Something other than a body had been dragged along the tunnel, perhaps a makeshift stretcher bearing the body. Yao was at the waterfall when Shan caught up with him, shining his lamp on the faded markings on the wall beyond. "Can you read them?"

They were words, written long ago in an elegant hand. He saw the letters for life, near small images of humans. "No," he said.

Shan had not had time to study the corridor along the stream when he had run down it toward the frightened American. As they continued along the passage he saw now that once the passage had been lined with frescoes, though most had crumbled to dust or were riddled with cracks and holes. But three had been recently destroyed, transparent tape over some crumbling sections, thin tissue paper glued to others. Someone had tried to saw along the top of one, to chisel or cut along the top of another.

An angry mutter escaped Yao's lips and he began examining the crumbling frescos in detail. "There were no fingerprints left at the imperial cottage," he said, "only traces of latex. This mess, it doesn't look like the same professional work."

"Old plaster can have many different constituents, many different properties," Shan suggested. "Even a professional might have to practice."

After ten minutes they moved down the corridor, discovering a series of doorways, half a dozen low entries close together.

"Meditation chambers," Shan explained. They aimed their lights inside each as they passed it. The walls were rough stone, the chambers unfurnished. Yao stepped inside the last one, followed a moment later by Shan.

A faint hint of incense hung in the air. A dust-covered scrap of cloth in one corner may have been a monk's blanket.

"They would sit in here," Shan explained, "sleep in here, eat in here, chant their beads in here. For days, sometimes for weeks." He studied Yao, whose face had shown a flicker of uncertainty. "When the Tibetans meditate they can go away, to a place unfamiliar to you and me."

Yao frowned but stepped to the blanket and squatted in front of it, pushing his light close to it. He seemed unwilling to touch it. "This is my fourth visit to these ruins," he said. "Each time I sense I hear something, and I strain to listen but there is nothing, only perhaps a lingering vibration, like an old echo. Not a sound, but an intuition of sound."

Shan studied Yao. It was a strange language the inspector spoke. Sometimes he sounded like a policeman, sometimes a party member. But other times he spoke more like a professor. Yao looked back at him with amusement in his eyes. Was he mocking Shan? Was he somehow mocking the gompa?

He stood and fixed Shan with a cool, steady stare. "You have a decision to make, comrade. There is another way to proceed, Colonel Tan's way. Saturate the mountains with troops. Bring every man, woman, and child in, every goat and yak, and see what kind of confessions spring forth. Tan says it always works."

"I need to know you are not lying to me," Shan said. "About my son. About your investigation."

For a moment Yao looked uneasily at the doorway past Shan, as if wondering whether Shan might try to prevent him from leaving the meditation cell, even try to fling him into the stream. Then his gaze hardened. "I've told you."

"What you are speaks louder than what you say."

"What—an investigator for the highest government offices? It's what you did for twenty years, comrade."

"Exactly."

One side of Yao's mouth twisted into something like a smile. "Colonel Tan said you might be desperate, that you would be irrational about protecting Tibetans. He said to weigh all your words carefully. He said you never did anything by chance or from stupidity. You may recall he wanted to send soldiers with us today, but I turned him down. This time. You were supposed to see that as a gesture of good faith. To show my commitment to your rehabilitation." He took a step toward Shan but Shan did not move. "All I want is the truth," Yao said.

"No," Shan said. "Like you said, I spent many years doing what you do. I know exactly what you want. What you want, all you want, is to close your file, get a politically palatable answer to close your file. There are prosecutors who have discovered that Tibetans are the answer to every open case. Social misfits. Genetically inferior, some scientists will testify. No one to defend them. Hostile to Beijing. By definition politically undesirable. But sturdy enough to contribute years of hard labor."

Yao frowned again. "So far," he sighed, "your rehabilitation appears to be a failure." The inspector pushed past him into the corridor, then paused and reached into his pocket, produced a slip of paper which he handed to Shan. It was a long grouping of numbers, in a familiar format. Without conscious effort Shan rolled up his sleeve and compared the digits. It was a lao gai registration number.

"It is his number. His facility is in northwestern Xinjiang," Yao explained, referring to the vast province north of Tibet, a land of deserts and remote, inhospitable mountain ranges, a favorite venue for gulag camps.

Shan gripped the paper in his fist. "You still haven't told me why you are here. It's not just because the FBI is here or because of the timing of the crime."

"Among the old papers in the Qian Long cottage Ming found a copy of a letter from the emperor saying he was sending something beautiful from his personal cottage, in tribute to his friends in Lhadrung."

"What friends?"

"We don't know. Like you said, he had lamas in his court."

"How do you know the letter was genuine?"

"Because Ming said so," Yao snapped. "It was Ming who reported the theft to the Chairman, and the letter."

"You're saying the fresco was taken as the tribute promised from Beijing to Tibet two centuries ago? That it was a political crime?"

Yao just smiled, then stepped away to explore the two remaining chambers that opened into the passage above the pool from which Corbett had almost fallen to his death.

One chamber was empty except for a corner where dust had accumulated, preserving the prints of heavy climbing boots, expensive boots, not the kind Tibetans would wear. There were over a dozen prints, in at least two different sizes. In the second, the last chamber, which had the benefit of the sunlight coming from the stream's outfall, they found chaos. Shards of clay pots littered the floor, which was carpeted with what had been the contents of the pots. Flour, sugar, rice, the contents of torn envelopes of dried soup. A small butane stove, its frame bent as if crushed by a boot. Tea leaking from the small bags used in the West, each with a tiny English label. A box of latex gloves, into which a jar of honey had been dumped. Down, from two sleeping bags that had been slashed open.

Yao pointed to the bootprints outlined in the spilled flour and sugar.

"At least three pairs of boots. The owners of the supplies," Shan suggested, and showed him how all the tracks were at the front of the room where those in the boots had surveyed the damage, except for one set that led straight to the farthest corner. Two pairs of tracks showed the heavy treads of Western-style boots, the third was smooth, from the type of soft boots worn by many Tibetans. He followed the single set of tracks to another clay pot in the corner, under a blanket. It held batteries, still in plastic packs, the size used in the metal light Shan had found on his first visit, and an empty package of cigars. Soaked in rum, the English label said.

Yao made a small satisfied sound like a purr, then began examining every inch of the room, shining his light in each corner, studying even the ceiling. Within five minutes the inspector had found a small battery powered saw, its circular blade covered with plaster dust, and, in another clay jar, loaded ammunition clips for a rifle.

"I can compare chemical composition of the plaster from the emperor's cottage," Yao announced as he held up the saw with a victorious gleam, then popped off its blade and inserted it into one of his glassine envelopes. "If even a microscopic portion remains we'll find it."

Shan simply stared and nodded. He had been studying the tracks as Yao worked. The soft imprints had been there before the final set of boot tracks, as if a solitary Tibetan had destroyed the supplies. Surya wore soft-soled boots.

Ten minutes later they found Corbett bent over a flat rock, holding a pair of long tweezers over a small piece of paper on which he had assembled the fruits of his fastidious search. Three cigarette butts, without filters. Another of the small cigar butts with the sweet tobacco. Four single-edged razor blades that had been shoved into a crack. A piece of wide adhesive tape, folded, stuck to itself. Several chips of what looked like bone. Fragments of a dark blue stone that might have been lapis lazuli, one of the stones favored in Tibetan artwork. More of Surya's prayer beads, over fifty. And tiny grey specks Shan could not recognize.

"Silver," Corbett explained. "Flecks of silver." He raised the largest in the tweezers and held one of the lamps close to it.

"For what?" Yao asked.

"Maybe there was other artwork here," the American suggested. "Something with silver and jewels that had to be pried loose perhaps." He lowered the flake, picked up another that had a small kernel shape. "This one is different. I spent a few years in a forensics lab. A silver filling from a tooth."

"The Tibetans that live in these hills," Shan observed quietly, "do not have teeth filled with silver. If a tooth goes bad it gets pulled."

"The blood drops start there," Corbett said, aiming his beam at the cell where Shan had found the manuscript leaf. "Where the first attack was made, where the wound was opened. He was bleeding severely by the time he got inside the door. Stepped in his own blood, I think." The American held the light on a point in the gruesome trail Shan had missed, where the toes of a boot had stepped over the blood. The sole of the boot made a waffle pattern, similar to those he and Yao had seen in the chamber below. Corbett continued to trace the trail with his light. "He fell, after trying to hold on a moment." Corbett lit the stone wall on the side of the doorway. There was a print, a red smear that showed part of a palm and fingertips. The spot of light followed the tracks on the other side of the pool Shan had seen before, the smudged prints of sandals. "Someone else was there while this one lay dying. Or just after."

"Surya," Shan whispered.

"This is not the crime we are investigating," Yao said with warning in his voice.

A strange stillness fell over the chamber as Corbett kept the light on the prints, showing how Surya had gone to the corner, then to stand in front of the nine-headed deity, below which the beads had collected in the crack in the floor. Corbett, Shan sensed, understood Surya had retreated to the corner in horror, then stood in front of the deity and broken the cord of his prayer beads.

"There is no partial truth," Shan heard himself say in a voice that was somehow sad. "There is only the whole truth." He looked up to see both men staring at him.

"What do you mean?" Yao demanded.

"I mean," Shan said with a certainty that seemed to well up from some unknown place within him, "you will never understand what happened in Seattle and Beijing without understanding what happened here, in this room, without seeing what that deity witnessed." He looked up at the powerful image on the wall above the pool of blood.

He expected anger, or at least ridicule from his companions. But they said nothing, only stared at the deity with the nine heads. Had it been blinded because it had seen what had happened?

"There's another thing," Corbett said, and aimed his light on the lower wall just outside the chamber. "He tried to leave a message." The American pointed to the oval with the circle and square inside. "Someone drew that and wrote a word." He pointed to what Shan had thought was another smear of blood above the drawing, perhaps where the dying man had supported himself as he drew. But in Corbett's light figures glowed through the smear.

"What glows is blood," Corbett said. "Over it is pigment, nearly the color of fresh blood." He switched off the purple light and the letters disappeared. "Someone wrote in blood, someone else covered it with paint, the same color that was used up at the tower to cover the writing." He switched back on his light. "What does it say?"

"Nyen Puk. It means Cave of the Mountain God," Shan said. "It must not be complete. Sometimes the dying will write one last prayer." Surya had desperately wanted to obliterate any reference to the Mountain God, but the dead man used his last breath, his last blood, to tell about it.

"You mean the dead man was Tibetan," Corbett said.

Shan's hands closed around the chip in his pocket. "I don't know," he said and pulled the chip out. "This was in the pool of blood. Maybe it was his." It was as if the dead man were Tibetan, but not Tibetan.

Corbett's eyes lit with excitement. "Not the dead man's!" he exclaimed. "Why didn't you—" He didn't finish the question, just snatched the chip and studied it. "He was here, this proves it." He tossed the chip to Yao, who frowned at it without examining it further. "The bastard killed again," he said in a tone that was almost hopeful. "He tossed it at the dying man, like a taunt, an act of contempt."

The American looked up at Shan. "We searched Lodi's recent travel history. Before Seattle he had flown in from London but spent three days in Nevada. Reno."

Corbett may as well have said he had proof the man came from a bayal, one of the mythical hidden lands. It seemed impossible, as if somehow life in two alternate universes had briefly overlapped in the dim chamber, leaving a dead man, the nine-headed deity, and a plastic gambling chip inside a forgotten earth taming temple of ancient Tibet.

"Surya came to the surface saying he killed here," Shan said. "I was here minutes later. He could not have carried out the body without being covered in blood, couldn't have dragged him away without leaving a trail of blood. When I came down minutes later, the body was gone."

"Because Lodi was still here," Corbett said. "Hiding, waiting to destroy the evidence of what he did."

"The thieves store supplies here," Yao reminded Shan, and explained to Corbett what they had found. "Your old monk must have seen him, could have been frightened and confused about what he saw. He ran to the surface."

"But why would Lodi steal a fresco already in Tibet?" Shan asked.

The American sighed, staring into the darkness again. "What the hell is this place?" he asked in a voice that was suddenly weary. It seemed he was speaking to something in the shadows.

They stepped into the corridor that led to the stairs, studying its walls this time. The space somehow felt incomplete to Shan. There was no gonkang chapel, only a place to prepare for the gonkang, a place to pray and compose one's self for meeting the fierce protector deities. He slowly walked twelve feet to the end of the corridor. The rock wall that formed the end of the passage, consisting of a solid slab with smaller stones along its edges, was canted slightly inward at the top. The mani mantra was painted on the smooth stone, in big red letters. Shan played the beam of light slowly over the mantra, studying the letters. In places the paint was flaking away. He touched the edge of the paint and another piece fell away. It had been applied with a wide brush, in thick, bold strokes, less refined than the other writing he had seen. He played the beam along the corners of the back wall, running his fingers along the cracks in the loose stone rubble that had fallen in the corner. There was an odd sense of motion. Air. He aligned his fingertips along one of the cracks. The flow was almost imperceptible, but air was moving out of the crack. He aimed the light beam slowly upward, following as it covered the stone above his reach, settling on a smudge of color over ten feet above the floor, where the ceiling met the rear and left walls.

"What is it?" a voice snapped behind him. Yao shined his own light into the corner.

"Nothing," Shan said uncertainly. "Something on the rock. Probably lichen."

"Lichen doesn't grow where there is no light," a deep voice said behind them. Corbett approached, shining his own lamp toward the ceiling before stepping closer to the rear wall. He bent with his light over the writing. "This paint is different from all the rest. Not the old stuff. It's like cheap house paint." He picked up one of the chips of paint and pulled on both ends. It stretched.

Shan gazed back at the smudge of color at the edge of the ceiling.

"I'm the heaviest," Corbett declared. "Which of you two wants to climb?"

A moment later the American bent, and Shan climbed onto his back. Then, with Yao supporting him, he put his feet on Corbett's shoulders. The American slowly straightened, Shan leaning on the wall for support. As the American reached his full height Shan's head was less than an arm's length away from the top corner.

"What is it?" Corbett asked with a groan.

"Someone is looking," Shan said slowly. An eye was painted on a fragment of plaster, partially obscured behind the broken wall. He recognized the eye. It was one of the symbols used in murals and thangkas, and probably had been part of a larger mural that covered most of the side wall. The back wall wasn't meant to be a wall. It was a slab that had collapsed from the ceiling, probably during the bombing of the gompa, but someone had carefully removed the remains of the painting, leaving only the eye hidden in the shadows. He put a hand on the rocks at the corner of the walls, aiming his light downward, quickly discovering that the rocks had not fallen randomly but had been carefully mortared in place. Someone had deliberately hidden part of the old ruins.

As Shan hopped off the American's back he realized the American had noticed. Corbett shone a light along the sides to examine the cleverly concealed mortar.

"What's back there?" Yao demanded.

Shan studied the two men uncertainly, then felt his hand close around the registration number Yao had given him. He asked Yao for a sheet of paper and sketched two maps. First, on the left side, he drew the gorge and the surface ruins as he recalled them, marking the point where the water poured out of the cliff face. Then he turned the paper over and drew on the left side the broad stairway corridor, the fresco chamber and the tunnel leading to the waterfall inside the mountain. He turned back to the top side and folded the paper in half so that the surface drawing covered the sketch of the underground complex.

"Very pretty," Corbett said. "What are you trying to prove?"

Shan pointed on the diagram to the pattern of buildings surrounding the stairs, flanked at the entrance by pedestals for prayer wheels, then to the lines he had drawn on the opposite side of the surface compound. "It was constructed to be symmetrical. The surface was almost obliterated. But if you climb the slopes above I think you could see an identical pattern of rock walls and prayer wheel pedestals on the other side. They line up, two hundred yards apart."

"Symmetrical," Yao repeated, uncertainly.

Shan nodded. "The entire compound was carefully laid out by artists and lamas." He lined up the sketches again. "The walls on the other side line up with the stairway here."

"Another stairway," Corbett said.

"Two stairs, at each end of a broad subterranean corridor. Which means," Shan said, "we haven't seen the main underground complex."

They climbed to the surface, Shan leading them slowly, watching for signs of Gendun. Five minutes later they stood on the opposite side of the gompa, gazing at the ruins of two rock walls, in a perfect line with those flanking the stairs to the west. At the end of each wall was a pedestal for statuary. Large statues, particularly those carved of stone, were not common in Tibetan monasteries, but in this, like so many other points, Zhoka seemed an exception. On the right another pedestal held a life-sized foot in a sandal, the only remains of its statue. On the left was a figure in a monk's robe sitting in the lotus position. It had been decapitated. Between the walls was a tangle of loose rock, shards and slabs that completely filled the stairway, overgrown with lichen and a few small struggling shrubs. A building above the stairs had collapsed into them.

Corbett wandered along the north wall, then stopped fifty feet away and called for them. He pointed downward as Shan reached his side, toward a shadow in the rubble, a shallow hole five feet across and seemingly five feet deep. But Corbett picked up a pebble and dropped it into the hole. It bounced upward. It wasn't a shallow hole. It was a shaft covered by a canvas expertly painted in browns and greys to blend with the rocks. Corbett leaned over and pulled away a corner of the cover. The shaft continued downward for another twenty feet, a makeshift ladder leaning on one side. Someone had been excavating a small passage through the rock debris.

"So someone else knows about your underground complex," Corbett muttered and turned to survey the grounds again.

"Why now?" Yao asked. "All these years, and suddenly someone starts digging."

Why now indeed, Shan thought. Could it have been the monks? Could it somehow be part of Gendun's plan to secretly revive the gompa?

Corbett bent and picked up a cigarette butt, extended it for them to see. It was recent, like the ones he had collected earlier. Someone other than monks had been here.

"Lodi," the American suggested. He pointed to the words on the filter. "He smokes American cigarettes. Same as I found near the pool of blood." He smelled the tobacco. "Still fresh. A few days old at most." Suddenly the American stiffened and leaned his head toward the south. "Do you hear that? Someone's crying."

Shan and Yao exchanged a glance. Shan heard nothing.

Corbett studied the harsh landscape in the south, then took several small hesitant steps in that direction. Shan and Yao began searching the ground for other evidence. They found several large squares of barren soil among the rocks, which probably had once been gardens. There were long shallow imprints in several, which could have been caused by the same boots that had marked the floor below, but the wind had eroded them, making it impossible to be certain. When Shan looked up, Corbett was gone. Yao was staring at the decapitated statue, wearing an oddly worried expression.

A sudden moan broke the silence. Shan darted to where he had last seen Corbett. The American was sitting on a rock, his face drained of color. He held up a warning hand as Shan approached.

"This isn't what I do," Corbett said in a small, tight voice. "What is this place?" he asked for the second time that day, toward the soil beneath his feet.

Yao darted past Corbett, around the ruins of a high stone wall beyond the American. Shan found him a moment later, staring at a macabre display in the center of what appeared to once have been a small courtyard. On a makeshift plank table were bones. Nearly twenty skulls, yellow with age, were carefully lined up in the center of the table, seeming to return their stares from eyeless sockets. Arrayed before the skulls were smaller bones. A fully articulated hand. Half a dozen femurs. At either end of the table was a small brazier, for burning the fragrant smoke that attracted deities.

Yao stared, transfixed, as Shan circled the display.

"Like a massacre," a deep voice said. Shan looked up to see Corbett standing beside Yao, his hand on his belly. "It must have been a massacre," the American said in a tight voice. "We'll need a forensics team."

Yao's eyes began to turn toward Shan, then his gaze dropped and he pulled out his pad of paper. "No one else is needed," he said in a voice that was nearly a whisper. "This is not our concern."

But Shan did not believe it. Someone had been excavating through the debris that had filled the deep stairwell. Above the stairs may have been a chapel, collapsed into the stairs that horrible day nearly fifty years before, a place where monks might have gathered as the end drew near. Perhaps it had not been looters but Tibetans, finally paying homage to the dead.

As Shan leaned over the rock table, Corbett took a step forward.

"There are curses," Yao said, pointing to a line of script that ran along the edge of the thick plank at the side of the table. "The kind of people who do this leave curses for those who try to interfere."

Shan looked back at the writing. It was recent, and had been made in chalk or with a piece of plaster. He struggled to make sense of the Tibetan letters. After studying the line of text he realized he could read the words, but could not make sense of their combination. He stared at it, reading it again and again. "It is not a curse," he said at last. "It says . . ."

"Says what?" Corbett asked, staring at the bones.

Shan had not realized he had stopped speaking to look back over the ruins with a new sense of wonder. "The words are these," he said, and pointed to them as he read. "Not time but beauty has claimed us."

He reverently placed his fingers along the side of the first of the yellowed skulls, as though resting his hand on the cheek of an old loved one. When he looked up Yao was staring at him with a strange defiance in his eyes.

"It only proves that it's Tibetans at work here," Yao said, finding his investigator's voice again. He lifted one of the femurs from the table. "You said you saw such a bone below," he observed to Shan. "Tibetans use them, don't they, comrade," he asked, as if he were trying to force Shan into a confession.

"They make trumpets out of them," Shan confirmed.

"And they gild them with silver," Yao added, "perhaps to sell them through Lodi's craft store in Lhadrung, or overseas, as antiques. If Lodi and his accomplices are so fond of collecting bones," Yao said from the shadows, "do you suppose they are particular in how they obtain them?" He walked away without awaiting a reply, reaching into his pack. As he disappeared around the ruined wall Shan saw a small black radio in his hand.

Corbett still stared at the skulls.

"Did you understand what happened yesterday when you almost died?" Shan asked. "I don't."

"What do you mean?"

"I mean the old writing on the wall. It had nothing to do with William Lodi, nothing to do with your case. But you took off your boots and stepped into the frigid water and nearly died. Because you had to see old Tibetan words on a wall."

Shan's words seemed to cause the American pain. He looked into his hands a moment, then stood and circled the table of bones. "I thought one of these could have been him, the one who died below. But none of these died recently, did they?" he asked after a moment.

"No."

"So who's been——? There must be graverobbers digging here."

"There are no graves in this part of Tibet."

The American gave a peeved frown. "Right. No one dies here."

Shan found his gaze drifting back to the skulls. "What do you know of Tibetan history, Mr. Corbett?"

The American said nothing.

"What did the inspector tell you about this place?"

"A school of some kind, they said. An old art school that closed a long time ago. Looks like a century or more. Yao and Tan put it on their list of places outlaws might use."

"It was a monastery. A gompa. The army and the Red Guard destroyed nearly every gompa in Tibet, thousands of them. Places like this, too remote for the infantry, were bombed from the air. I've heard eyewitness accounts about places like this. A lot of monks had never seen planes before. They waved at them as they began their bombing runs because they thought they were some kind of sky deity."

The American's gaze shifted from Shan to the skulls and back to Shan. He appeared troubled, then just confused. "Look, the history here has nothing to do with me. It's not my land, not my country. I'll be here a couple weeks, then I'll be going home, never to come back." His gaze drifted slowly back toward the skulls. "They just bombed them?" he asked after a long silence. "Monks?"

A shiver ran down Shan's spine and he turned to see Yao in the ruined gateway, glaring at him. "Even in your country, Mr. Corbett, I suspect criminals have their own peculiar views about their society and its history."

Corbett nodded slowly. "Still," he said pensively, rising and walking to the table. "A funny thing about these skulls. I spent a year in a forensics lab." He pointed to the seams joining the plates of the skulls. "They all died young. Not one of these was older than forty, I'd wager." He shrugged at Yao then stepped past him out of the courtyard.

Yao's face was flushed. His eyes were like two blades stabbing at Shan. "I think Colonel Tan was wrong," the inspector growled. "You really are stupid after all. Spreading reactionary views hurts us all, most of all you. I'm not sure why you were released from prison. It was on Tan's order, that's all I know. But Tan's orders can be countermanded."

Shan stared at him impassively. He warned himself again not to be fooled by Yao's disheveled, undisciplined appearance. The man was a top official, doubtlessly a high-ranking party member, and he could easily summon the cold calculation, the casual cruelty that were usually bred into such men. "If you want to understand the people of these hills," he said after a moment, "you have to understand what you see on this rock, you have to understand what they have experienced in the past fifty years."

"No," Yao shot back. "Tibetans commit crimes out of fear, out of greed, out of passion, just like anyone else. It's always the same. In the end it is because the criminal mind fails to embrace the socialist imperative."

Shan did not break away from his intense stare. "You must be wildly successful in Beijing, Inspector Yao."

Yao's jaw clenched and unclenched several times, then he shrugged and raised the radio. "Helicopter patrols report six or seven Tibetans in the mountains south of here. A man and a child, another group of three or four with sheep. We'll pick them up, let them make their contribution. You've changed my mind, Shan. I very much want to know what happened to the man who died here, where his bones wound up. Right now I can think of nothing more important."

A man and child. The patrols had seen Lokesh with Dawa.

"You can't," Shan blurted out.

"A squad has already been dispatched."

"Send more helicopters into those mountains and every Tibetan for miles will scatter," Shan warned, trying to control his own sudden anger. "They will run so deep into the ground they won't be seen for days, weeks even." He looked back at the skulls for a long moment. He sensed he was betraying someone, but not certain whom. "I know where the dead go to," he said in a low, resigned voice. "I know who can tell us about bones. Call off the soldiers and I'll take you to the dead."

Chapter Seven

"She was floating face up, her eyes looking right at me," Corbett said in a brittle voice. The American was explaining how, incredibly, he had encountered the body of the murdered governess. They had paused at a stream in their steady ascent toward the southern peaks. "Must have been a hundred people there, looking over the rail, crying out, fainting, shouting for the crew. But she was looking at me." He had turned his gaze from the distant mountains back toward Shan and Yao, with an awkward, forced grin. "I know a medical examiner who says sometimes the dead can be like that, their eyes looking nowhere and everywhere, following you like some zombie Mona Lisa."

"Mona Lisa?" Shan asked. He squatted to scoop water from the stream.

Corbett shrugged. "A painting. I went out with the harbor patrol to recover her. I helped pull away the seaweed that was wrapped around her arms and legs." He looked into his hands. "Twenty-three years old. She was wearing earrings shaped like little silver turtles. Supposed to bring long life, turtles, isn't that what Chinese say?"

"How do you know about Chinese things?" Shan asked after a moment, cupping the water in his hand for a drink, then sluicing another palmful over his head.

"I started as a policeman in San Francisco. When I made detective I worked Chinatown for seven years."

As they started up the trail again, the American's strangely despairing mood vanished, and he walked beside Shan, almost lighthearted, asking him for words in Tibetan, the names of flowers, more than once exclaiming about the spectacle of the snowclad Himalayas in the far southwest, even picking up a stone that lay by the trail, carved with figures nearly obscured by lichen. "It's a prayer, isn't it?"

"A *mani* stone," Shan explained. "Pilgrims buy them, or make them, and leave them behind, to bless others, to gain merit. This one could be centuries old."

Corbett stopped, insisted that Shan teach him how to correctly recite the prayer, the mani mantra on the stone, then repeated it as he made a little mound of gravel and laid the stone upon it. "I pray to find William Lodi," he said as he rose. "Double murderer."

"It's unsettling work, to be looking for bodies in water," Shan said when they paused again a quarter hour later.

"I wasn't," Corbett said. "She found me. I was just on the ferry crossing the bay. I didn't even know she was missing. I had been assigned to the Dolan theft, but no one had mentioned her. There had been a back-page story about a missing college girl I hadn't even read. But suddenly she was there in front of me, the Dolan governess whom nobody had seen since the night of the theft. A few hours later I made the connection. An eyewitness caught and disposed of by Lodi before he went out and celebrated in those bars."

"So you're here because of the girl?" Shan asked.

Corbett seemed to resent the question. "I told you. I was assigned to the case. I could speak Chinese. Someone had to follow Lodi." The American clenched his jaw and continued up the trail. He was finished talking.

They passed through some of the steepest, most treacherous land Shan had ever seen, walking in a brooding silence most of the way, Yao clutching his radio like a weapon. Half an hour after passing the trail intersection where Lokesh, Dawa, and Liya had camped, they entered a chasm with nearly vertical two-hundred-foot walls. When at last they exited the darkness of the chasm, Corbett gasped and stepped back into the shadows as if frightened. The slope they had emerged onto was jammed with sculptures—eerie, twisted shapes of stone that seemed to have been placed to warn travelers from the southern route. They were not human forms, but hulking shapes that suggested the vague, dark creatures of nightmares.

"It was just the wind," Shan said uncertainly. "It's just how the soft rock was carved by wind." He found himself searching for signs of Lokesh and Dawa. It was the kind of place his old friend would linger for hours, wandering among the distorted columns with awe on his face, touching the stones, because Lokesh would be convinced it could not be the wind. Shan found himself stepping to the first of the columns, a ten-foot-high formation that looked like a human contorted in pain. In dimmer light they would look like giant skeletons and grotesque, misshapen animals. If this was the way the local deities shaped the land, how had they shaped its people?

Movement in the shadows caught his eye, and for a moment he thought Lokesh was there after all. But the man who stood with his hand on one of the skeleton columns, gazing at it with intense curiosity, was Yao. Shan watched the inspector for a moment, then hurried on, following the winding trail through the columns, Corbett close behind.

When they reached the end they paused, waiting for Yao.

"Is it true, Agent Corbett, that in America justice is simply a matter of facts?"

"Of course. The evidence tells it all."

"Then you must be very careful here," Shan warned in a low voice. "You are in a world that is not constructed of facts."

"I don't give a damn about Beijing politics. And I know a fact when I see it."

"I'm not speaking of politics now," Shan said, and gestured toward the nearest column of rock. "What do you see there?"

"Crumbling sandstone."

"Many Tibetans would not see stone at all, but the work of powerful gods. Others would consider them perfect symbols for meditating on the frailness of the world. Many would travel a hundred miles to pay homage here."

The American frowned and looked expectantly toward Yao, as if hoping for rescue.

"Two years ago an old man was stopped on a road near Lhasa with a golden statue. He had sold everything he owned to buy the statue, so he could leave it at a holy mountain to gain merit for the soul of his dead wife. He was certain she had died because he had cut down the prayer flags that always flew over their house to use the rope to tether their last two sheep. He was arrested because he told someone he had killed his wife. Someone else reported that he had given a man money for the death of his wife. It was the money given to the goldsmith but no one bothered to explain. He was accused of having stolen the statue and did not deny it, because the house he had sold to buy it had belonged to his wife."

"What happened?"

"He was sent to prison and died in three months." He fixed Corbett with a hard stare. "The government had all its facts right. He did say he killed his wife. He did pay money because of the death. He did feel like a thief with the statue." Shan pointed to a small ledge cut in the rocks above the stone columns. It held several small weathered statues of saints. "There is the truth of this place. People here live by truths, not by facts."

"And what is the truth I should be following?" the American asked as he stared at the little statues.

"Godkillers," Shan said, and quickly explained what had happened to the shrines in the mountains.

An hour later as they climbed down a steep ridge Yao stepped in front of Shan and threw a hand up to block him. "Enough," the inspector growled.

"Are you seeking to trap us, maybe lose us in the wilderness? You will give me directions I can transmit to the helicopter now." The midsummer days were long, but they had no more than two hours of daylight left.

"Before you learn to solve a mystery in Tibet," Shan said, "you must learn how to learn."

Yao grimaced and turned to Corbett. "We are being held hostage by a convict. It is well known that most convicts suffer from some form of mental disorder."

"Right," the American said with an amused grin. "Almost as bad as those suffered by investigators."

Shan shrugged, not understanding what was passing between the two men. Something burned intensely inside each of them, but it was clearly not the same thing. "I had a teacher in my prison barracks. He said that to truly learn, turn your back on what you know, leave it all behind. He said to know the world you must immerse yourself in what is not your knowledge."

Yao pulled out the army map he had been consulting most of the afternoon, turning it one way, then another. Shan was certain Yao had no clue where they were.

"I read a book about that once," Corbett said, mischief in his tone. "It's called having a beginner's mind."

Yao frowned at the American then waved the radio in front of him. "You said you knew where to go," he said to Shan in an accusing voice, "but I think you have never been in this land."

"I have not," Shan admitted. "But the place we are going to is right there," he said, and pointed to the crest of the next ridge, half a mile away, where a dozen large birds spiraled above an outcropping that had the appearance of a huge rock nest.

Halfway up the ridge Shan paused. "It would be safer if I went ahead," he warned his companions.

Corbett seemed to be looking for a place to sit among the boulders when Yao stepped in front of Shan. "Not a chance. If you say 'stay' I know I must go. You will wait here. I will not have you warning them, laying a trap for us."

Four wispy columns of smoke could be seen from the far side of the ridge, beyond the birds, a sign of habitation. Yao motioned Corbett forward, and set off up the trail toward the crest.

Shan leaned against a rock wall, wiping his brow as he watched the two men advance toward the crest. They had gone less than three hundred yards when he saw the American jump back. Four small figures, mere children, materialized out of the rocks, waving clubs, leaping at the two men, hitting them.

By the time Shan reached them Corbett was curled up against a boulder, hands clasped around his neck, taking blows from two young girls, cursing each time one of the clubs hit him but offering no resistance. Yao was futilely trying to fight back as two boys pinned him against a ledge. The inspector wrenched one of the clubs from a young boy's hand, then abruptly stopped, stared at the thing in his hand, then threw it onto the ground in revulsion. The weapon was a human thigh bone, and not one of the old yellowed ones they had seen at Zhoka.

Shan leapt to Yao's side as the children closed around him. The inspector's discovery of the bone had seemed to paralyze him. Fear entered his eyes. Shan stepped in front of him, muscles tensing, ready to take a blow himself. But one of the children, a boy of no more than eight, called out and pointed to Shan's chest, then lowered his club. The others, eyes round, did likewise. As a group they retreated a few feet then spun about and ran up the trail.

Shan looked down. The boy had pointed to his gau, the silver Tibetan amulet box that hung from his neck. In his frantic run up the slope the gau had slipped out of Shan's shirt. When he looked up the children had disappeared.

"Like phantoms," Corbett said as he straightened, rubbing his arm where he had been hit. "They were just there, out of thin air. Who—why would they . . ." His words drifted away as he watched the children appear near the crest and run toward the nest of rocks.

"What these people do, they prefer to do in secret," Shan said. "Even among Tibetans the *ragyapa* are a people apart. For centuries it has been like this. In a way they are outcasts, but they accept it because they are performing a sacred duty. It is not for outsiders, not for tourists. Even Tibetans just deliver the body to the village and leave a payment."

Corbett looked at the birds that flew over the circular outcropping. "Christ. I've read about it," he said in a haunted tone. "I never thought . . . this is the twenty-first century. It's from another time."

"It's called a *durtro,*" Shan said, pointing to the outcropping, the charnel ground where the ragyapa dismembered the dead, stripping away the flesh, even pulverizing the bones so the vultures could eat them.

"If someone wanted to kill someone this is how the evidence would be destroyed," Yao said, anger in his voice now. "Which makes Tibet a murderer's paradise," he added. He was holding his radio again.

"A durtro is a place of great reverence," Shan warned. "No helicopters."

"Crushing bones to feed to birds," Yao shot back with a sour tone. "Butchery. Tan said the people up here had one foot in the Stone Age."

"They are returning bodies to the earth," Shan said as he watched figures running from the circle of rocks over the crest, away from them. The people of the village were fleeing.

The cluster of houses on the far side of the durtro appeared to be abandoned when they reached it. They silently walked past the stone and wood structures toward the ring of rocks where the birds waited above several lines of prayer flags. Yao stepped past Shan and was the first to enter into the ring of huge boulders. He stood speechless as Shan and the American reached him.

"Bloody Christ," Corbett muttered, then turned, his face pale, his hand over his nostrils and mouth as he retreated outside the ring.

A lean boney man squatted in the center of the small clearing, staring angrily at them, a long heavy blade in one hand, an intact human arm in the other. Beyond him, atop the tallest rock on the opposite side of the clearing, three vultures gazed at them with the same expression as the man. Shan struggled to keep his eyes fixed on the squatting man but his gaze kept drifting, snaring images of the gruesome scene. A human knee, the femur and tibia still attached. A hand, flesh on the palm but not on the fingers. A column of vertebrae, bloody tissue clinging between the discs.

"Who has come from Zhoka?" Yao called out. "We demand the body from Zhoka!"

The man's only response was to lower the arm to his cutting block and swing his blade, splitting the arm at the elbow.

"I doubt he speaks Chinese," Shan said.

"Then you ask," Yao snapped.

Shan fixed his gaze above the man, on the vultures. "I knew a ragyapa in prison. He had killed a Chinese tourist who came to take photographs of his father cutting bodies."

"You brought us here," Yao growled. "You're not going to scare us away now."

"The man said that for many of his people cutting bodies was like a meditation. He said sometimes he could sense a deity in the hand that stripped the flesh, that even if a Tibetan had walked away from Buddhism in life, that visiting the durtro in death was a return to it, that sometimes when he cut flesh his father spoke with Buddha himself."

Yao winced. "These people are no priests."

"I don't know," Shan said after watching the ragyapa for a long moment. "There are old stories, even in China, of people who would collect the pain and sorrow of others, to bear it so others could live in peace." Shan looked back at the squatting man with the cleaver. "These people are like that. Like the priests who sit with the dying. But they do this all day, with reverence, every day of their lives. How could any man bear such a burden?"

Yao cursed as Shan left him alone, joining Corbett outside the rocks. A moment later Yao was beside him, glancing back nervously toward the clearing.

"These people did nothing. They just stay here and do the job they have always done," Shan said, although he could not understand how the village could sustain itself on the offerings of the slim population of the southern hills. He gazed back at the durtro. There may have been two bodies brought from Zhoka. The Tibetans had not told where they were taking old Atso.

"Barbarians," Yao said. "How can we allow such a thing in China?"

"Let me ask you something, Inspector," Shan said after a moment. "Of all the things you know in the world, how many have stayed unchanged for a thousand years? I think to do what they do, all their lives, all their generations, takes something that is probably very different from barbaric."

Yao gave an impatient snort and moved back toward the village.

Corbett lingered, staring at Shan with a new intensity. "Prayer," the American said in a low, uncertain voice. He surveyed the village with a respectful, inquiring gaze. "Like on that rock today. That never changes, does it?"

Shan found himself looking at Corbett with the same curiosity, as if they were just meeting. "Like art maybe," Shan said. The mysteries of Zhoka were still weighing on him. "The act of translating your deity onto cloth or paper."

Strangely, Corbett smiled and nodded, as if it were exactly what he had expected Shan to say.

Yao was hovering near the rough plank door of the nearest of the buildings when Shan and Corbett reached the village. He was examining implements leaned against the front walls: a hoe with a crooked handle, an ax, a leather bucket.

"Obviously a den of international art thieves," the American observed.

More vultures appeared, flying low over the village, as if they sensed the visitors and expected a new meal. From the distance, in the rocks below the houses, someone called out. Shan could not make out the words but the tone of warning was unmistakable.

A solitary goat appeared and began walking from house to house, pausing several times to study the intruders. At the fourth house it pushed its nose into a pile of blankets by the front door. The blankets began moving, and a gaunt hand reached out to stroke the animal's neck.

Shan raised his arm, cautioning his companions, and slowly approached the house. The goat looked up, cocking its head at Shan for a moment before burying it in the blankets. A dry rattling laugh erupted and another bony hand emerged, the two hands embracing the animal's head.

The old woman who rose out of the blankets wore a tattered grey felt dress, the same color and material as the blankets. Heavy silver earrings dangled from her lobes, a necklace of thick turquoise beads framing a silver gau hung from her neck. Her hair was streaked with grey, her face spotted with age. Her eyes, which did not follow them as they approached, were milky. She was blind.

"Two Chinese," she declared in an amused tone, then hesitated, lifting her head as if to smell. "And another outsider, but not Chinese." The goat turned and pressed close to her side as if to defend the woman. Shan put an arm around its neck. The woman's head shifted back and forth a moment, settled in Shan's direction, and she abruptly reached out, grabbing his arm. "Are you prepared?" she asked in Chinese.

"For what?" Corbett blurted out in English.

The woman paused. The bright smile that appeared on her face revealed nearly toothless gums. "Give you joy," she called in a thin, dry voice, in English.

The three men looked at each other in confusion.

"Do you speak English?" Corbett asked.

"Inchi?" the woman asked with a flush of excitement.

"She wants to know if you are an Englishman," Shan explained to Corbett.

"Close enough," Corbett said in Chinese. "How could she speak English?" he whispered to Shan.

"Give you joy," the woman declared again in English, more loudly. She cast a smile in Shan's direction. "Mostly we speak goat," she said in Chinese again.

"A man died in Zhoka," Shan said. "He could have been brought here. We need to know about his death."

"It is a season for death," the woman sighed. "Uncle Yama has come to live in the hills this summer," she said. Shan felt something cold travel down his spine. She was referring to the Lord of Death. She embraced the goat's head again. "We must be very careful when speaking about the dead," the woman added, addressing the animal now. She reached to her belt to clutch a string of prayer beads and dropped her head, as if she had abruptly fallen asleep.

Yao continued his investigation of the compound, lifting the lids of the clay jars that lined the front of the next house, the largest in the village. Shan knelt closer to the woman, whispering. "Grandmother, I am seeking an old man and a girl, and a woman named Liya." The goat pushed Shan's shoulder with its head as though warning him away now.

"Liya," the woman said, not raising her head. "Trying to keep a leg in both worlds stretches her too thin. I pray for Liya."

"The Englishman," Corbett interjected, in Chinese. "Have you seen him? He calls himself Lodi."

A dry crackling sound came out of the woman's throat. "Too thin to see at all," she said with a sad smile and began working her mala, whispering the mantra in the goat's ear. The goat settled onto its back haunches with a contented expression, as if welcoming the prayer.

Yao was standing now, staring into the last of the large clay jars, that nearest the door of the house. Shan slowly stepped toward him, carefully replacing each of the lids Yao had dropped onto the ground in front of the jars. Barley was in the first two jars, some kind of white tuber in the third, then small shriveled apples and bricks of black tea. By the time he reached the inspector's side, Yao had his pad out, writing feverishly. Corbett reached the last jar a step ahead of Shan and gasped.

Inside the large clay pot was a small black radio-cassette player, a battery-powered razor, and a blow dryer.

"Like you said, nothing's changed in a thousand years," Yao observed in an acid tone.

Shan lifted the cassette player. It was covered with dust. He turned it over. The batteries inside were corroded. He set it back in the basket and lifted the hair dryer. It had a cord, to be plugged into an electrical outlet. But there were no outlets for at least twenty miles. As he lowered the dryer back into the jar he noticed for the first time a small shape that dangled from a roof beam directly over the jar. It was made of twigs, fastened in a diamond shape, with colored yarn interwoven around the frame to form a series of diamonds, ending in a small red diamond in the center.

"What is it?" the American asked.

"A spirit trap," Shan explained, "to catch demons." He stepped closer. It seemed new.

"There's another," Corbett said in a nervous tone, pointing to one more of the traps hung unobtrusively under the eaves. They quickly surveyed the other buildings. Every house had one or two of the traps hanging in the shadows under their eaves. "If you're a ragyapa, doing what they do," the American said in a contemplative voice, "what demon could you possibly be frightened of?"

Yao had stepped away and was staring down the slope, toward a small wood plank structure fifty yards away. It stood in the shadow of two old wind-twisted junipers. A ragyapa girl stood in the doorway, looking not at the three strangers but inside the hut. Shan jogged to join her, followed closely by the American.

The girl did not notice their approach until they were only a few steps from the shed. Fear clenched her face as she spun about. She stood, mouth open, gulping air, then bolted toward the cover of the nearest outcropping. As she reached it a woman in a red dress appeared and swept the girl into her arms.

Shan ran past his companions to the crude plank door of the shed, which hung ajar a few inches. Someone inside was chanting. The sweet acrid scent of incense wafted through the cracked door. He pushed it open. The single chamber of the hut was dimly lit with four butter lamps, three of which stood in front of an open peche. An adolescent girl sat against the wall in one corner, apparently asleep. The man who read the book paused only a moment as Shan reached his side, turning to offer a sad, familiar grin and returning to the book. It was Lokesh. Shan glanced back at the girl, finally recognized a dirty, haggard Dawa with tangled hair, her dress torn, her hands caked with dirt. Her jaw was moving, clenching and unclenching. Perhaps she wasn't asleep, he realized, perhaps she was just frightened. For Lokesh was reading the Bardo, the death rites, and in front of him, in the center of the rear wall, was the shadow of a dead man.

A hand closed around Shan's forearm. It was Yao, squeezing tightly. Shan started to pull away resentfully, thinking Yao was again worried Shan would flee. But then Shan saw Yao's face. The inspector was looking at Lokesh and the effigy in front of them with a tight, worried expression. For the first time Shan saw uncertainty in Yao's eyes.

The five-foot-high shape hanging over the rear wall was a crude representation of a man, a brown shirt stretched over a frame of sticks, with the top stick extending eighteen inches from each shoulder to represent arms, two vertical sticks extending below the shirt as legs. An expensive watch and a string bearing three gold rings hung from one stick arm. The face was a piece of beige cloth stretched across a smaller frame of sticks lashed above the shirt, with eyes, ears, and mouth drawn in charcoal. Colors had been added by what may have been wax crayons. Brown hair. Red circles on the cheeks. Brown eyelashes.

There was movement behind them. Shan did not turn but heard the American's startled groan.

The crude effigy had a macabre power about it, a haunting presence that seemed to be warning them away. Shan understood why Dawa was keeping her eyes closed. He had learned of such a practice from the old lamas in the gulag, but never had he seen one of the effigies. It was one of the very old customs that still lingered in isolated pockets of Tibet, probably dating from before Buddhism came to the country.

"When a body isn't available for the customary three days of preparation," Shan explained in a whisper, "or when mourners chose to observe the full forty-nine days of traditional death rites, a likeness of the dead might be substituted for the body, to be the focus of those who would talk the departed spirit through his transition."

"The manuscript is very old and faded," someone suddenly said, in a quiet voice. Shan realized Lokesh had stopped reading and was speaking to him. "Written in the old style," he added. "They have difficulty with it, and asked if I could read it, at least the early chapters."

Corbett stepped to Shan's side, staring intensely at the effigy, then shook his head, hard, as though struggling to pull his gaze away. He moved to Dawa, lifted the girl into his arms, and carried her outside.

"Who was it?" Shan asked Lokesh.

"A man who was not prepared, is all they said," his old friend replied.

Not prepared. The Tibetans usually used the term to describe a devout Buddhist who had died unexpectedly, but it could mean anyone who had not prepared his spirit to pass on. Someone, for example, who had been murdered. Shan took a step forward, toward the effigy. Near the side wall he saw two more butter lamps, unlit. He tipped them into the flame of a lit lamp to ignite them and set them by the effigy.

Yao squatted at the legs of the figure, to which were attached thick black woolen socks, then poked tentatively at a blanket which lay on the floor below the stick feet. As Shan lifted the blanket Yao's breath audibly caught. Exposed in the dim light was a row of what must have been the dead man's possessions: A portable compact disc player with earphones, an expensive Japanese model that showed signs of heavy use. A small magnifying lens that swung out from a hard plastic case. A pair of hiking boots. A compass. A complicated pocketknife with perhaps a dozen blades. Three short bristled brushes, bundled together with a rubber band. A roll of American currency. A clay tsa-tsa image of a saint, identical to those Shan had seen at Fiona's house.

Yao pushed at the items with his fingertips, as though uneasy about lifting them. Shan gazed at the brushes a moment, realizing they were not for painting but for cleaning dust from delicate objects, then lifted one of the lamps toward the effigy's head. Yao followed his gaze, emitted a small cry of surprise. He darted outside, where he had left his small pack, and returned a moment later with his hand lantern, fixing its beam on the crudely drawn face. An instant later he ran back to the door, calling the American. The eyes of the effigy were blue.

The discovery seemed to ignite something inside Yao. He forgot his wariness about the effigy's belongings and began lifting them, pointing with them toward Shan as if accusing him of something. After a moment Yao growled he was going to call the soldiers to arrest the entire village. Corbett's breath caught as Yao lifted the disc player. Underneath was a passport, a British passport. Corbett grabbed it, scanning the inside cover, and angrily slammed it down. Shan lifted it and read the name. "The bastard!" Corbett spat. He seemed to take it as a personal affront that William Lodi had gotten himself killed.

Shan sat silently, letting his companion's anger burn away, then calmly introduced them to Lokesh, explaining the death rite, reminding them again that if they brought soldiers into the mountains there would be no more Tibetans to speak with, no evidence to follow. The two men stared at him grimly, Yao fidgeting with the radio, which he kept in his hand. Then Shan directed them to gather firewood.

"We are going to make a meal for the village," he explained when Yao hesitated.

"It will take all the supplies we brought," the inspector protested.

Shan nodded. "And money. I will need money, too. You owe it to them, to apologize for disturbing them, for being so rude. If they accept the apology we may learn some answers to our questions."

Corbett reached into his pocket.

A quarter hour later they were boiling water at the edge of the village. Shan, having purchased butter and tea and borrowed a churn and kettle from a curious villager who had materialized between two of the houses, was laying their supplies out on a blanket: A bag of raisins, a bag of walnuts. Half a dozen apples. A bag of rice. Four cans of peaches, three of tuna fish.

"It's not enough," Shan said as ten, then fifteen Tibetans materialized from the rocks.

"We have no more food," Yao protested.

"Anything," Shan said.

Yao tightened the top of his pack and held it to his chest. Corbett stared into his own then withdrew a small black leather case and handed it to Shan. It was the American's evidence kit. Shan opened it, extracting one of the little rubber syringe bulbs that held the powder used for highlighting fingerprints. He upended the bulb and squeezed it, shooting powder into the air. The nearest Tibetans gave an exclamation of surprise, then pressed closer as Shan handed it to an old man. They thought, Shan realized, it was a device for shooting flour into the air, a technology for celebrating.

A woman appeared with a pot of barley flour, for which Shan offered the remainder of the money Corbett had produced, and as Shan helped with the fire she began roasting the flour in a pan, chatting with Shan.

As more ragyapa warily appeared, Shan returned to Yao and Corbett, who sat together on a nearby rock, both wearing the same uneasy, suspicious expression.

"The body arrived early yesterday," he reported. "It was taken right to the charnel ground, right to the birds."

"Destruction of evidence," Yao said.

"It doesn't figure," Corbett said. "They made that effigy. That's not a cover-up."

"I think those who brought the body wanted the birds to begin immediately," Shan said. "But the people here knew Lodi, and had to mourn him as well, in the best way they knew how."

"The gifts, those electric devices in the basket," Corbett said.

Shan nodded. "I think they are from him."

"He looked Tibetan," Yao said, "but he had a British passport." Yao, like Corbett, had studied the passport, even looked as though he were going to take it as evidence. But just as he had seemed about to stuff it in a pocket he had glanced at Lokesh then returned it to the makeshift altar.

"Tibetan but not Tibetan," Shan said. If Lodi's killing still made no sense, at least some of the evidence left where he had died now did. There had been something else in the hut, an old thangka of a blue figure with the head of a red-eyed bull bearing two pairs of horns, its head surrounded by a red halo, standing, holding a spear and a sword in its front hooves, its back legs trampling humans and animals in the cosmic dance of death and rebirth.

"It means you can go home," Yao said in a hopeful tone as he handed the American some of the buttered tea.

"Home?" Corbett muttered. "Now I can never go home." He lifted the bowl of salted tea to his lips, sipped, and seemed to gag. He stared doubtfully at the bowl, then looked at the Tibetans, as if he couldn't believe they were drinking the same brew. "You don't understand," he said. "Never have I not recovered the art that was stolen in my cases. I don't close incomplete files. Not once in my career. If I could have arrested Lodi, I would have found the art eventually. But now . . ." He shrugged. "Now I have to follow his trail. Where the evidence leads—" he paused and looked doubtfully at the village"—is where I go."

Yao reacted to the news with a weary expression. He set his bowl of tea on a rock without attempting to taste it, watched as the old blind woman slowly approached their fire. Shan saw him lean forward as if to rise and go to her and placed a restraining hand on Yao's arm. They watched as the other villagers greeted her and assisted her to a seat, a place of honor on a blanket by the fire, then Shan poured her a bowl and Lokesh handed her a handful of raisins, which she began to consume one at a time, working each one with her gums.

"Grandmother," Shan said in Tibetan. "I have never before seen the deity on the thangka in the mourning hut."

She raised a hand in warning. "Its name may not be spoken." She grinned, as if Shan had attempted mischief and been caught. "I am the only one of the village who may touch the painting, because I was born away from the hills and it has no power over me."

She had not told him the terrible name but she had told Shan enough. It was the image the godkillers sought. It was why Ming snatched Surya from Zhoka, to understand the shape of this particular four-horned dancing bull god. "William Lodi was still very young," Shan said. "How did he die?"

"A terrible wound in his side, they said." She was stroking the back of the goat which lay at her side. "He will be missed by his clan."

"He was stabbed?" Shan asked.

She did not respond. She had warned him about speaking of the dead. "All these years, no Chinese has ever come to these mountains," she said after a long silence. "Soldiers were in the distance once but they were frightened of our birds and fled. Now two come, and another *goserpa* from far away," she said, using one of the Tibetan words for a Westerner. "Some of us are scared, some confused." She drank deeply from her bowl. "You have good raisins."

"Where was his family, his home?"

"Treasure vase, in the south," she said. "I visited as a child. We sang the queen's birthday."

Shan glanced at Lokesh, who listened attentively. His old friend had the same frustration in his eyes Shan felt. She was speaking true words, Lokesh would say, but they did not have the listening.

"Was it people from there who brought Lodi to the birds? Were they with him at Zhoka?"

"There are no monks here, haven't been these forty years. We have to be monks and nuns in our own way. People trust us like they would a monk."

Shan cast a wary glance toward Yao and Corbett.

"I wasn't always blind," the woman explained suddenly. "I was not always with the ragyapa. I saw more beautiful things while my eyes were alive than most see in a lifetime. Sometimes I think it is why I went blind."

"You mean at Zhoka?"

"This is a special land, where the hands of deities can work uninterrupted. Those who come from down in the world must be careful in ways they have never been careful before."

Shan hastily translated, in a whisper, for Yao and Corbett, offering no explanation for her words, for he had none.

The woman's blind eyes were strangely expressive, filled not with fear but with a sad wonder. Lokesh filled her bowl again, sitting close, reciting the mani mantra with her. The old Tibetan had a special reverence for the blind. More than once he had told Shan how those without eyes were not distracted by all the meaningless activity of the world around them, that those with reverence could learn to use unknown senses to see the movements of deities.

"I am sorry you lost your home," Lokesh said quietly, after several minutes.

The woman's hand reached out and without hesitating found Lokesh's own hand and closed around it. Lokesh had been there the day before, he had said mantras with the village. Shan watched as the two sat in silence, remembering the woman's words. I was not always with the ragyapa. She was not one of the fleshcutters but, incredibly, she had chosen to live with them.

"It was a long time ago," she said to Lokesh. "I had brought my father's body here, and had promised his spirit I would stay to perform one hundred thousand mantras to the Compassionate Buddha. While I was here there were many explosions and guns firing in the north and west, from the valley. Two days later a shepherd came with five yaks, carrying more bodies. My mother. My husband and three children. The army had passed through," she added, as if reporting a violent storm that had randomly struck her home.

"Grandmother," Shan said. "Where did you learn your English words?" He switched to English. "I met another woman in the hills who knows some."

"Give you joy," she said again, in the Western tongue.

"Her name is Fiona," he said, still in English.

She gave no sign she understood anything he said except the name of the sturdy, enigmatic woman Shan had met. A smile grew on the blind woman's face. "Fiona," she whispered, with sudden excitement. "Give you joy," she repeated, and when Corbett echoed the words over her shoulder she dabbed at her eyes, suddenly moist, then slowly rose from the ground and, incredibly, began to dance. Hers was a slow, stiff gait, and it took only a glance at Lokesh's confused expression for Shan to know the dance was not one of those from Tibetan tradition. As fragments of a tune came from her throat, however, Corbett seemed to recognize it, coming forward hesitantly, an uncertain grin on his face as he warily touched his fingers to the blind woman's hand. Her breath caught, but then as Corbett began humming the tune loudly, she gripped his hand tightly and they danced together.

The entire village stopped, the ragyapa gathering close in the fading light, parents calling children, Lokesh, then others, softly clapping their hands in rhythm, Dawa quietly laughing, the goat standing, softly bleating, an old man in the shadows beating time with a wooden spoon on a clay jar as he hummed the same tune. Time itself seemed to stop. Shan, surprised by joy, watched with the others as the American and the old Tibetan woman danced by the fire, below the rising moon. The gait grew faster but the woman seemed to have no difficulty following. Indeed, the years seemed to drop from her face and in the dimming light Shan glimpsed a much younger woman laughing, eyes gleaming, overflowing with life.

"We have to go," Yao interjected uneasily, pulling Shan's arm. "We have to call a helicopter. We have to . . ." Then Yao, too, was captured by the magic of the moment, seeming to forget his thought as he watched the two dancers silhouetted by the moon.

At last, spent, the two collapsed into each other's arms, Corbett embracing the woman tightly before releasing her.

"God save the queen!" the woman cried out in a final rush of excitement, then she let one of the children guide her back to her blanket.

Corbett cocked his head, as if wondering if he heard correctly, then took a bowl of tea proffered by Shan, mixed in the Indian style with milk and sugar. The American sipped cautiously, grinned, and drained it before speaking. "My grandparents used to do that dance when I was knee high," he explained. "Though there should be bagpipes and fiddles. It was a Scottish reel." He seemed to consider his words a moment. "Damn me. A Scottish reel," he said again, in disbelief, then wandered out into the darkness, wonder on his face.

"We need to call Tan," Yao said. "We need to make the fire brighter so the helicopter can find us."

Shan still studied the blind woman, who seemed to have fallen into a deep reverie now. "No. We still need to understand Lodi."

"It's the living I want to know about," Yao protested. "Lodi's accomplices."

"Then forget the helicopter," Shan said. "We keep going south."

"Not without soldiers. Death has become too commonplace in these mountains."

"Don't go south unless you are ready," a voice said behind them. It was the woman who had helped Shan prepare the meal, cleaning the pans now.

"Ready for what?" Shan asked.

"The south is not a place for strangers. It is a hard place with long memories. A terrible battle was fought there hundreds of years ago. Thousands of soldiers died. None of them prepared. None with anyone to keep vigil. Wandering souls. Thousands."

"But the south is where I will find the clan of Lodi," Shan said. No one seemed able to speak of the south except in words like code.

The woman frowned. "If you get lost there will be no way out."

"Nonsense," the blind woman said, from across the fire. Lokesh was sitting next to her now, handing her more raisins. "People don't really get lost in these mountains. This is the land of the earth temple. There are places here that seek people out. The right people."

The words seemed to build a new resolve on Yao's face. He disappeared into the shadows, toward the packs they had left near the mourning shed. Moments later loud shouts broke the quiet, and Yao reappeared, his pack in his hand, a snarl on his face. "They took it!" he declared. "They stole my radio and my map! They must be searched!"

Shan studied Corbett, who sat gazing into the fading fire. "You won't find them," Shan said.

Yao glared at him. "Why not?"

"Because I took them," Shan declared in a wooden tone. "I threw them away. Destroyed them."

"You'll be back in jail for this!" Yao hissed and seemed to about strike Shan with his pack.

Suddenly Corbett was between them, turning to Shan. "Why the hell would you say that?"

Shan returned his steady stare. "Because none of these Tibetans would have stolen anything."

Corbett studied the frightened villagers and turned back with an apologetic glance at Shan before addressing Yao. "He thinks he should protect me for some reason."

"You?" Yao barked.

"When I was dancing with her the old woman said something," Corbett said, suddenly very solemn. "She said in these mountains you either fight demons or you become demons."

"You're speaking the same gibberish as these people. I must have my radio and map."

The American stared at Yao for a long time before replying. "I threw them off the side of the gorge. Gone."

"Why?" Yao demanded, his voice flat, his eyes forlorn.

"Because you were talking yourself into turning around."

"We're helpless without that radio," Yao said.

"You haven't been listening to Shan," the American said in a somber voice. "He's been trying to explain that we're helpless *with* it. I'm not sure who you're after anymore. But I know who I want. And we'll never catch godkillers with soldiers."

CHAPTER EIGHT

A hand reached for Shan in the darkness, a small trembling hand that found his arm and pulled. It was his son, and they were going to watch the dawn from one of the sacred mountains. They would throw the Tao sticks, speak of the old verses, and eat sweetened rice cakes made by Shan's grandmother.

"Aku Shan," a tiny voice called, and the hand pulled again. "Uncle Shan, he is dead."

The words stabbed him awake. He sat up. He had been asleep on a blanket outside the mourning shed. The hand and the voice belonged to Dawa, whose face he could barely see in the shadows. Behind her stood a boy, one of those who had pummeled Yao and Corbett with bones, and behind the boy the horizon held the first blush of dawn.

"Who died?" he asked as he rose, anxiously surveying the landscape. Corbett and Yao lay wrapped in heavy felt blankets by the fire, the blind woman sitting between them like a sentinel. He could hear the low drone from inside the shed that meant Lokesh was still speaking to Lodi.

Dawa did not reply, but pulled him away from the shed onto one of the paths that led to the main southern trail. The ragyapa boy followed hesitantly, seeming more afraid of Dawa than Shan.

They walked, then trotted, Dawa leading him more than a quarter mile down the main trail then halting, hand up in warning. She picked up a short stick that had been left leaning against a boulder and advanced on a low slab of rock that jutted over several smaller boulders. A cairn, no more than a foot high, had been erected on the slab. Several freshly painted mani stones, the mantra depicted with soot in crude, poorly formed strokes, were arrayed on the ground around the front of the slab, before a burrow under the stone.

"He won't touch it," Dawa said. "He just said a deity was killed here two days ago. I told him to prove it." She bent and fished out a large twisted piece of metal with the stick.

"It was a god," the boy said in a voice full of warning. "But now it died. You must leave it in peace.

Shan knelt by the metal. It had been an old sculpture, an exquisite image of Manjushri, one of the Buddhist saints, its bronze glowing with the patina of age. In the rising light he could discern a serene face, with an oval beauty mark above the nose, a slender arched body, finely detailed fingers, one hand holding the mythical sword that dispelled ignorance, the other the stem of a lotus wrapped around a manuscript. Behind him sat a lion, the saint's mount. Until recently, it had been perfect but for a patch of corrosion along the figure's left shoulder. But now the saint had been brutalized, its head smashed nearly flat and bent back at the neck, the upraised sword arm twisted and folded back at the elbow, the finely wrought lotus flowers hacked and splintered with something sharp. The entire body had been pounded so, the metal stretched and cracked, it lay almost flat. It had been a beautiful piece of art, probably rendered centuries earlier, but here, at the durtro, the day after Lodi had been killed, it had been destroyed beyond repair. Yes, Shan almost said in despair, the deity is dead.

"You saw this happen?" Shan asked the boy, who seemed emboldened by Shan's lifting of the sculpture from the ground. Shan turned the statue over. Unlike the others neither its back nor its base had been cut open.

The boy nodded. "From a distance. I sit and watch the trail sometimes, see the people who pass the village, see where the people go after they leave bodies. I try to imagine what the world is like."

"You followed the ones who brought Lodi?"

"Two others were waiting in the rocks here. A big one and a small one. With Chinese faces. The big one had a rifle. The others ran away, all except her. She yelled at him, and he acted like he would kill her. He forced her to give him the sack she carried. They took the statue out and attacked it. With their boots at first. Then the butt of the gun. I thought the big man was going to shoot it, but the little one stopped him. Then they got rocks and hit it. They laughed and threw it against the boulders like a ball. She cried."

"Who cried?"

The boy grew quiet, looking worried.

"Did you know the Chinese?"

"They weren't Chinese," the boy whispered. "Just godkillers using Chinese faces. The little one was in charge. He put a boot on it when he was done and told her to go home, and tell everyone how things had changed now. I didn't know what to do. I brought my grandmother and we buried it. Our birds can't eat the metal."

"You did right," Shan said, and shot up as footsteps rose behind him. Yao emerged from the shadows, gesturing to Shan, silently taking the statue from him. He sighed heavily at the sight of the wanton destruction, then set the twisted metal on the rock beside the cairn, studying it intensely in the first rays of sunlight.

"If there are words that must be said for a dead man," Dawa said quietly, "what must be done for a dead god?"

The question hung in the air.

"It is only the image of a god," Yao said after a moment. Shan looked at the inspector in surprise.

"In the hut," Dawa said, "it is only the image of a man."

The words seemed to confuse Yao. He just turned and gazed toward the south.

"We need to pack," Shan said.

"I'll wait here," Yao offered, reaching for his pad. "I'm not going back to that place."

For an hour they walked southward in silence, as they had left in silence. The villagers had kept apart as Shan and Corbett had gathered their packs, watching no longer with resentment, but with something like worry, as if they feared for Shan and his companions. Corbett had silently gathered flowers and set them in the blind woman's hands. "Give you joy," she had whispered.

Shan saw that Lokesh had strayed off the trail, up the slope of a small ridge with a long flat top. He urged the others on, promising to rejoin them with Lokesh soon. The old Tibetan sat at the crest of the ridge facing a small half-mile-wide plain at the top. A familiar expression had settled over Lokesh, the odd, sad joy he showed when walking through the ruins of gompas or watching aged herders labor over their beads with arthritic fingers.

"It's taken a long time," Lokesh said as Shan approached, sweeping his hand toward the plain.

The plain was filled with rock cairns, hundreds of cairns, some covered with lichen so thick it bound their stones together. Shan slowly stepped among the cairns at the edge of the field. The ones with the thickest lichen were all tall, over six feet high. Where the lichen had not covered them he could see carvings, not just of the mani mantra but of elaborate images of Buddhist teachers and deities. The oldest and tallest were arranged in a circle around a small chorten of white stone, eight feet high, that itself was beautifully carved with the faces of protector deities.

But the vast majority of the cairns were smaller, more recent, though none less than decades old.

"The battlefield," Shan said. "They spoke of a terrible battle in the mountains."

"Living so close to the dead," Lokesh said with a reverent whisper as he gazed back in the direction of the ragyapa village, "you would be brushed by many spirits. It would be like a wound." He stood and stroked the top of a cairn. "Maybe you would have to keep the wound open, always, because of the scar that would grow over your spirit."

Shan remembered the hollow but wise expressions of the ragyapa, even the children. They had chosen to keep the wound open, for the honor of being brushed by many spirits.

Shan saw that Lokesh had found something new. Tucked into a cleft in a ledge wall was a statue, a finely detailed image of the Future Buddha, serenely gazing over the battlefield. No, Shan saw, it had not been inserted into the cleft, it had been carved from the living stone. The workmanship was masterful, the inscription of the mantra carved into the base so fine it seemed as though it had been left with a brush.

"Zhoka," Lokesh said.

They stared at the beautiful Buddha a long time. It was a work that belonged in a temple, or a museum, not in such a high, lonely place where living eyes almost never saw it. But Shan somehow knew Lokesh was right. It was not for the living. The monks of Zhoka had given it to the dead.

"I don't understand what they are doing, those two policemen," Lokesh said after a long silence.

"Trying to find the thieves," Shan said, confused.

"Surely taking such things of beauty is a sin," Lokesh said, "but I don't see how the government can help. Policemen are supposed to be concerned about crime. It is far easier to punish a crime than to resolve the sin."

For the first time Shan realized that Lokesh, too, was investigating in his own way. The battered statue with Atso, the deity paintings in the old tower, the disturbance in the harmony of the durtro, these were the clues he followed. Lokesh was on the track of godkillers, not to punish but to resolve their sin. The old Tibetan pointed to a rock formation at the side and walked toward it. A stick had been jammed into the rocks, and a makeshift prayer flag hung from it, a piece of cloth ripped from a garment, inscribed in soot. Below it, in the shadows of the rocks, were the remains of a recent fire. Shan squatted and studied the ground. Several people had been there recently, wearing the soft-soled boots of Tibetans.

In another hour the southern trail began to sharply ascend, and after two more hours of hard climbing they found themselves on a wide, high plain framed on the south and west by the distant snowcapped Himalayas. The broad, arid plateau was unlike any land Shan had ever seen. It was strewn with high spires of rock and narrow flat-topped buttes, twenty or thirty of the structures, some hundreds of feet tall, scattered across the plain. Like cairns, giant cairns arranged by the gods.

"It's like the end of the earth," Corbett said.

The wind suddenly found them, a cold, battering wind that seemed to want to push back down the trail, off the plateau.

"We have no food. There's no water. We have to go back now," Yao muttered. "We can't sleep up here. I must be in Lhadrung, I have to call Beijing."

"No. There are places that seek people out," Lokesh said in a level voice, echoing the words of the ragyapa woman. "We are being pushed toward what must be done. It is just stripping us of what holds us back. Your money. Your map. Your radio. Your food."

"My camera," Corbett added. "My evidence kit."

"This is no place for thieves," Yao snapped.

Shan surveyed the rugged terrain they had crossed. He, too, had reasons to go back. Ming was still searching for a monk. Gendun was still somewhere at Zhoka, while the godkillers stalked the hills.

"No one could live in such a forsaken place." Yao said, then paused, looking at Lokesh, who was quickly walking toward a long ledge a hundred feet away.

Shan followed his gaze and stared, disbelieving. "Someone did," he said, and trotted to Lokesh. Words were carved into the rock in front of the old Tibetan, an inscription facing the barren, brutal plateau, not far from where their trail had entered.

"What does it say?" Corbett asked, over Shan's shoulder.

"Study Only the Absolute," Shan translated, glancing at Lokesh with a strange thrill of discovery.

The sudden appearance of the words seemed to take all protest out of Yao. They walked slowly along the edge of the plain. After several hundred yards Corbett pointed to an eye, two feet wide, painted on a high rockface. Soon after they passed a long slab of rock with the eight sacred symbols carved along its edge. Suddenly Corbett stopped, hand in the air, pointing. "She looks so lifelike," he said in a whisper.

Fifty feet away in the deep shadow of a huge pillar of stone was a statue of a woman wrapped in a blanket staring out over the plain. Dawa gazed a moment, uttered a little cry, and bolted forward. As Shan followed the figure slowly moved, opening its arms to embrace the girl.

The woman who sat so still in a grey hat and a grey blanket was Liya and not Liya. She seemed stiff, unwelcoming, and acknowledged them only with a small, reluctant nod. "The brown wind will come soon," she said impassively. "You cannot be on the plain then." She took Dawa's hand and began walking up a worn path that wound around a series of ledges and natural pillars.

As the others followed, Shan paused to survey the plain again. The wind had indeed increased, and a low cloud of dust had risen along the floor at the far end so that the monoliths there seemed to be floating in an eerie brown fog. Now that the deities had gotten them there they seemed loath to let them leave.

They moved down the tortuous narrow path for several minutes, stepping through a short tunnel then over a narrow channel cut into the rock to emerge into a landscape like none Shan had ever seen. It seemed as if great square blocks had been cut out of the high steep ridge, each nearly a hundred yards wide, perhaps half as deep, and fifty feet high, creating a series of four giant steps leading to the top of the ridge. The tiers of rock had sprouted juniper and hemlock trees, and houses made of stone and wood. The houses were built along the mountain walls, connected by stairs carved along a small stream that cascaded down the ledges. At the base a small wooden waterwheel caught the water as it tumbled into a pool at the base of the ridge. People could be seen on every level—not many, not enough to populate all the houses. Some stared at the newcomers suspiciously. Most glanced at them and went about their labors, as if they had been expected.

Half a dozen of the inhabitants gathered behind Liya, as if they expected her to protect them. "What do you call this place?" he heard Yao ask.

"*Bumpari Dzong*," Liya said, in a voice full of warning. "It is a very old place. They say before people lived here, gods did."

Bumpari Dzong. It meant Treasure Vase Mountain Fortress. The old blind woman had referred to Lodi's home as Treasure Vase, Shan remembered, the traditional place where spiritual treasures were stored.

Lokesh rubbed his palms together, seemingly delighted at her response. As Shan stepped to his side he began pointing, low sounds of pleasure coming from his throat, at two women pressing wool between two wet blankets, the first step in felt-making. Then to a small wooden frame loom where an elegant rug was being created. And a woman crushing plant stems with a stone pestle, making incense in the old style. They were things, Shan realized, Lokesh had probably not seen for years, decades even, things from his childhood he may have assumed were lost forever.

The extraordinary terraced settlement was indeed living in a different century. The houses, the implements, the reverent relief carvings on the rock walls, even the homespun and embroidered clothing of most of the inhabitants could have been from the eighteenth century or earlier. But as he studied the inhabitants, Shan saw that the young woman sitting at the loom wore an expensive gold watch, and a teenage boy who worked at the waterwheel had stylish running shoes on his feet.

Corbett pulled on Shan's sleeve. "The entrance path," he said.

Shan turned to see a team of yak straining, pulling a huge slab of stone with braided leather ropes down the stone channel they had stepped across, sealing the tunnel that led to the village. Beside it a dark, compact man stood like a sentry, holding a musket. The man did not look like the others in the village. Shan suspected he was from across the border, from Nepal, probably of the Gurka people. In his wide belt was a curved blade, and what looked like an automatic pistol.

Liya ushered them toward a small clearing under a half circle of juniper trees growing at the base of the cliff that defined the western wall of the settlement. Vines grew up the cliff, and peeking through an opening in the vines was an animated, excited face carved in the stone, the laughing countenance of a Tibetan saint. Inside a ring of mortared stones a fire burned, a kettle on its grill of iron bars. Others arrived as the tea was being churned, one of them a middle-aged woman in a red embroidered dress, who brought a copper teapot which she filled from the kettle, then from a pouch at her waist dropped in several green tea leaves. She poured the green tea into four matching white cups—for Shan, Yao, Corbett, and herself—as the other Tibetans silently accepted bowls of traditional buttered tea. They sat in a circle, studying their visitors with expectant faces.

"We have waited long," the woman in the red dress said in a warm tone. "Welcome to our village." She spoke the words two times, once in Mandarin, once in English. As she sipped her cup the sun broke out of the cloud cover, washing the little clearing in a brilliant light.

"Your eyes!" Dawa blurted out, pointing at the woman. "What is wrong?" Then she paused and looked to Corbett and back at the woman. "They are like his! Like a goserpa's," she said.

Blue. The woman's eyes were blue. Shan studied the other villagers, some of whose faces were obscured by hats. More than half of those he could see had blue eyes. They had found the blue men who lived in the south.

"Yes," the older woman said, and handed the girl a wooden bowl of shelled walnuts. "A wonderful man lived here many years ago, an Inchi teacher. He was the grandfather and great-grandfather to most who live here today. He came from England a hundred years ago."

The words caused Corbett's head to snap toward the woman. "British?" the American asked.

The woman nodded. "In the Wood Dragon Year, hundreds of British came to Tibet. Many became good friends of our country. And more," she added with a mischievous glint, then refilled their cups.

She was referring to the Younghusband expedition, Shan realized, in which Great Britain, reacting to exaggerated reports that Russia was establishing a military foothold in Tibet, had sent troops to force political and trading links with Lhasa. The year had been 1904.

"They came as soldiers," she said. "Ready to do war. But for many the real fighting they did was inside themselves. They had not known about Tibet, about Tibetans."

Shan searched his memory, recalling Western history books he had read with his father. There had been a few small battles, with heavy casualties among the Tibetans, who fought with charms and muskets against Maxim machine guns. The British had surprised the Tibetans by giving medical aid to the wounded Tibetans. The Tibetans had surprised the British by using the Buddhist scriptures as guidelines for negotiations. After leaving Tibet, Colonel Younghusband, the expedition leader, had been a changed man. He formed a new council for world religions, and spent his life working for global peace.

"You are our guests," the woman said. "You may wash," she said, pointing to a stone trough by the pond. "You may explore our world. We ask only that you respect the mourners," she added, gesturing toward a small structure beyond the junipers that had the appearance of a temple. Two braziers flanked the door, each emitting a column of smoke. "And that you will not go to the top level, where there are sacred things. Later we will share food."

Shan studied Liya as the woman spoke. Her face was clouded with worry, and she looked away when she met Shan's gaze.

Dawa pulled Corbett toward the pond. Lokesh started up the path to the next level, where gardens of flowering shrubs led to a long elegant timber frame building.

Liya stepped toward the temple, as if to avoid Shan, who watched, sipping tea as the circle around the fire dispersed. He studied the strange, beguiling landscape, his gaze settling on a cottage at the opposite end of the first level, a sturdy wooden building with a gracefully sloping wooden shingled roof and a narrow porch on which were suspended a large prayer wheel and several flower boxes, spilling blue and red blossoms down the porch railing.

As he stepped onto the porch of the cottage, Shan found himself touching the exquisitely worked copper prayer wheel, turning it as he walked by. At the end of the porch was an old rocking chair, its rockers worn thin from long use.

The interior of the building, like everything else he had seen in the terraced village, had been constructed with great skill and attention to detail. Beams were tightly joined with precisely fitted mortice and tenon joints, and carved with climbing vines. Stained and varnished planks of wood had been joined to form wainscotting that rose four feet from the floor along the walls of the main chamber, with smooth white plaster above. On one wall hung a small Union Jack flag over shelves of Western books, on another a dozen framed photographs were hung over a simple stone fireplace. On the other two walls hung several cloth thangkas, one above a small wooden altar with a bronze Buddha. The chamber had the air of a small, intimate museum. Shan investigated the doors that led out of the room. The first chamber held a simple wooden-framed bed covered with a thick down quilt, framed drawings on the walls. The second room was a small kitchen, the third another bedroom with two wooden beds, a shelf over the farthest holding an array of compact electronic devices. A floorboard creaked and Shan returned to the main chamber to find Yao staring at the British flag, Liya at his side.

"My great-grandfather built this house and raised his family here," Liya explained. "There is a photograph of him holding my mother in that rocking chair outside."

Shan stepped to the framed photographs, and quickly found the black and white picture of a Western man, large whiskers on the side of his face, proudly holding a baby, one arm around a beaming Tibetan woman who stood at his side. The man's expression was jovial, almost impish. In another picture the same man appeared, much younger, attired in a uniform, holding an elongated helmet in the crook of one arm. In the center were separately framed images of two nearly bald men, each seeming to wear the same enigmatic grin. One Shan recognized as the Thirteenth Dalai Lama, who had died over sixty years earlier. The second man, a Westerner in a suit and tie, he remembered from pictures in his father's history books. Winston Churchill.

Under the photo on the fireplace mantel was a box with a glass lid, displaying several medals and a calling card. "Major Bertram McDowell," Shan read out loud, "Royal Artillery."

"McDowell!" Yao repeated in a surprised whisper, and stepped to his side.

"The major was stationed at a trading post in Gyantse for a year," Liya said over their shoulders. "He had always been a painter and a writer. In Tibet he began to compile material for a book, the first English book on Tibetan art. When he asked to be taught as Tibetan artists would, a lama told him to sit in a meditation chamber with nothing but a Buddha for a week, that he had to expand his deity, let it reach his fingers."

"A lama from Zhoka," Shan suggested.

Liya nodded, still facing the photographs. "He never turned back after that week. He declined home leave, requested extended tours of duty. Eventually he resigned and the lama brought him here, where artists had helped the Zhoka monks for centuries."

"Why would this place be so hidden?" Yao inquired.

Liya turned, not toward Yao but toward the little Buddha on the altar. "Study Only the Absolute," she said.

"Major McDowell lived in this house," Shan said.

Liya nodded. "He became a great artist." She gestured toward a line of framed sketches surrounding the door to the first bedroom. "He had a teacher, the daughter of a metalsmith. They married after the first year, had six children. Two of the boys became monks of Zhoka, the other children had many children themselves and populated the hill country." She moved to a table by the door and picked up an object Shan did not recognize at first, a small wooden bowl with a stem attached. Liya stroked it affectionately. "He was beloved by all the people. Each December he would have a festival and give gifts to everyone. He played a violin and taught everyone dances from his youth."

She put the bowl to her nose, then set it back on the porcelain tray where it had lain. It was a tobacco pipe.

Outside, a boy went by the cottage with a bundle of juniper sticks for burning.

"Are they mourning Lodi?" Shan asked.

Liya nodded again, then looked out the window in the direction of the temple. "He was our provider, he kept us protected. When he was sixteen Lodi left, to go across the border. We were suffering terribly. More and more people abandoned the village every year, some to the hills to farm and herd, some to Nepal and India. When I was young there were winters when some of the children and old ones starved to death. William took some of our art to sell, and sent new friends from Nepal with food for us. Then we didn't hear from him for a long time, more than a year, until a letter came from England. He had gone to meet our relatives."

"Elizabeth McDowell," Shan said.

"She had studied Asian art, was an advisor to a number of museums. She and Lodi said it was predestined that they work together. When he came back she was with him, bringing medicine, bringing orders."

"Orders?"

"For art. Things they could sell in Europe and America."

Liya's eyes brimmed with emotion and she turned away, stepping out onto the porch. Shan followed.

"I am sorry about William," he said. "But I need to understand what happened at Zhoka. For Surya's sake."

"His body had been carried down the tunnel. After I found it, I convinced some of the hill people, my cousins, to help me carry him away."

"But who killed him?"

Liya looked down, one hand twisting the fingers of the other.

"The ones who attacked you at the fleshcutters?"

"I don't know. If Surya had found Lodi in the tunnels, with that fresco stolen . . . I don't know."

"Who were those two men?"

Liya shrugged. "There are others who work with Lodi sometimes, from the outside. They were angry because Lodi was supposed to give them that statue."

"Then why would they destroy it?"

"They said they were taking over for Lodi, they said the terms had changed. They said the only chance to save the hill people was to help them. I didn't know them. A short Chinese with a crooked nose, and a big man, a Mongolian I think. William kept his dealings down in the world secret from us. It was safer for everyone that way, because he had to keep Bumpari secret. They ruined that beautiful thing, that old statue, because of what I said to them." She lowered her head into her hands a moment. "I am so afraid, Shan," she said abruptly. "It is the end for us. They will find us and will make us their slaves. They know we have no registrations, that one call to the authorities will destroy us. Our people are so scared. Most of them speak of fleeing across the border."

"Why didn't those two follow you from the fleshcutters?"

"I don't know. They acted like they had urgent business elsewhere."

"It would make no sense for them to kill Lodi without knowing how to find you." He paused. "But you said Elizabeth McDowell already knows this place."

"Punji would never tell. She is part of our family. All we want is to live in peace here, and make our art. She would never work with those two men . . . they were like animals. Nothing makes sense." Liya looked up as if suddenly remembering something. "The little Chinese demanded that I give him what Lodi had from the emperor."

"What emperor?"

"I don't know. I told him so, and he slapped me."

Shan looked out over the tiered village. "Did the emperors have art from Bumpari or Zhoka?"

"What we make has always been for Tibetans, for Buddhists."

"The emperor Qian Long revered the Buddhists. He had lamas in his court. He collected Tibetan treasures."

"If those men wanted more of our art they would have followed me."

"Perhaps they had to leave because they needed to obtain new supplies," Shan ventured. "After you destroyed what they had at Zhoka."

"When I found Lodi's body in that supply room I sat with it a long time. I was so sad at first, then angry. I had never felt such anger."

"If it was their supplies you destroyed, then they are the ones who are taking frescos from Zhoka."

Liya closed her eyes a moment. "Lodi would never harm Zhoka," she insisted. "He only sold things we made here. He would never loot the old shrines."

"That night at the camp with Lokesh and Dawa, did you leave because of Tashi?"

"Everyone who is smart stays away from informers."

"You were going north again, but then you came back here."

"I listened to Tashi from the shadows. I knew they had found a way to make you help them. I knew that eventually you would find this place."

"I am sorry," Shan said.

Liya shrugged. "You didn't start this." She began watching Corbett now, on the stairs to the next level, playing with Dawa and the children of the village.

"Why did Lodi come back to Lhadrung?" Shan asked.

Liya shrugged. "He wasn't due back for weeks. He just appeared, very excited and scared. He went into the room he kept here—" she nodded toward the room with two beds—"to search for something, then left for Zhoka the next morning."

Corbett now had one of the children on his back, climbing the stairs. The sight seemed to intrigue Liya, and without another word she stepped off the porch and walked toward the next level.

Shan turned back inside, entering the first bedroom, which had the air of a shrine. The framed sketches there seemed to match those of the main chamber. They showed a light, subtle hand that perfectly captured the smiles of playing children in one, the powerful energy of a harnessed yak in another. But the first of the frames held not a sketch but a piece of paper, letterhead printed with the caption Royal Artillery, flanked by crossed cannons. Under it, in an elegant hand, was a verse in English. He read it several times before he found himself grinning:

> *In a letter I have written, my mama's*
> *I report I did outwit the lamas*
> *They said we're not here, you're not there*
> *'cause we're made of thin air*
> *then why says I, wear red pajamas?*

He paused and pulled out the peche leaf he had found in the cell at Zhoka. The haunting script matched that of the limerick about the red robes of the monks. It had been written by Bertram McDowell, the primogenitor of the strange clan in the southern mountains.

Shan found Yao in the second bedroom, sitting on one of the beds, sketching in his notebook. The inspector was drawing a map.

"Ming has lied to you," Shan said. Yao kept drawing as he explained what Liya had revealed. "You don't know that these people are involved," Shan said.

"She would lie to save herself. Do I believe her or a ranking party member? This entire village is a nest of criminals. They gave aid to William Lodi, the thief and murderer. Illegal weapons are here. They admit smuggling across the border. No registrations, no taxes. Tan and Ming will be so pleased they will probably let you go back into hiding." He paused, and looked at the wall, as if consulting something unseen to Shan. "With so many to arrest, it will take a month for the interrogations alone."

Shan looked at Yao's crude map. It was worthless. Yao had no idea where they were.

The inspector opened the closet door. Stacked on shelves inside were boxes, apparently for the devices arrayed over the second bed, most bearing glossy labels in English and Japanese. A portable air freshener. An emergency desk lamp. An electric nose clipper. A metallic model of a car called a Ferrari. A pen with a lightbulb in its top. Something called an atomic alarm clock. A television remote control, though there was no television. An entire shelf of pharmaceuticals with English labels. Antibiotics. Sleeping pills. Pain relievers.

Shan looked back at the beds. The shelf over the second bed was an altar of sorts for the puzzling man who had been killed at Zhoka. In the shadows beyond was another altar, a traditional one, with a small brass Buddha, a paint brush, and a faded photograph of a young Major McDowell, posing by a cannon, a sword raised over his head as if he were about to lead a charge, his mouth obscured by a huge moustache.

On top of a short bookcase were perhaps two dozen elongated beads, the brown dzi beads prized as protective charms, the kind Lodi had given away in Seattle, each bead with a different pattern of white lines etched into it. Below the beads were several bound books, dusty, apparently neglected for years. Shan lifted one. It held heavy paper, blank, bound as a sketch book. On the first page, in a child's hand was written, in Tibetan, the name Lodi. The sketches that followed were crude but somehow confident, images of flowers, of the faces of dogs and yaks, of the sacred emblems. Like all the children of the village, no doubt, William Lodi had started at an early age to hone the skills of his clan.

Shan lifted another of the books. It, too, was a sketchbook, with many of the same subjects, though drawn with a more mature hand. The human faces had become sadder, some gaunt and emaciated. New images appeared, sketches of airplanes and automobiles. Photographs from magazines were pasted onto some pages, images of Western women, sleek cars, Western food, even of telephones. The last of the books contained drawings of women's faces with deep alluring eyes, of Gurkhas and Gurkha's blades, of Chinese war machines being blown apart. In the last pages a new series of faces appeared, all Western, all sharing certain features as if of the same blood, including one Shan recognized. Elizabeth McDowell. Confirming that Yao was engrossed in some new discovery on the other side of the room, Shan tore the sketch of the English woman out of the book and placed it inside his pocket.

As he returned the book to the shelf he realized his hands were shaking. He had been wrong about everything. He had struggled to be led by his compassion, as Gendun would have wanted. He had been so certain Surya was an innocent who could not possibly kill. He had thought anyone trying to excavate at Zhoka must be doing so out of reverence. He had taken what he had seen at Bumpari as a sign of hope, a stirring symbol of how the Tibetans could still find ways to shield themselves in their Buddhist traditions to maintain their spirit, and identity. But it wasn't compassion driving events. It was greed. Lodi had been supporting the art colony not to keep traditions alive but for reasons that had to do with the things he worshiped on the altar over his bed. Liya might not believe Lodi capable of looting Zhoka, but she did not know of the murder he had committed in Seattle.

A small chirping sound behind him pulled Shan's gaze from the bottom of the closet. Yao had opened the hinged top of a flat box on his lap, which was now glowing. It was a laptop computer. As Shan stared over his shoulder, the inspector began quickly opening and shutting files, making small guttural sounds of satisfaction. Bank account records. Travel records. Inventory records, showing long lists of art objects, classified in categories of thangkas, sculpture, ritual implements, and masks. Everything was in English.

As Yao scrolled through the files, glancing nervously at the closed door, Shan stepped back to the chest which had contained the computer. Shan put his hands down along the edges of the chest, probing. From beneath the blanket that bore the rectangular imprint of the computer he retrieved a small felt bag. Inside were half a dozen computer discs. He studied the labels on the discs a moment then extended them toward Yao, fanned out in his hand like playing cards.

They were red discs, bearing computer-printed labels. *Nei Lou,* the labels warned. Classified, a state secret. Below the legend were a series of numbers, ten digits all the same, followed by a hyphen and a single digit. Number one on the first disc, two on the second, through six. He handed the last disc to Yao, who inserted it into the computer.

"This computer may be all I need," the inspector said, then blinked in confusion as the photograph of a familiar building from Beijing appeared on the screen. "The Museum of Antiquities," he said in a puzzled tone. "Ming's museum." The photo faded and the words Nei Lou appeared, in huge figures that filled the screen. A moment later the screen was filled with dense, tiny ideograms under the heading Chapter Forty-five.

"Another *neyig*," Shan said in confusion. "A pilgrim's guide."

Shan gazed at the discs with the emblem of Ming's museum, then as Yao continued to scroll through the files, he probed the room again. On a small table by the bed was a cigar box, filled with photographs. He quickly leafed through them, seeing none that showed Zhoka or the village, then returned to those on top. People were gathered in front of a house, all Westerners except for Lodi, who stood in the center. His English cousins, including a younger Elizabeth McDowell. There were tourist shots from England, capturing castles and cathedrals.

In a separate envelope on the bottom were photos of a different set of people, taken in a sandy, windblown place. It appeared to be an archaeological excavation. He saw Elizabeth McDowell kneeling in the dirt, Director Ming beside her. Shan stared at the next photo a long time, not believing his eyes, looking toward Yao, then back at the photo. It was a group picture that included McDowell, Ming, and a number of Chinese who had the air of scientists, some wearing aprons, some holding hammers and chisels. At Ming's side was Lodi, and in the center of the group, more photogenic than the others, was a well-dressed Western man. At one of his shoulders was a huge man with the features of a Mongolian, a short cigar jutting from his mouth. At the other shoulder was a thin-faced Han who was looking at the Westerner, not the camera, highlighting his crooked nose. Shan put the photo in his pocket, then added the next one, which showed the same group lifting glasses in a toast, inside a large tent at a banquet table on which stood small flags of the People's Republic and the United States.

A deep bellow broke the silence in the cottage. Yao's head shot up and he slammed the top of the computer down. Shan darted out of the room, through the central chamber and onto the porch. From the next level someone was blowing a *dungchen,* one of the long telescoping horns used to summon monks at a gompa.

As Shan and Yao jogged up the rock steps, the horn stopped blowing, and jubilant cries came from a handful of villagers who bounded down the steps from the upper levels, toward the long frame building beyond the gardens.

Shan paused, stopping Yao behind him, and watched as the Tibetans ran inside the building.

By the time Shan and Yao reached the gardens everyone else except a man who stood like a guard at the stairs to the fifth level, was inside the elegant building. They stepped into a small chamber with a workbench holding a nearly completed statue of a deity with the head of a horse. Beyond the workshop was a large chamber, its arched passageway flanked on both sides with large prayer wheels handsomely worked in bronze, with the mani mantra inscribed in gilt lettering near the top rim on each and small images of the sacred symbols worked into the sides. Shan paused at the first, realizing he had seen a nearly identical wheel before, bent and corroded, lying half buried at Zhoka.

The building appeared to be divided into two great halls, the first of which had the air of a temple except it had no altar. The Tibetans had apparently gathered in the second hall but Shan paused, studying the first room. Incense burned in several small samkang. Along the edge of the room, lining the walls, were bronze statues on pedestals. Shan had seen similar statues before, in temples and gompas, even in museums, but never had he seen so many. Through the haze of the incense he counted forty of the bronze images, some only a few inches high, others two feet or more. He saw Lokesh standing, seemingly entranced, in front of one of the statues. Inside the perimeter of statues were tables, defining a central square in the chamber, and inside the square were a dozen stretching frames used for painting thangkas, cushions in front of each frame for an artist to sit, pigments and brushes by most of the cushions. But only one cushion was occupied.

A middle-aged woman sat at a frame, contemplating her unfinished work, on which the images had been outlined in pencil. The woman gave no acknowledgment as Shan and Yao approached. She was completely absorbed in her painting, though her brushes were at her side. She seemed deeply troubled, and repeatedly glanced past the stretched cotton cloth toward another, completed thangka that sat ten feet away, still in its frame, surrounded by burning butter lamps.

"Did you see?" an excited voice asked from behind Shan. Lokesh had found Shan. "Did you see?" Lokesh repeated, gesturing toward the completed thangka.

Shan stepped closer, recognizing the style. "Impossible," he gasped. "It's Surya's. But it can't be."

"It can only be," Lokesh said in a confident, yet wondrous tone.

"My children and I found him on a mountain when we were visiting our cousins who herd above the valley," a soft voice interjected. "He was painting a

Buddha on a rock." The painter spoke from where she sat, still staring at the unfinished face of her deity. "We were scared at first. My children had not seen a red robe their entire lives. I had not seen one for decades. Some would have said it was a ghost. We crept closer, not thinking he saw us as we hid under a ledge thirty paces away. But then he turned and he had the end of a brush balanced on his nose, and spread his arms like bird wings. My children could not stop their laughter. He came and sat in front of us. He called us rock pikas, and began squeaking like one."

The woman rose with a sad smile and approached the finished thangka. "When we crawled out he asked us to meet the deity he had painted. I started to cry. I don't know why. I cried like a little girl, then after a long time he took my hand and placed it on the deity. Something seemed to shoot through my arm, a strange tingling, and then it seemed like what was crying was not part of me anymore."

"But when did he come here?" Shan asked.

"We brought him nearly a year ago, for his first visit. Most of us had stopped painting years ago, working only in the metal shops. He helped us discover what was wrong."

"Wrong?"

The woman wrung her hands. "For centuries our people had helped make paintings for the earth temple. The living god paintings. There are old books here that speak of how a lama once came here and said he had entered one of the heavens where blessings fell off the tips of brushes and homes for gods were made of cotton and pigment." She looked at her hands as she spoke, as if embarrassed.

"But we lost the way," she continued after a moment. "We could make the things collectors wanted, even museums, but not the ones that could serve in temples. We lost the ways of spreading fire onto the cloth. Lodi said it didn't matter anymore, because there were no more temples, that we made no money from temples. But we knew better. My father was one of our best painters in generations and he spent half his time praying. Then we had terrible winters, three in a row, when all the old ones died. I think we forgot how to pray." She turned and nodded a greeting to Liya, who was standing by Surya's painting now.

"When Surya came to us that first day, it was like the sun had come out after years of storm. He put a hand on all our heads—everyone, even the children— then he came inside the workshops. He spent two hours inside, alone, studying our work. Afterwards he told us to take everything away, to empty this entire chamber. Then he put a little stool in the center of the room with a little bronze Buddha on it, saying after he left we had to meditate on that Buddha, do nothing but meditate on that Buddha, and the Buddha inside us, night and day, stopping only to eat and sleep, until he came back.

"When Lodi found out he was furious because we had stopped working, because his order was not ready on time. But we did not stop the meditation. Two weeks later Surya returned and began teaching us how to paint, starting with us as if we were children. He painted this for us, finished it on his last visit. He said soon the world would change. . . ." Her voice fell away and she looked up, blinking away tears. "Liya told us what happened. He labored to help us find our deities and then lost his own."

There was a long silence as they stared at Surya's painting. Something opened in the back of Shan's mind and he heard Surya's voice reading one of the old sutras. When he finally walked away, Lokesh at his side, Yao still stood staring, not at the painting, but at the painter.

The second chamber of the long building seemed to hold most of the population of the village. The woman who had served them tea was there, half a dozen children, and perhaps twenty more adults, standing in a tight knot at the center of the wood-paneled chamber, quiet murmurs of excitement rippling through the assembly. Shan and Lokesh eased their way to the side of the group. The villagers were gathered around Corbett, some of them venturing to pat Corbett on the back, a woman offering him fresh berries, another tea.

"He was outside in the garden," a small voice whispered. Dawa had found Shan. "There was a tablet of parchment, a brush, and some ink. I saw it happen. He dipped the brush in the ink and made a few strokes, smiled, and did it again. It was a flower on a branch, a perfect little flower with only six strokes. He saw me and motioned me to sit by him, then an old woman came to him and gasped when she saw the flower, saying it was as if it was growing from the paper. She laughed for joy, and started giving prayers of thanks. She cried out that this one is born of the rainbow. People started running. Soon someone starting blowing that long horn."

"What old woman?"

Dawa pointed to a woman in a brightly colored apron who sat at Corbett's side, showing him a collection of old paint brushes.

"The head of our painting halls," Liya said over Shan's shoulder. "The oldest of our painters."

"What did she mean, Corbett was born from the rainbow?"

She welcomed the question with a broad smile. "Many saints were said to have passed through here in the early centuries, going on to live at Zhoka. They taught that art was a spiritual practice, that the best artists, like the best lamas, were those who had benefited from many prior lives."

"Surely you don't mean he says Corbett is reincarnated from one?"

"Not exactly. It is more like art is a spiritual power, Corbett has the power of many prior artist lives focused in him. Not one specific artist. Our old teachings say the rainbow is the vehicle for passing the power, that where a rainbow touches down, an artist is born in that spot."

Shan looked at Corbett. "And he's been told this?"

"Oh yes. It pleases him. He is part of the prophecy, that the world is changing," Liya said. She glanced at Shan and flushed with color. "I mean people are saying that."

"He is an agent of the United States government," Shan pointed out.

Liya shrugged. "He is an artist, a translator of deities. The rest is unimportant."

Shan watched Corbett and the villagers, the American awkwardly accepting gifts of food and paint brushes, the lama grinning, the children singing.

"When I met you, you were with the purbas," Shan said. "I never saw you with a paint brush."

Liya offered a smile that was somehow grateful. "I was going to be an artist, as all of us are brought up to be. But after my mother died and Lodi left there was no one to watch out for everyone. He calls me—he called me—the village business manager."

"That's not what I would have called you when you were helping the monks with the festival."

Her smile seemed sadder now. "That seems like a long time ago. That was when Surya was going to open Zhoka again, and I was going to bring new art for the temples."

"What was Lodi's business with Ming?" Shan asked abruptly.

"We make art and Lodi sells it. Punji introduced him to Ming, who helped him learn about art markets. She got him assigned to some of Ming's expeditions."

"Was Ming buying art from Lodi?"

Liya frowned, and did not answer.

"Was he stealing from Ming?"

"Lodi was no thief."

"Yes he was, Liya." Shan explained what he knew about the theft of the Dolan collection, and murder of the young American woman.

Liya stared at a row of lotus flowers carved into the wall near the ceiling, her eyes growing moist. "I don't believe it. He was no killer, no thief. He had reverence for our art, he would not steal sacred things, it would be disrespectful."

"People change. He had money. He traveled, he had friends in the West.

Bumpari was part of his life, but not all of it." What would she say, Shan wondered, if he told her that Corbett had proof that Lodi visited casinos? She would not even understand what a casino was. And stealing from a rich American might not seem disrespectful, especially if Lodi was indeed bringing the artifacts back to Tibet.

A lonely despair grew on Liya's countenance. "All I want is for things to be the way they were, the way they are supposed to be." She gazed at the children playing at Corbett's feet as she spoke. "We spoke about looters, Lodi and I. There have always been thieves looking for treasure. He always thought he could protect Tibetan things while still—" Liya searched for words, "still conducting his business in the West. But then I saw him at Zhoka before dawn on the festival day. He was upset. More than upset. Remorseful. He said nothing that was about to happen had been his idea, he wanted me to believe that. He said we should seal some of the old shrines and he vowed that he would find something that would make up for everything, something wonderful for the people of the hills, something Surya had been seeking for months. He had that statue of Manjushri with him, and gave it to me before dawn the day of the festival, to protect it. I hid it in the ruins and brought it back with his body."

She grew silent again, and moisture filled her eyes again. "I feel responsible for his death. I took him there, months ago. I asked him to go to Zhoka with me because Surya was going to show us how to make it live again, and I wanted Lodi to be part of it. He didn't want to go at first, but when we began finding things he seemed to change, and did not protest."

"Did he assemble the skulls on the table?" Shan asked. "Did he make the writing beneath them, about being taken by beauty?"

"We both gathered the skulls. There were old chambers where they were scattered about the floor. All these years, and everyone has been too frightened to return to pay homage. We weren't sure what to do with them. Lodi wrote the words. It should have been a prayer but we know so few," Liya added in a whisper.

"Ming was his partner. Don't you think he would have told Ming about Zhoka? They had dealt with ruins before, for the museum."

"I don't know. Lodi was becoming distrustful of Ming. He said Ming was too interested in emperors and glory to be trusted." She turned her gaze back to Shan.

"Ming spoke to Lodi about emperors?"

"That's what Lodi said, nothing else."

"What were they doing, Liya? Ming and Lodi were doing more than distributing art."

She clenched her jaw, and acted as if she had not heard the question. "He never said more about Ming on his last visit, except that he said we should be prepared to resist if Chinese came from the north. He said it would not be soldiers, but men like soldiers. He sent for the Gurkhas who help him get by the border patrols."

"The ones with guns."

"Some of us argued with Lodi, said we must not have guns. He said we did not understand how dangerous things had become. He said something happened long ago that is finally going to destroy us. He even asked me to begin to move everyone away across the border."

"But you haven't."

"I will not be the one who abandons Bumpari after so many centuries. I will be the last one here, if it means I live alone."

Liya's tone, as much as her words, frightened Shan. "What did he mean long ago? The Chinese invasion?"

"I don't think so. The last time he was here he was looking for old books, old peche that spoke of the history of Zhoka. He would not tell me why. But he got drunk one night, and said only fools think emperors put deities first."

A deep hollow ring reverberated outside, three peals in succession. Liya looked up in alarm. "There is trouble," she gasped, and darted out of the building. The circle of Tibetans began to break up, the other villagers also leaving the building, some running.

Only Corbett remained, still sitting on the floor, his lap full of brushes and flowers and fruit.

"I think," Shan observed, "they want you to stay here and teach them how to paint gods."

Corbett's only reply was a melancholy grin. After a long moment, he looked up at Shan. "My mother was an artist, and her sister. They took me with them when I was young, gave me an easel and watercolors to use as they painted seascapes. But eventually they packed me off to college, telling me I couldn't support a family on art."

"Ming has not been telling us everything," Shan said, glancing toward the gathering of Tibetans below, by the gate." There was a photograph of William Lodi," Shan said, extracting the picture of the banquet in a tent and handing it to Corbett. "Ming knew Lodi."

The contentment disappeared from Corbett's face as he gazed at the photo. He abruptly rose, letting the brushes in his lap fall to the floor, then stormed out of the building without a word.

Shan caught up with him in the garden, where the American stood facing the distant peaks, his face dark, his eyes lit with anger. He waved the photograph toward Shan. "It's him! They knew him! Ming and Lodi both knew the famous Mr. Dolan. The son of a bitch Ming must have planned it all." His mouth twisted and he kicked a stone, which flew through the air, knocking a flower from its stem.

"Ming is laughing at us," Corbett spat. "They knew of Dolan's collection, knew how wealthy he is. It was probably irresistible to Ming. A conspiracy against a rich American capitalist, with his friend the international art thief. Who would know better how to dispose of such a collection than Ming and Lodi? Ming has been laughing at us all along, knowing that politically he can't be touched."

"Except Lodi was killed," Shan pointed out. "And Ming didn't do it, he was in Lhadrung."

"Maybe it was your monk who killed him after all."

"It doesn't explain what happened in Beijing."

Corbett nodded slowly, offered a curse under his breath, then sat on a nearby bench, watching the villagers as they gathered below, near the gate. The stone barrier had been rolled back, and one of the Gurkhas was addressing them, waving a gun as he spoke. Half a dozen of the villagers stepped out of the gate, packs on their backs. "I don't know," Corbett said in a worried voice. "I understand less now than when I arrived in Tibet." He stared into his hands a long time, then pulled a paper and pencil from his pocket and began writing. "Can you use a computer?" he asked Shan.

When they stood up from the bench half an hour later the villagers were still assembled below, but their mood had grown somber. Yao sat apart, as if shunned, gazing into the pond. The Tibetans would not look into Shan's eyes as he approached.

Liya intercepted him before he reached the others, pulled him toward the old cottage, then waited on the porch as Yao joined them.

"I am sorry," she began. There was a deep anguish in her eyes. "I tried to make them see reason. But . . ." She turned, fixing both hands around the old prayer wheel as if she were about to fall. "The Chinese are in the mountains blowing up old caves. Our people sometimes hide in those caves, and some could be trapped inside. They know you work with Ming. They say now that Ming is leading the godkillers. And now they attacked an old woman, a cousin of ours, stole all her old statues and scriptures, then destroyed her kiln."

"Fiona?" Shan asked in alarm. "Was she injured?"

Liya looked at him with new curiosity. "You mean our Dolma? She was not hurt. But the Gurkhas insist you two were part of it, that you are just spying for the other Chinese, that what you really want is to destroy Zhoka and Bumpari, wipe all traces from the earth. They say you came to finish what was started the day Zhoka was bombed. Others are saying you are some of the earth demons come to end the taming."

The villagers began staring at the cottage now, some approaching cautiously.

"Go inside," Liya urged. "I will speak with them, try to make them understand." But then she paused and put a hand on Yao's arm. "Is it true, Inspector? Would you destroy us if you could?"

Yao did not hesitate. "Everything you do here is illegal," he said in a steady voice. "You are illegal. The entire village is illegal."

"Would you destroy us?" Liya pressed.

"It is my duty," Yao shot back.

Liya searched Shan's face as if asking him for a solution, then closed her eyes a moment. "Thank you for your honesty," she said to Yao, then she escorted them into the second bedroom and closed the door.

Yao instantly began opening the chests in the room. "A weapon," he whispered urgently. "We must find a weapon."

Shan did not help him but studied an old framed sketch by the door. It was one of those done by the major. He took it off the wall to gaze at and sat on a bed. It was of a laughing lama, sitting on a yak. He felt suddenly very tired and fell into an odd meditation, in which the disjointed events of the past three days floated before him. The lama on the yak seemed be to mocking his lack of understanding.

He did not know how many minutes passed before the door opened and Liya entered. She silently studied the disarray from Yao's search, and sighed. "There is tea," she announced in a tight voice, and turned back into the main chamber.

Shan followed Liya, Yao a close step behind him, holding the little computer.

Corbett sat sipping from a white porcelain cup, Dawa on the floor beside him, showing him pictures in a book. Liya handed Yao and Shan each one of the dainty cups, gesturing for them to sit at the table, then extended a plate of dried cheese and apricots. He sipped at his cup, then studied its contents in surprise. It was heavy black tea, with milk, in the Indian fashion. It was sweet and invigorating, with a strangely metallic aftertaste. Liya nibbled a kernel of cheese, seeming careful not to look them in the eye.

Shan was about to ask where the others were when he froze. Corbett was slumped in his chair, unconscious; Liya carefully lifted the little cup from his hand.

Shan stood in alarm. "Lokesh!" he called, or thought he called, but then he realized his tongue felt thick and heavy. His knees began to buckle. The room swam. He took a step forward, and fell to his knees as he heard the computer drop to the floor beside him and saw the inspector clutch his throat.

Liya stepped close to Shan, taking the cup from his hand. "Lokesh will not be harmed," she said forlornly, as if she owed Shan one last favor. Then she put out her arms as Shan fell forward. In his last moment of consciousness he saw several figures run into the room, dim shadows of people surrounding him. "Make sure it is quick," was the last thing he heard Liya say. "I do not want them to suffer."

Part Two

CHAPTER NINE

The light Shan kept reaching for stayed just out of reach, a tiny brilliant patch in a long black tunnel. A child kept calling to him down the tunnel, crying out that everything was safe, to come back now. A man cursed, in Chinese. A girl prayed, in Tibetan.

Suddenly something like lightning exploded in Shan's head, and there was nothing but light, glaring, painful light. He threw his arm over his eyes, and heard himself moan.

"Come back," the girl said in an anxious voice, pulling his arm from his head. "Aku Shan, please come back." She squeezed his hand repeatedly.

Shan's eyes finally found their focus. He was lying in a meadow of tall grass, and Dawa was holding his hand. She smiled as his confused gaze settled on her, then helped him sit up. They were on the gentle slope of a long high ridge, much of it carpeted with wildflowers. The sun was perhaps two hours above the horizon. Larks sang nearby.

"You didn't die," Dawa offered, then gestured toward the sitting figure of Inspector Yao, as if his presence were proof enough Shan had not reached heaven. "Some people in the village wanted you dead," the girl reported in a matter-of-fact tone, "but Liya gave you medicine, she said, so you would feel better today."

Shan studied the girl's face. Medicine. He stood, filling his lungs with the cool morning air. So he would feel better. So he would remain alive, he realized as he recalled the events of the night before. Some of the villagers had wanted Shan and Yao dead. Liya had drugged her Chinese visitors to save them.

"How did we get here?"

"Tied over the backs of horses. They only had two horses in the village. I rode on Liya's back."

"But where's Lokesh? And the American?"

Dawa shrugged. "They stayed at the village."

A spring bubbled out of the earth thirty feet away. Shan rubbed the cool water over his face, drank deeply, then gestured for Yao to do the same.

"Kidnapped," the inspector growled. "Attempted murder of a government official."

Dawa stared at Yao in confusion. "It was medicine," she repeated.

"Liya saved us," Shan said, and explained what the girl had told him. "She let you go even though you said you would destroy Bumpari."

"She just found a less violent way to kill us," Yao shot back. "We're stranded in the wilderness, without food, without a map, without transportation." Yao paused, patting his pockets, and pulled out his notepad. He leafed through its pages, as if to confirm they were intact, then pushed it deep into his pocket. As he did so he paused, then pulled something from his pocket, a long brown bead with an intricate pattern etched in white.

Shan searched his own pockets and found another of the beads. "Liya," he said. "She gave them to us for protection."

Yao frowned but put the bead back in his pocket. "The American," he said in a worried tone. "A foreigner is in even greater danger than we were. People like that just rob foreigners and dispose of the bodies."

But Shan did not believe Corbett was in physical danger. Corbett hadn't been singled out because he was a foreigner, Shan suspected, but because the villagers had decided he had awakened from a rainbow. "Why did they send you away?" he asked Dawa. "They would never hurt you."

"Liya said people would keep looking for me if I didn't go back. She said you would know the place to take me."

"I don't know any—" Shan began, then stopped as she extracted a piece of paper.

"*Iwin how,*" she said, struggling with the word, and handed the paper to Shan.

He grinned as he read it. "To Ivanhoe."

Dawa nodded energetically. "Yes! She said find Ivanhoe, that there we can help each other."

"Which way?" Shan asked the girl. "Which way did we come last night after leaving the village? Up that long plain? Down the trail we arrived on?" He did not recognize any of the surrounding landscape.

Dawa shrugged. "It was dark. I was sleeping when they carried me." She pointed to a cloth sack on a rock near the spring. "Liya sent that for you."

"It's been twelve, maybe fourteen hours," Shan calculated as they retrieved the sack. "We could be thirty or forty miles away," he exaggerated, not wanting to make it easy for Yao to find the village again. He doubted they had come more than ten miles over the rugged terrain. "We came south, closer to the Himalayas."

Yao upended the sack onto the grass. Six apples and some dried cheese tumbled out. "It just means we die more slowly of starvation," he groused.

"No," Shan said as he studied the landscape again. "She picked this place carefully. Water close by. High enough to see the road, far enough from it to avoid onlookers." He pointed to the southwest, where a plume of dust could be seen in the distance.

Yao stood and stared at the plume. "A truck!" he announced excitedly. "Going north. But we'll never catch it!"

"There'll be another," Shan said, repacking the food. He slung the sack over his shoulder.

There were no vehicles in sight when they reached the rutted gravel track an hour later. But after thirty minutes of walking northward a battered truck with four sheep in its small cargo bay appeared.

"Lhadrung market," the nearly toothless driver replied when Shan asked his destination. Shan handed him three apples and the man gestured them inside the cab. Shan opened the door for Dawa, handing her another of the apples as she climbed inside.

Yao began to follow the girl but Shan gripped his arm. "We're riding in back," he said.

Yao shot him a venomous glare but closed the door and climbed with Shan over the rear gate.

As the truck accelerated with a loud rumbling and a cloud of exhaust smoke, Yao settled against the rear of the cab. The sheep all stared at him. "Maybe you told Liya to do it," he said with ice in his voice. "You could have staged it all just to get me out of that place." He raised a hand as though to threaten the sheep. They kept staring at him. "The first time I begin to find answers to my questions I am forced away. Because you know the guilty ones are Tibetans."

Shan's only reply was a steady stare, matching that of the sheep.

Yao glared angrily at him, then extracted his notepad and began writing feverishly. Confidence seemed to build on his face as he worked. "An entire village of thieves," the inspector declared with a satisfied tone. He seemed to regard the sheep as an audience now, and spoke toward them as if testing his theories. "An unprecedented affront to socialism."

"Yesterday he was admiring their art," Shan observed quietly, to the sheep.

Yao ignored him. "They can't stay hidden forever. Colonel Tan can send troops to sweep south from Zhoka. Aerial reconnaissance can find them in two or three days. Border commandos can be deployed. We will conduct a mass trial in Lhasa. This will get national attention."

Shan grimaced. "That's how you're going to find the emperor's missing frescoes? Dolan's missing artifacts? I saw mostly women and children in that village. A mass trial for twenty or thirty women and children. Is that the victory you came to Tibet for?"

Yao frowned. "We don't have to arrest the youngest or the oldest."

"Just destroy their lives."

"Introduce them to the twenty-first century."

Shan stared at him in silence. "Corbett awakened from a rainbow," he said at last, "and you? What? You crawled from under a rock?"

Yao glared at Shan again, then turned toward the distant mountains.

"Soldiers will never find them," Shan continued. "They will probably find the village if they look long enough. But it will be abandoned by the time soldiers get there. They keep lookouts. They will have hiding places even deeper in the mountains." But once Tan found Bumpari, the damage would have been done. Soldiers would destroy the village in any event, annihilate the mysterious little oasis that seemed to live in several centuries at once. "It will ruin any chance of finding Lodi's killer, or the lost art."

The truck stopped to let a flock of goats cross the road. Shan reached into the bag and pulled out the last two apples, tossed one toward Yao, who frowned at it but took a bite. He chewed and swallowed, then broke off small pieces which he tossed to the sheep.

There was something else in the bag, a smaller cloth pouch Shan had not seen before. He extracted the pouch, untied the knot that bound it, and pulled out a rolled-up magazine. Not a magazine, he saw, as he straightened the glossy pages. It was a thin catalog dated the year before, perhaps thirty pages long, a listing in English and Chinese for the special Tibetan exhibit in the Beijing Museum of Antiquities. Ming's museum. The pages were filled with detailed photographs and descriptions of the artworks. Someone had written Arabic numbers in black ink by several of the photos. He leafed through the pages and found the numeral one near the center of the catalog, by a small seated Buddha, fifteenth-century, in painted brass with an alms bowl in his hand. Number two was near the back, a fifteenth-century protective deity in gold-plated bronze with nine heads and thirty-four arms. Numbers three through five were twelfth-century thangkas of incarnate lamas surrounded by mythical animals. Quickly Shan counted the other entries. Fifteen items in total had been marked, the last a silver statue of Tamdin, the horseheaded protector. On the inside back cover, which held no print, the numbers appeared again, with figures in dollars hand-written beside them. Number one, $10,000, it said, with a date three years earlier. He went back through the pages more slowly, reading the entry for each of the hand-numbered items. The twelfth was a fourteenth-century bronze statue of the saint Manjushri, sword in one hand, lotus flower in the other.

"Liya wants us to find the truth," he said slowly. "She didn't send just food, she sent evidence."

Yao looked back with a scowl. "What do you mean?"

Shan extended the catalog to Yao. He quickly pointed out the numbered items.

"Could be anything," Yao said. "Someone's marking of favorite pieces."

"Not someone's favorites. Look at them carefully. They are the most detailed, the oldest, the most valuable. And the prices shown are far too high for museum shop reproductions. Far too low to be the true market value for the original pieces."

"Meaning what?"

"Look at item twelve."

Yao flipped through the pages and paused, wrinkling his brow. A low curse escaped his lips. "We saw this yesterday, broken. At the fleshcutter's village."

"We saw that, or a perfect duplicate. Not a reproduction. If not the original, it was an exact replica." Shan pointed to the little beauty mark on the forehead, "even the same little patch of corrosion on the shoulder. Done by a true artist."

"They stole it, the bastards."

"No," Shan said. "Look at item fifteen, the statue of Tamdin. We saw that, too, in the workshop. But it wasn't finished."

Confusion clouded Yao's face. "It was here, in Lhadrung, that very sculpture. But the one we saw wasn't finished." He quickly leafed through his notebook and turned an open page toward Shan. It was his sketch of the ruined sculpture they had seen the day before. "Lodi had stolen it and his killers destroyed it." He stared at the catalog. "But Ming never reported it stolen."

"There's only one reason someone would make such an exact duplicate, reproducing every tiny imperfection. So the original could be replaced with the duplicate."

"Ridiculous!" Yao leafed through the catalog, pausing at each of the marked photos. "You're saying each of these others have been switched? Impossible. They would have been reported as stolen. Someone would have noticed." But as he spoke Shan saw something deflate in Yao. The inspector knew the answer.

"Not," Shan said, "if Ming was arranging it. The director can always remove a piece. For cleaning, say, or some special scholarly study. Ming and Lodi were friends," he added, and explained what Liya had told him about their relationship.

The inspector sighed, and gazed back at the mountains a moment. "But the originals could never be displayed, never be publicized. And they would be priceless."

"Right. They went to a private collector, for whom money is no object. As the middleman Ming could become wealthy, if he sold to a wealthy collector. A billionaire collector."

Yao was silent a long time. "You have no proof it was Dolan who bought them," he said at last in a low voice. "It would make no sense. Lodi stole Dolan's art. Someone else stole the Qian Long fresco."

"I was explaining the old crime," Shan said, "not the new ones. An old one, in which Lodi and Ming were partners. With Elizabeth McDowell," he added.

Yao gazed at the sheep again. "There is an audit," he said. "Ming's museum is being audited. Outside experts are being brought in to examine the collections, spot-check pieces. Special equipment is being brought from Europe, thermoluminescence gear that can verify the age of metal and ceramic pieces." When he looked at Shan apology was in his eyes.

"When was the audit ordered?"

"Four months ago."

"Has it started?"

"No. The equipment will arrive soon."

In the silence Shan reached for the dried cheese in the pack and discovered one more object secreted by Liya: a rolled piece of rice paper, ten inches wide and nearly twice as long. It had been printed from a woodblock in bold, forceful ideograms which had been faded by sunlight along one side. Perplexed, he showed it to Yao, then read the text out loud.

Esteemed subjects of the heavenly empire, it said, *let it be known that Prince Kwan Li being lost to us for more than the span of six months we commit to whomsoever shall deliver him unto us a reward equal to his own weight in gold. Whomsoever shall be found to have hidden his holy person shall be punished by slow death. Whomsoever shall be found to know of information and not brought it to us shall be punished by the ax. Be it known in all the lands. Tremble and obey.*

At the bottom, reproduced in vermilion ink on the printed page, was a complex seal that Shan had seen years before. "It has the chop of the Qian Long emperor," Shan said in a slow, incredulous voice.

"Liya's notion of a joke," Yao said.

"I don't think so. Tests could be made. Probably one of those students at the guest house could do so, but I think it is genuine. I think it is from the old imperial court. I think Ming has been keeping many secrets from us."

They both stared at the name. Kwan Li. It was the name Shan had seen on the easel in the conference room. He saw something else now, scrawled in Tibetan along the bottom, covered by the curling edge of the paper on Shan's first reading. *Dead, by order of the Stone Dragon Lama,* it said in faded ink. *May the gods be victorious.*

The driver cheerfully agreed to a quick detour, dropping them not in Lhadrung but at the base of the ridge that marked the eastern hills, nearly a mile from the grey trucks that marked a new prison work site. Tan had ordered the prisoners to clear fields in the valley below the high cliffs that marked the beginnings of the mountains. Half an hour later they were on top of the ridge, walking along the crest. Shan smelled woodsmoke again, also something new. Cordite, the scent of explosives. He hurried, carrying Dawa, until he could see that Fiona's sturdy little house was intact, though the top of the kiln and its structure were gone, lying in pieces over the little plot of barley, which had been trampled.

The door of the house was open again, and Shan looked inside to see Fiona sitting at the table by the little kitchen, arranging colored shards into piles. Porcelain, Shan saw as he approached. The porcelain tea set had been smashed, and she was arranging the shards of the cups, pot, and saucers into piles.

"Jara says he can get some glue in town," she said without looking up.

"I am sorry, Fiona," Shan said. "I am glad you are not hurt."

"They did not touch our Ivanhoe," she said with a sad smile, rising slowly to her feet. "They wanted to look at old Tibetan things. They took some of the peche, all my old statues. They demanded to know what pilgrim guides I had. They saw the English books and asked if Lodi was in my family. That's when they threw a little bomb into my kiln."

"Did you know them?"

"No. Two men, a big one and a little one with a crooked nose." He extracted the group photo from his pocket and pointed to the men who stood beside the American Dolan.

"Yes," Fiona murmured, her face darkening. She raised a finger and touched another face, sighing. She had recognized her nephew, Lodi. When she looked up she offered a sad smile. "They did not know where to look." She gestured Shan toward the sleeping alcove, where she pulled away three blankets to reveal a small prayer table, where scriptures might be laid for reading. Shan stood in silence, glancing outside, where Yao and Dawa were patting the brown dog, then watched as Fiona pried up the top of the table and extracted two old peche and a bundle of felt. She leaned back and unfolded the bundle on her legs to reveal a brilliantly colored piece of yellow silk with blue brocade along the edge.

Shan stared, dumbfounded, momentarily forgetting Yao and Dawa, as he dropped to his knees to study Fiona's treasure. It was a robe, elaborately embroidered with images of cranes, dragons, and pheasants.

"It was given to my family many generations ago, in payment for a ceramic statue of Buddha."

"Do you know by whom?" Shan whispered as he leaned to study the symbols on the robe. Arrayed around the animals were axes and bows.

Fiona shook her head. "That is lost."

But Shan did not need to be told. He did not touch the intricate symbols, but lifted the cuffs, which were cut to resemble horse hooves. The row of five-clawed dragons along the bottom of the robe said it all. There was only one family allowed to wear such dragons. As impossible as it seemed, the garment came from someone in the family of the Chinese emperor. The hoof-shaped cuffs were in the Manchu fashion, from the Qing dynasty. And in the bag from Liya was a document with the seal of the Qian Long emperor, of the Qing dynasty.

"It is very pretty," Fiona said as she folded the garment back into the felt.

"Yes," Shan stammered. "Did the two intruders ask for the robe?"

"Not the robe. They demanded, what did I know of the Chinese prince."

"What prince?"

"Kwan Li," she said in a matter-of-fact tone.

"Why him?"

She shrugged. "He is missing. But I pretended not to know him."

For the first time Fiona seemed to notice the figures outside. "Have you brought friends? I should make tea."

"One is more than a friend," Shan said, with sudden guilt for forgetting who waited. "Forgive me. She has come to help you." As he spoke a small eager face appeared at the entrance. "Help her great-aunt."

He looked back to see Fiona standing, her eyes welling with moisture, her long arms extended. Dawa rushed forward and fell into her embrace.

Outside, he found Yao staring at the clay tsa-tsa tablets Shan had seen on his first visit. They were still in a line, but all were crushed, as if someone had carefully, heel to toe, walked on top of the fragile deities.

Frantic activity filled the guesthouse compound when Shan and Yao arrived two hours after noon. A military truck had picked them up as they walked down the highway toward the turnoff to the compound. The sergeant at the wheel, one of Tan's staff, excitedly radioed ahead with the news of their appearance. Yao, who had maintained a brooding silence since their discussion on the truck, kept glancing at Shan as the truck approached the compound, then suddenly he opened the small pouch, which he had clutched for the past hour, and ripped out the back page of the catalog. He handed Shan the page, bearing the list of fees paid, or to be paid, then gave Shan three of the six discs he had taken from the cottage, gesturing for him to stuff them into his pockets. He was dividing the evidence, giving half to Shan.

Why, Shan kept asking himself as they entered the compound, why would the inspector trust Shan with such vital evidence? It was as if Yao had suddenly decided to worry about Ming, perhaps even fear him. The inspector had not asked questions when Fiona had described in more detail how her home had been raided. But he had carefully recorded in his pad her description of the two men who had done it, the small Chinese with the crooked nose and a large Mongolian who smoked sweet-smelling cigars.

At least thirty people were working in the courtyard, with wheelbarrows, buckets, hammers, and brooms. The bilingual sign at the gate that had identified the compound as the Lhadrung Guest House had been replaced with a new one, bigger, with two rows of freshly painted foot-high ideograms. ANNEX, MUSEUM OF ANTIQUITIES, read the top line. BUREAU OF RELIGIOUS AFFAIRS was painted below.

As the sergeant herded Yao into the main building, Shan paused at the door and studied the courtyard. There were army soldiers, Tan's soldiers, supervising Tibetans laboring along the back wall and far side of the yard. Two Tibetan men and a heavyset soldier with his tunic stripped off were hammering with sledges at a large bent piece of metal. It had been the head of a large statue of Buddha that had been stored along the rear wall. The soldiers were pounding chisels into the metal, splitting the back of the head. At a long makeshift table of planks supported by sawhorses several dozen smaller artifacts were piled, the small statues of deities and saints that typically adorned the private altars of Tibetan families. Half a dozen well-groomed Han Chinese men and women seemed to be supervising the work of perhaps ten Chinese men, clad in blue denim work clothes, several of whom were digging a trench along the wall. Shan stared at the workers in confusion, then suddenly he felt weak and leaned against the wall.

The oldest of the men in blue clothing, a stocky man Shan's age, sat on the plank table and was amusing himself by throwing stones at a row of the smaller altar offerings placed at the edge of the stagnant fountain pool ten feet away. Another, a lanky young Han with greased hair and a cold sneer on his face, hovered over a barrow of dirt pushed by a middle-aged Tibetan man. As Shan watched the man lost his grip and the barrow tipped over.

"Damned locusts!" the young Han growled. Locusts. It was one of the epithets for Tibetans used by some Chinese, for the buzz of their mantras. The youth kicked the barrow, then kicked the Tibetan in his thigh. Shan was at the man's side the next moment, stepping between the weary, frightened Tibetan and the surly Han.

"*Thuchechy,*" the Tibetan whispered. Thank you.

The young Han kicked out again, striking the dirt this time, sending particles into Shan's face. As Shan straightened, he saw something familiar in the angry, empty eyes of the youth. The youth, like the other Han in blue, were themselves prisoners, trustees deployed to help manage the Tibetans.

Shan broke away from the youth's glare and studied the yard once more. He recognized several of the Tibetans now. He had seen them at the chorten, in the ruins of Zhoka. Some of the fugitives from the festival had been detained. He hurried into the building, suddenly very concerned about what Yao might be saying to Director Ming.

The inspector was standing in the door to the large chamber where Shan had been confronted on his last visit, staring with his own perplexed expression into the hall. Ming was at the long table, sitting across from an aged Tibetan woman, speaking to her in rough tones. Another fifteen Tibetans were seated on the floor on the opposite side of the hall, watched over by two armed soldiers. Several of the Tibetans were crying. Several were staring into their hands, anxiously working their beads. None appeared to be younger than seventy.

Ming nodded at Yao and dismissed the woman in front of him with a flick of his wrist. She was pulled away by another soldier who stepped from the shadows at the end of the table.

As Yao lowered himself into the empty seat at the end of the table, where Shan had sat earlier, Shan stepped toward the shadows six feet behind him, leaning against the wall. On the adjacent wall, along the table, photographs of Tibetan paintings had been pinned, all of them images of different forms of the death deities. Not one matched the image Shan had seen on the wall of Lodi's mourning hut. Beside them sheets from the large easel had been taped to the wall. Prince Kwan Li, the first said, at the top, followed by what appeared to be a chronology of his life, starting with his birth in 1755, ending with an entry that simply said "last seen a day's ride south of Labrang." Labrang was hundreds of miles to the north.

"A patrol was dispatched to look for you," Ming announced.

"We got lost," Yao said quietly.

Ming seemed to find the words amusing. He glanced at Shan. "Even with your famous guide."

"We followed the evidence much deeper into the mountains than expected," Yao declared. "Our radio malfunctioned." The inspector looked toward the old Tibetans. "What are you doing with these people?"

Ming ignored the question. "Did you find him? The thief?"

Yao hesitated, made a movement as though to look back at Shan, then he stopped and looked at the old Tibetans. "William Lodi is dead," he announced slowly.

Director Ming stared at Yao, uncertain, as if deciding whether to believe him. He seemed about to speak when a sound behind them broke the silence, the sound of someone stumbling, and what might have been a muffled cry. Ming grimaced and seemed about to move toward the door, then froze and stared down at the table, clenching his jaw tightly.

"Did you recover the artifacts he had brought with him?" Ming asked in a tight voice.

"None," Yao replied tersely.

"Then Lhadrung has become a dead end for you, Inspector," the museum director said. "And for the American."

"Not at all," Yao said. "It proves we are in the right place. Now we just have to find Lodi's killers."

Ming frowned. "What have you done with Agent Corbett?"

"Still in the mountains."

Ming shot an accusing glance at Shan. "That might seem negligent."

Yao ignored the comment, studied the frightened Tibetans again. "I don't understand what you are doing with these citizens, Comrade Director."

"I made a trip to Lhasa in your absence. Bureau of Religious Affairs. Very resourceful people. They are not sufficiently appreciated in Beijing. They explained things about Tibet I had not understood. I discovered that the office of the director in Lhadrung County is vacant."

Shan stiffened, feeling Ming's cold stare again. The Religious Affairs office was vacant because the year before Shan had provided evidence that had sent the director to a firing squad. "They said officially Colonel Tan has authority in the absence of a permanent director. But they gave me a letter for Tan to sign, granting me temporary powers as director for the purposes of my investigation."

Shan saw Yao's fingers tighten on the arm of the chair. My investigation.

"Then they instructed me in techniques."

Shan found himself stepping toward the old Tibetans. The words stopped him. He turned back toward Ming. "Techniques?" he asked with a chill.

As Ming raised his head in Shan's direction a cool grin grew on his face. "Certainly you are familiar with them, comrade." He gestured toward the table. "Please sit. There is tea."

The porcelain panda cups appeared again, on a tray carried by a young female soldier. Shan sat and clamped his hands around his cup as Ming continued.

"Religious Affairs explained two things. First, Tibetan treasures are never randomly deposited. Second, the State Domain Decree." Ming seemed genuinely pleased at the confusion on the faces of Yao and Shan. "An artifact stolen by Tibetan resisters would not simply be hidden. They are chained to old traditions, to the reactionary culture of the old lamas who enslaved them. Artifacts would be hidden according to those traditions, not just in any cave or shrine, but very particular caves or shrines, one corresponding to the deity deposited."

"With what deity would the emperor's fresco be deposited?" Yao inquired in a chill tone.

"The most important, the most powerful shrine. The most sacred place in Lhadrung County." Ming paused to light a cigarette, blowing a stream of smoke toward his aged prisoners. He leaned toward Yao and spoke in a low voice. "The Bureau has studies that show that spending one's childhood in these high altitudes impedes brain development. They are all like children," he added, gesturing with his cigarette toward the old Tibetans on the floor. "You have to know how to speak with children." He directed a glance toward Shan. "Right, Comrade Shan?"

"You mentioned a decree," Yao observed stiffly.

"The Domain Decree," Ming confirmed. "One of the guiding laws of the Bureau. All religious artifacts are the property of the state. Enforcement has obviously been lax in certain parts of Tibet."

"And these people?" Shan studied Yao. The inspector had turned his back on the old Tibetans, as if he did not wish to see them.

"They are the ones who cling most fervently to the old ways, and therefore know the ways of the old hidden shrines. Much more efficient than trying to gather intelligence through pilgrims' guides."

Ming rose and led them with a triumphant air back into the courtyard. "I am afraid people still keep artifacts in defiance of law. These," he said, pointing to the dozens of altar objects on the makeshift table, "are just those confiscated in the valley." He picked up a small bronze figure of the Future Buddha and turned it upside down, showing Yao a slit in the bottom of the hollow figure. "When these are made things are put inside. Messages. Writings from monks. Possible references to mountain shrines. We are cross-referencing them with the information in the pilgrim books and tracking the most frequent references. I have devised a matrix, and my assistants are integrating the data into our computers." He gestured with obvious pride toward a team at the end of the table. A man wearing a leather apron, heavy gloves, and a gauze mask was seated at a bench saw. Ming handed the bronze figure to the man, who hit a switch with his foot. The saw screamed to life, the man deftly passed the figure over the blade several times, then handed it to a young Han woman with short, stylish hair seated at a table beside him. With a pair of pliers she pried back the metal from the gaping incision left by the saw. Half a dozen objects fell into a basket in front of her: several small rolls of paper tied with dried stems of grass, a small bar of black metal, a chip of bone, and a turquoise stone. She worked with chilling efficiency, tossing the stone, the metal bar, the bone chip into a trash bucket at her knee, then handing the rolled papers to another colleague, a well-dressed Tibetan woman seated beside her.

The Tibetan woman produced a pair of surgical scissors and cut the bindings that held the first paper together and unrolled it. She read it quickly then tossed it into a bucket below the table. She raised a scrap of cloth and examined it with a magnifying lens for a moment before discarding it as well. As she did so the oily young Han Shan had seen earlier at the barrow picked up the bucket and replaced it with another, empty. He clowned with the bucket full of prayers, amulets and relics, balancing it on his head a moment, drawing a laugh from one of the guards who leaned languidly against the wall, then headed across the yard.

With a chill Shan saw his destination, a steel barrel in which a fire burned. Two guards flanked the barrel. They were more alert than the other soldiers. They had obviously noticed how the Tibetan prisoners watched the barrel. Some stared in anger, some in fear, some with tears streaming down their faces.

Shan stared at Ming as he stepped back inside the building. Ming was not just destroying small figurines, he was destroying the place where, for many families, reverence and hope resided. Many of the altar figures, especially those packed with prayers and artifacts, had been used for generations. What was burning in the barrel were the prayers of their grandfathers and great-grandfathers, the link of reverence that connected them directly to ancestors who had lived centuries before. In some families, there was a custom that each member contributed at least one prayer during their lifetime, secret prayers that sometimes took years to compose, like works of art. It was their chain of compassion, unbroken for centuries, an old woman had whispered once to Shan when, seated at their family altar, she had explained the custom. Unbroken until now, until Director Ming had arrived from Beijing in his strange quest for a fresco and an official who had been missing for two centuries.

The Han youth stopped ten feet from the barrel, lowered the bucket, and lifted a rolled prayer into the air, extending it overhead for all to see. Then with a quick, exaggerated motion, like that of a basketball player, he flung the paper in a long arc into the burning barrel. Some of the guards cheered. He repeated the performance, then he unrolled a prayer, waving the nearly three-foot-long paper into the air. Shan stepped forward, slowly maneuvering through the crowd as the youth took a second paper and unfurled it, waving the papers like streamers, mimicking the streamer dances popular in Chinese parades.

Shan reached the bucket and scooped it up, taking a step toward the burning barrel as if to help.

"You!" the youth growled at Shan. "Old man! I'm not done!"

Shan feigned surprise, spun about, the bucket leaving his hand, propelled outward by a quick thrust, so it landed among the seated Tibetans, ten feet away, spilling its contents.

The trusty glared at Shan but said nothing. He was trying to gauge Shan. Shan was not Tibetan, did not wear the rough blue clothes of a trusty. But one of the prison guards at the barrel seemed to recognize Shan. He was at Shan's side in an instant, and just as quickly slammed the butt of his rifle into the back of Shan's knee.

Shan collapsed, and found his hands covering his neck, an instinct he had acquired during his years in the gulag.

But no blow came. The guard retreated. The Han trusty continued his strange dance, swirling his streamer, kicking dirt at Shan, then with a final flourish deposited the two prayers into the fire. When Shan looked up he was staring into the moist eyes of a Tibetan woman, who clutched her beads with trembling fingers.

"In some parts of China," he said quietly, in Tibetan, "people burn prayers as a way of delivering them to the deities." The woman nodded her head and offered a sad smile. He saw she had retrieved one of the fallen prayer rolls and held it tightly in her other hand. Near his fingers lay another. He pushed it under her leg, out of sight of the guard who was trying to collect the contents of the spilled bucket. The soldier returned no more than ten of the old prayers to the bucket, then straightened, cursing, and emptied the bucket into the flames.

"Lha gyal lo," a hoarse voice called out from the crowd.

"Bzzzz," the young trustee offered in reply, flapping his arms like wings as he mocked the Tibetans. "Bzzz. Bzzzzzzz."

The sound of a heavy door opening and shutting at the far end of the main building interrupted the performance. The guards and trusties fell instantly silent as a slender red-haired figure appeared. Elizabeth McDowell, clad in tee shirt and blue jeans, appeared from the shadows with a bucket and a dipper, moving toward the Tibetans in the courtyard. The angry young trusty seemed to forget what he was doing and just stared at the British woman. Her eyes were swollen, her gaze lowered to the ground. No one moved, no one spoke as she left the water bucket with the Tibetans and stepped back inside.

As she did so Shan saw Yao standing by the main door, arms akimbo, glaring at him. Shan started back across the yard.

Inside, Ming was at the table, interviewing an old man. A soldier was video-taping the interview. The old man was shaking. His words came out in sobs. "There are no treasures left. There are no deities left." He scrubbed his eye with a trembling hand. "The age of deities is past."

The wave of emotion that swept through Shan was so powerful he felt nauseous. Hand on his belly, he stepped back out of the room.

No one stopped him when he stepped through the gate out of the compound past the vehicles parked along the wall. The soldier who had picked up Yao and Shan on the road, Tan's sergeant, was sitting against the rear wheel of his truck, asleep. Shan walked a hundred yards down the dry, dusty road to the edge of the woods and settled against the trunk of a hemlock facing the far side of the valley. He could see the steep rugged slopes, miles away, that stepped upward toward Zhoka. Gendun was there somewhere, and Corbett, and Lokesh, all in danger because of thefts in Beijing and America. He stared at the ground in front of him, trying to calm himself, trying to forget for a moment the torment on the faces of the Tibetans Ming had detained.

Shan found his hands driving his fingers into the soil on either side of him, as if something inside was struggling to hold on. He kept them in the soil and closed his eyes again. After what seemed a long time, he caught a whiff of ginger, a passing scent from some door that had come ajar in his memory. With a sad smile he cupped his hands and lifted them, depositing each handful of sandy soil in front of him. Leveling the two small piles he drew with his finger, without thinking, letting his unconscious direct his hand as his father had shown him, as a meditation technique. After a moment he saw that on the first little platform of soil he had drawn a figure like an inverted Y inside a large U, with a long tail. On the second he had drawn a more complex figure, which he absently traced again with one finger.

"What do they mean?" a quiet voice asked.

He looked up into the green eyes of Elizabeth McDowell. "Nothing," Shan said, and moved to erase them.

"Please don't," she said, and knelt beside him. She had been crying. "They're old ideograms. What do they say?"

"My father used to use them, like poems," Shan said after a moment, pointing to the inverted Y, "This is the sign for human, and this"—he outlined the U shape, "means a pit. A human falling into a pit. Together they mean misfortune. Disaster." He let the words sink in a moment. "I know Lodi was your cousin. I am sorry. He was also a criminal."

"Not much of one," McDowell said. "He had too big a heart. Like a Robin Hood." She looked up. "I'm sorry. Robin Hood was—"

"He stole from the rich to give to the poor. And you must have helped him," he added.

She offered a melancholy smile. "I'm just a consultant. What is the other one?"

Shan erased it and drew again, starting with a flat line with a short perpendicular bar in the middle, small marks like apostrophes on either side of the bar. "This is a roof, keeping out the wind and rain." He drew a rectangle below the marks. "A window under the roof." He added a line through the window. "A pole," he explained, then drew a loose waving shape from the pole. "A banner. It is a banner that flies always, no matter what the weather. Together they mean Absolute."

The British woman stared at the figure soberly.

"What people from the outside never understand about the traditional Tibetans, like those in the deep mountains," Shan said, "is that they deal only in absolute terms. There is no in between, there is no maybe, there is no borrowing, there is no tomorrow. There are only the true things, and the need to devote everything to those things. Nothing else matters. Not political power. Not money. Not electric blow-dryers."

McDowell seemed to think Shan was criticizing her. She leaned backward, her sorrow seeming to deepen. "I never thought Ming would do this, would bring in these people, or raid their altars. I was at the clinic. I would have tried to stop it if I had known. He just wanted to find some old shrines, that's all. He wants to know about some symbols of the death deities. He's . . . he's obsessive."

"He's ripping the prayers out of sacred figures," Shan said woodenly. "And you call it obsessive."

McDowell pressed her palm onto the second ideogram and pushed it, holding it there as she looked up at Shan. "Just let him finish and leave. No one wants the Tibetans to get hurt."

"Did Ming have your cousin killed?"

She stared him, not with surprise but with sadness. "Of course not. We were all friends."

"You were partners," Shan suggested.

McDowell shrugged. "People in the archaeology and art business often engage in a little trade, to help pay the bills. Ming and I know the markets, Lodi could supply original pieces of art."

"And the men in the mountains, they were your partners, too? The short Chinese and the Mongolian."

"No." The pain returned to McDowell's eyes. "The big one is called Khan Mo, the other Lu Chou Fin. They work for the highest bidder. They will do anything for the highest bidder. Ming introduced them to us, but they are not working with Ming."

Shan studied her face, which was wracked with worry. "They are competing," he ventured, "looking for what Ming is looking for, trying to get it before he does."

"I never would have thought so."

"Until Lodi was killed."

McDowell nodded, then traced her own finger over the ideogram for misfortune.

"Why does Ming care about a prince who died two hundred years ago?" Shan asked.

"Because he is so interested in power and gold. But he's no murderer," McDowell said. She suddenly stood, turning away.

"He's just a godkiller," Shan said to her back. The words stopped the woman, but she did not turn, and after a moment moved on toward the compound.

When he reached the trucks on his return to the compound the sergeant was awake, sitting on the hood of his truck, smoking a cigarette. He grimaced when Shan approached but did not move away.

"You're in and out of government center," Shan said. "Have you seen the old man who was begging? His name was Surya."

The soldier slowly exhaled a plume of smoke. "The killer monk?" he asked with a mocking grin. "Colonel Tan took care of him."

Shan felt his breath catch. "Took care of him?"

"Kicked him off the square. No more begging." As the sergeant inhaled the cigarette he studied Shan with amusement. "Had no job," he continued as smoke drifted out of his nostrils and mouth. "People were coming to watch him, as if begging was something to be admired. The colonel had one of his officers make a little speech in the square, saying it was a form of hooliganism."

"Where was he taken?"

"The colonel told him to go get a job in a factory, like good Tibetans do. He had him dropped off on the road to Lhasa, five miles east of town. But one of my men said he saw him back in town sitting with the shit dippers. If that Ming sweeps for old ones again he'll be picked up." He turned his head languidly toward the compound gate as a truck roared out. Its door was marked 404th People's Construction Brigade, its rear bay crowded with Tibetans.

"Trustees stay here," the sergeant said. "Locked in the stable after the meal."

Shan stared at the man in confusion. "Trusties?"

"He's a wild one. They cautioned us when they left him here, said he attacked a guard with a shovel last week. You saved him from a discipline squad."

"Saved who?"

The soldier shook his head and sighed, as though astounded by Shan's stupidity. "Your son, you fool." He gestured with a thumb over his shoulder, toward the courtyard.

Shan took a step backward, his heart suddenly racing, then ran through the gate.

The men in blue clothes were all in the open front shed opposite the main building, eating handfuls of steamed rice that had been brought to them in a bucket. A guard watched them from a stool by the wall. Shan slowed, looking for the smallest of the figures, trying to find the battered, frightened teenager among them, the one with a scar on his chin from falling on an icy street when he was a boy.

"Shan Ko!" a rough voice boomed behind him. The sergeant had followed Shan.

No one moved in the shed.

The sergeant advanced, hand on his truncheon. "Tiger Ko!" He shouted.

One of the old trusties was shoved aside and a figure emerged from the shadows. But it wasn't his son, it was the surly prisoner who had taunted the Tibetans.

The sergeant pulled the prisoner by his sleeve, into the light of the yard. "Meet your daddy," he said with immense amusement in his voice. The guard on the stool laughed.

"This old thing?" the youth snapped. "Bullshit. My father is a leader of a powerful gang." He turned slightly, as if speaking for the benefit of the other prisoners. "He eats soldiers for breakfast."

The sergeant turned to Shan, grinning widely. The soldier on the stool rose and took a step forward, as if expecting still greater entertainment.

Shan became small and cold inside. There was a flicker of a shadow on the prisoner's chin. A small scar where he had fallen on the ice. Shan stood, paralyzed, barely hearing the laughter now, feeling only the baleful glare of the young prisoner.

"*Cao ni ma!*" the youth spat at the sergeant, and disappeared back into the shadows. Fuck your mother.

Clutching his belly, Shan stumbled back toward the main building, finding and staying in the shadow of the entry hall, calming himself, gradually becoming aware of a loud voice coming from the main chamber.

Inside, Ming was presiding over a dinner meeting with his team of well-scrubbed assistants. Heaping bowls of fried rice, chicken and vegetables, fried pork, and several other dishes lay at the far end of the table. Ming's assistants sat eating around the table, watching Ming, who stood in a corner, writing on the large easel. Yao sat near the door, balancing a plate of food on his lap. The elderly Tibetans who had been in the room were gone, the only evidence of their having been there a stack of four videotapes on a chair by the door.

"A breakthrough!" Ming was proclaiming as Shan stepped into the chamber. The museum director proceeded to explain how the old altar messages had provided vital clues that would lead them to the criminals they had sought for so long. He was going to telephone Beijing with the good news, and turned the discussion over to the earnest young Han woman Shan had seen extracting the prayers outside.

Yao gestured Shan toward the food but Shan had no appetite. He sat in a chair by the stacked tapes as the group applauded Ming, who disappeared through a rear door. The woman began to explain the results of what she called their excavation of reactionary messages. Based on the repetition of names in the artifacts, the matrix devised by Ming had identified half a dozen primary sites as candidates for illegal hordes of state assets hidden by the monk class who had formerly ruled the people because, as everyone now understood, the monks always kept the wealth of the people for themselves. The messages had pointed to places called Bear Cave, Cave of Light, Miracle Cave, and Lama Throne Cave, each now identified with caves in the mountains south and east of Lhadrung. The messages gave no indication of the exact locations, but did refer to geologic features such as peaks shaped like spires which, with the help of the People's Liberation Army, surely would be found, the woman assured her audience.

Shan rose and quietly slipped back outside, pausing to gaze with a cold, painful emptiness toward the trustees, then walking back out of the gate and into the trees. After fifty paces he turned, confirming no one followed, then sat, trying to understand the emptiness his son's appearance had caused. Not finding understanding, he instead pushed it back inside, reminding himself the Tibetans in the mountains still needed him. He pulled a videotape from his shirt. It had not been difficult to lift the top tape from the pile as everyone's eyes had rested on the woman. He smashed the tape against a rock until its case broke away in splinters, then he pulled some of the exposed tape out, breaking it from its spool. With a small flat rock he scraped a shallow hole in the soil and buried the remains of the video.

"I've seen everything you've done," a stern voice cracked. It hit him like a blade between his shoulders. Shan stared into his own hands a moment, then slowly looked up at Yao, who leaned against the nearest tree. "Destroying the tape recorded by Ming as evidence. Deliberately spilling those old prayers today so Tibetans could recover them. Ming would be furious." Yao looked at the earth covering the tape with a strange mixture of amusement and anger on his countenance. "I begin to understand the kind of mistakes you made in your career, Inspector General Shan."

The last words caused Shan's head to snap back toward Yao. "I read your file again this afternoon, all of it this time. Model worker in your Ministry. Nominated for party membership but you declined. Never in my life have I heard of someone declining such an honor. You may as well have put a gun to your own head."

"It didn't feel like an honor at the time," Shan said. "I was investigating a senior party official for corruption. He arranged for the nomination while I was writing my report."

Something like a dry laugh escaped Yao's lips. "Did you get your man?"

"The Ministry of Justice exercised its discretion not to prosecute."

"And so you start the process all over," Yao said with a shrug, taking a step toward Shan. "You must understand that what Ming is doing is correct." He pushed his boot into the loose soil and dug in, plowing back the dirt to expose the tape. "The artifacts belong to the state. The mass interrogation is also a highly effective technique for dealing with indigenous populations."

He picked up the shattered, dirt-encrusted tape, frowned at Shan, then began using it like a shovel, digging the hole wider and deeper. He quickly finished, stood, pulled the other three tapes from his jacket, and tossed them into the hole with the first tape, kicking the soil on top of them. "But he is so overzealous. I find it distasteful. Old people crying on a video, with a soldier hovering over them. I will not have such evidence in my trials." His face hardened as he looked back up at Shan. "Try something like that again, and I'll have you back behind wire, buried so deep in the system no one will ever find you." He pounded the earth over the tapes with his boot. "What I just did was an exercise of my official discretion. What you did was a crime against the state."

Ming was holding court again in the hall when Shan and Yao returned to the compound. They stood at the entrance to the chamber a moment, listening to the director explain why one of the targeted caves was thought to be on a high, square mountain facing west. An army officer with a wooden pointer indicated possible locations on a topographical map now pinned to the wall.

Shan took a step inside the door, staring at the map, but Yao pulled him away. Shan followed him silently through a smaller door at the end of the entry hall, into a long corridor with half a dozen doors. They passed an unoccupied office with a desk strewn with paper. Through a second door, closed, came the sound and smells of a kitchen. Three more doors held numbers like hotel rooms. Inside one of the rooms a Chinese matron was making a bed. Yao opened the last door and gestured Shan inside as he studied the corridor behind them, then closed the door and switched on a brilliant overhead light.

The high-ceilinged room had the atmosphere of a small chapel. The wall opposite the door was covered with cedar planks, lustrous with the patina of age. Planks covered the other walls as well, but they had been painted with yellow enamel. A red flag, its upper left field consisting of a large yellow star with four smaller stars arrayed in an arc beside it, hung on one wall, flanked by portraits of past party dignitaries. A ten-foot-long table topped with plastic laminate filled most of the chamber. Yao rushed to the far end of the table, where a laptop computer sat, and turned it on, impatiently tapping the frame of the machine as the screen lit. After a moment he inserted one of the discs from Liya. The logo of the Museum of Antiquities appeared, then a familiar title, another pilgrim's guide.

They quickly examined the other discs, including the two Yao had given Shan. Three were more pilgrim's guides, and a file showing the results of a computer search. Someone had looked for patterns in references, for the location of certain repeating Tibetan place names: Dom Puk, Zetrul Puk, Kuden Puk, Woser Puk. Bear Cave, Miracle Cave, Lama Throne Cave, Cave of Light. As Shan would have expected, the search showed the names to be used repeatedly, each in several locations across old Tibet. But Ming had now identified local sites bearing the names. The fourth was a log of transactions. Yao stared at a small box of discs behind the computer, bearing a label with Ming's name on it. He glanced at the door then opened the box and inserted the first of the discs.

A new legend appeared. *"Nei Lou,"* it said in large figures, over a Chinese flag. State secret. Project Amban, the next screen said, over a short biography of Prince Kwan Li. The prince had been a nephew of the emperor, and a fierce general renowned for several victories in the western lands where the empire kept trying to subdue the Moslems. He had been appointed *amban,* imperial ambassador to Tibet, in recognition of his achievements on the battlefield. Next came a series of meeting records, all dated several years earlier.

The task group and its name had the air of a high-level government project. Shan pointed to the list of task group members at the bottom of the memorandum. They were all Chinese names, and many had their official affiliations listed. A senior official from the Public Security Bureau, a ranking officer of the Party secretariat, the Bureau of Religious Affairs, the Minister of Culture, the head of the People's National Library, the Chief Curator of the Forbidden City Museum. A professor of history from Beijing University.

"They were discussing a new public information campaign drawn from historical experience," Yao said as he scanned the next screen, and glanced at Shan. It was one of the peculiar holdovers from the era of Mao, the occasional announcement of a new hero, often a dead hero, as a way of underscoring correct socialist thought. "To honor the heroic nephew of a revered emperor. It says the amban was to return to the capital for the festivals declared in honor of the long reign of the Qian Long emperor and the enthronement of the emperor's successor. But he was lost en route from Tibet. The available histories did not agree on his fate. The committee established that he had stopped to settle a war between two small tribes that had taken a terrible toll on the local peasants and was killed, making the ultimate sacrifice in the service of the downtrodden."

Yao scrolled through several pages in silence, then looked up and shrugged. It seemed nothing more than a record of Beijing's process for coronation of a new people's saint. Such heroes were discovered once or twice a year. A book or two would be written, party officials were to include references in speeches, a statue of the new hero might be commissioned, passages written to be inserted in school curricula. "It's nothing," Yao said. "Eventually they dropped the amban in favor of a new hero, better suited to a new political theme."

"Except that even though he was not on the task group Ming suddenly decided to assemble all the files, even the secret files. Two months ago." Shan pointed to a date at the bottom of the file. "Three days after the robbery."

Yao stared at the screen in silence. "There's no sense in it. Maybe he does buy forgeries from Lodi, and sell the originals to people like Dolan. It's got no connection to the amban."

"The connection," Shan said, "is the Qian Long emperor."

The next disc did not display text in a computer font but the image of an old document that had been scanned, a letter on what looked like a rolled parchment elegant Chinese ideograms. Yao began to read out loud.

"Son of heaven," he began, "esteemed of all peoples." Yao muttered a syllable of frustration as he stumbled over the old ideograms, then scrolled down. At the bottom of the page was a museum inventory number. It was a document from Ming's archives in Beijing. Another letter followed, and another with the same flowery salutation. Ten letters in all, each with the bright smear of vermilion that was the sign of a wax seal.

The next four documents held more letters, numbering forty in all, all in the same elegant script, all with the same greeting, all with museum inventory numbers. Each of the letters had been processed into a computer font on the next four discs. They seemed to follow a similar format, opening with the same stiff formal language, offering news of troop movements, rumors about foreign agents, harvests, caravans, and weather. Most closed with an expression of affection, some with poetry, some with small ink sketches: A line of ceremonial hats used in Buddhist ritual. A yak in profile. The Potala Palace in Lhasa. The front line of the Himalayas, viewed from the north. An old wrinkled hand, holding a string of prayer beads. They were primitive drawings, but done with a simple grace.

Suddenly Yao gave a small exhalation of surprise. Shan stepped to his side and followed his finger to a legend where the museum registration number had appeared on the other letters. This one had a more complete explanation. Imperial Ching Collection, it said, personal correspondence of the Qian Long emperor. Ming had been secretly examining letters sent by the nephew of the Qian Long to his uncle the emperor in Beijing, over two hundred years earlier.

"We have to read the letters," Shan insisted. "They may hold the answer, the missing link."

"There's no time," Yao protested. His fingers tapped a single key, calling up more letters, until he reached the last, scanned onto the disc only three weeks before. Yao muttered a low curse. The last document, but only the last, was encrypted. They could not read it.

Shan darted to the cabinet at the rear of the room, quickly searching its drawers. From the third drawer he extracted a disc, lying loose among pencils and paper clips, extracted the disc in the computer, putting it in his pocket and placing the new disc into Ming's case.

Yao's notepad appeared in his hand. As the inspector began writing, Shan went to a second computer, connected a phone line, and began typing. In less than a minute he was staring uneasily at a new screen, displaying text under a red, white, and blue emblem.

"What have you done!" Yao gasped behind him.

"Corbett gave me his access code. He wanted me to send some questions to his team." Bold letters appeared on the screen: The Federal Bureau of Investigation. He was inside the internal network of the agency.

"About what?" Yao asked in a sharp voice.

"About Lodi. About Dolan."

"It's a crime for you to do so."

"Not a Chinese crime."

"He could be fired."

"Which means he considered the questions important." Shan entered another code and the mail account of Corbett appeared.

"What questions?" Yao demanded.

Shan did not need to look at the list the American had given him. He had it memorized. He entered the name Bailey, as Dolan had instructed, and began typing: When had Dolan visited China during the past ten years? What is Dolan's relationship to Director Ming of the Museum of Antiquities and to William Lodi? Where did Dolan go on an expedition with Ming in China? Was there a business connection between Dolan and Elizabeth McDowell, citizen of the United Kingdom?

"Dolan was the victim of the crime." Yao observed.

Shan paused to study Yao. "Dolan," he said slowly, "is a friend of Ming's and McDowell's." He showed Yao the photographs he had found in Lodi's belongings.

"Why didn't you tell me before?"

"Because by telling you I compromise you."

"Ridiculous. I work for the Council of Ministers."

"What if Dolan had discovered Ming and Lodi arranged the theft of his collection? What if he told the Council to send you to Lhadrung, to put pressure on Ming and Lodi?"

"Impossible."

"Dolan is an important benefactor to Chinese cultural activities. And a significant foreign investor."

Yao's glare softened, and he looked back at Ming's box of discs.

Shan continued typing—a new set of questions, not on Corbett's list: Inquire whether Elizabeth McDowell traveled on same flights as William Lodi from Seattle. Was Lodi's flight from Beijing to Lhasa reserved in advance? Do a media search and try to obtain published photographs of Dolan's Tibetan art collection. Find out purpose of Ming's museum expeditions to Inner Mongolia.

Suddenly he became aware of Yao looking over his shoulder again. "Confirm what contributions Dolan has made to Ming's museum in Beijing," Yao added in a solemn voice. "Provide a list of any calls between Dolan and Beijing during the past six months. Send passport records of—"

Yao was cut off by the abrupt opening of the door. Director Ming was suddenly staring at them. "We missed you," Ming said. "You would have learned something about your thieves."

Shan finished typing, hit the send button, and shut down the computer.

"I am sorry, Comrade Director," Yao said impassively. "It sounded like a history lesson."

Ming circled the table, pausing in front of the now blank computer screen. "I need you on the teams going into the mountains tomorrow, Inspector. The army has developed search quadrants."

"I came to find thieves," Yao declared.

"Exactly. The thief was taking the stolen art into the mountains and was killed by Tibetan reactionaries who took the art treasures to one of the old hidden shrines."

"You revised your theory," Yao pointed out.

"We must adapt to circumstances."

"It could be dangerous to send your—" Yao searched for a word—"scholars into the mountains. It would be safer to wait."

Ming silently returned Yao's stare for a long moment, then shrugged and smiled. "We can wait no longer. It is urgent now. We have discovered there is a long tradition in Lhadrung of stealing art, of killing people for their art." He stepped toward the door, paused and turned. "It's one of the reasons the army is assisting. You have been assigned to a team. Both of you." He grew silent and stepped to the door, turning just before he disappeared. "Be prepared for great things," he said.

Shan and Yao were in the corridor thirty seconds later, moving into the shadows at the rear, where it reached the outer stone wall of the compound. An old plank door led outside. Shan put his hand on the latch and paused. There was a sound like a moan coming from another old door, locked with a small beam set in two metal brackets. Yao lifted the beam and cracked open the door. An acrid odor of ammonia and soap wafted out of the darkness inside. As Yao lowered his hand from the door it swung open, propelled by a limp arm that had apparently been braced against it. Blotches of fresh blood were on the hand that landed at their feet. Yao leapt back. Shan knelt, touching the hand. It was warm, had a strong pulse. He pushed the door against the corridor wall, letting the dim light inside. It was an old meditation cell, converted to a janitor's closet, cleaning chemicals on its shelves, mops and buckets arranged against the walls. A Tibetan man had been dumped inside. He was sprawled atop a pile of musty rags, one leg over a bucket. His face was puffy and bruised, blood oozed from several small cuts on his face. Shan thought he must be unconscious, but after a moment the hand moved. It was missing two fingers.

"Tashi, it's Shan," he said as he bent over the injured man. The informer leaned forward, nodded, the effort bringing obvious pain to his eyes.

"Please no more!" Tashi cried.

"It's me. I will not hurt you." He lifted a rag and dabbed the blood on the informer's face. "Who was it? What did he want to know?"

"That old man with you in the mountains," Tashi said. "Lokesh. After you left we spoke about the old ways, about my life. He told me to tell my mother there were monks in the mountains." Tashi pushed himself up against the wall.

"Was it Ming?"

"Now she won't let me tell them anything about Zhoka." Blood trickled down the side of his face.

"What is it you can't tell him?" Shan asked.

"He asked about the Lord of the Dead, like he asks everyone. But I know nothing about that. Then he made everyone else leave the room and he asked about the Mountain Buddha. He said he could make me rich."

"The Mountain Buddha?"

Tashi forced a smile and took the rag from Shan to wipe his face. "My mother told me about it. The golden Buddha of Zhoka, who lived in Nyen Puk."

Nyen Puk. The cave of the mountain god, the words Lodi had written and Surya had covered. As Shan studied the informer Yao darted into one of the rooms along the hall, reappearing a moment later with a bottle of water which Tashi gulped down. The informer held onto the doorframe and stepped into the hall. "I have to get them to listen to me. They think I lie for the Chinese. I never lie, that's how I stay alive. This isn't the time. They have to bury it, hide it again. My mother, she rejoiced when she heard the eyes of the golden Buddha were open again."

Tashi closed his eyes, took a deep breath, and cast a plaintive gaze at Shan. "In the mountains they think it will protect them. There's an old lama who appeared at Zhoka. He says they will use it to liberate all the prisoners in the construction brigade. They understand nothing," he said wearily. "But these people from Beijing, when they come worlds change. People dying, that means nothing to them. What that Ming wants most of all is to interrogate the dead."

Without another word he rushed past Shan and Yao, pushed open the door, and disappeared into the night.

CHAPTER TEN

He made it sound like some sort of monster coming out of the hills," Yao said as he drove toward town in the half light of dawn. "Mountain Buddha. What is it?"

"I don't know," Shan admitted. "I've never heard of it." Surely he had not heard correctly, he kept telling himself, or surely Tashi for once had it wrong. No one could possibly think they could liberate the prisoners.

"Ming beats Tashi to find out about it, and when Tashi, Tan's top informant, refuses to speak for the first time in his life," Yao pointed out, "Ming decides he urgently needs to be back in the mountains." He had been silent for most of the drive, withdrawn into the same brooding silence that had seized him the night before, after Tashi's escape.

The inspector had led Shan into the room assigned to him as sleeping quarters, and silently written in his pad for half an hour before throwing a blanket and pillow onto the floor for Shan. The dilemma that troubled Yao, Shan knew, wasn't how to make sense of his investigation but how to make sense of the politics. Yao had arrived in Lhadrung at the head of a criminal investigation in alliance with Ming. Now Ming had commandeered his resources, opened communication directly with senior authorities about the investigation, even obtained new authority on his own in Lhasa. Ming had seized the political initiative in the strange game they were playing.

Shan had tried to slip away in the middle of the night but Yao's hand had closed around his arm as he had opened the door to the corridor, pulling him back inside.

"It isn't going to end like this," the inspector said. "Just because Ming may not be after the same thing anymore doesn't mean anything. I will get what I came for." He seemed to be arguing with himself.

"I have a teacher," Shan said. "He says strong spirits have to be careful about the truth they seek, for that truth may come back to seek them."

"What do you mean?"

Shan looked down the corridor of shadows. "When the stakes grow high enough, even the most senior investigators become expendable."

Yao glared at him. "You think I'm scared?"

"I am frightened for you."

The inspector's eyes narrowed. "Sometimes I think you are nothing but a political officer. For the Tibetans."

Shan stared into the shadows.

Yao released his arm. "I still need a guide."

"I refuse."

"Then I need a helper," Yao countered.

"For what?"

"To catch an art thief."

"Then you're a fool. You'll destroy yourself if you still think it's only about art theft."

Yao gazed down the darkened hallway. "To stop Ming," he muttered.

Shan met Yao's gaze and nodded. "I need a helper," Shan said.

Yao's eyes hardened. He gestured Shan inside the room and switched on the light. "A helper for what?" he asked, closing the door behind him. "To regain your son?"

The question silenced Shan for a moment. Yao and the others seemed to wield his son like some weapon, attacking when he least expected. "I will tell you exactly what I want when you tell me the same," he said at last.

Yao gazed at Shan with an intense expression. "How will I know when what you seek begins to interfere with what I seek?"

"You won't."

"Will it? Will it interfere?"

"Almost certainly."

When Yao finally nodded he seemed almost grateful. He stepped to his bed and hastily packed a canvas bag.

They had nearly reached the courtyard outside when Shan held up a hand. A quiet, irregular tapping sound was coming from the assembly hall. Yao cracked open the door. The earnest young woman with the short hair who had been assisting Ming sat at the table, working at a laptop computer, with no light but that from the screen. The woman's head jerked up in alarm as she discovered the two men staring over her shoulder.

"Are you cleared for the Amban Project?" Yao asked sternly as she began to lower the screen.

"Of course," she said defiantly and, as if to prove it, raised the screen again.

She was working on what appeared to be an essay, or article, complete with footnotes. Across the top of the page was the title POLITICAL ASSASSINATIONS IN LHADRUNG COUNTY.

"Director Ming's discoveries are too important for us to wait for the return home," the woman declared. "He wants a draft sent to Beijing this morning."

"I wasn't aware he had made his discoveries yet," Shan said.

"If someone had been assassinated here," Yao observed, "we would have known about it."

"State secret," the woman replied. "That's the whole point, isn't it?" she asked in a patronizing tone. "The way the local population has cleverly concealed the truth."

"But no one has been assassinated," Shan pointed out.

"The missing amban was killed by reactionaries right here in Lhadrung," Ming's assistant stated. "We are going to correct the history books."

"The nephew of the Qian Long emperor?" Yao asked. "It's been centuries."

"It makes no difference. The people's justice knows no bounds." The woman frowned as she saw the skeptical expressions both Shan and Yao wore, as if deciding her audience was not sophisticated enough to understand. "This is vital work. The final copy will be circulated to the full team later this week," she said and dismissed them with a wave of her hand.

Outside, they searched the army vehicles until they found a small utility truck with the keys in the ignition, then Yao climbed in behind the wheel. "I never asked where we are going," Yao said.

"I'll know when I smell it," Shan explained.

Now, as they entered town, Shan rolled down his window. Five minutes later he directed Yao to park the truck two hundred feet down the road from a small complex of mudbrick buildings. As they approached the buildings, Yao began to slow, lagging behind Shan, his hand over his mouth and nose. The stench of human waste was almost overpowering.

"So far the main secrets of Tibet you have shared with me seem to be a charnel ground and this place," the inspector observed. "No doubt next we'll be tunneling into a garbage heap." He waved Shan on.

Shan passed a line of battered bicycles, each with heavy wire racks mounted on either side of the rear wheel, then three sturdy wooden carts with a heavy U-shaped front handle, designed for two people to step inside and push. As he stepped into a shadow of the first building a woman appeared, a yoke on her shoulder, balancing two large clay pots. A brown crust extended down the side of each pot. A man in a coat that was so tattered it seemed about to disintegrate appeared behind the woman and headed for the row of bicycles. The sun was rising. After dawn large ceramic pots of night soil would be waiting behind houses and tenements all over town, to be transported to the fields as fertilizer, an occupation as old as China itself.

"I came to see Surya," Shan said to the woman. "The old monk."

The woman gave a bitter laugh. "We have no monks. Look in the mountains. Look in the prison."

"I mean him no harm. I am a friend of his."

The woman did not speak but reached into one of the carts and produced a long wooden ladle. She dipped it into one of the jars lined up behind the building and it came out dripping with a brown sludge. Shan took a step forward. The woman flung the contents of the ladle at him. As he stepped to the side the sludge landed where he had been standing. From behind him he heard Yao curse. Shan held his ground. Two more women appeared, each grabbing a ladle, each filling it with night soil. "Chinese!" one of them hissed, and flung another ladle of waste at him. Splatters hit his shoe.

"You want to give us shit, leave it on your doorstep," one of the others barked. Shan glanced behind him. Yao had retreated to the truck. He heard a murmur of alarm among the Tibetans and turned to see them lowering the ladles. In the rising light they had recognized the military markings on the truck.

"Surya came down from the mountains," he tried again. "He was asking for alms. Tell him it is Shan."

The first woman disappeared around the corner, returning less than a minute later. "He says he knew a man who once knew Shan," she announced in an uncertain voice.

Shan ventured forward a step. When no one reacted, he pushed past them into the yard of the little compound. Surya sat on the stone wall of what looked to be a central well. Three small children sat in front of him. Behind them half a dozen men and women, dressed in the soiled, tattered clothing of the gatherers, stood before what appeared to be an old stable. Shan glanced about the compound. Sleeping pallets had been pulled outside to air. A blackened kettle sat on a smouldering fire. The gatherers didn't just work from the compound, he realized, they lived there, shunned, no doubt, by the rest of the town.

Surya seemed not to notice when Shan sat beside him. He was making a small doll out of dried rushes, tied with straw.

"Rinpoche," Shan said, "we must go back. They need you. They are frightened for you."

Surya absently looked up, not at Shan, but to his own side, then over his shoulder, as if to see whom Shan spoke to.

"Gendun. Lokesh," Shan said. "They need your help. There are things that have to be understood at Zhoka."

Surya's eyes slowly found Shan's. "I am sorry, comrade, you have mistaken me for someone else. Our fragrances sometimes confuse strangers." The children laughed. Surya finished tying the doll and handed it to a young girl.

"You met Director Ming at the old stone tower. Did he ask about the death deity?"

"He met a young Chinese, a great abbot. No one can understand the great one's ways," Surya said. His voice had a strange absent quality to it. "The abbot makes beautiful paintings, holy paintings, with one finger, one word."

A cold shudder passed down Shan's spine. Surya was still speaking of his prior life in the third person. "Why is Zhoka so important to Ming?" he pressed. "Is he one of the thieves you feared?"

"The things that are important at Zhoka seem to be different, depending."

"Depending on what?"

Surya lifted his head and grinned, exposing a row of crooked yellow teeth. "Whether you are Chinese or Tibetan," he said and chuckled, the sound rasping over his dry throat. "Comrade," he added, and laughed again.

Shan pressed his hand to his forehead in frustration. He was not speaking with Surya. The man in front of him was truly different, the way Lokesh had said people become different when struck by lightning. "If I don't know the secrets how can I protect the lamas?"

"It is not secret. It just has no words. It cannot be explained between people, only between deities." The words that rushed out of the old man's mouth seemed not to belong to him this time. He looked deeply confused, almost shocked. He touched his tongue with a finger, and something in him seemed to sink, as if disheartened.

Shan stood and took a step toward the stable. Two of the men sitting there stood, blocking the entry to the building.

Shan turned back toward Surya. "What happened to Kwan Li?" he asked.

Surya made a strange spiraling motion toward the sky. "Something wonderful."

Shan studied him a moment. His mannerisms had changed from the monk Shan knew, his face seemed to have new lines in it, his eyes even had a different, sadder, more callous glint. "What was hidden at Zhoka?" he asked.

Surya shrugged. "That is for the monks to know."

"You are a monk."

When Surya shook his head there was a new emotion on his countenance. Not sadness. Pity, as though he felt sorry for Shan. "He might have discovered it if he had stayed there. But," Surya said with a sigh, "he died at the festival."

Shan reached into his pocket and handed Surya the paintbrush he had kept there since the festival day. "The only one who died was Lodi," Shan explained, fighting to keep his helplessness from his voice. "The one you saw in the tunnel. He was a thief. I think you saw him stealing. There was an argument, perhaps, an accident," he ventured.

The old Tibetan stared at the old brush in his hand like he had never seen one before, then pocketed it and stood, supported for a moment by one of the children. "I have soil to bring back to earth," he declared, stepping away toward the bicycles and carts.

It seemed to take a huge effort for Shan to reach the truck, as if a great weight had landed on his shoulders. By the time Yao eased the vehicle away Surya was pulling one of the handcarts down the road, filled with four oversize ceramic pots.

"Did he know that mountain deity?" Yao asked.

"Not any deity," Shan said in a worried whisper.

Shan did not have to ask their next destination. Yao aimed the truck toward the highest building in town and pressed the accelerator hard, as if he were suddenly desperate to get to the government center. Because, Shan realized as Yao parked the truck near the front door, it was too early for the offices to be occupied, too early for any of the senior officers to be in their offices, the perfect time to find idle computers and telephones. They had to review the other letters, understand the two-hundred-year mystery that drove Ming.

The guard at the door nodded at Yao, glared at Shan, then waved them through. Shan protested as Yao pressed the elevator button for the top floor. "There are computers upstairs," Yao explained as the elevator slowly climbed, "in the visitor's room by Tan's office."

As the doors opened, Yao darted toward the central office complex. Shan stood in the corridor, fighting a strange weakness that suddenly gripped him. It was here where he had met Colonel Tan; here where Tan had begun the strange torture of forcing Shan to become an investigator again; here, too, where Tan had abruptly given him his freedom.

When he finally joined Yao in the office, Shan sat at a terminal and quickly typed in the codes Corbett had given him. It had been the middle of the day in Seattle when he had sent the prior message, and Corbett's team had not been idle.

Hey boss, we were getting worried—glad to have you back on line, the first reply opened. *We've been monitoring messages day and night just in case. Received queries, back soonest, Bailey.* The second message had been sent two hours later, and was captioned *Dolan travel to the PRC.* It spanned ten years and listed an average of two trips a year. Next came a message entitled, *Donations, Dolan to PRC*. It listed nearly a dozen in the past three years alone: to an archaeology project in Inner Mongolia, to three special exhibits in the Museum of Antiquities, computer labs in five cities, a restoration project for an imperial temple in Manchuria. *Ming archaeology expeditions were for the recovery of frescoes from old temples buried in the desert,* Bailey added.

Next came a report captioned simply, *D's phone accounts/calls to PRC*. Shan called Yao to the screen. Yao began pointing to numbers as they scrolled through the long list of numbers. "The Museum of Antiquities," he said in a tight voice, "the Minister of Culture. The Minister of Justice."

As they stared at the screen a soft beep announced several new messages, each followed by Bailey's name. A list of Dolan's Chinese investments: Dolan's private companies owned seven factories in eastern Chinese cities, interests in a dozen joint ventures. There was a hurried message Shan did not understand: *The boss found out you opened papers on the babysitter. He ordered it closed.* Then came two short lines on Elizabeth McDowell: *Art consultant to Dolan, part own-er of Croft Antiquities, with offices in Seattle and London. Confirmed traveled on same flights as William Lodi to Lhasa. Neither McDowell nor Lodi reserved flight to Lhasa in advance.*

The final message contained files of photographs and a compilation of articles on Dolan's famed Tibetan collection. Shan silently pointed to several small images on the screen as he held up the catalog Liya had given them, including the fourteenth-century saint wielding his sword of wisdom. They were all in Dolan's collection, but excluded from his report of lost property.

"Dolan could still have them," Yao said in a hollow voice.

"No," Shan said. "Corbett had records of the crime scene, saw photos of all the shelves and display cases. Every Tibetan piece was reported stolen. Lodi was carrying the pieces from the museum back to Beijing, because of the audit. Maybe they were all he really cared about in the theft. The rest was cover, the rest might have stayed in America. But something happened to change his plans. He unexpectedly came straight to Tibet."

"What do you mean?"

"I mean the saint with the sword that he was carrying, the one they destroyed at the fleshcutters, it was the original from Dolan. Lodi gave it to Liya for safekeeping. Lodi was planning to stay at a hotel in Beijing, but didn't. He had no time in Beijing to exchange it for the copy."

"But why destroy it?"

"Liya said because they were sending a message to Bumpari. But I think the message was for someone else. The one who would be most hurt by its destruction."

"Ming," Yao spat. He stared at the screen a moment, then typed in a new question. Verify Director Ming's travel the week after the robbery. He exchanged a wary glance with Shan. It was a question he could not safely ask in Beijing, but the FBI could access airline records.

Half an hour later they had finished examining the old letters Ming had collected, failing to find any clue to the fate of the amban. But the letters made it clear that the amban had given up his career as a general and come to Tibet at the request of his uncle, not just to play the role of the senior Chinese representative, but to find lamas who would be willing to travel to Beijing to serve in the imperial court. In his first year the amban had not only sent a dozen lamas but, with the help of his powerful uncle, had arranged for the construction of Tibetan Buddhist temples in half a dozen eastern cities.

A clink of porcelain caused them to turn. Tan sat on a table by the door, sipping from a mug of tea. "Once," the colonel said in a tight voice, "all my visitors from the outside were behind wire at the 404. Then last month two more came, Ming and McDowell. Now, at last count, there are a dozen, brought in by Director Ming. I received a fax from Central Command. I was instructed to provide maximum support to all of them. Now my general has called. He wanted to share a secret. Director Ming has been advanced two grades in the party during the past year. He will be of minister rank in another year or two."

Yao stood and studied Tan, as if composing a response. Tan gestured to the thermos of tea and extra mugs on a table outside the office, and the inspector followed Shan to the table without speaking. When they had settled back into the chairs by the computer with their steaming mugs, Shan explained Ming's interest in the long dead amban, and showed Tan the letters on the discs.

"There's a report being sent to Beijing today about the amban," Yao announced. "It's called Political Assassination in Lhadrung County."

Tan's lips curled in a silent snarl. "A lie. No one gets assassinated in my county."

"It was over two hundred years ago," Yao pointed out.

Shan knew the date mattered little to Tan. Newly reported murder whenever it occurred, especially political murder, would bring unwelcome attention to the county, and to its chief official.

"A new martyr," Tan said, gazing out the window. "There was talk of this Kwan Li four or five years ago, at a conference I attended in Lhasa. The dead always make for safer politics than the living. I thought they had dropped the idea. Someone must have decided the people needed new lessons on integration of Tibet with the motherland. Now we'll have little buttons with his likeness. Speeches to schoolchildren, speeches by schoolchildren." He paused and looked back at them. "But he can't know the amban died in Lhadrung. It's impossible. The Chinese ambans never had business in Lhadrung. It's not on the route back to Beijing. Prince Kwan died in the north." Tan lit a cigarette. "He's here for the fresco. If he's not finding the fresco he should leave." He seemed to be talking to himself, staring out the window now. "I made some inquiries. His fieldwork was supposed to be back in Mongolia. He changed it to Lhadrung on two weeks' notice, with a satellite project in the north. He said it was to research herding cultures. But I checked. It was where Kwan Li supposedly died two hundred years ago. He starting making arrangements too." When he turned to face them his eyes were lit with a cold anger. "He changed his field project days after the theft of the fresco."

Tan rose and disappeared down the hall, returning in less than a minute with a dusty folder from which he pulled a report bound between two clear plastic covers, extending it to Shan. "In the back," the colonel said.

The final pages were a transcribed report from an imperial official sent by the emperor to find the missing amban. The high-ranking mandarin had delivered a report to the emperor a month before the emperor left the throne, explaining his frustration at failing to find the amban, alive or dead, but reporting that many witnesses had signed sworn statements that the amban had departed from tradition and left his regular Chinese bodyguards in Lhasa, to travel in the company of Tibetan soldiers as a sign of good faith. The party had been deep inside rugged mountains five hundred miles north of Lhasa when the amban had encountered two warring tribes fighting over the rights to pastureland. Confident that he could negotiate a solution, and without regard to his personal safety, the amban had ascended to the mountain battlefield. He had met with the chieftains and indeed negotiated a solution that provided for sharing of the pastures, but at the banquet celebrating the accord an angry warrior who resented the outsider's intervention had shot an arrow into his throat. Kwan Li had died asking for the emperor's forgiveness. The tribes, terrified of the emperor's likely reaction, had slain the guard party and withdrawn deep into the mountains, taking the bodies with them, leaving a group of lamas who had appeared on the scene to conduct death rites.

The emperor's investigator had traveled on to Lhasa to complete his work, finding no contrary evidence but that of a drunken tailor formerly employed by the amban who insisted that on the eve of the amban's departure he had been asked to make Tibetan soldiers' uniforms for several monks. The story could not be verified, and the tailor disappeared after the first interview. The investigator suspected a conspiracy of Tibetans against the amban, that there had been no soldiers with the amban but only disguised monks. He insisted the emperor should dispatch troops to find and destroy the mountain tribes since they had either killed him, or been part of the conspiracy. He requested to return to Tibet to find the monks who had conspired with the tribes. The report closed with an annotation by an imperial secretary, noting that the emperor had declined to send troops or authorize further investigation, and had sent the mandarin to a senior post in a southern province.

"I didn't understand why after coming here Ming spent half his time on the phone with Beijing," Tan said as Shan closed the report.

"Because it's all about political opportunity," Shan said. "What he's doing is not how a scientist conducts fieldwork. But it is exactly the way you would do it if you were aspiring to become a minister."

"There was one more document," Shan added after a moment, gesturing toward the computer screen, "but it was encrypted by Ming."

"Because it explains too much?" Tan suggested.

They sat in silence, Tan looking at the screen displaying the encrypted letter, Shan out the window. "The inspector knows you tried to hide me, Colonel," he said in a tentative tone. "He knows I haven't said anything about his failure to verify whether Director Ming and Lodi had a prior relationship."

"What are you talking about?" Tan growled.

Yao sighed and stepped to the computer. "He's talking about me. He's talking about rough bargains being made, and how I haven't reciprocated." He began tapping the keyboard. "It is not a high-level code Ming used. He doesn't have access to the most secret ones. There's probably a thousand people in Beijing alone who have this one," he stated, punctuating his remark with several emphatic strikes of the keys. Suddenly the image on the screen blurred, and the figures rearranged themselves. The text of the last document appeared.

It was not one more letter from the amban, but five letters placed together in the secret file, short missives drafted over the course of a year, letters not included in the official files of the Amban Project. They lacked the flowery prose of the early correspondence, had the air of communication between two old friends who no longer had use for pretense. The first thanked the emperor for accepting that the amban had embraced the Buddhist faith, thanked him likewise for speaking in the words of the sutras. He prayed his uncle's forbearance in the amban's delayed departure for Beijing, because the amban was using the time to accumulate the most precious treasures the emperor had ever beheld. The second letter indicated that the amban's effort to gather Tibetan artists to create masterpieces to honor the emperor was proceeding, although the amban found it necessary to journey to some artists because they were so aged, had even gone to nearby caves to visit hermit artists, caves named Dom Puk, Zetrul Puk, Woser Puk, and Kuden Puk—the names that had been searched in Ming's pilgrim guide database, the ones he had just that day identified with local landmarks. The third reported that the amban had discovered the source of the greatest art he or the emperor could ever hope to find, and was now in the old monastery befriending its lamas, and visiting the priceless Mountain Buddha. A wondrous mechanical mandala was being built of gold and silver, and in honor of the emperor an artist was dedicating a black stone statue of Jambhala, the protective deity, on which he had been working for two years. The fourth, the longest, months later, announced a still greater revelation. The lamas had discovered that Kwan Li was in fact the reincarnation of their greatest leader, their abbot, and he had been installed as the abbot of the old earth taming temple, a place where deities were grown the way flowers were grown in gardens. The fifth reported that the abbot had received the humbling offer of the emperor, which he dared not write of further for fear of the secret being discovered. Great preparations were under way, and the abbot needed to go on retreat before returning to the capital. Meanwhile the abbot would secretly arrange for the shipment of the emperor's treasures. He would deliver to the imperial messengers in Lhasa half a thangka of the protector deity of the gompa, a special form of the Lord of Death. If anything happened to the abbot while on the arduous journey he would hide the treasures and entrust the other half of the thangka to a trusted lama, who would present it to the emperor. Once joined the two halves would tell the emperor where to find the treasures. *And later, like the sutras,* the last letter closed, *I will explain the rest of death.*

"It's not just about politics," Tan said in a low, frigid voice. They had discovered why Ming was so zealous about finding information on the deities, why he had demanded to know the word, the name of the protective deity, and what it looked like.

"Ming wants it all," Yao growled. "The political treasure, for his public face. And the treasure of gold and silver, for himself and his partners."

"What does it mean, the offer of the emperor?" Tan asked.

"It doesn't say," Shan said.

"What temple?" Tan asked.

Shan and Yao exchanged a silent glance. "It doesn't say," Yao said.

"But in Lhadrung," Tan said, his anger rising again. "Ming is reporting that the amban was killed in Lhadrung." He pounded a fist into his palm. "Why now? What happened?"

Yao shrugged.

"What happened," Shan suggested, "was the robbery in the Qian Long's cottage. In removing the fresco, I think they exposed something unknown to anyone before. The secret letters of the amban."

There was a final screen they had not viewed. Shan pressed a key and a photograph appeared, an image of a torn thangka, the upper half of a blue deity with the distorted head of a four-horned bull. As they stared at it the adjacent computer chimed and Shan opened the FBI message screen. Director Ming, it said, had flown to Lhasa on the same flight as Lodi, returning on the very next flight to Beijing. Shan quickly typed a reply, as Yao printed out a copy of the image of the torn thangka. Search travel records for Lu Chou Fin and Khan Mo, arrived in Tibet during past month.

Suddenly boots pounded the floor of the corridor. The door flew open. A young officer, one of Tan's adjutants, burst into the room. "Colonel," the man said in an urgent voice. "Director Ming is calling troops out of the base. He's talking with Lhasa and Beijing. He says they found bodies. Dead Chinese, a massacre," he said. "Killed by Tibetans." As he spoke phones began ringing at the desks outside and a siren rose from the street.

Thirty minutes later they stood at the edge of a field in the southern valley, surveying a chaotic scene. Ming stood in the middle of the field, fifty yards away, frantically directing workers with shovels and buckets, ordering soldiers onto the field. Two military police cars sat on the road, emergency lights flashing.

"By the time word spreads in Lhasa people will be saying there is an uprising in Lhadrung," Tan growled. He called for a radio operator, with orders to reach army headquarters in Lhasa.

The troops had not known what to expect, Shan saw. Most were in combat gear, with grenades slung on their belts. Two dozen had formed a perimeter guard, establishing a square fifty yards to the side, while others were erecting a large military tent, a command post, near the center of the square, where Ming was assembling a field station of his own.

A heavy truck arrived from the direction of the guest compound and soldiers began unloading tables, chairs, and metal cases under the supervision of one of Ming's assistants. Ming himself strutted along a trench, barking orders as soldiers hastily dug, pausing to exclaim excitedly to his assistants, or pose for a photograph, jumping into the trench, then jumping out again. The young woman with the close-cropped hair was at a folding table near the trench, several artifacts arrayed before her. A soldier presented her with one of the metal cases. She opened it and began removing small trays packed with brushes, lenses, and metal instruments.

A farmer had come to the compound the night before with a small jade object which he had plowed up in a low mound in his barley field, the woman explained in answer to Yao's questions. She pointed to the farmer's discovery, which sat on a towel in the center of the little table. It was the front half of a dragon, intricately carved of jade, part of what had been a handle, perhaps for a cane or fly whisk. With a needle-like probe the woman pointed to what had excited the museum team.

"The claws?" Yao asked.

"There's five," Shan said. "You found it in these trenches?" he asked.

The woman dropped a cloth over the jade, studiously ignoring Shan.

Shan met Yao's stare. There was only one family authorized to use the five-clawed dragon in imperial China. "What have you found?" Yao demanded of the woman in a slow, simmering voice.

"The farmer's family already had been digging when we arrived. Started the trench around the old foundation they had uncovered. Director Ming himself found the Chinese artifact," she added. Jade was not commonly used in Tibet. "By the time the rest of us arrived he and the farmers had excavated a stone chest. Inside was a grand treasure. She bent and lifted the lid of a long metal case, revealing an elaborate silk robe, in yellow and blue, embroidered with cranes, dragons, pheasants, and other creatures, including one whose leg appeared around a fold, a leg bearing five claws. "It's centuries old. Ching dynasty. And this was found with it, from the ancient reactionaries. Things unseen for two hundred years." She uncovered an old piece of rice paper. "It removes all doubt."

But Shan had seen the robe, only the day before at Fiona's house. And Yao had a similar piece of rice paper in his room, given to them by Liya. The woman had another of the bounty posters, as if people in Lhadrung had collected them two hundred year ago, kept them for a special reason. Yao pointed to two lines of handwritten Tibetan script at the bottom of the poster. "Killed by order of the Stone Dragon Lama," Shan read. The letters were faded, probably had been placed there two hundred years before. It would be the perfect closing to the political parable Ming was writing. A senior lama had killed the amban, and Tibetans had essentially admitted it. Shan leaned over the writing to better see the second line. "Conquered in Zetrul Puk," he read. But to Shan's eye it did not appear old. Someone had recently added the reference to the Miracle Cave.

"But you reported that people had been killed," Yao interjected.

The woman pointed toward the far side of the mound, where a knot of soldiers stood. Yao and Shan stepped cautiously to their side. They were guarding several skulls, and the remnants of skeletons. Another, deeper trench had been dug nearby, exposing a stone wall and a small square portal, a doorway no more than thirty inches high. As they watched another skull was placed beside the others already in front of the soldiers.

The colonel had taken Ming aside and was speaking to him. Tan's face seemed as tightly clenched as his fists. As they watched, a dozen soldiers climbed back into one of the trucks, which drove away.

After several minutes Shan stepped as inconspicuously as possible toward Tan's car and the remaining trucks, leaving Yao making notes by the trenches. Perhaps he could slip onto a truck as it left. He searched the faces of the soldiers. There may be some who recognized him, who would be willing to help him leave, if only because they knew how much his presence usually upset Tan. He recognized a middle-aged sergeant who acknowledged him with a scowl. But as he approached the man a hand closed around his arm.

"We still need you, comrade," an oily voice warned. Ming.

"Surely your work is done," Shan said, after a long moment. "You can return to Beijing a hero."

Ming acknowledged the comment with a pleased nod. "But I still will not have my thieves, or the American his killer. We have not changed the plans. The supplies are to be ready by noon at that prison. Four teams are going into the mountains, with scientists and soldiers, and trustees," he added, staring pointedly at Shan.

For once Shan agreed with Ming. Shan needed to be in the mountains. "Nothing has changed," he confirmed. Nothing, and everything. Yao and Corbett had not caught their criminals but now it was Ming who worried Shan the most.

Ming glanced at his watch. "Things are under control here. Now that we know what we have found, the tedious work begins. For professionals," he said with a nod toward his white-aproned assistants. "I am leaving to supervise the departure of the mountains teams. Would you indulge me on the way?" he asked, gesturing toward his car. As Shan climbed inside he saw Yao standing with Tan. Both men were staring at him. Ming followed his gaze and waved at the two men.

"What's that they say?" the director asked in a quick aside to Shan. "Ah yes. The gods will be victorious," he called out in Mandarin to Tan and Yao, then started the car. "Tremble and obey!" he called out through the open window, and laughed.

"Look in the backseat," the director said as he accelerated out of the field, spinning dirt and gravel into the air. There was another metal case lying on its side on the seat. Shan twisted and unfastened the latches, opening it as Ming gave a little sound of amusement. The bottom half of the case was filled with ice, which cooled several bottles of carbonated orange drink. Shan opened two, handing one to Ming.

"You and I started badly," Ming said. "We had to overcome our natural distrust," he suggested. "But now so much has happened. I never expected that this county hid so many opportunities. I will need someone on the ground who knows how to get things done among Tibetans. An operations director, let's say."

Shan lowered his drink halfway through a swallow. "You are offering me a job?" he asked in disbelief.

"It would give you a future. At least a way to build a future. We could do something about your status. Your current arrangement is little better than prison," Ming added.

"You mean you want me to be in charge of recovering and destroying Tibetan artifacts?"

Ming frowned. "I run a museum, not a scrapyard."

"I was there yesterday," Shan pointed out.

"Those little ornaments? They were worthless. Political handicaps. Removing them from use was a service to the country. These people have to be shown everything. They are like children. It is part of their education about life in a new century."

"I had a friend named Surya who told me once that art lies in the deity that beholds it. To those people those things were art. And more."

Ming drained his bottle. "Deity this, deity that. It seems to be the excuse every Tibetan uses for doing nothing. A way to justify being lazy."

Shan stared at the bottle in his own hand, remembering the anguish on the faces of the Tibetans in the courtyard as their beloved altar sculptures were ripped open. An old woman had held her belly, as though what was being ripped apart was in her womb.

He felt Ming's glance and heard the director sigh. "I must be more tolerant," Ming said. "I apologize. I salute you. No doubt it is your sensitivity that makes you so valuable."

The words made Shan stare out the window a long time. He replayed the events at the field in his mind. The director had separated him from Yao for a reason. "I have no work papers," he said.

"A phone call can fix that. I could arrange living quarters at the compound. A car, or at least a utility vehicle." Ming slowed the car and began weaving in and out of the throng of bicycles that marked the approach to town. "I could authorize you to hire Tibetans," he said in a careful tone. "Say five or six. I will negotiate with Religious Affairs to take over the compound in the name of the museum. You could restore it as you see fit, with money from Beijing."

"There's Colonel Tan and Inspector Yao," Shan said, intensely attentive now.

"Tan is a dinosaur, easily disposed of when it is time. Yao can be recalled. It may be he misunderstood something, perhaps overreacted. There would be no shame in it, no mark on his record. He is just in danger of mischaracterizing the crime. You of all people know the damage that can be done. By helping him understand you help all of us, especially yourself and your Tibetan friends."

Shan's mouth was suddenly very dry. He fought the urge to retrieve another drink from the rear seat. "Perhaps," he said slowly, "I could demonstrate that the thief was Tibetan, acting on a political pretext, that the thief is dead, perhaps after destroying the stolen art."

Ming offered a respectful nod. "For a man with your instincts rehabilitation may come swiftly," he said, then paused and cast an ironic grin toward Shan. "I read something about lamas," he added after a moment, "how sometimes they help the dying find their new incarnation. Let me be your lama."

They moved through the town quickly, Shan keeping an eye on the streets. For a fleeting moment he saw an old man in ragged black clothes, pushing a cart down an alley. It could have been Surya, hauling night soil, or just another Tibetan peasant carrying his meager produce to market.

"Someone who would help you would need a map of the sites you intend to study. The old gompa, the caves."

Ming shrugged. "Every team leader already has one," he said, and pulled a paper from a folder on the seat between them, handing it to Shan. "You can be my eyes. Something new has surfaced. A huge golden Buddha is somewhere in the mountains. I want it, Shan. Find it for me and you'll get your new life."

Was it his arrogance, Shan wondered, or just his political ambition, that made him so blind? "Before we are finished I will find it," Shan vowed.

"Excellent. Our little secret."

"Surely Miss McDowell knows," Shan ventured.

"Our little secret," Ming repeated.

It might be difficult to understand what was happening among the Tibetans in the mountains, Shan thought, but it seemed impossible to grasp what was passing among the strangers in Lhadrung. "All power is based on secrets," he observed after a moment.

Ming shot him an amused glance. "Meaning what?"

"Secret prayers. Secret caves. Secret letters from the emperor. A lost secret letter implicating Lhadrung in the theft of the fresco in Beijing."

Ming slowed the car and studied Shan warily. "Because of the incompetence of the Beijing police."

"You're the one who found it, who explained what it said."

"Not so surprising. The cottage was my project. I was there within an hour after the robbery was reported."

"But such a coincidence, to find that letter just then."

"Not at all. There was some kind of old vault in the wall behind the fresco that had originally opened into the room on the far side, but it had been sealed in years ago."

Ming, Shan realized, had just told him where he had found the secret amban papers. "You said the letter proved the theft was a political crime. But to be so the thieves would have to go public, make a statement."

Ming lit a cigarette. "We scared them, drove them into the hills. They're hiding for now. The fact that you found Lodi proves my point." He blew a stream of smoke toward Shan.

"Lodi's killers are still up there," Shan said, watching Ming's face carefully.

"Killers?" Ming smiled thinly. "There is already a confession. Perhaps I neglected to tell you. I had it typed up, and signed. By Surya, with two army officers as witnesses. Just in case."

Shan stared at him in disbelief. "No," he said in a level tone. "It was a big Mongolian named Khan, who smokes sweet cigars, and a short Han named Lu."

Ming slowed the car. In his eyes there was no alarm, only a tremor of excitement. "You have such capacity for subtlety, comrade, that I am surprised I must explain. You are the one who confirmed that Lodi was indeed killed. I have in my possession a signed confession from Surya saying he killed a man in the mountains. There would be no need for an investigation. You've done all the necessary work, proven the crime. All I have to do is have an official file opened, submit the confession with my supporting statement, and Surya goes to a firing squad."

If Shan were to pursue Khan and Lu, Ming was saying, Ming would see that Surya was executed. Khan and Lu were somehow opposing Ming, but Ming still could not afford to have them arrested. "What exactly do you want me to do?"

"I told you. Work for me. Share in my riches. Prove yourself in the mountains. The monks were fastidious about keeping records of what they did in the old monasteries. Even two hundred years ago. Bring me the records. Find the location of the Mountain Buddha. Find the details of the amban's travels. You're the one who can do it. Perhaps the only one."

Shan fixed Ming with a cool stare. "Tell me what you did to him, to Surya, when you met him in the mountains."

"Nothing. We spoke about art. I told him I collected paintings, had more art than he had ever seen."

"Did you tell him you were an abbot?"

Ming's thin smile returned. "You have to speak in terms these people understand. I couldn't simply say I was a museum director, now could I?" He seemed pleased with the hopelessness that entered Shan's eyes.

Shan suddenly realized where they were, what road they had turned onto at the last fork. His throat was bone dry again. His skin crawled. "This isn't where—" he protested. He found himself sinking into the seat. The road had only one destination. The 404th People's Construction Brigade.

"It is," Ming said, amusement back in his voice. "The colonel said it was most convenient. Secure. Hidden. Close to the prison trusties, close to the soldiers."

As the car skidded to a stop two minutes later Shan discovered that his hand had clamped around the lao gai tattoo on his forearm.

A single huge military tent had been erected fifty yards from the razor wire gate of the prison camp. Four military trucks were backed up to the tent, being loaded with stacks of equipment and boxes on wooden pallets. Shan forced himself out of the car and began to examine the supplies going into the trucks but could not stop his gaze from repeatedly drifting toward the prison camp. He found a spot in the shadows by the front corner of the tent and squatted, studying the compound inside.

Most of the prisoners were on work detail, still clearing fields by the cliffs at the far end of the valley. But as usual the sick, the injured, and the dying stayed in camp. Figures in tattered pajama-like clothing hobbled around the yard between the barracks, carefully avoiding the line of white lime laid on the ground ten feet from the fence, the dead zone where prisoners were not permitted to enter. He fought wave after wave of emotion. Inside the wire were men Shan knew, some of the bravest, strongest, and yet most serene men he had ever known. The men who had preserved him, who had given him a new life, who had forever changed the universe Shan lived in. They still lived there, in rags, half starved. Images flashed before his eyes, of an old man lying on the ground, a tooth kicked out because he had been caught with prayer beads, of a young monk shot in the head for leading a protest against the warden, of Lokesh sitting in the snow with two old lamas praying for the souls of the guards. Suddenly he found himself standing in the rough grass on the far side of the road, an arm stretched toward a bent figure walking between the huts. He meant to call out a greeting but the sound came out like a sob. There was abrupt movement beside him, prison guards jogging toward him, muttering curses. They seemed somehow distant and unimportant, despite the anger in their voices. He stepped away from them, toward the fence, into the dead zone that surrounded the camp, suddenly desperate to look into the faces of the prisoners.

Something hit him behind the knees, a baton, and he dropped, instinctively curling into a ball, his head tucked into his chest, knees up, hands over his neck. After a long moment he realized nothing had happened, no stick had landed on his head or back, no boot had kicked him. He looked up to see two guards hovering over him, cruelly grinning, batons in their belts. Beyond them others were watching, half a dozen soldiers, several trusties. And Yao. As Shan straightened his limbs and stood, the inspector stepped into the shadows as if he did not want Shan to know he had seen.

"Idiot," one of the guards growled.

"There will be time enough, Shan," the second hissed. "We have a place waiting for you inside. You'll be back." He motioned Shan back toward the tent, slapped his companion on the back with a laugh, and marched back toward the gate.

A strange weakness overcame Shan. He sat on the running board of one of the trucks, watching as Ming and Colonel Tan conferred forty feet away. The loading was proceeding at a near frantic pace. He noticed several of the prison guards who had been at the guest compound the day before, followed the steely gaze of one to a slim worker in the blue clothes of a trusty. Ko still wore his cold sneer, and Shan began to wonder if it was a permanent part of his expression. Ko was carrying a box onto a truck, moving slower than those around him, his hooded eyes restless, watching everyone, studying the open wooden crates from which backpacks were being loaded with cooking kits, sleeping bags, and other supplies, casting furtive glances toward the guards.

A trusty carrying a small plastic drum of water suddenly stumbled, dropping the container, the drum popping its seams and launching a spray of water onto those nearby. Work stopped a moment as prison guards shouted at the man, soldiers laughed, and one of Ming's assistants jogged forward with a reprimand, directing the man back to work. But Shan watched the scene only out of the corner of his eye, for as the others had watched the little drama, Ko had kept moving, changing his route, carrying a box near the stack of crates where with a quick motion he snatched something and stuffed it into his shirt without breaking stride.

As Ko carried his load to a waiting truck Shan stepped toward the crate where his son had stopped. It was a receptacle for several types of equipment. Binoculars, belt packs, canteens, even folding shovels. But Ko had taken something small. Near the front were compasses, rugged military compasses, and pocket knives. Ko must have taken a compass or a knife, perhaps both.

Shan watched the youth weave through the crowd of workers, cutting in front of older men who clearly struggled with their burdens, setting another box on the tailgate of a truck then stepping along a line of soldiers, two fingers raised, until a soldier gave him a cigarette and lit it for him. Ko leaned back on another truck with a superior air, studying the others as he smoked, watching one of Ming's assistants set a tin mug of steaming tea on a table then quickly, carefully stepping by the table and stealthily lifting the mug, carrying it back to the truck, where he drained it. He dropped the empty mug into the shadows under the truck, observing the scene with sleepy, hooded eyes, pausing to look at Shan long enough to direct a plume of smoke toward him, not moving a muscle when an old Tibetan trusty dropped his load near Ko's feet, scattering a box of butane fuel canisters and canned goods across the ground.

"I had him assigned to us," Yao suddenly interjected from Shan's side. "As one of our porters. You haven't had a proper reunion."

"No," Shan shot back. "No reunion." He turned and faced Yao, saw that Yao was stuffing one of the pilgrim guides into a pack. "Take him off our team. Send him away," Shan demanded. The aching he felt now was alien to him, a strange mix of revulsion, anger, fear, and guilt. And an unexpected sense of loneliness. Not love, certainly not affection, just a stabbing loneliness. He recalled the years he had spent imagining Ko running, happily playing with other children, reading old teachings, going to temples on festival days to make offerings to ancestors the way Shan always had. But the real Ko was a cruel, arrogant, drug-dealing gang member. The bigger the lie the more bitter the truth.

CHAPTER ELEVEN

E lizabeth McDowell." There was reluctance in Yao's voice as he spoke the name, as if it were a truth he did not wish to acknowledge. There had been one more message from the FBI when Yao had gone back to Tan's office. "They had decided to check the travel records of everyone whose name they had. She was with Lodi all the way, not only from Beijing to Lhasa, but from Seattle to Beijing."

"She knew the Dolan collection. Lodi needed help," Shan said. He was not surprised at the news, only surprised that Yao seemed so upset by it. "They were partners in everything." He looked back toward the valley. "She would be one to appreciate the irony of what happened today," Shan said tentatively, glancing about to be sure no one else was within earshot. "Sort of a tribute to Lodi."

Yao turned to face Shan, inquiry in his eyes.

"The tomb was as fake as some of the artifacts he displays in Beijing," Shan said quietly. "It was just the foundation of an old chorten, an old shrine. The farmers in the valley probably know of a dozen such places, buried when the shrines above were demolished."

"But that robe, the old decree."

"They were real, planted to lend authenticity."

"You're saying Ming faked his discovery."

"No, someone else, to trick Ming. You know Ming lied about finding a letter suggesting the emperor's fresco had been taken to Lhadrung, to have an official excuse to come here. Now someone is lying to him. There were no complete skeletons there. Many people know where old skulls and bones can be found. I had seen the robe in the hills." Even as the words came out Shan was not certain whether he was offering himself, or many others, up for sacrifice. There were parts of Yao he had grown to grudgingly trust, other parts he would never trust.

"The robe—why would anyone give up anything so precious, just to fool

Ming? And surely whoever it was would have wanted him to think the amban's grave was in the north."

"They still do. But they are desperate now. All they can do is distract him here, because here is where they are. They gave him political treasure today, enough to distract him for a few days. Soon enough he will realize it was faked for his benefit. He will keep to the official story, because it is so politically convenient. But what he wants most of all is the amban's treasure. He thinks his competitors do not know about the Tibetans uncovering the Mountain Buddha in the hills, so he can take that at his leisure, that was why he wanted to hire me, to slowly reap the fortunes lying in shrines here. But he is desperate for the records that will tell him where the amban's treasure can be found. When he realizes the tomb was faked, he will decide it was because his competitors are close to victory, that they have confirmed the treasure is in the north, and wanted to keep him in Lhadrung."

Yao nodded agreement. "He will conclude that Khan and Lu would never give up something so valuable as that robe unless they were confident that they had something much more valuable."

"That will be his biggest mistake," Shan said, "thinking that it was Khan and Lu. He would never consider that Tibetans could devise such a trick. And all they wanted was to keep Ming in the valley, to protect something more valuable than the robe."

"His workers are going into the mountains."

"They know nothing of his true purpose, only that they must call Ming if they find anything. They are no threat to his plans."

"He won't stop," Yao stated. "Not until he finds the records that tell him where in the north the amban's treasure was left."

"Which means you're investigating the wrong crime."

"What do you mean?"

"We'll never get to the truth about the emperor's fresco and Dolan's stolen art until we unlock the mystery of the amban's death. That is why we're not going to the cave Ming assigned us to," Shan said. "The emperor has told us where we need to be, even Ming has shown us where we need to be."

"What do you mean?"

Shan pulled out the map he had taken from Ming's car. "It marks the destinations of each team," he explained, pointing to circles drawn in the remote ranges, a double circle around each of the suspected pilgrim shrines which were the targets of the new search teams. "Ming has concluded that Lodi was killed at Zhoka for a reason. He will go back eventually, when he thinks it safe. But the imperial decree at the tomb today was also a decoy. Whoever wrote the words at the bottom was trying to push the search to Zetrul Puk." He pointed to a location twenty miles north of Zhoka. "Of all the search targets, that is the most distant from Zhoka. Whoever created that tomb wanted Ming as far from Zhoka as possible, wanted to buy some time."

"The ones who killed Lodi must still be there," Yao said after a moment, "hidden underground. Corbett will eventually understand that as well and return to the ruins. But how can we go there, with all of them?" Yao asked with a gesture toward the column of figures ahead of them. "They have radios. If we leave they will tell Ming."

"One of us is going to fall, and twist an ankle. Here," Shan said, indicating a place where a path to the south crossed their trail. "About an hour from now. The other will stay to help while we send the party on. I can find the way to the gompa."

"Not much of a plan," Yao said, then shrugged. "I have weak ankles," he offered quietly.

But a quarter hour later the soldier in the front of the column halted and raised a hand in warning. A figure was frantically running down the trail above them, stumbling one moment, leaping over rocks the next, pausing to look behind him then lurching forward at a desperate pace. One of the herders, Shan assumed, it must be one of the hill people trying to avoid the soldiers. The soldier at the front of their column studied the solitary figure with binoculars, cursed, then motioned them into the rocks by the trail.

Shan hid with the others for nearly a minute then ventured a look. The figure, nearly upon them now, wore a black wool cap pulled low over his head and a dirty green army jacket. He was fifty feet from Shan when the soldier leapt out of the rocks and slapped the stock of his rifle against the man's lowered head. As the figure swayed and crumpled to the ground, the cap dropped from his head. It was Ko.

Shan was not aware of leaping forward, of scrambling over the loose rocks on the trail, only of being at the boy's side, cradling his head, dabbing at the blood where the rifle had struck.

"Damned escapee," the soldier growled, and reached for his radio.

Ko's eyes fluttered open. They looked about wildly, unfocused, then settled on Shan a moment. He seemed to recognize Shan, and pushed away Shan's hand with a look of revulsion.

"You're bleeding," Shan said in a tight voice.

Ko's lips curled into his familiar sneer. He pushed himself up on his elbows and crawled away, then started to rise. The soldier gave an exaggerated sigh and thrust a boot onto Ko's leg, pinning him to the ground as he lifted his radio.

Shan stared numbly at his son, his fingers reaching out toward Ko, then retracting, the boy glaring at him hatefully, as if Shan had been the one who had hit him.

"You don't know anything," Ko snarled at Shan.

Shan became aware of voices arguing and looked up to find Yao pushing the soldier's radio down. "Not what you think," Yao was saying. "No need to over-react."

"He's a criminal," the soldier growled. "One of those trusties, escaping from his team. A little too much trust. Should never have used them. They're like animals after a year or two behind wire. I could shoot him and no one would question it."

Shan stood and stepped between the soldier and Ko. Yao glanced at Shan nervously. "He's not from Lhadrung, not from the 404th," Yao told the soldier. "He was brought here from Xinjiang just to help us. And he's not escaping."

Shan watched as Ko's fingers wrapped around a sharp stone he seemed about to slam into the soldier's shin.

"I asked him to meet us," Yao announced. Ko stopped moving. "I lost my navigation unit and I asked him to bring me one from the stockpile."

"We wouldn't trust the likes of him with that kind of equipment," the soldier grunted, shifting his eyes back and forth from Shan to Yao.

Yao pulled out the small leather folder with his identification card, and held it in one hand, flipping it open. "I did," Yao said, and extended his other hand, palm open, toward Ko.

The rock slipped from Ko's hand. He stared at Yao, jaw clenched, glancing at the rifle, then the hand reached inside his jacket, extracted a palm-size plastic instrument, and handed it to Yao.

The soldier seemed to deflate. He looked at the navigational device, then at the leather folder in Yao's hand. "Yes sir," he said, then pulled his boot from Ko and signaled the others to continue up the trail. "He's your problem now, Comrade Inspector," the soldier said in a resentful tone. "I'll let the other team know. They'll be glad to be rid of him. Criminals," the man spat, staring not at Ko this time, but at Shan, then slung his rifle onto his shoulder and turned to follow the column.

As Ko turned in the opposite direction, Yao stepped in front of him, blocking the trail down the slope. "Like he said, you're my problem now," he said, and pointed to the party moving above them. "I saved you because of your father," he said, indicating Shan. "Only once. Run from us and I'll not stop them from shooting."

Confusion passed over Ko's face. He studied Shan silently with squinting eyes. "Bastards," he snapped, then turned up the trail.

An hour later, just after they passed a trail that led to the south, Yao cried out in pain and Shan looked up to see him sprawled on a rock, holding his ankle as the soldier jogged back to investigate. Shan darted forward to reach the inspector's side before the soldier. He lifted Yao's pant leg and quickly began wrapping it with his rolled up handkerchief.

"Sprained," he explained to the soldier as he tied the makeshift binding in a tight knot. "Won't be walking much more today."

Yao quickly ordered the party on, saying he and Shan would meet them at the cave the next day.

"We'll need help," Shan called out as the soldier pulled away. "He may need to be carried."

Without hesitating the soldier jerked his thumb toward Ko, ordering him to help rearrange supplies for the three into the packs Shan and Yao had been carrying. In ten minutes the main party was over a ridge and out of sight. Yao was bending to untie Shan's handkerchief when Ko dropped one of the packs at Shan's feet.

"You lied to them." There was a glimmer of curiosity in his voice.

"We decided to take a different route," Shan said.

Yao picked up the pack and shoved it toward Ko. "Here's how it is. You run and I won't trouble over you. I'll just call in troops. Not prison guards, mountain troops. They'll use helicopters with infrared. If you're lucky a snow leopard will get you first. If the soldiers find you they will put you in a helicopter. Then they will throw a party. Do you know what that means?"

From the grim way Ko studied the barren, rocky landscape Shan knew he understood. Ko shouldered the pack and, his face taut with anger, gave a mock bow then gestured for Shan to lead the way.

They reached Zhoka an hour before dusk, approaching in a wary silence. The ruins seemed unusually cold. A steady wind moaned through the broken walls. Ko hung back, uncertainty on his face. He removed the pack and held it in front of him, as though he would need to defend himself.

"It's an old prison," Ko said when they stopped at the edge of the ruins. "I can tell, I can feel it. Just look at it," he said in a voice that had suddenly gone cold and hollow. His words stopped Shan. Shan studied the ruins again, looking as if for the first time at the maze of rock walls, the dust that swirled in the chill wind, making shifting, foreboding shadows, the patches of blackness that marked entrances into the subterranean passages. "They've always had prisons, always killed thousands," Ko said. "You can feel it." He wasn't speaking to anyone in particular. When he looked and saw that Shan was listening, his sneering expression returned. He shouldered the pack and pushed past Shan.

"Not a prison," Shan said to his back. "A monastery. A place of lamas."

He did not think his son had heard. But Ko called back. "You're a fool, not to know it's a place of death," he muttered, then kept walking.

They circled through the outer rim of the ruins, watching, pausing often to listen. They walked through eerie pools of silence, where old walls blocked the wind. When a pika scurried along a wall Shan looked up to see Ko crouching, one hand clenched in a fist, nervously watching the walls. Ko seemed to sense Shan's stare and he cut his eyes resentfully, straightened, then pushed on to the lead. "There!" he warned when he reached the next wall. "People are waiting in the shadows. An ambush!" There was a new sound, faint but regular, a quiet murmuring.

Shan stepped ahead, staying in the shadows, until two figures came into view, hovering by a dim yak dung fire: a big man in a brown felt hat and dirty fleece coat, holding a girl on his lap, comforting her, patting her back. As Shan approached he realized the man wasn't speaking or crying but humming.

"Do you need help," Shan called softly, in Tibetan.

"If you're asking if I'm okay," came the reply in English as Shan stepped forward, "I could do with a pizza and a beer." It was Corbett, holding Dawa.

Yao darted to the American, handed him one of their water bottles.

Dawa seemed in a state of exhaustion. She murmured a greeting, then rolled over in Corbett's arms, her head on his shoulder. As he drank Corbett seemed to notice how Shan's eyes searched the shadows. "I had to come back here, to understand why Lodi died here. Lokesh said he understood, but he said I was wrong about why, that I came for the same reason he was coming, because of the sleeping deities. He said imagine a house full of slumbering saints, and people trying to kill them in their beds."

For a moment, as Corbett looked at Shan there was helplessness in his eyes. "Lokesh isn't here," he said. "I mean he's here but not with us. The three of us arrived yesterday. He said he had to find an old lama here. When Lokesh couldn't find him in any of the surface ruins he said he had to find the way underground. It's been over ten hours," he added in a worried whisper.

"Into the place with the blood," a small muffled voice said from the American's shoulder, "into the blackness where death waits."

"Fiona," Shan said, "is she—"

"She is safe," Dawa said, lifting her head. "But when she learned I had not had time to understand Zhoka she sent me back with Uncle Jara. She said if I have only a limited time in the mountains this is where I should be. But as soon as we arrived Liya appeared and took Aku Jara away. When I asked him why, he just said it was the Mountain Buddha."

"You mean he was frightened of it?" Shan asked.

"Yes. I don't know. What is it, Uncle Shan? What is the Mountain Buddha?"

"I don't know, Dawa," Shan admitted uneasily.

As they made camp around a small fire in the sheltering corner of two crumbling walls, Corbett explained that when he had regained consciousness he had found his clothes stripped off, replaced with Tibetan homespun. They had taken his passport, wallet, notes, and put a prayer box around his neck. He spoke of the events without rancor, in a strange, distant tone. "They wanted me to think you were dead. I think some of them thought you were dead. But Liya came back by the next afternoon and confided in me, said you would be safe. She said she knew I would have to leave, but that I should please try to understand the importance of the words spoken about me, about the rainbow, because they were one of the true things about my life. She said even if I didn't believe them everyone in the village did, and it had given them great hope. She said she was sorry, that they must seem like barbarians, that she kept my things in a sack. She gave it to me, asking only that I wear the clothes of Bumpari until I left, she begged me, to let the people there keep believing. I could go anytime and just think of my time there as a little Tibetan vacation."

"You're still wearing the clothes," Shan observed.

The American offered an uncertain grin. "They're just getting comfortable." Corbett abruptly turned at the sound of running feet behind them. Ko appeared, back from looking for firewood with Yao, walking now, trying, but not succeeding, to hide his alarm. "There is blood," he announced, turning to point in the direction he had come.

Ko led them to an intersection of two ruined alleyways, where Yao waited, studying the bright crimson drops that stained a flat rock. "Boots here," the inspector said, pointing to imprints in the dry soil. "Soft shoes here," he said, pointing to nearby indentations. "The boots waited for the soft shoes, and leapt out. There was a struggle then the one in shoes broke away," he concluded, and pointed over the wall, at the top of which were more drops of blood. "Impossible to follow."

They ate in wary silence, and Yao was laying out blankets as Shan read the pilgrim's guide for Zhoka, when Ko muttered a low, frightened curse and pressed his back against the nearest wall. Shan turned to see a figure in the shadow, curling up against a rock. As Corbett coaxed the fire brighter, and Yao found one of the battery lamps, Shan stepped to the newcomer with a blanket.

"We missed you," he said.

Lokesh gave only a small murmur of acknowledgment. Shan brought him tea, but he would not drink. Corbett brought him an apple but he would not eat. Finally Dawa just sat with him, holding a hand, until both were asleep.

"That bounty for me," Shan said as he and the American studied the pair. "I presented myself. You should pay me a hundred dollars."

"I suppose . . ." Corbett began uncertainly.

"I will give it to Lokesh, for bus fare for Dawa's parents. They should come home."

Corbett smiled. "The American taxpayers would be honored."

When Shan awoke at dawn Lokesh was sitting cross-legged on one of the walls surveying the ruins. Not surveying, Shan saw as he approached his old friend. Praying. His hands were wrapped in a ritual gesture Shan stopped to study. It was not a mudra Lokesh used often. The right hand was crossed over the left, the middle finger and thumbs touching as if he were about to snap his fingers. It was a warrior mudra, meant to invoke a wrathful deity.

Shan sat beside his old friend and tried to find words, starting to speak more than once but stopping short, the sound hanging on his tongue like a small groan.

"Where did you journey inside the rock, all those hours?" Shan asked at last.

"I saw no one. I visited old paintings. I sat in every chamber I could find. It was very dark. It is hard sometimes in such darkness to know if you are moving or the world is moving about you."

Shan studied his friend. Lokesh was still investigating, seeking in a different way, trying to sense the true nature of the enigmatic gompa.

"Gendun is in there," Lokesh said.

"We don't know that for certain."

Lokesh sighed. He seemed disappointed in Shan's words. "Not the way that inspector knows things. But he is in there. He is doing what Surya was going to do. He is putting Zhoka back in its place. If it is not too late," the old Tibetan added.

Shan looked back over the ruins. The words might have had the air of witchcraft to some, senile ramblings to others. Shan didn't entirely understand himself what Gendun was doing in the dark recesses of the old Buddhist power place. He suspected that putting Zhoka back in its place had something to do with changing the people in the lands that surrounded it. Perhaps restoring it was little different from what the monks who had originally built the earth taming temple had done. It was as if Gendun had gone inside to find an old furnace whose coals had been stoked and banked decades earlier, to revive the last dim spark before it died. But how did anyone, even the holy men of Yerpa, restore such a place?

Shan still didn't fully understand what Zhoka had been. Perhaps that was the greatest mystery, the one that would explain all else. It was a place of great history, of deep magic, of saints and deities, connected even to a faraway emperor in a faraway time, a place the old Tibetans would die to protect.

"I went into every meditation cell I could find," Lokesh said suddenly. "I descended into every hole, hoping it was a tunnel. I found many old paintings, some of images I had never seen before. We have seen only a tiny part of what was meant to be."

"But the passages leading farther inside are all collapsed," Shan said.

"Yes. I found some small tunnels leading to shrines but the shrines led nowhere else. They were all places of preparation. For somewhere else."

Corbett appeared, with a bowl of tea for each. After he drank, Lokesh looked up, and rubbed his eyes, as if just coming awake. "I found the beginning place for pilgrims. Come." He did not elaborate but climbed down and began briskly walking to a ruin nearly fifty yards away, as the others followed. Shan had taken the huge pile of rubble to be a collapsed hall. But the hall was not fully collapsed and Lokesh had found a narrow passage inside.

They climbed down a narrow flight of stairs and entered a chamber inhabited by demons. Every inch of the surviving walls and ceiling had been painted with the images of wrathful protector demons. Yao, carrying his small pack, produced his copy of the pilgrim's guide and leafed through the pages. "Newcomers may only enter the earth temple through the garden of the demons who watch over it, to all sides and the sky above."

Yao looked up from his reading for a moment and seemed to lock his gaze with that of a blue demon above him. "Here is where you leave your life behind, for only by doing so may you attain the heaven beyond. Be terrified, or do not continue to the four gates. Become pure or you will not know which is heaven and which is hell. Be always a pilgrim or you will be blind to what you seek."

"The pilgrim meditated on the demons to become pure," Shan explained.

"And then descended to the four gates of the mandala," Lokesh said.

"But there were only two gates," a voice said from the shadows behind them. The beam of Corbett's light found Liya, who sat against the wall. The side of her face was bruised, a line of dried blood where the skin on her cheek had been split. As Dawa ran and embraced her she extended her hand as if to ward off any aid. "I'm not really hurt. They jumped me, those same two. I scratched the big one on the cheek when he grabbed me. He hit me and I ran." She straightened and looked at Shan. "Two gates, only two stairways down."

Lokesh reached into a pocket and extracted a stone. "I found this by that waterfall. I think it had fallen from above, where it is all shadow now." He handed Shan a small piece of rock, no more than two inches long.

Shan rolled it over in his palm, looking inquiringly at Lokesh, then studied it closely. One side was painted green. Shan and the old Tibetan exchanged a knowing smile, then Shan gestured for the others to follow him outside, showing them how the entrance to the tunnel was lined up with the end of the collapsed hall. "Probably it was all one structure, so from the time of entering to greet the demons the pilgrim had the sense of being inside the earth." He squatted at the top of the stairs and made a circle in the soil.

"One of the basic symbols in Tibetan tradition is the circle, the fundamental shape of the mandala," he explained. "Symbolism was used throughout the construction of gompas, incorporated into the architecture. Several old gompas had central structures built on the scheme of a mandala, three or four stories high, creating three-dimensional mandalas to represent sacred mountains and the ascent to Mount Meru, the center of the universe, the summit of heaven."

"But everything here was destroyed," Corbett observed. "Even if there had been a mandala palace, the army leveled it."

"If you were trying to reach the earth deities, if you were taming the demons who lived in the earth, where would you put your mandala? In the earth," Shan suggested, and pointed toward the tunnel that led down to the fresco room and drew a line at the base of the circle on the ground, and another at the top, representing the collapsed tunnel on the opposite side of the ruins, then asked for Corbett's compass. "These tunnels are on an east-west axis." He demonstrated his point using the compass. Traditionally a mandala had four gates, aligned in the cardinal directions, each associated with complex symbols, each represented by a separate color. "The arrangement of the gates would depend on the deity at the center." Shan cast a look of inquiry toward Lokesh. "If the earth is to be tamed then it must be the Lord of the Thunderbolt." Lokesh nodded. "Then the east gate will be white, the south yellow, and the west red. And here," Shan said, marking a point in the circle halfway between the east and west, "is the waterfall with the old writing on the wall. The green wall. Marking the north gate."

"But there is no gate, no other sign of a mandala," Yao protested.

"Somehow it is the way inside the sacred mountain mandala," Shan said. "Carved out of rock, incorporating natural features like the underground stream. It is the palace of the artists, the place the amban referred to, the place of secrets. There will be three or four levels, in concentric circles, each smaller than the one below."

But it did not feel like heaven as they stepped through the dimly lit fresco room, packs on their backs, half an hour later. Dawa, who had found Surya there, covered with blood, buried her head in Corbett's shoulder. Yao had found an old staff and held it like a weapon, keeping behind Ko, as if he expected the youth to flee at any moment.

Shan paused, Liya at his side, shining the light on the patterns of blood on the wall. "Lodi made these shapes," he said, "as he lay dying. On the top he wrote about the cave of the Mountain God."

The words had a strange effect on Liya. She clamped her hand on his arm as if in warning and glanced around as if to see who else might have heard, then shot him an angry glance.

"Where is it?" Shan pressed. "Where is the Mountain God, the golden Buddha?"

"That has nothing to do with the stolen art, nothing to do with dead emperors," Liya said, her voice full of warning.

"People will die if you try to liberate the prisoners," Shan said in a desperate whisper. "Many people."

"People will die if we don't," she shot back.

As Liya turned to step away Shan touched her arm. "Wait," he said, and pointed to the long oval with the circle inside, and the square inside the circle, then reached into his pocket. "Something occurred to me when we were climbing the mountains yesterday." He pulled out the dzi bead Liya had given him at Bumpari and extended it, fingers on each end. "He collected these beads, and each has a set of symbols."

Liya's gaze did not leave the drawing. "You're right!" she exclaimed. "He drew it like a bead! A square means access to earth, a circle access to heaven. An earth door inside a heaven door," she said in a perplexed tone.

"Was he trying to tell you how to get inside?"

"No," Liya replied. "He did not know the way in, none of us do, only that the palace exists and must be saved."

"Then perhaps he was explaining how to find the Mountain Buddha," Shan ventured, watching Liya turn away as if she feared revealing something by her reaction. "Or saying someone else had found a way in." He left Liya staring at the drawing with pain in her eyes.

Five minutes later, at the side of the frigid channel, Shan borrowed the staff and stepped into the stream at the base of the falls, one end of the rope tied to his waist as Corbett held the other end. He probed the waterfall with the stick, each time hitting solid rock five feet behind the cascade. He tried the base of the falls, behind the rock bed of the stream, and could find no bottom. There was a deep pool directly under the falls.

As he reached the far side he extracted the small lantern from his pocket and studied the faded images. He saw now that there was a small painting above the old writing he had seen before, two robed figures seated on top of a mountain. One wore the conical hat of a teacher.

"Life," a familiar voice rasped behind him. Lokesh was there, nearly knee deep in the frigid water, pointing to the faded letters, one hand on the safety rope. "And nature," he added, pointing to another. He paused, studying the images of the lama and student, then a soft laugh escaped his lips. "He asks the novice a teaching riddle."

"What is the nature of life," Shan said. As he turned to call out to the others, explaining the words, he saw that Lokesh had released his grip on the guide rope and was staring at the base of the falls, into the blackness of the pool, his eyes suddenly serene, his mouth turned upward in a grin.

"We know the nature of life," the old Tibetan said and leaned forward until the water began to pour onto his crown.

"No!" Shan shouted, and lunged to grab his friend.

But it was too late. Lokesh, grinning, spread out his arms and let himself drop forward, into the falls, disappearing into the black pool. The nature of life was a man falling into a well, his eyes wide open.

CHAPTER TWELVE

He's killed himself!" Liya gasped. "The waterfall will trap him at the bottom!" There was no thrashing, no sign of Lokesh beneath the black surface of the water.

The terrible stillness left by her words was broken by a flurry of movement to Shan's side. Ko grabbed the light from Corbett's hand, shoved Yao against the wall, and leapt into the water, exactly where Lokesh had disappeared.

Shan stared in horror, vaguely aware of Corbett cursing, of Dawa crying. Then he dropped the pack from his back, stripped off his coat, and stepped into the water. He did not look back, just clenched his light tightly and dropped into the waterfall.

The churning, frigid water wrenched his body, driving him down, deeper into the blackness. The pool seemed to have no bottom, no side after he left the narrow chute where he had jumped. He pushed with his legs, fought to move through the water with his one free hand, the other aiming the light to find something ahead. But there was nothing. Lokesh and Ko, both of whom had worn more clothing, might still be sinking, falling through the blackness until their lungs burst, until there was no chance of ever rising again. The old land gods, a voice moaned in his head. Lokesh had gone to meet the ancient land gods, who would never give him, or Ko, back. Then he realized his own lungs were screaming. He pushed upward, fighting the coldness, struggling against his panic, and broke into a dark chamber, gasping its cold air, fearful at first that the blackness below would pull him down again, then fearful of the strange sobbing he heard.

He swam toward a tiny light, collided with a black rock wall, and pulled himself up onto the wall. The sobbing was closer. He wiped his eyes, trying to make out the dim shapes before him. It was Lokesh and Ko. But they weren't sobbing, they were laughing. They had taken off their shoes and were wringing water from their socks.

Ko saw him first, his amused expression instantly changing to a scowl.

"Welcome to the real Zhoka," Lokesh exclaimed, and shined his light on the walls.

A minute later, Shan was back in the tunnel, excitedly explaining their discovery. "It is the north gate," he confirmed. "The chamber is full of paintings and words." He quickly described how a wall had been cleverly built across the pool by the ancient builders, to give the appearance of the falls cascading down a natural rock face, leaving a chute in the center for those pilgrims who could answer the old teaching riddle.

"I can't swim," Liya said in a low moan as she began to grasp Shan's meaning.

"It isn't really swimming," Shan said. "You just fall and move toward the lights. Lokesh and Ko will shine their lights in the water. We just need to protect the gear."

Corbett began emptying the packs, and produced rope and two heavy plastic bags that had been packed as ground covers. As he began lining the packs with the bags Shan stopped him. "Your clothes. The water is freezing. Keep room for your clothes, so you will have dry ones to put on."

Yao looked at him, aghast.

"Swim in your underclothes," Shan said. "It's dark, no one will see. Follow the light."

Corbett, grinning, tossed two tee shirts for Dawa and Liya to wear, then finished repacking and extracted a long length of rope, explaining he would go first with the rope tied to his waist, Yao holding the other end, so Dawa and Liya could follow the rope, then they could pull the packs through from the other side.

Ten minutes later they were all on the other side, making tea, after Corbett showed them how to use the small gas stove the army had provided. As Dawa sorted what extra dry clothes she could find for Shan, Ko, and Lokesh, Yao began studying the chamber with his lamp. The pool carved a long half oval into the room, whose curving back wall had two stairways cut in the living stone, leading to passages extending to the east and west.

"The circular tunnel," Yao said as Shan joined him. "We are inside your mandala." He looked back at the black pool. "Surely pilgrims weren't expected to enter that way."

"There were many ways," Lokesh said in a solemn voice. "But each was a test. You read the guide. Be terrified or do not continue. Surely there were pilgrims who needed to come through the water, may even have been told by the lamas here they must do so. The heart of the world is not to be easily attained. Here is where your life is left behind," he said, repeating the words of the pilgrim guide.

"What do you mean, the heart of the world?" Yao asked.

"The mandala is a form of the universe. The essence of the world." He gazed at Yao with an expression of sudden curiosity.

Yao frowned. "You mean a model of the universe," the inspector said uncertainly. "A pretend place."

"No," Lokesh readily replied. "The opposite. More real than real." He saw the confusion on Yao's face and shrugged. "Outside, the universe can be difficult to see. But here—" he gestured toward the walls, which seemed alive with color and shapes, "it is within the reach of your arms."

Dawa pushed against Lokesh, her hand reaching up to hold his arm, staring uneasily at the walls.

"Acala, Tamdin, the gatekeepers," Lokesh said, speaking to two of the images in a happy, nostalgic tone, as if greeting old friends. He moved slowly along the wall, pausing at a vivid painting of a figure holding a staff, surrounded by flames, a mongoose in his hand. "The king of the north," he explained, passing his palm over the surface, as Shan had seen Gendun do at the Stone Tower. When he stopped there was a new glow in his eyes. He rubbed his palms together then leaned toward Shan. "There have been prayers," he whispered.

Shan stared at him, but before he could press the old Tibetan to explain Lokesh stepped beyond the tunnel, to the wall directly opposite the underwater entrance, raising his light. An inscription was painted in gold over a painting of the Historical Buddha. "Does one who has immersed himself in the stream that flows to enlightenment," Lokesh read, "say of himself I have entered the stream?" He looked back with a grin. It was a familiar line, taken from the ancient Diamond Sutra.

"Is every writing to be a riddle?" Yao demanded in a frustrated tone. "And why here?" he added, echoing Shan's own thought.

"The answer to the riddle is no," Shan said slowly. "Because having conscious thought of being in the stream means you have not attained the selfless state of enlightenment."

"So we must not recognize the water," Corbett said in a new, eager voice, as if warming to the game. He paced along the pool. "And if the water wasn't here, what? We'd be dry," he mused. "We'd be warmer." He paused and examined the room again. "We'd be able to look up and make sense of that," he said, shining his light on the ceiling.

The ceiling was uneven, each side curving sharply inward to meet at the center, as if being folded along a long, even seam, each side visible only to those who stood directly beneath it. On the side where Corbett and Shan stood it had been painted with half of a white snow lion, with a turquoise mane, its mouth open in a traditional pose, a ferocious expression that somehow looked more like a laugh than a roar, one paw raised and bent, a tiny monk cradled in it.

"Half a lion," Yao called from the opposite side, "a garland of skulls wrapped around its front leg."

There was a wrathful lion protector on the ceiling, one side of its body painted on each half of the segmented ceiling.

After studying the chamber another quarter hour, finding no other riddle, no other way to interpret the words from the old sutra, they ventured into the western tunnel. Yao counted paces as they moved, pausing often to add to the rough map he was drawing in his pad. Their progress was slow. The inner wall was lined with chapels, many tiny, no more than six feet wide, some twice as long, each filled with dazzling paintings, some with altars lined with small figures of saints, aspects of the Buddha in bronze, copper, silver, and gold.

Lokesh lingered, refusing to be rushed as he visited the chapels. Shan and Yao found him sitting in the third one, before a hanging thangka of protector demons, Liya standing beside him. "Someone's been here," she said, and pointed to a tiny column of ash, the remains of an incense stick extending from a stone holder on the altar.

"It could have been long ago," Yao said.

"No. You can smell it," Liya said. "It's fresh. And a butter lamp."

"But I told you," Lokesh said, "Gendun has been here. He knows how to bring the deities back."

"I didn't think . . . Alone in the caves . . ." Liya began, then with a shudder seemed to accept Lokesh's words.

After they examined the first six chapels, Corbett protested that it would take hours to study all the art. "If the corridor follows the pattern of a circle," he said, "then if some of us go ahead we can't get lost, or separated for long."

Yao agreed. "If we find nothing in an hour, we leave," the inspector warned as he took a step down the tunnel. "This is not an archaeological expedition. We are seeking criminals."

Archaeological criminals, Shan almost reminded him as he glanced at Lokesh, engrossed in a painting, then followed Yao. Had Surya found his way inside the mandala palace, he wondered. Had Shan somehow betrayed the old Tibetans by bringing outsiders into the ancient temple? One moment he was eagerly looking for Gendun, the next worried about what would happen if Yao and Corbett stumbled upon the old lama. Or the Mountain Buddha.

When they reached the rock debris of the collapsed western gate Shan aimed his light toward the ceiling at the right corner, where they had found the watching eye on the far side of the collapsed rock. He saw now that the eye had been one of over two dozen painted in a line below a blackness that marked where the slab had fallen out of the ceiling to block the stair corridor. Beneath the watching eyes was a huge mural of a fierce protector deity, wearing a garland of skulls. It was an image Shan had seen often before—except for one small figure, hanging over the shoulder of the wrathful deity, a small white lion holding a lotus blossom. He pointed it out to Yao.

"Could be a signature of the artist," Yao suggested.

"Tibetan artists almost never signed their works in any manner. It could be a sign, part of the trail the old ones left for pilgrims." Shan aimed his light at the other painted deities. Several had similar lions at their shoulders.

Suddenly Yao switched off his light and pushed Shan's arm down. "Listen!"

Shan extinguished his light. Someone was coming out of one of the chapels they had passed, using an electric light covered with a cloth, perhaps a shirttail. Shan felt Yao push him sideways, realized the inspector intended for them to flank the intruder, one on either side.

The figure approached slowly, sometimes crouching, sometimes turning about as if wary of being followed. Even when he stood from his crouches he did not fully straighten, Shan saw, for he held something heavy in the crook of one arm.

From down the passage a jubilant voice called out. "Blessed Buddha!"

The unexpected exclamation from Lokesh caused the figure to spin about. As he did so the muffled light rose toward his head, illuminating his face in a hollow mask of jaw, cheeks, and forehead. It was Ko.

When Shan and Yao switched on their lights there was an instant of fear in the boy's eyes. As he recognized them his body visibly tightened and he leaned against the wall, hiding the object in his hand, which glittered in the dim light. His lips curled over his teeth and he brandished his own light like a weapon.

"You should be careful," Yao said to Ko in a quiet voice. "There are thieves in these ruins." Shan glanced at Yao. The inspector had decided to refrain from the obvious, the thing that stuck like dry sand in Shan's own throat. Ko was stealing from the chapels.

"Let's see what evidence you have uncovered," Yao said and stepped forward.

For a moment Ko's face had the look of a cornered animal, a savage resentment, then it stiffened and seemed to collapse as the inspector pulled the object from his arm. It was a small gold Buddha, ten inches high, inlaid with precious stones around its base.

"Excellent," Yao said, extending the statue for Shan to see. "Proof that we have discovered a place the thieves have not yet looted. It will allow us to focus our search."

Ko's pockets bulged with angular objects. A gilded trumpet hung on a braided cord from his shoulder. Ko stood in silence, looking at the floor as Shan lifted the trumpet and slipped the cord down his son's arm. "This was made from a human thigh bone, Xiao Ko," Shan said. "Probably from a holy man who lived centuries ago."

Ko looked up with revulsion, and Shan somehow knew it had nothing to do with the bone. Without thinking about it Shan had addressed him as Little Ko, a traditional term of affection fathers and uncles might use. His son seemed to despise the words more than he hated Yao's confiscation of his treasure.

"My name is Ko," the youth snapped. "Tiger Ko," he added, using the gang name in his criminal record. Abruptly he pushed Shan, shoving him against the wall, and bolted into the darkness.

"Children," Yao said with an exaggerated sigh, handing Shan the little Buddha.

Shan looked into the darkness after Ko. His son couldn't go far. The tunnel circled back.

Shan retraced their steps, looking into the chapels, and found an empty space in the third chapel he entered, a small clean place outlined in the dust that covered the rest of the altar. "Forgive him," he whispered to the blue deity above the altar as he returned the statue to its place. "He was not raised well." Noticing a heavy peg halfway up a side wall amid a row of painted skulls, he hung the jewel-encrusted trumpet on it, then paused. The peg was inserted into the eye of one of the skulls. He swept his light over the wall. There was another hole, incorporated into the eye of another skull. The holes were invisible to the casual glance. On the floor, by the altar, was a dust-encrusted peg, the same size as the first. He lifted it hesitantly, wary of disturbing anything in the ancient chapels. It fit perfectly into the eyehole. He searched the walls again and found four more holes, all the same size, all disguised as part of the painting. They formed no pattern. It could simply have been another clever way the builders had integrated the beauty of the wall with functionality, a way to hang robes, whisks, trumpets, and other ceremonial implements. But as he proceeded back toward the north gate, Shan found more holes in the corridor, in no regular spacing, only three or four every ten feet, all worked so perfectly into the overlaying paintings as to be effectively hidden to the casual observer. Zhoka's heaven was intended only for those who earned it with both their wits and their faith.

As Yao and Shan followed the curve of the tunnel toward the south they seemed to pass through pockets of scents. Incense, Shan smelled, some recent, most older, musty, the complex scents made in the traditional ways with ten or twenty fragrant ingredients. Decay was sometimes in the air, interspersed with the fragrance of cedar. And, very faintly, something different, something alien to the temple.

"You smell it?" Yao asked.

"Tobacco," Shan nodded. "Cigarette smoke." He remembered the cigarette butts they had found above, near the excavation, and the cigar butts Corbett had found near the blood stains. They followed the tunnel as it curved to the south, passing more chapels, but found only ruin where the gate should have been, broken pieces of stone bearing the yellow paint of the southern king, huge slabs that had tumbled from the ceiling, blocking the passage, broken timbers, signs perhaps of a wooden stairway. There was no sign of Ko, though twice Shan heard sounds that may have been running feet. Each time he fought the urge to run and find his son. Ko, Shan sadly knew, was unlikely to stray far from the riches of the temple.

Yao caught Shan staring into the darkness. "It was a brave thing he did, jumping in to save Lokesh."

Shan offered a nod, not because he agreed, but in gratitude for Yao's tone. Shan knew his son had not gone into water to help anyone, only to escape them.

Ruin was in the east as well. The collapse of the eastern entrance had been more devastating than that of the opposite side, with great shards of rock on the floor of the approaching tunnel, the collapsed roof almost blocking their passage, obliterating any artwork or message at the entrance that might have yielded a clue.

They walked quickly back, silently, as if Yao, too, felt the sudden need to find the others. When they reached them in the chapel near the collapsed western gate, below the line of eyes, Lokesh had a serene glow on his face, a kind Shan had seen on his friend's countenance only a few times in all the years they had known each other.

But they had found no answers to the riddles of the tunnels.

"There is no sign of the amban," Yao said to Shan. There was a hint of accusation in his tone. "Not even any sign of the thieves except some smoke. Smoke," he repeated pointedly.

"But this is the palace," Lokesh said, as if not understanding Yao's frustration.

Yao ignored the old Tibetan. "There is no other level. This is not the amban's palace, and if this is not where the amban hid, the thieves would have reached the same conclusion. They could be miles away. We have wasted the day, and unless we are going back into that black water," he said in a tone that told them he was loath to do so, "we have all but imprisoned ourselves in this place."

"The snow lions are the message," Shan suggested in a tentative voice. "The snow lion at the northern gate must mean something." He took them back to the ruins of the western gate and showed them the small lions hovering near the shoulders of the deities.

"There's more words!" Liya exclaimed, holding her light close to one of the lions to reveal a few tiny Tibetan letters. "And more, over each lion."

"The true nature of things is void," Lokesh read slowly. "The clear light of emptiness is the dawning of awareness." They were words from the Bardo, the death rites.

"Emptiness." Corbett aimed his light into the black tunnel. "We've got lots of emptiness."

"But the words are incomplete," Shan said, turning to Lokesh. "The actual words of the rites are different."

Lokesh nodded. "One phrase is left out. 'The clear light of emptiness, without a center or a circumference, is the dawning of the awareness.' Those are the correct words to be spoken."

"What is emptiness with a circumference?" Shan asked. "A hole," he said a moment later, then quickly explained what he had found in the chapel, the oddly disguised holes and pegs.

Shan gathered what pegs he could find as they searched the chapels again. Ten minutes later Dawa called out excitedly from a chapel halfway between the east and south gates. As Shan arrived with Corbett, Liya and the girl were standing with their fingers in four holes, all on one wall, each a spot on the coat of a small snow lion, the four small lions arrayed around a larger image of a wrathful protector deity, the topmost lion cradling a tiny monk in his paw.

Shan inserted the long, heavy pegs he had gathered into the holes. They were evenly spread, diagonally left to right, the bottom left one eighteen inches off the floor, the top one, three feet to the right, a foot from the top of the wall.

"A stair!" Liya cried.

"But it leads nowhere," Corbett pointed out.

Shan stepped onto the first peg, then the second, bending to fit under the ceiling. At first the rock above appeared to be solid but as he probed with his light, pushing at several spots, a piece of the ceiling lifted. "It's wood," he explained. "A door." The hatchway had been carefully carved and painted to look like the stone roof, its edges irregular, matching a curving seam in the rock. Shan pushed the cover out of the way and illuminated a chamber above. Musty, incense-laden air drifted down as he stepped back off the makeshift ladder.

He turned, gesturing for Lokesh to have the honor of leading them into the ancient chambers above. But a slender figure burst into the room, hit the first rung with a leap and with a blur was up and into the shadows overhead. The only sign he had been there was a small bright object that fell from his pocket as he scrambled up the ladder.

Corbett picked the object up and examined it, an elegant silver figure of a god. "Your son," the American said to Shan, "has very good taste."

The small entry hall on the second level was lined with paintings of demon protectors. Beyond it, however, was not a curving tunnel as below but a sprawl of arches, entries to small chapels, each opening into at least two other chapels. It was a labyrinth.

"There still must be a ring shape to the design, a chain of chapels that circles the rest," Lokesh said. "Just hidden in the chaos." He gestured toward the largest of the paintings in the hall and the words beneath it.

Shan recognized Atisha, one of the greatest of Tibetan saints, framed by smaller images of lesser saints, each in a little square. Atisha wore the close-fitting contoured cap ending in a point that was associated with him. The smaller images were in the traditional formal style, but Atisha sat in a relaxed, asymmetrical pose, one foot extended beyond the edge of the large square that surrounded him, as if he were about to step out of the painting. The painting had a whimsical air. As he stepped closer to it his foot knocked another large peg. On the floor in front of him were four of the long wall pegs, as if someone had climbed up and pulled the pegs out behind them to conceal their passage.

"The greatest meditation," Liya said. Shan looked up to see her reading a line of text below the painting. "The greatest wisdom." That was all.

"It's an abbreviation," Lokesh observed in a contemplative voice, "a summary. The full verse goes 'The greatest meditation is a mind that lets go, the greatest wisdom is seeing through appearances.'"

Yao pulled out the rough map he had made of the lower ring, and turned it over, sketching the chamber they occupied.

"And here," Lokesh continued, pointing toward more writing under a mendicant's staff suspended on hooks over one of the doorways. "'It is the only thing that is ours yet we look for it elsewhere,'" he read. "An old teaching. It means we carry the truth with us, just don't recognize it."

Shan took at step into the maze of chapels. "Rice," he said, looking at Corbett, who carried the food supply.

The American looked at him quizzically, but silently opened the pack and handed Shan a small white cloth sack. Shan pulled open one corner. "We must stay together," he said as he slid the cover over the hatch that led to the lower floor. "From here we will make a trail," he explained, sprinkling a line of rice as he moved.

They had reached the fourth chamber when Yao called Shan's name. Shan looked away from another of the rich paintings to see that the inspector's light was aimed at a black cylinder on the floor, a metallic lamp matching the ones the soldiers had packed for them, its lens and bulb broken. It was the one Ko had carried.

Corbett studied the floor around the light. There was dust on the floor, from crumbling plaster overhead, showing patterns of bootprints in the dust. "He was running," the American said. "He must have looked back and hit the wall." Corbett gestured toward the pillar that separated the two doorways in front of them.

Shan stared into the blackness ahead. Without a light Ko could fall to his death, could wander aimlessly in the eerie labyrinth, could even stumble into the thieves, the killers, provoking a violent reaction.

He saw movement to his side, and watched as Dawa pulled Lokesh's arm. "Aku, you are right!" she exclaimed in a loud whisper. "Some of the gods are still alive!" She bent and pointed, causing the old Tibetan, then Shan, to squat to make sense of her words. They saw nothing, but then Dawa took Shan's light and held it low to the floor, creating a new pattern of shadows. At first Shan saw only smudges along the edge of the dust, but then he realized they were in a line. And at the end of two of the smudges were small ovals in an arc. The fresh prints of bare feet, extending into the darkness, lost as the dust disappeared and the floor became smooth bare rock again. Gendun never wore his boots inside a temple.

As Shan stared into the blackness ahead he became vaguely aware of a discussion behind him, of Corbett asking Liya where the clue was, insisting there had to be one, of Liya futilely asking Lokesh the same question. But as Shan turned toward his old friend he saw Lokesh was lost in one of the raptures that periodically seized him, staring at another painting of Atisha the gentle saint. His hands were together at his chest, the heels and fingertips of each hand touching, the fingers bowed outward as if clasping an invisible sphere. It was the treasure box mudra.

Yao began walking deeper into the network of chapels, busily sketching the layout.

"We should go now," Shan said to Lokesh. The old Tibetan seemed not to hear. But when Dawa grabbed a fold in his shirt and gently pulled, Lokesh followed the others, walking like a blind man, the smile still on his face, his hands still acknowledging the treasure. Not the treasure the others hoped to find, Shan knew, but the treasure the ancient paintings had already deposited in Lokesh's heart.

Shan gazed at the painting until, looking about, he saw that he was alone. But as he took a step someone behind him made a small murmuring sound.

Corbett was there, with his light out, looking at the ancient saint with the same longing awe that Shan had often seen on the faces of old Tibetans.

"It doesn't feel like we should be here," the American said in a barely audible voice.

"This is where we will find them," Shan said. "The criminals you seek."

"I don't mean it that way."

Shan studied the American. "Not in an investigator's way, you mean."

Corbett nodded slowly and looked into the darkness. "Somehow I feel like this is the farthest from the world I have ever been, or ever will be. Lokesh was right. It's more real than real. People sat here centuries ago and did things more important than we will ever do."

Shan stayed silent a long time. Corbett's words were like a prayer, offered to the deities. "Lokesh sometimes speaks of true places," he said at last, "where you can glimpse the essence of the earth, or life as it was meant to be."

Corbett nodded again. "He also told me of the bayal, the hidden lands. Maybe it's the same thing. The true places are all hidden from the damned world we've created. When I swam through that black pool it didn't feel like water. It was like shadow so thick it was almost solid, like a pit where darkness became concentrated." He covered his face with a hand for a moment and breathed deeply. "How could there be criminals here?" Shan thought the investigator was speaking again, until Corbett asked another question, addressing the saint. "How could they stay criminals?"

The American reached for his water bottle and drank deeply, almost desperately, as if doing so would break the spell that held him. "Sorry," he said with a small gasp when he lowered the bottle. "I'm short on sleep I guess." He pushed past with an awkward glance and Shan began dropping rice again.

A quarter hour later they stood in the twentieth chamber since leaving the entry room, making no progress in finding a pattern in the maze of rooms or a clue among the paintings. Yao's map had become a meaningless tangle of lines. Every room had a curve built into at least one wall, there were no straight paths, at no place could they stand and see more than twenty feet away. The walls continued to be painted with scenes of the Buddhist pantheon, each room a little exquisite palace unto itself. Lokesh had returned to awareness, but strangely, the dreamlike state seemed to have shifted to Dawa. The fear that had been on the girl's face when they entered the underground complex had not stayed with her, or grown as Shan had expected, but had disappeared entirely. She had begun to smile, had even shown something that seemed close to serenity.

Suddenly Shan heard his name urgently called from the next chamber. Corbett gestured for him to hurry.

The room had no art, or at least no colorful images of deities or saints. The surface of the walls were covered with faded words. Liya quickly paced along the perimeter then pointed to the upper corner of one wall. "It begins here," she said, and slowly read. "I create a wisdom palace," she began. "It will not be small." She grew silent, scanning the text, looking at the next wall before speaking again. "It is a very old prayer," she explained. "A song really, called the Prayer for the God of the Plain." She looked at Corbett and Yao. "I think when the old artists began, this is where they started. When the Buddhists first tried to build temples in Tibet they were always torn apart by the gods in the earth, by earthquakes. This is one of the original prayers used to placate the main land gods, to calm the land so temples could be built." She looked at Shan with a small knowing smile. They stood in a place where the earth taming began, a thousand years before.

Half a dozen more rooms with only writing adjoined the first. Lokesh and Liya studied each wall, calling out excitedly as they identified the sutra or other teaching from which it was extracted. Yao, looking exhausted, sat on the floor with a water bottle and laid his map between his legs, asking if anyone could make sense of the rooms, could find anything like a passage that might lead to another gate. Shan stepped into the shadow of the next chamber. He held his hand over his light to muffle it, watching in near darkness, fighting the urge to call out for his son. At last he turned off the light and sat in the black stillness, listening.

The silence of the temple had a texture all its own. He had been in many caves, but this did not feel like a cave. There was a strange lightness to the air, an invisible energy. After several minutes he sensed a low sound, an animal-like moaning, rising and falling. He rose, still in darkness, and walked, no longer dropping rice, one hand in front of him, touching walls at first, then, inexplicably, finding he could sense where the openings lay, walking from chapel to chapel without colliding with the walls until, suddenly, a frightened groan rose a few feet in front of him. Shan froze, still not switching on the light.

"It is a very old place," he said. "If you let it, it will give you strength." He heard a sharp intake of breath.

"I was tired," Ko snapped. "I was sleeping and now you woke me."

Shan began to take a step toward the voice, stopped, turned back into the adjacent chamber long enough to silently lower his unlit lamp to the floor before advancing toward his son.

"I have food," he said. "Some walnuts." He extended the small sack he had kept in his pocket.

When Ko did not respond Shan frantically thought he had fled. Then he

229

heard a rustling of clothing, and a hand, sweeping through the air, touched the sack. Fingers closed around it and pulled it away.

"You have no light?" Ko asked in a tight voice.

"No."

"How did you find your way here?"

"I don't know," Shan said truthfully.

He heard a nut crunch in Ko's mouth. "I need a drink," Ko demanded.

"I have none."

A snort, a sound of dismissal, came through the blackness.

Shan remained still, facing the sound, trying to push back the pain in his heart. He was in one of the most beautiful places he had ever known, and his son was stealing from it, his son was feeling nothing but anger and greed.

"No one can stop me." Ko's voice in the darkness was like the growl of some cave creature.

"No one will stop you. We are here for something else. But afterwards, if you get out alive, they will send troops to find you. The soldiers in this county are bored. You heard Yao. They will make sport of it, the way they hunt leopards sometimes."

"I'm not scared of any damned soldier."

Shan sighed, wondered what deity was looking down from the walls. "I do not know how to be a father," he said very slowly. "But I could try to be a friend." He could only have said it in the darkness, without seeing the eyes of his son, or of the deities.

He heard the snorting sound again. "I'm sorry. I'll go," Shan said, and he took a step away from Ko. The darkness somehow seemed different, as if closing in about him. For a moment he felt a desperate need to be on the surface, in the light and air, away from everything.

Then an uncertain voice called to his back. "Your gang," Ko said. "What happened to your gang?"

The ten years Shan had waited to have a real conversation with his son had seemed like a century. And now, when Ko seemed ready to talk, he wanted to know about Shan's gang. Shan turned. "I told you, there was no gang. I was sent to prison by some powerful people to stop me from sending them to prison."

"I thought you lied, that you were saying that to impress that damned inspector."

Shan took a step back toward his son. "My job, it was like what Inspector Yao does today."

"If you were so important, you could have gotten me out of that prison."

"I told you. I was in prison myself." He heard his son eating the walnuts again. "If we stood back to back, walking slowly," he offered after a moment, "we could watch for lights and find the others."

"They won't want me."

"They need you. You'll just have to remove the things you put in your pocket."

"Why?"

"Because you're a trusty. Because if he learns he can rely on you there's a chance Inspector Yao may have you made a trusty when you return to your prison." Because, Shan wanted to add, you must stop offending the deities who live here.

"Right," Ko said slowly.

Shan heard the rustle of fabric, a metallic sound, of small objects clinking together. After a moment he sensed Ko rising, and felt his hand touch Shan's arm. Shan turned and they stood back to back.

"They're hard places, the coal mines," Shan observed after watching the darkness for another minute.

"Think of your worst hell," Ko said in a whisper, "times ten. They work you for twelve hours a day, every day, all year. In the cold, the rain, the snow, the heat, it doesn't matter. Barely warm rice gruel twice a day, and you pray you find an insect or a worm to eat with it. First day I was there I saw a man catch a bird and bite its head off and chew it, then stuff the whole body in his mouth, feathers and all. After a month I was looking for birds. Every night you drop with exhaustion, but the fucking lice keep waking you, chewing on your skin."

Something inside Shan prayed for Ko to stop speaking. He didn't want to hear any more. He was powerless to help his son, knew his son would have to go back to the hell he described.

"They never issue gloves," Ko continued. A distant fascination had entered his voice. "And almost no tools. Old hammers and dull chisels. My first week, I saw a man with little white caps on his fingers and asked what they were. He laughed and said they were the reward for prisoners who survived ten years. It was only later, when I saw more men that way, that I understood that it was the bones of his fingers. The skin on the tips wears away. After ten years the flesh starts shriveling and the bones show like little white knobs. Fuck me," he added, his distant voice cracking for a moment. "It's true."

Shan found himself trembling. He knew it was Ko, the nineteen-year-old convict speaking, but he heard the words in the voice of Ko as an eight-year-old boy.

They moved in silence.

"In one of those rooms I felt someone," Ko said suddenly. "I touched his shoulder. A ghost I think. He said if I would sit with him I could learn to understand. I ran and hit my head again. I imagined it. He couldn't have been real."

Shan stopped, fighting the temptation to call out Gendun's name.

"I see light!" Ko exclaimed.

Shan turned to see a glimmer in the distance. As they approached more light could be seen, then the moving beams of hand lamps, and he heard familiar voices speaking in urgent whispers. Lokesh and Liya were at another wall of text as Shan and Ko reached them, struggling with the translation.

Yao frowned at Ko, and extended a water bottle to Shan. As Ko stepped in front of him to grab the bottle Shan saw that his pants pockets had been emptied of the artifacts he had taken, but his jacket pockets were now full. His son had not discarded the artifacts, only moved them.

Shan noted the confused expressions shared by Liya and Lokesh. They seemed to be understanding the words but not the text. It was not one of the old teachings. Along the top were painted small white birds that looked like doves, along the sides flowers that looked like roses with heavy thorns.

"It's not as old as some of the others," Corbett said, bending to examine the paint. "Only a century or so."

"To all things exists a season," Lokesh said slowly, pointing to the first line. "And an hour for every intention under the gods' palace."

Shan heard Corbett's breath catch, and the American bent to the final words, near the floor, then stood. "To everything there is a season," Corbett recited in English, "and a time to every purpose under heaven. A time to be born and a time to die."

Lokesh, nodding his head, looked at the American in confusion.

Corbett pointed. "At the bottom, the source is given, in English. Ecclesiastes. The Christian Bible. A time to plant," he continued with the verse, "and a time to pluck up what is planted."

As they stared in mute astonishment a woman's voice rose from the shadows. "Bloody wonderful, isn't it? I wish I could have known the old major. His life was a miracle, don't you think?"

Elizabeth McDowell stepped into the chamber. Corbett frowned, and patted his pockets as if looking for a weapon. Liya grabbed Dawa and pulled the girl behind her. McDowell looked at the Tibetan woman with a hurt expression, shrugged, then offered Shan a small apologetic nod.

"All these years," she said with a vague gesture into the labyrinth, "we never had a clue about the amban. There's a key to a fortune somewhere in these walls. If Lodi and I had known," she said, and shrugged again, "we never would have had to work so hard."

"Lodi wouldn't let you do this," Liya said. "Not the earth temple. He would protect it."

"Not the temple, cousin. The amban's records. Lodi wanted to know about the amban as much as the rest of us. The lost treasure belonged to the emperor. It's not stealing from Tibetans."

"You can't do it," Liya protested. "They'll hurt the temple."

"You misunderstand, Liya. We want to learn where in the north we can find the amban's treasure, that's all. Kwan Li and the emperor liked a good mystery. All these old gompas keep detailed records. I assumed they were destroyed until I heard about the underground temple. Help me find the records, help me solve the mystery, and no one has to damage the temple."

"Someone already stole a fresco here," Shan pointed out. "Damaged others."

"I didn't know, you have to believe that," the British woman said in a strangely plaintive voice. "Lodi didn't know. People get overzealous. Good professionals always keep their skills honed," she said with a glance to the shadows. "It won't happen again. Look, let Ming get famous, let him get rich. I'll make sure Bumpari gets part of it. You'll never have to worry about food or medicine again. I want to get them away from here as much as you do. I can do it. Just trust me."

"You'll never get away, McDowell," Corbett said between clenched teeth.

"Punji. All my friends call me Punji," the British woman said in an oddly gentle, almost vulnerable tone. "Somehow you seem like an old friend, Agent Corbett, following my tracks, trying to get close to me."

"I didn't know you were one of them," Corbett growled.

"Not one of them," Punji said with a melancholy glance toward Shan and Liya. "Just call us an alliance of people with certain mutual interests." She seemed to force a grin as she studied Corbett and Yao. "But just so we have no more unpleasant misunderstandings, we'll have to check things."

Liya moaned as two men appeared out of the shadows, the huge Mongolian and the gaunt Han whose faces Shan had seen in the photos with Ming and Dolan. "This is Mr. Khan and Mr. Lu."

Liya visibly shuddered, then grabbed Dawa and stepped between Shan and Corbett. Shan saw the long scratches down Khan's cheek, where Liya had raked her nails. Khan fixed her with an eager, hungry stare.

"Godkillers!" Liya spat at the two men. Lu laughed, then the two men began searching each member of the party. They took the packs, stuffed inside them the radio, pocketknives, the compass, and all the lights.

"Even if you thought of running back," McDowell said, "you'll never find the path." She opened a palm to show a handful of rice.

Chapter Thirteen

Brother Bertram's life was a miracle. The British woman's unexpected words about her ancestor stayed with Shan as she escorted him, with Corbett and Lokesh, deeper into the maze of chapels while Khan guarded the others. The woman was an enigma, an art thief and humanitarian, partner of Director Ming, cousin of the Bumpari clan, organizer of relief for Tibetan children, and, according to Corbett, a murderer.

"I can give you a deal," Corbett said in English to McDowell's back as they walked. "Maybe it was Lodi's idea, maybe you were just duped. If I ask for leniency a judge will listen."

"Deal?" she asked with a laugh. "For what?"

"For the prosecution that will take place in Seattle."

"Seattle? Last I checked you were my prisoner in a labyrinth in a cave on the opposite side of the planet. And also—" she turned and pretended to struggle to recall something. "Oh yes," she said with a finger on her chin, "you have no evidence. No stolen art. No proof of who was at the scene. Nothing. Like the lamas say, your thieves were made of thin air."

"We can place you and Lodi in Seattle, and know you left the next day, flew back to Tibet, to transfer what you stole from Dolan to Director Ming."

"Why would we do that?"

"Because Ming stole it from the government of China. Because he had to get it back before the audit. Give me Ming and you can walk. If I find the art without you there will be no more room to negotiate," Corbett warned.

"But you'll never find it. You know the routine. The collection gets broken up, sent to dealers in Europe. Impossible to trace." She shook her head and gazed at the American, seeming to notice his Tibetan clothes for the first time. It seemed to soften her somehow. "What is wrong with you?" she sighed. "You're obsessing. Wealth gets redistributed. No one gets hurt. Dolan gets a check from his insurance company."

"What about the girl who died?"

The smile faded from Punji's face. "What girl? No one died."

"The nanny. Abigail Morgan. Her body was found in the bay five days later."

The British woman searched Corbett's eyes for a moment. "Not a chance. No one died."

Corbett looked at Lu, who walked in front of them. "He doesn't speak English," McDowell said, and grabbed a handful of Corbett's shirt to force his gaze back to her. "Damn you, what girl?"

"She disappeared that night. She went back to the house for something and must have seen something. She was killed, thrown off a bridge."

"Impossible." McDowell said in a slow whisper, then looked at the wall for a long moment, at an image of a lama with his novices. "You have no evidence. Of anything. I am telling you nothing. But theoretically, if two people flew in for a job like that, they would be the kind of people interested only in the art. Just business. Theoretically," she said, fixing Corbett with a somber look, "the alarm sensors were cut in three places, at the video feed, the house alarm box, and at the remote police alarm mounted on the fence. Theoretically, the entire Tibetan collection was taken, but only the Tibetan collection. Let's say the back-door lock cylinder was popped out, and the thieves wore latex gloves, leaving no fingerprints." It was practically a confession. But she was telling him to make Corbett believe her, Shan realized, to make him understand she and Lodi were not murderers.

"Theoretically, there was a third person who wasn't always with you," Shan ventured.

"No way." McDowell kept studying Corbett as she spoke. "You don't really know she was killed there." It was a statement, not a question. "There's no official inquiry into a killing. If there was, the press would have gone into a frenzy over a nanny killed at the Dolan estate."

Corbett frowned but said nothing. Shan stared at him, suddenly perplexed. The FBI agent had told him the death was why he had come to Tibet. He recalled his first conversation with Corbett. The American had stated her death as a fact connected to the robbery. But he had told Shan of the strange, accidental way he had been involved in the discovery and recovery of her body, had admitted to Shan that finding her had not been part of his robbery investigation. There had been a message, on the FBI computer. *The boss found out you opened papers on the babysitter, ordered it closed.* Shan had thought it was about another matter. He had not understood the word babysitter. It must mean the nanny, the college student who died. Corbett had been ordered to stop investigating the death of the young woman. Yet here he was, in the earth temple, risking his career, perhaps his life, to find an answer.

Punji McDowell looked away, took a step further into the maze. "Why did you bring the little girl?" she asked abruptly, staring into the darkness. The anger in her voice was gone, replaced with something like worry.

"Dawa was lost," Shan said. "She came to find her Tibetan family. To hear about the old ways. She is from these hills originally. Descended from the Bumpari clan."

McDowell sighed and offered another small, melancholy smile.

"She came to teach us how to learn about the temple," Lokesh said, as if correcting Shan, reminding Shan of the words Surya had spoken.

"The old ways are a bit obtuse," the British woman said. "I thought gaining entry to the temple would be the hardest part." She eyed Shan, and switched to English. "We're looking for the same thing. Get me to the upper chambers, where the records must be, and I'll let you go. All of you."

Shan studied her. "First you must tell us something. Why you made that tomb Ming found."

McDowell's green eyes flashed. She returned Shan's steady gaze for a moment, then slowly smiled. "I think I like Ming better as an enemy than a partner. It was quite entertaining."

"You had to give up the robe from Fiona."

"I was sorry. But she understood. Cousin Fiona and I have drunk tea together many times, for many years. I told her it was for Lodi. She sent a herder on horseback to Zhoka for the bones, with a prayer to protect him. I promised when it was over I would stay with her for a week and read all her books out loud."

"What do you mean an enemy?" Yao asked, and studied McDowell intensely. "You mean a quarrel among thieves."

"Another mistake. I'm not a thief," she said in a voice grown suddenly fierce.

Yao frowned and threw up his hands. "You just told us you . . ." He paused and noticed how Shan and McDowell stared at each other.

"Do the FBI files show any other thefts ever committed by Lodi and Miss McDowell?" Shan asked Corbett without breaking from the woman's gaze.

"None," the American replied. "Not even a record of a parking ticket anywhere on the planet. What's your point?"

"She wasn't a thief," Shan said, his mind racing to understand what McDowell was telling them, and not telling them. "She was a courier. Someone else was there, someone else disabled the security system. Lodi and Punji just carried the collection away."

McDowell offered a thin smile then turned away and stepped closer to the nearest wall, acting as if suddenly interested in a painting of a green deity.

"They all worked together for years," Shan explained. "Lodi, Ming, Khan,

McDowell, and someone else close to Dolan." He turned to Corbett. "Dolan had to know the pieces Ming sold him were from the museum. He was a sophisticated collector, and Ming never would have risked it unless he was paid a fortune. Maybe there was a middleman, an art dealer somewhere, but Dolan knew he wasn't buying reproductions. They were partners in crime against the Chinese people. But then, because Ming was in trouble, Ming urgently had to have the art back in Beijing and Dolan decided to extract a huge price for helping him. So this time there were two sides, two teams. Ming directed Lodi and Punji in taking the artifacts from Seattle, Dolan or his agent had Khan and Lu at work in Beijing, to steal what was to be Ming's payment for the return of the artifacts."

"Dolan wanted the fresco?" Corbett asked. "No way."

Shan did not reply, but looked at McDowell's back. "Everything had to be balanced, coordinated. It was why the crimes were committed at the same hour, because Ming and Dolan had grown suspicious of each other."

"Dolan," Corbett repeated with a chill in his voice. "He would never get his hands dirty. But he has an art dealer in Seattle." The American fell into deep thought. "None of that makes Ming her enemy," he said after a moment.

"That came later, more recently," Shan offered, still watching McDowell, "when Ming started arresting old Tibetans and raiding personal altars. I believe it when she says she wants them all gone, wants the strangers out of Lhadrung."

Punji turned back toward Shan and offered him a grateful nod. "Ming's arrogance will keep him from seeing the truth for a while. If we hadn't planted that tomb last night he would be here right now. He's so obsessed. He would bring soldiers, have them shoot anyone who gets in his way. He is feeling invincible."

"You're in his way," Shan observed.

"But I know him. I know them all. Don't you see that I am the only one who can do this, who can save Zhoka from them, with no one getting hurt." She returned Shan's steady gaze, her eyes so hopeful now he wanted to believe her. "You said something about showing us the next level."

"Enlightenment is the goal of the temple," Lokesh said. "You must approach the temple as a pilgrim."

Punji winced. "So enlighten us on how to get through the labyrinth."

"I think," Lokesh said slowly, "that there is no labyrinth."

The British woman threw her hands up in frustration and aimed her light toward the chapels they had not yet explored.

"There is no maze for those who see through appearances," Shan ventured, stepping closer to his old friend. Punji turned back to face them.

"In the entry there were two writings," Lokesh explained. "The first said the greatest wisdom is seeing through appearances. The second was another old scripture. The only thing that is ours we look for elsewhere."

"You think the entrance to the next level is right there," Shan said.

"I didn't then," the old Tibetan said, stroking his grizzled jaw. "But now I think at least the answer to the riddle is there."

McDowell turned, shining the light behind them now. "Go," she said.

Moments later they reached the chapel where Khan was guarding the others. Ko squatted close to the big Mongolian, speaking to him in a low, casual voice.

McDowell quietly spoke to Khan, smiled at Ko, then ordered Lu to stay with Khan and the rest of the group, to hold Dawa, Liya, and Ko as hostage so the others would not run while they unlocked the secret of the maze.

"Why should we help you solve the puzzle?" Corbett demanded as they arrived at the entry chamber. "Because of you that girl was killed."

"I will do whatever it takes to show you Lodi and I killed no one," the British woman said. "But right now there's something more urgent. You get me upstairs to the record chambers that must be up there and let us get out of Zhoka. You're the genius art sleuth—help me figure out where the amban took the torn thangka. Then we'll talk about Seattle."

Yao glared at her. "I don't make deals with criminals."

Punji gave another of her exaggerated winces. "I've commited no crimes on Chinese territory."

"Foreigners are here at the government's discretion. We can deport you merely for associating with criminals. Permanently close the door."

"Deport a British aid worker? Imagine the diplomatic tempest that will create."

"No one is to get hurt," Shan said. "When we finish we go our separate ways."

"Except for the one called Lu," Yao interjected. "We take him with us, back to Lhadrung."

There was worry in McDowell's eyes as she gazed at Yao. "You don't know that one. Be careful what you wish for."

"He was the one who took the emperor's painting," Yao declared. "The gear we found, the gloves, the tools, they were too small for that Khan. Lu must be the plaster man. He stole the fresco here, he stole the Qian Long fresco in Beijing. I want him. Cooperate now if you ever want to leave China."

"A moment ago you were going to ship me out. Now you won't let me leave. Make up your mind."

"Sign a statement, tell us what you know. Enough for Lu to expect hard labor for twenty or thirty years. That will be enough for me to obtain what else I need."

"Lodi's dead," Shan reminded her. "It's never going to be the same."

"I don't betray people. He's just doing a job. Why should I ruin his life?"

"So we can get Ming. He betrayed the trust of the Chinese people."

"If you don't help us you will have betrayed all the people of Bumpari," Yao added with an apologetic glance at Shan. "Your family."

"What do you mean?"

"If we have no way to link Ming to the stolen fresco, then we will have to try to stop him with evidence of the forgeries from the village," Yao said. "We have Lodi's accounts."

Punji clenched her jaw. "All the more reason not to cooperate."

"Make a deal," Shan urged, "Yao can promise to keep Bumpari out of this."

"I never said—" Yao sputtered.

Shan cut him off with a raised hand. "If everyone compromises a little Bumpari can be protected. It would be what Lodi would want. What Brother Bertram would want. What the lamas would want. That is my price for helping." He looked at Yao. "Every investigation of a man like Ming ends in compromise," he said, challenge in his voice.

Yao frowned but said nothing.

Punji bit her lip and stared at the image of the saint, and slowly nodded. "We still have to find the old records. And you'll never get out of here safely without me."

She returned their lights to them, and they began examining every inch of the walls, studying the smaller images in the murals, reading the painted text, studying the patterns in the colors. Corbett pointed to the top of the wall, which was bordered in small renderings of sacred symbols on colored backgrounds.

"White, blue, yellow, green, red, black," the American said, pointing to each in turn. "Then it starts again."

Lokesh shrugged. "The seed syllables," he said, as if he thought everyone understood.

"Seed sounds have colors associated with them," Shan explained. "White is *om*, blue *ma*, yellow *ni*, green *pad*, red *me*, black *hum*."

"Om mani padme hum," McDowell said. "The mani mantra. The faithful must keep invoking the Compassionate Buddha to find the true path."

Corbett stepped to the wall, looking at the patterns of color in the murals. He pointed to the squares surrounding the image of Atisha. "There is only one white, and one blue," he said, pointing to a square by the saint's shoulder and another near his lowered right hand. He turned to the next painting, pointing to the only yellow and green squares in the mosaic of small portraits, again in the same pattern as the first two, then to two red and black squares on the third wall. "Put a line through each and they point to the bottom right corner of each wall. He bent to show them that the bottom right corner of each was a brown square, part of a different color pattern along the bottom of each vivid wall.

The fourth wall had no pointers. "What was it you said," the American asked Lokesh. "We must see through appearances. And the thing we seek elsewhere is always right there with us." Corbett knelt in the corner and an instant later gave a small cry of discovery. "The other walls were telling us to look at the corner of the fourth wall," he said, showing how the square was a hole, not black as it appeared at a quick glance—a dark hole disguised by the pattern. "Something goes inside. A handle."

Shan looked at the mendicant staff that hung over the door.

Moments later Corbett inserted the long handle of a staff into the hole. He pushed it tight and lifted. Nothing happened.

"I thought I heard something," Yao said. "A click, maybe a release of something." He pushed the wall above the hole. Nothing. Corbett and Shan pushed together, shouldering it, Yao joining in. Still nothing.

"It could be another false lead," Corbett said, then rested against the adjacent wall and gasped as he began slipping. The wall behind him was shifting, opening on a central pivot. As the wall stopped, Corbett fell into the darkness.

Shan quickly followed, aiming his light at the American, who lay on the floor of a wooden landing below a steep, eighteen-inch-wide stairway, leading up.

"Christ they were good," Corbett said, as he stood and aimed his own light at the back of the moving wall. It was constructed of heavy wood, joined so tightly and painted so cleverly that from the outside it looked like another stone wall.

As they climbed to the third level they reached a chamber unlike any of those below. Punji groaned as she topped the stairs, Lokesh gave a cry of delight.

The walls were lined with the heads of demons. Not those of the paintings below, but three-dimensional heads, the intricate, horrible masks of Tibetan ritual dancing, the heads that according to tradition could be inhabited by the demons themselves when the right words were spoken.

They stood for a moment, in the center of the room, their moving hand lights giving motion to the wrathful faces.

Shan's light settled on a piece of paper framed in wood, hanging by one of the chamber's two doors. It was not Tibetan, not part of the rituals, but a greeting of sorts.

As he lifted the dusty frame from the wall and handed it to McDowell, Shan heard her breath catch. "Dear Uncle Bertram." She smiled and quietly read the text out loud:

> How you made it this far I am curious
> Since the chapels make pilgrims so furious
> Was it our monkish crew
> Or the deities who
> Told you the maze was just spurious?

The door from the mask chamber led into a curving tunnel, matching that of the bottom floor, though with a smaller, tighter radius. The outer wall of the tunnel was broken at regular intervals by doorways leading to a series of chapels, each separated from the next by a meditation cell. They walked quickly, not pausing to study the images of the chapels. The inner wall was plastered, as intricately painted as the chapel walls, but with a simple wooden door every thirty feet, each constructed of heavy planks and held shut with an iron latch, each with a segment of rainbow painted between the top of the doorframe and the ceiling. They passed a painting of a deity on a lion throne, the wall behind painted yellow. It was the symbolic southern gate. Shan paused at the wooden door opposite the yellow wall and opened it.

It was an apartment, a living quarters for one of the gompa's senior lamas—a spare, simple chamber, with a single thangka on the wall opposite the door, a low platform bed against the right wall, a wooden trunk against the left wall, and a simple altar under the thangka, all constructed of fragrant wood. The bed had a pallet and a single felt blanket, crumpled, pushed against the wall. As Corbett opened the trunk, Shan looked over his shoulder, seeing that it was divided with a slender plank. On one side there were two robes, two grey underrobes, sticks of incense, and several jars of herbs. On the other were four peche, the manuscript leaves neatly tied between elegantly carved end-boards. As Shan ran his finger over the delicate birds carved into the topmost end-board, he noticed Punji staring toward the center of the room. He followed her gaze to see Lokesh, gazing with sudden anguish toward the bed. Under it was a pair of worn sandals.

"What's wrong?" Corbett asked as he noticed the old Tibetan. Then he muttered a low curse and stepped silently to Lokesh's side.

"He ran out, sprang up from his bed," Punji said in a pained voice.

The blanket, left in disarray in the otherwise pristine room, and the sandals forgotten under the bed, spoke eloquently of the day forty years before. "They came at dawn," Shan whispered.

The blanket had not been touched, left where the lama had cast it off as the alarm was sounded, perhaps as the first bombs fell, as he sprang out the door without his sandals.

They silently stepped out of the room and ventured behind the next wooden door. The chamber appeared nearly identical to the first, except that its blanket was neatly folded on the bed. But an easel rested on the floor by a cushion and a wooden tray with paints and brushes. The piece of stretched cotton on the easel held the shapes of a complex thangka outlined in charcoal. In one corner the artist had started applying pigment.

The next chamber held another blanket thrown off in haste, and a clay jar upturned by the door. Suddenly Shan realized Lokesh was no longer with them. They retraced their steps and found him in a nearby chapel, staring at the murals, his lamp close to the wall.

"They aren't the same as the others," Lokesh observed, as Shan stepped to his side.

Shan's lamp, quickly followed by the others, rose to illuminate the walls. The colors and the patina of age in the panels were like those of the other chapels. But instead of being surrounded by smaller images of the reincarnate lineage or panels of sacred emblems there were rocks and trees and clouds in the background. Mountains were behind the saint, with small birds flying over an open landscape.

"It's not Tibetan," Corbett said.

But Lokesh pointed to the saint in the center, with his hand to his ear. It was without a doubt Milarepa, the famed ascetic, flanked by other Tibetan saints.

"Tibetan but not Tibetan," Shan said. "The background is in the Chinese style." He pointed to a small group of five curving marks in the lower right corner, like commas, all rising from the top of a small arc. "This I don't know."

Corbett confirmed that the marks were in the corners of the other two paintings in the chamber. "It's like a painter's mark, a signature. But you said Tibetans don't sign their paintings."

"Almost never, except sometimes a handprint or word on the back of the painting."

"Who is at the side?" Yao asked, pointing to the two robed figures who stood behind another Tibetan saint, one robed figure at each shoulder, their faces drawn in painstaking detail. He pointed to one of the men. "His face is not Tibetan," the inspector said. "He looks somehow familiar."

Shan and Lokesh lingered behind the others, still gazing at the strange paintings. Though they departed from the traditional form of Tibetan art, the artist had been skillful, had created a different form with its own simple, stirring beauty. When Shan finally stepped into the corridor he saw the others standing in front of the next wooden door, gazing at its frame. Several pegs hung from the frame, and from them hung at least twenty khatas, ceremonial offering scarves. At the base of the door were several dust-encrusted bronze figures, rolled prayer papers tied in vines, and shriveled brown shapes that may once have been butter offerings.

"It's some kind of altar," Punji said. "These were put here a long time ago, before the bombing."

At first, in the beams of their lights, the interior seemed like the others, with a spare plank bed, a small, low writing table with a chair, a shelf with peche manuscripts, a wooden trunk, and an altar under a thangka. But the pallet was tied with a length of silk, and on top of the trunk was a small stone statue of a dragon.

No one seemed willing to step over the offerings in the entryway. Finally Yao sighed and stepped inside. As the others waited he walked to the bed, rested his hand on the rolled pallet a moment. He paused, gazing at the dragon, then he turned to sweep his light along the other walls. Suddenly, with a sharp intake of breath, he dropped his light. He did not bend to retrieve it, but stared at the wall around the door, the wall that could not be seen by the others. After a moment he recovered and took a tiny step, then seemed to stumble, dropping to one knee but not recovering, just staring at the wall, forgetting his light, supporting himself on one knee.

Shan stepped inside, followed by the others, and turned to follow Yao's gaze. For a moment Shan thought his knees were about to buckle.

"Ai yi!" Lokesh cried.

"It's him!" Punji gasped.

"It's who?" Corbett asked in confusion, staring at the two magnificent Chinese scroll portraits on the wall.

Shan instantly recognized the elegant middle-aged man in a fur hat who stared down from the throne in the painting on the right. It was the Qian Long emperor.

"He brought a picture of his uncle from Beijing," Punji whispered.

"And of himself," Shan said. On the opposite side of the door was a matching painting, of the same size, with the same silk brocade border, of another man in a fur cap, seated on a bench, his kind intelligent face a younger version of the emperor's own.

"The saints we didn't know," Lokesh said. Shan suddenly realized why one of the men in the murals had seemed familiar.

"It was the emperor," Punji said in an awed voice, "painted as a lama. And the other was his nephew."

"Not the amban," Shan corrected. "By then he had become the other."

"The other?" the British woman asked.

"The reincarnate abbot." Shan gestured to the dragon statue on the trunk. "The Stone Dragon Lama."

"Killed by order of the Stone Dragon," Punji uttered in a surprised whisper, and looked up at Lokesh and Shan. "The lama Kwan Li ordered the death of the amban Kwan Li." The handwriting on the bounty poster had been something like a joke, a taunt, written by members of the lama's own flock.

"He signed his work," Lokesh whispered, his voice still full of wonder. His finger rested on one of the stone dragon's outstretched feet.

McDowell, opening the trunk by the bed, looked up from a neat work tray of brushes and dried pigments that sat inside. "What do you mean?"

"The paintings with the marks. They were his," Shan said. He realized none of them were speaking above a whisper. "The five marks. It's the footprint of the imperial dragon. Five claws."

In the shadows by the altar a match flared. Lokesh was lighting a stick of incense, setting it in a stone holder on a low table Shan had not noticed before. Beside the holder was a large wooden tray, holding an odd assortment of objects: Several little tsa-tsas, the traditional clay images of deities, painted in brilliant colors. Over twenty rolls of paper, tightly bound with silk threads. What may have been a piece of bone. And a round piece of brass in a small dome shape, with a short shaft on its back. The collection appeared to be another makeshift altar.

Another soft gasp came over Shan's shoulder. Punji pushed the brass object with a finger, turning it over, her hand hanging over it. It was a button, an ornate military button, with two cannon barrels, crossed, on its front surface.

McDowell's face seemed to swirl with emotion, then she folded her arms across her chest and turned to face the picture of the amban, approached it as if about to ask him a question, then slowly stepped back into the hall, and walked into the darkness.

When Shan followed, a light was shining into the next doorway, thirty feet away. Corbett stood in the opening. Shan watched as the British woman reached the American, stared into the chamber a moment, then darted inside as Corbett laughed.

The only thing about the chamber that matched the others was the fragrant wood walls. The bed was higher, elevated on wooden blocks, and three trunks were arranged along the wall straddling the door. The wall opposite the bed consisted of floor-to-ceiling bookshelves. Shan stepped to the shelves. Most of their contents were unbound peche, but one shelf was packed with Western books. On a finely worked table beside the bed were several candle stubs, pieces of paper, and two images in matching frames. Shan stepped closer to examine them. One was of the Dalai Lama, as a boy of perhaps ten. The other was a photograph of a large Western woman, in a dark dress with a lace collar buttoned tightly at the neck, sitting in an ornate chair. Shan recalled seeing her face in another photo, at the cottage in the village. As Corbett lit the candles another laugh escaped his lips. Punji appeared and lifted the frame with the woman.

"It's his queen," she said, still in her tone of awe. "The queen of his boyhood. Queen Victoria."

On the wall along the side of the bed was a peg holding a wooden tube suspended on a leather thong, open at the top end. Inside was a pair of wire-rimmed spectacles. Above the peg was a space on the wall where something large and rectangular had hung, its shape made visible by a lighter layer of dust within the five-foot-long rectangle.

Yao appeared and began opening the trunks. The first had robes and under-robes, incense, and socks—heavily darned woolen socks. There were paintings hung along the entry wall, above the trunks, paintings like Shan had never seen before. They were skilled works, painted as thangkas but without the formal structure used by the Tibetans.

The first was the future Buddha riding a magnificent white horse, bearing a lance like a warrior, facing dim shapes on horseback at the edge of a forest. There was a monk standing on the ramparts of a British-looking castle, the wind whipping his robe. Shan looked back at the first painting and smiled. The figure on the white charger was Buddha, as Ivanhoe.

In the corner was a huge painting that looked like a European battle scene, with Western soldiers in tan helmets, some urging hordes that pulled cannon, some wearing bandages over bloody wounds, a group of officers apart, on a hill, their faces very detailed, as if based on actual men the artist had known. But all of the soldiers, including the officers, wore the maroon robes of monks.

Corbett called out and lifted a long object from one of the trunks. It was a violin, worn from heavy use.

Shan sat on the stool, staring at a peche leaf, blank except for a sketch of a flower on the margin. It had been waiting under Brother Bertram's pen, about to capture a thought that was now lost forever.

Corbett opened another trunk and pulled out a pair of red trousers with gold trim, part of an officer's dress uniform. Shan stepped to the bound books. There was a Bible, several British novels, a guide to the birds of Asia, and a thick untitled leather-bound book. He opened it and discovered that it was a journal, written in English in a careful, elegant hand.

December 10, 1903, read the first entry.

We have redefined the word chaos today by taking four thousand mules over the snows of the Jelap La mountain pass, altitude 14,000 feet, with three hundred handlers speaking four different languages.

It was a description of the progress of the Younghusband expedition over the Himalayas. He leafed through the pages. The entries were weekly for the first year, the early ones short factual descriptions of the work of soldiers, the later entries speaking of Tibetan art and monk artists. The major had been posted at Gyanste, established by treaty as one of the British trading centers. A long period passed without entries, over a year, until there was an entry marked Lhasa 1906, then more entries about a magical secret place his teacher had taken him, from which he wanted never to leave. Shan paused, and read a joyous passage about the birth of a daughter.

Then, after an entry in 1934, there was a blank page, with a single word. Zhoka, followed by the first entry by Brother Bertram.

My dear friends and teachers have insisted I occupy honored quarters adjoining those of the Twelfth Stone Dragon, whom they speak of as they might a cherished grandfather, and revere now as a protector deity. They say he, too, was a traveler from another part of the world who came to translate things for the spirits of men. They have let me read his correspondence. I never knew the emperor read Tibetan.

Before laying the book on the table Shan went to the final entry, dated May 24, 1959.

We celebrated the queen's birthday today. I played the fiddle in the foregate, and helped the lamas dance a jig. We threw flour in the air and drank a spot of brandy. Victory to the gods.

"Lha gyal lo," a soft voice said over his shoulder. Elizabeth McDowell had been reading too.

"Is that true, Miss McDowell?" Shan heard Lokesh whisper. "Do you wish victory to the gods?"

The question seemed to disturb Punji. She looked away, but her gaze slowly drifted back to the open journal. "I've seen letters my great-grandmother wrote about Bertram. He was full of mischief. Girls' pigtails in inkwells, that sort of thing." She produced a pencil, then leaned over the open book, at the last entry, and wrote for a minute, then straightened and walked toward the empty bed.

Dear Uncle Bert, Shan read. Then she had written the mani mantra in Tibetan, and added, *We will make the gods victorious. Give you joy, Punji.*

Shan joined Corbett, who was at the third chest now. The American lifted out several bundles. A peche wrapped in silk, another wrapped in fur. On the bottom was a long piece of cotton, unadorned, folded, and sewn along the bottom like a pouch. As Shan lifted it out and laid it on the table, Punji was suddenly at his side. She reached into the pouch and pulled out a piece of yellowed cotton, with two handprints in the corners, the back of a thangka. With a gasp Punji pointed to the edge of the cotton. It was jagged from being torn. She did not move, did not speak as Shan reached over and turned the cotton over, revealing four pairs of hooved legs trampling humans and animals.

"Zhinje!" Punji whispered, then she clamped her hand over her mouth, her face draining of color. She had spoken the name which had not been heard in nearly fifty years. After a moment's stunned silence Punji began rolling up the thangka. "The monks must have brought it back from the north, when he died. With this," she said in a suddenly urgent tone, "we can beat them. Go to the first level," she said in English. "Past the eastern gate there is a meditation cell with a piece of grey felt draped over the back of an altar. The chapel has a shelf of old peche, some of them open for reading. The felt covers a hole. Lu and Khan found air flowing through a crack in the rock and chipped out a small tunnel. I'll say you ran into the maze, that you're lost. Go. Go now. I don't want more people hurt. Lodi and I, we never meant for people to be hurt." She looked up for a moment at the journal, then grinned at Shan, excitement in her eyes, and stepped toward the packs they had dropped in the corner, holding the precious thangka.

But as she slipped into the shadow of the far corner, a figure hurtled through the doorway, falling, landing heavily beside the bed. It was Liya, holding her belly as if she had been struck. Two figures entered the room. Lu, the cruel-faced plasterman, holding a hammer in one hand like a weapon, and Ko, holding a staff, wearing a victorious smile.

"She was trying to run," Lu spat. "But our new friend stopped her. He's fast with that stick. I didn't know he was an escaped prisoner." As he spoke Dawa appeared behind him, following closely, tears on her cheeks. Lu shoved her forward and she ran into Liya's arms.

Shan felt something strange course through him as he returned his son's cool gaze, an odd heat that was unfamiliar at first. Anger.

Ko pulled something from a back pocket and extended it toward Punji with a businesslike air. It was a small gold statue.

The British woman, shouldering her pack, hesitated, then offered a weak smile. She glanced at Shan, took the gold figure, then closed her fingers around Ko's hand. The action seemed to pleasantly surprise Ko. The perpetual sneer left his face as she squeezed his hand, for a moment replaced by an awkward grin. Then he gestured for Liya and Dawa to stand.

"That's not polite, boy," Corbett said in English as Ko raised the staff as if to use it on him. "Bad company breeds bad manners." The American threw an apologetic glance toward Shan then lowered the light in his hand and turned it off. As if on cue Yao turned off his light and stepped to the candles, blowing them out. As Lu glared at them suspiciously Shan extinguished his own lamp, leaving only the lamps held by Lu and Punji to light the room.

Suddenly Yao seized the light from Lu, throwing it against the wall, the bulb flickering then dying. Corbett grabbed Ko's staff, slamming it into Ko's jaw, knocking him to the floor as Liya grabbed Dawa's hand and the two disappeared out the door. Shan darted to Punji's side and put his hand on the lamp in her hand. She glanced at Lu, who was lashing the air with his fists, trying to connect with Yao's jaw, and relinquished the lamp.

Shan tossed the light to Corbett as he and Yao grabbed their backpacks. Corbett offered a small salute to Punji and disappeared out the door, Lokesh and Yao close behind. Shan lingered, staring at his son, opening his mouth to say something. But he had no words, and let Corbett pull him into the corridor.

They found the tunnel behind the altar on the first level as Punji had described, hidden by the felt that blended with the shadows. The six-foot-long shaft exited onto an open ledge, which they quickly surveyed with the beams of their lanterns, discovering rows of old wicker storage baskets, coils of heavy yak-hair rope, stacks of old blankets partly covered with chips of rock, and a dozen old wooden pulleys, heavy enough to take the thick rope. Yao found a ladder made of rope, new nylon rope tied to a pillar of rock, and threw it over the edge. In an instant he was over the side and Liya began climbing down. Shan lingered, confused, as the others followed. He knew now where they were, above the chamber with the stolen fresco, the room where Lodi had died. He walked along the ledge, opening the first of the baskets. It was filled with old musty barley. Several chisels, some nearly two feet long, and hammers lay beside it, and beyond them a long, three-foot-high curvature, a cavity carved in the rock that ran the full length of the ledge, over fifty feet long. It would have been the perfect place for the storage baskets, but they were not in it. It was empty. He stared at it in confusion then turned toward a strange rustling sound and watched as a loose peche leaf tumbled out of the tunnel, blown from the altar by the air current, floating down into the lower passage. It was, he realized, how Brother Bertram's verse had found its way to the level below.

Corbett urgently called for Shan to join them below. He lingered another moment, gazing at a brown stain underfoot, then climbed down, pausing once more to look at the two rectangular holes cut in the stone. They were for a ladder. There should have been a ladder to the storage shelf. He paused, recalling the splinter of wood he had found in the passage to the stream, then ran as the American called again.

Only when they reached the foregate yard on the surface did they rest, panting for breath, Yao producing the last of the water bottles as Lokesh sat against the wall, cradling Dawa.

"She's going to break it wide open," Corbett said in a victorious tone. "Punji. She knows exactly what happened in Seattle and she's going to tell me."

"You don't know that," Yao interjected between swallows of water.

"I do. I saw it in her eyes."

Shan studied the American. "You mean you've decided she had nothing to do with the girl's death."

Corbett frowned, but nodded. "I don't need to arrest her. No extradition. No blacklist for entry into the United States."

Yao grinned. He too seemed to sense victory. "Are you feeling affection for her, Agent Corbett?" he asked in a playful tone.

Corbett flushed with color. "Right," he said slowly. "The international art smuggler and the art theft investigator. How opposite can two people be?"

"I think," a dry voice interjected from behind them. They turned to see Lokesh, helping Liya to her feet. "I think somewhere she must be very beautiful," he said, as if they had not truly seen her yet.

Corbett stared at Lokesh so intensely he seemed to have forgotten the urgency of their flight. As the others began to move into the shadows Shan pulled him toward the path that led to the old stone tower and the valley beyond. But as they reached the entrance to the path, between two crumbling walls, Liya reappeared, walking backwards, then Yao and Dawa. The big Mongolian, Khan, was herding them back, raising one hand in a pushing gesture, the other hand casually holding an automatic rifle, a glint of cool amusement in his face as he motioned for them to sit with their backs to the foregate wall, facing the chasm forty feet away.

A moment later Lu appeared, Ko at his side. Shan was aware of movement out of the side of his eye and turned to see Punji, her pack lowered to the ground beside her, kneeling beside Dawa, wiping her grimy face with a red bandana.

"What a sight," the British woman sighed. "You look like a family of moles."

When she was satisfied that the girl's face was clean she straightened, hands on her hips, and paced in front of them as Khan wiped his rifle with an oily cloth.

She looked at Dawa again. "Children shouldn't be here. Or Americans," she added with chagrin in her voice, glancing at Corbett. Khan pulled something out of his pocket and showed Lu, whose eyes lit with excitement. It was the small gold Buddha Ko had stolen from the temple. Lu produced his own trophy, a little statue covered in gemstones.

"Here's the way it will be," Punji explained. "We're going to get on with our business. We have what we need here. We'll need some lead time." Lu tossed his little deity from hand to hand with a gloating expression, then wandered behind the wall. "We're going to put you in one of the cave storerooms, tie you up. We'll leave you some food and blankets. I'll send someone to free you in a day or two."

Shan heard a new voice behind the wall. The words were drowned out by the wind, but someone, a stranger, was talking urgently.

"Then my colleagues go north to retrieve the treasure and you go home. We can all laugh about the good jokes the old monks played on us." She looked back at Corbett. "I want you to know something. A third of what I make goes to the relief fund. To the children."

"Help us," Corbett said. "Your uncle the major would."

Ko stepped to one of the army packs and helped himself to a bag of raisins. Punji smiled. "It's because of him we're here. Look at all he gave us."

"What he gave to you," Shan said to the British woman, "was Zhoka. It was Tibet. He was a soldier when he started, as you were in a sense, a soldier of fortune. But when he finished he was a monk." Shan pulled the rolled-up peche leaf from his pocket and let Punji read it. *Death is how deities are renewed*. She puzzled over the words a moment, taking the leaf, turning it over, holding it one way then another as if to better catch the light.

Finally she sighed and the sad grin returned to her face. "He was a deep old thing, our major."

When she handed the leaf back to Shan, he declined. "Keep it. It's a piece of him, from your family."

Punji seemed uncomfortable with the notion at first, running her fingers through her auburn hair, and seemed about to refuse, then slowly rolled up the old paper. "What was he trying to say?" she asked no one in particular. "Renewing deities."

"You always have another chance," Corbett said.

Punji gave one of her exaggerated sighs. "So predictable. You're obsessed. Get some lives, all of you. Renew your own deities. Mine fits perfectly fine. Restoring art, that's what I do, getting it to people who appreciate it. Letting the global market extend itself."

Shan stepped closer to the wall, away from the others. The wind died at that moment and it seemed to Shan he was very near the unknown man speaking behind the wall. He caught brief sentences, without meaning. They were in English. "Of course we will do it," the man said. "From here on it's easy."

"A few days at most," Punji said. "Then we'll be gone." She looked at Dawa. "I'll send some candy for you. I have candy somewhere in the packs."

Lu appeared at the far end of the yard. But it could not have been Lu speaking, since McDowell had said he spoke no English. A knot began tying itself in Shan's gut as Lu squatted by the big man with the rifle and spoke in a whisper. Khan frowned, seemed to argue, then sighed and for a moment seemed somehow melancholy. Lu straightened, patting the big man on the shoulder as if for encouragement.

The big Mongolian called Punji to his side, opened the pack at his feet and pointed inside. Lu picked up the rifle then nervously stepped away. As Punji bent over the pack Khan swung his arm in a wide arc over his head.

There was something in his hand, Shan saw, a large jagged rock. "No!" Shan shouted in alarm.

As Punji looked up Khan slammed the rock into the back of her skull with a vicious strength, once, twice, three times until there was a sickening crunch, and a crack of bone shattering. As she crumpled to the ground Corbett leapt up with a roar. Lu fired the gun into the ground in front of him, shouting, stepping between Corbett and the Englishwoman. Her assailant stepped back, his eyes wild, as she got up on her hands and knees, blood streaming down her neck. She pushed up, a trembling hand reaching behind her neck, a dull, vacant expression on her face. She stood with great difficulty, looking around the clearing, swaying, studying them absently, as if she no longer recognized them. The big man scooped her into his arms, lifting her like a child, one arm around her neck, one under her knees. As he did so Punji's head sagged to one side and she looked, without focusing, at Shan. Her mouth opened, round and wide, and a wrenching sound came out, a hollow confused syllable that might have been the beginning of a word. Then she watched her hand, which seemed to be moving of its own accord toward the peche leaf in her pocket.

Lu shouted a warning at Shan, leveling the rifle, and Shan realized he had run forward. Shan halted, raising a hand out toward Punji. Khan paused, looking at Punji, then Shan, with sadness in his eyes. Lu spat a curse at him. Khan turned, reached the side of the cliff in three long strides, and dropped Punji into the void.

CHAPTER FOURTEEN

The sound that came from Dawa was like no scream Shan had ever heard. The quivering howl of torment seemed to be a living thing, shooting through them, shaking the old walls. It seemed the old gompa itself was speaking, all the ghosts calling upon the girl to express their horror. It roiled the air, ebbing and rising again, like a jagged rip in the atmosphere, holding them all in a trance for a moment, even Khan, who looked forlornly down into the abyss where he had dropped McDowell.

Suddenly Lu was staggering. Ko was on his back, beating him about the shoulders, pounding a fist into his skull. As Khan launched himself toward Ko, Corbett threw himself through the air, slamming into the man's legs, knocking him off balance. Khan hit the ground heavily, the wind knocked out of him as Shan grabbed the rifle in Lu's hands. Lu twisted the weapon, hitting Shan's crown with the barrel, then Shan wrenched it from his grip. Ko kept beating Lu, who did not fight him but twisted and turned, backing against the wall. Suddenly Ko seemed to see the rifle in Shan's hands and dropped off the man's back. He stared at his father for a moment, then looked at Lu—who was darting away into the maze of rocks—and at his own hands, as if not understanding anything, perhaps as shocked by his own action, which would deny him refuge with the thieves, as by Punji's sudden death.

Corbett and Yao began to circle the big man, joined by Liya, a piece of a broken beam raised over her head. Punji's killer raised his fists at those surrounding him, but his eyes were on the rifle in Shan's hands.

Ko looked up and nodded, not at Shan but at the rifle. Shan, too, looked at the rifle a moment, then reversed it, took it by the barrel, and flung it far out over the chasm. The big man grinned and bent over, shoving Liya aside, then grabbing Punji's pack with the torn thangka. He lifted the pack with a taunting expression and ran into the ruins, Corbett and Yao at his heels. Shan glanced at Ko, whose expression rapidly changed, from confusion to anger to disdain. Shan glanced about to make sure Lokesh was still holding Dawa, then ran in the direction he had last seen Lu.

He found the short Han in the shadows of an alley less than fifty yards away, his back to Shan, speaking into a black instrument. Shan slowed, wary of making a sound. Lu was speaking excitedly, gesturing with his free hand. Speaking in perfect English. He heard Lu say, "yes," and "tomorrow," then heard him give an assurance that there would be no more problems now. Lu could not speak English, Punji had insisted, and she had used English when explaining to them how to escape. Lu had entered the chamber a moment later. He must have been at the door, must have been listening, and reported to someone on the black box who had then ordered Punji's death. Now he was calling to confirm she was dead.

Shan lifted a stone and threw it in a long arc, over Lu, so it landed in front of him. When Lu spun about to flee in the opposite direction Shan was less than three feet before him, blocking his way.

"Tell him he can't hide behind lies anymore," Shan said in English.

As Lu spun about Shan grabbed his arm. The radio dropped to the ground as Lu twisted, pushing Shan into the rocks, and broke free. In an instant he was gone.

Shan was in the foregate examining the device Lu had dropped when Corbett and Yao returned. Punji's killer had eluded them.

"Ming," Yao spat the word like a curse.

Corbett nodded as he took the device, then his face clouded. "It's not a radio," the American explained, as he studied the buttons on its face. "It's a satellite telephone. He could have been speaking to anyone. He could have—" his voice faded as he stared at the little green screen above the rows of buttons. A cold fury grew on his face. "There's a recall button," he said after a moment in a chill voice, "to let you contact the last number dialed." He showed the number displayed on the screen. "It's in the U.S. A Seattle number." He pushed a green button and held it out so Yao and Shan could hear.

After a moment there were two rings and a woman answered, speaking in crisp, refined tones. "Croft Antiquities."

Corbett lifted the phone to his mouth. "Is Mr. Croft there?"

"Mr. Croft has departed," the woman said after a moment's hesitation. "Who's calling please?"

Corbett looked at Yao as he spoke. "Tell him it's Investigator Yao of the Chinese Council of Ministers. Tell him the Chinese government has some questions for him. Tell him he just changed everything."

Yao did not protest, did nothing but stare at the little phone, a sad, defeated look in his eyes.

Corbett pushed the disconnect button. "We'll get the phone records," he vowed. "In a couple days we'll know everything there is to know about Croft Antiquities."

"But what you won't have is its connection to Beijing, to Ming," Yao said, gazing into the chasm. "The answer is in what happened that day at the Forbidden City, what the police didn't report. We have only the letters from the amban. We don't know what was finally communicated about the treasure. How can we stop them without knowing what happened between the amban and his uncle? The amban's missing treasure connects them all. That's where they will be."

"We know the emperor kept copies of his correspondence," Shan said. "But I don't think Ming had it all."

"What do you mean?" Yao asked in a distant voice.

"It's still there, in the Forbidden City."

"You can't know that."

"The amban told us. He thanked the emperor for using the words of the sutras. The emperor Tibetan. He meant the emperor was writing in Tibetan. Major McDowell's confirmed it, that the emperor spoke Tibetan. It would have been the perfect language for keeping secrets from his mandarins. Even if he found them Ming would never have thought a letter in Tibetan to be important. He speaks no Tibetan."

A glint was in Yao's eyes as he looked at Shan. He stepped to Corbett, who was still staring at the little telephone.

Liya was standing at the edge of the cliff, tearfully looking into the chasm when Shan stepped to her side. He squatted and drew in the bare soil: an oval with a circle inside, a square inside the circle. "Earth door inside the circle of heaven."

Liya's hand went to her mouth. "The tunnel. He was trying to tell me that Lu and Khan had cut a tunnel through the earth, into the mandala temple."

Shan nodded and remembered the pattern of bones he had seen below the drawing, pointing upward. As he lay dying Lodi had tried to find a way to tell Liya, only Liya, what he had discovered that day in the tunnels. "And he wrote of the Mountain Buddha. Where is it, Liya?"

"Sleeping," she said, warning back in her eyes.

Shan glanced about to be sure no one else was in earshot. "You don't understand," he said. "Ming knows about it from one of the old books. He thinks the golden Buddha should be his. Even if he can't find the emperor's treasure he intends to finish with new political power and the golden likeness of the Buddha."

"There are some things that must be left to Tibetans, Shan," Liya said.

"That is between the people of the hills and Colonel Tan. Nothing you can do will change it. Gendun himself has given his blessing." She added the last words like an apology. Liya knew Shan would not oppose the old lama.

"But Gendun probably thinks Surya is among the prisoners," Shan protested. He searched her face as she shook her head from side to side, pleading with his eyes.

Liya offered a thin, sad smile. "It is the only chance in fifty years our people have had."

"Hide it at least."

"It was hidden, for fifty years. But Lodi found it. It was his last gift to us."

"Lodi?"

"You forget I was there too, after he died. I didn't understand his drawing of the dzi. But I saw the bones. They were pointing to something else."

"On the ledge?" Shan tried to recall the scene. The barrels on the ledge may well have hidden the tunnel but what else had been there? Heavy yak ropes. Pulleys. Long chisels.

Liya put a finger on her lips as if to quiet him, then extended it toward Shan's temple. "You're hurt."

When Shan touched the spot where the rifle had hit him three fingers came away bloody.

"In the food pack," Corbett said, "there is a medical kit."

But when Liya reached into the pack she froze, then looked up in confusion. She slowly extracted a long white cotton pouch, the one they had seen in the major's chambers.

"The thangka!" Lokesh exclaimed.

Liya opened the pouch and pulled out the top of the old painting. Punji had had her final word, had tricked Lu, putting the torn thangka in Shan's pack instead of her own.

"With that we have a chance of trapping the bastards," Corbett said. His voice had a new edge, a sound of vengeance. "Ming and this man Croft."

As Lokesh straightened the ragged-edged eighteen-inch square of cloth onto the ground Yao quickly produced the folded image of the upper half of the death deity they had printed from Tan's computer, placing it on the ground above the cloth. The amban's puzzle for the emperor was to be solved by having both halves. But they could make no sense of it. The combined image seemed no different from the one Shan had seen in the mourning hut at the ragyapa village. Lokesh dropped to his knees, bending over the artwork, the others squatting beside him. They looked for patterns in the colors, anomalies in the images of the great bull deity and the lesser deities that surrounded it, convinced the message they so desperately sought must be hidden in the art like the messages so cleverly disguised in the temple. Lokesh murmured a mantra as if to entice the gods to speak to them.

But they found nothing, nothing except five small claw-like marks at the bottom of the torn cloth, five more showing at the top of the printed image. The amban had made his mark on each.

"Speak to us," Yao moaned, and made a hurrying gesture toward Lokesh, as if to encourage the mantras.

Finally Corbett rose, warning them that Khan and Lu might have another weapon secreted in the caves. As Shan rolled up the thangka he glanced at the pair of painted handprints on the reverse, then explained that they could reach Fiona's house by dusk.

They moved quickly, running when they could, Dawa riding on Corbett's back, then Shan's, then Liya's. It was late afternoon, the sun shining brilliantly, a warm wind on their backs, and as they left Zhoka behind the darkness slowly lifted from their faces. There was little speaking, even when they paused to drink from springs, but Shan saw something new in the eyes of his companions. Not fear anymore, but a calm detached resolve, the kind Shan often saw in Tibetans when they faced insurmountable odds.

Ko alone seemed unable to leave his torment behind.

"Thank you for what you did," Shan said as they knelt by a stream. "You saved us."

"I had never known a woman like Punji," Ko said in an uncertain voice. "I mean . . . we didn't really know each other. But she made jokes with me in the tunnels. Me being a prisoner, that didn't matter to her. I remember her eyes. She was so beautiful. For a few minutes she and I were partners, and we were going to flee to the West, and I forgot everything else. . . ." He glanced at Shan, suddenly seeming to remember to whom he was speaking. "Forget it," he snapped, and seemed to make an effort at anger. After a moment he just rose and offered to carry Dawa on his back.

"If we cannot catch them for what they did," Corbett said as they watched Ko step away with the girl, "then we must take them for what they are going to do. Then they'll talk, then they'll tell us where to find what they stole."

Yao offered a stern nod. "The amban's treasure belongs to the government of China. But to find it we have to make the old thankga speak to us."

"The key," Shan observed, turning to Yao, "is knowing what was said in those last letters between the Qian Long and his nephew, the ones Ming has not seen. The amban said he was going to explain the rest of death. I thought he was speaking of Buddhist teaching."

"He meant the thankga!" Liya exclaimed. "He meant the rest of the death deity, the other half of the torn thankga. He was going to explain the puzzle of the torn thangka to the emperor so there would be no mistake!"

"Like the sutras," Shan said as he recalled exactly what he had seen on the computer screen. "Kwan Li said, like the sutras, he would explain the rest of death. He meant in Tibetan. He would write a letter in Tibetan to explain the secret."

"But the letters are still in Beijing," Corbett said. "We have to go."

"I have no one in Beijing," Yao said with a frown. "No one who can read Tibetan, no one I can trust." He fixed Shan with a sober stare. "If you want to help the Tibetans here you must go with us there."

PART THREE

CHAPTER FIFTEEN

Shan drifted in and out of a dark grey haze that was sometimes like sleep, sometimes like the edge of a deep meditation. He could find no calmness. Everywhere his mind turned he encountered something like the dark turmoil of clouds that he saw whenever he looked out the window. Part of him hated Yao and Corbett for forcing him onto the plane, for forcing him away from Surya and Gendun and the other Tibetans who so desperately needed help. Part of him hated himself for being unable to communicate with Ko, for being unable to crack the hard shell that had grown around the boy. He wondered with cold fear whether he would ever see Tibet, or his son, again.

Once Yao finished with him in Beijing the inspector would have no reason to return Shan. Except to be rid of him. Once in Beijing Shan would be near those who had first sent him to the gulag. Some had died of old age, but not all.

Even when he was able to force such doubts from his consciousness, even when he tried to sleep, he could not close his eyes for long, because of the images that haunted him. The confused, childlike expression of Punji, her brain destroyed by the blow of the rock, her killer cradling her as he carried her to the abyss. Surya, carrying night soil, speaking of his days as a lama as though they belonged to someone else. Gendun, speaking with deities in Zhoka's dark labyrinth. Sometimes through a fog there was another image, from some dim corridor, a serene Chinese man in a dragon robe playing checkers with a jocular British officer, their hands without flesh, the hands of skeletons.

Eventually sleep must have overtaken him, for suddenly the plane lurched and they were on the ground, taxiing toward a low grey building under a low brown sky, the dust-laden atmosphere of a Beijing summer.

Yao cautioned Shan to stay seated, and they did not move until the plane was emptied of other passengers. Even Corbett left with only a quick nod in their direction. Two young men appeared in the grey uniforms of Public Security, pistols on their belts, nodding deferentially to Yao, casting suspicious glances at Shan as they escorted him out a door in the side of the jet ramp into a black car waiting beside the plane. Yao did not introduce Shan, did not speak, but simply stared out the window as they drove into the city, staring at the skyline.

It was a different skyline than Shan remembered, a different city in many ways, he realized with an odd pain in his heart. New highways had appeared in every direction, choked by new automobiles, tens of thousands of new automobiles. Unfamiliar buildings towered over the highway, Western-style buildings with empty faces, some with the names of Western companies affixed to their sides. Advertising signs sprouted like weeds over the landscape.

Some things had not changed. A sea of humanity still flowed down the sidewalks, overflowing into the streets, cascading into subway stations, rippling around street vendors. Familiar smells of fried pork, chilis, noodles, garlic, cardamom, ginger, and steamed rice wafted into the car, cut with the acrid fumes of diesel and gasoline. He stared at the window. He wasn't there, he couldn't be in Beijing, it was another of his strange, empty dreams.

They drove directly to the ancient complex, parked along the huge outer wall of the Forbidden City, entering through the massive arches of the Meridian Gate. The grounds were not open to tourists for another three hours, and as they walked across the vast empty courtyards memories pressed on Shan, recollections of his first visits with his father and mother, even of walking the grounds with Ko on one of the boy's rare visits with Shan, as a youth of four or five. There, in the Hall of Supreme Harmony, Shan's father had pointed to the emperors' dragon-legged throne and explained how officials had approached the ruler with the ritual of three kneelings and nine kowtows. Beyond, in the Gate of the Great Ancestors, his mother had read him a poem written by an emperor a thousand years before.

Suddenly something stirred inside Shan, a new excitement of discovery. They were in a small quiet courtyard before the simple elegant cottage of the Qian Long's retirement. Not until now, until the moment of stepping across the threshold of the private home of the emperor, did Shan feel the weight of the history entwined in their mystery. The fate of so many seemed inextricably linked to what had transpired between the powerful emperor and his nephew over two hundred years before.

Yao spoke quietly with the police guard at the cottage entrance, who unlocked the door and stood aside. The interior of the cottage had none of the grandeur of the imperial halls. It seemed the comfortable living quarters of a genteel scholar, full of scrolls and paintings, its furniture and rooms designed not for formal audiences but for relaxed reading and conversation. Its centerpiece was a dining chamber, an interior room with three cedar walls, red lacquered pillars flanking each of its two entries, a magnificent scroll painting of an early emperor on one side of the table. Shan studied the chamber a moment, then stood facing a long section of exposed lathwork opposite the painting, the plaster still open, still dropping its particles onto the wooden floor, where the fresco had been taken. On the elegant mahogany table, its legs carved like those of dragons, sat a stack of manila folders.

"It's all there is on the theft," Yao explained. "The police reports, interviews with the staff here, background on the stolen fresco, even reports by art experts on how the fresco was removed and the precautions needed to transport it. You've got two, maybe three hours."

Shan looked up with questions in his eyes.

Yao hesitated, glancing toward the young policeman who stood at the entrance and a new figure in a grey uniform who seemed to be waiting for him, then stepped closer.

"I lied," he said in voice heavy with apology. He seemed unable to look Shan in the eyes. "We didn't bring you from Tibet just to help in Beijing. You're going to be arrested. Corbett is getting papers. He is making preparations. He will—" The figure in grey appeared in the door closest to the front hall. The guard called Yao's name. Yao frowned as he departed. "Read the files. If only you could find something."

Shan's throat was suddenly bone dry. Arrested. How could he have been so wrong? Abruptly, it was over. Everything was over. It made no sense but nothing ever did in dealing with those who hated Shan, who had finally reached out across the span of years to snare him one last time. He looked about the chamber again, feeling in his last hours of freedom, a strange connection with the Qian Long emperor. Somehow it felt as though the Qian Long had taken a hand in Shan's destiny. In his doom.

But then one of the guards appeared at his side, extending a folded paper toward Shan. "Excuse me. Inspector Yao said give this to you. Sir."

It was a hastily scrawled note. *You are going to America with Corbett as a material witness. The flight is this evening.*

Shan read the note twice, turned it over, read it again. It was impossible. With every hour he wanted more to be back in Lhadrung, where he could do some good. But Yao and Corbett were conspiring to take him to the other side of the planet. Gradually he became aware of his fingers. They had formed a mudra, the diamond of the mind. He stared at it a long time. Then he began to read the files.

When Yao returned two hours later Shan had finished with the files. "There really isn't a question that Ming arranged the theft," Shan said.

"Only a question of proof. I'm still no closer to recovering the fresco." Yao walked along the hole in the wall, leaning close to the exposed laths, pausing at the small ten-inch square in the lathwork, running his fingers around its edges. "I thought this was just some defect in the construction. But it's where Ming got the letters, the ones he encrypted, the ones that changed everything."

Shan stared at the photograph of the stolen fresco he had found in the files. It was beautiful, a scene of water with reeds and bamboo, and huge cranes that looked as if they were about to fly out of the wall. The wisteria vines that grew along the border were so lifelike they seemed to tremble in the wind. "Did you ever see the letter," he asked Yao. "The one he reported to the Chairman, the one that suggested the emperor owed tribute to Lhadrung?"

"A photocopy."

"How did the police lose it?"

"He had a courier from the museum deliver it in an envelope. The envelope was found but it was opened, and empty. Why do you ask?"

"Because Ming's biggest offense wasn't taking the fresco, it was lying to the Chairman. You know he fabricated that letter."

Yao nodded slowly. "But still there is no proof." He placed a hand on the file. "Ming's museum was in charge of the restoration of the cottage," Yao said, reciting the evidence. "Crews from the museum were working here almost every day, here and at two of the small halls on the far side of the complex. Ming approved the assignment of workers, even the schedules, even frequently visited the projects. I checked the full roster of workers cleared by Ming. The last two were added two weeks before the theft. Lu and Khan. No effort was made to hide their identities. They had worked with Ming before, on two expeditions.

"Every worker on duty confirmed that no work crew was assigned here the day of the theft. Khan and Lu were interviewed, said they saw nothing. Ming confirmed Khan and Lu were on the opposite side of the compound. The area was closed off to the public, with no guards except those stationed a hundred yards away. No witness could be found who saw any activity here. A police investigator said the thieves were invisible, that they had not passed through any of the security barriers. They looked for tunnels, for signs of secret egress over the walls, even checked the records of all helicopter flights that day. Ming gave a public statement about how disappointed he was in law enforcement."

Shan turned and put his hand on the file. "There are interviews of only half a dozen of the maintenance staff. There are more than a half a dozen that work in this quarter."

"The others confirmed they saw nothing."

"To you?"

"To policemen."

"And the ones who gave the statements, how old were they?"

"What could it matter?"

"How old?" Shan pressed.

"I don't know," Yao admitted, staring in confusion as Shan rose from the table and gestured him toward the door.

It had been years since Shan had visited the imperial servants' chambers, which he had discovered during his first wanderings through the complex nearly two decades before. The rooms, converted to crude sleeping quarters for some of the maintenance staff, were dim and dustladen, accessed through an arched gateway overgrown with wisteria. Shan told Yao to wait near the gate while he probed the interior.

An old man with a crooked back was in one of the chambers at the end of the long corridor, sitting cross-legged by a pallet, heating a tin mug of water over a cluster of three candles. He looked up but seemed to have difficulty seeing his visitor.

"My name is Shan," Shan said softly. "I used to sit in the small gardens. Sometimes I would play checkers with you and your friend, the one called the professor. You both taught at the university once."

The old man's smile revealed several missing teeth. He motioned Shan to sit beside him. "I have only the one cup," he said, and offered the sooty, dented mug to Shan, who declined it. "That was years ago," the janitor said. "What happened to you?"

"I had to go away. I live in Tibet now," Shan said in a slow, conversational tone. "You used to sit in the shade of the wisteria and throw your sticks to recite the Tao te Ching, or sometimes read a book of poetry."

The old man nodded. "Your father was a professor, too, I recall."

"A long time ago," Shan said.

There was a movement in the shadows. Yao appeared, and stood behind Shan.

"I am permitted to live here," the janitor said, gazing apprehensively at Yao.

Shan gestured for Yao to sit. "You are fortunate," Shan said, and realized the room was like a meditation chamber, its walls and ceilings lined with wood.

The old man stared at the candle flame, his lips quivering, fear in his eyes.

"We are trying to understand what happened that day the fresco was stolen," Shan said in a soft voice. "I think there are many secrets in the Qian Long cottage. I think the thieves were surprised at something they found, something other than the fresco. Something in that box in the wall."

"On National Day," the old man suddenly said in a hoarse voice, "Professor Jiang likes to go out on the square and sing patriotic songs with the crowds. He brings me back a bag of roasted pumpkin seeds then chides me for not doing my duty."

Shan could read the glance Yao shot him. They should leave. The old man was crazy, was wasting their time.

"In the night we would sit in the dark and hear the voices of those who used to live in the rooms, from the emperor's court. Some mornings we would tell each other we were going to work in some official duty in the emperor's court, and at night speak about how those duties had gone. One of the good emperors."

"Like the Qian Long." Shan said.

The old man nodded. "That was the professor's special interest. The Qian Long era. He used to give lectures about it at the university. I would have him recite the lectures for me, here." He slowly passed his fingers through the flames of the candles, watching with an odd, distant fascination.

"Where is the professor?" Shan asked.

"Now I hear his voice at night, with the others."

Yao muttered and shifted as though to rise. Shan put his hand out to stop him. "You mean he died. When?"

"They beat him that day when he found them."

"The police?"

"The thieves."

Yao froze, then settled back to the floor. "He saw them?"

"But he was already dying," the old man added. "He had a cancer, he knew. There was a big lump in his belly." He sighed and gazed at his candles. "In the newspapers the police said it was a perfect crime, said the thieves knew everything about how to get inside. I said the police were fools. But Jiang said no, to the police such men are indeed invisible."

Shan felt a new sorrow as he studied the old man. It had been a common thing, during the mad years of the Cultural Revolution, when institutions of higher learning had been shut down, for teachers to be assigned to manual labor. Shan's own father had been a member of the intellectual class which Mao had reviled as an enemy of the people. Most had been rehabilitated and eventually, sometimes ten or twenty years later, gone back to their former jobs. Some, like his father, had not survived the initial round of violent persecutions. Still others had been lost in the ranks of the proletariat, forgotten in back-breaking jobs that were little more than enslavement, left without pensions, without government support, often without surviving family.

"You mean men like Ming," Shan said.

"I told him to go to the hospital but he said they would think he was involved in the theft. They would interrogate him. He couldn't stand police.

They made him shake, made him so upset he could not speak. The thieves knew he was no threat."

"What did he see that day?"

The old man did not acknowledge Shan. "They always leave us alone, the professor and me, the two crazy old men. No one cares that we work slowly, stopping often to discuss the artifacts, to do what we can to protect them. I taught about the early dynasties, whose courts were in the south. But Jiang, he was the greater scholar. He knows things about the Qian Long no one else knows, he is always making new discoveries and taking notes." The old man kept mixing his tenses, as if he weren't sure that Jiang was actually dead. "He knows how things get protected."

For the first time Shan became aware of shelves around the top of the room, below the high ceiling. They were packed with hundreds of items: Scrolls, incense braziers. Jade seals. A small bronze horse.

"It isn't time for everything to be known," the old man said. "Perhaps one more generation, perhaps then people will not be so greedy."

Shan found himself looking into the flames. The two old men must have lived in the cramped room for decades, exiles in their own city. They had seldom spoken with him of their past when he had seen them in the gardens years earlier. Shan himself had often hidden from the staff when he saw them, for fear of being ejected from one of his private retreats. Those who had survived the years of Mao had learned to be wary of strangers.

"I remember sitting in one of the old courtyards once," Yao suddenly said in a slow voice. "I saw a mouse carrying a small jade bead. He took it into a hole in the foundation."

The old janitor looked up with a grin. "Sometimes we have helpers."

"So Professor Jiang was worried about the secrets of the Qian Long," Shan ventured.

"The Qian Long had many reasons for secrets, many places he kept secrets during his last years." He looked up toward the shelves. "It isn't stealing what we do. These things don't belong to us. But they also don't belong to those others."

"You mean the men from the museum."

"That Ming. He would yell if we got too close to their work. They were just children he had working on the restorations, students who didn't know what they were doing. I don't think it ever occurred to him that we had keys, too, to clean the buildings at night."

"They were not supposed to be working at the cottage that day," Shan said. "But two men came anyway, with a key, a big Mongolian and a small man, a plasterman."

"Jiang would go and just sit sometimes in the old cottage and read poetry, like a scholar in the old court. He said sometimes it felt like the emperor was listening. It is a big job, removing a fresco. They were probably waiting for some glue to dry so they were walking around the cottage. That's when those two found him, asleep at a table in a back room. They beat him and kicked him, that big one and his small friend."

The words brought a brittle silence.

"You must tell us about the emperor's secrets," Yao said.

The old professor looked into the flames again. "Near the end, he and the amban played a trick on the court."

"They corresponded in Tibetan," Shan suggested, and paused. "How did you know we are interested in the amban?" Shan asked.

"The amban lived in Tibet, the amban correspondence was the most important thing to the emperor in his last year of life. The disappearance of the amban was a tragedy from which the emperor never recovered. Letters about the amban get stolen. Now you arrive from Tibet. It is too big a coincidence, eh Jiang," he called to the shadows.

Shan reached inside his shirt and pulled out the piece of old cloth, unrolled it, and produced the torn thangka. "We know about the amban's treasure," he said. "We know how the thangka was supposed to tell where it could be found."

The professor emitted a long groan of excitement, his eyes bright as a child's. "It's the one, Jiang!" he whispered toward the darkness. "It is the one the emperor waited for, the one thing he ever wanted that he never received." He gazed at the torn painting a long time, turning it over, examining the pair of handprints, turning it back to the front to hold the deity images close to his face.

"How do you know about it?" Yao asked.

"The Qian Long had several secret compartments. Safes. One was in the wall of the dining chamber with the fresco, several in the Tibetan altar room where he met with his lama teachers. Once, inside the altar, we found letters and secret plans showing the compartment in the wall, and a note saying the Qian Long had placed the torn thankga there, with several of the amban's letters, but we had left them there in the wall, thinking they were safe, never dreaming what would happen."

The old professor was lost for a moment in the thankga, taking it from Shan, holding it close to his eyes, grinning like a boy. "You found this in Tibet, where the amban hid."

Shan and Yao exchanged a glance. "How did you know that?" Yao asked.

"After the fresco was stolen, when Jiang was lying here injured he had me go back for the letters in the altar room, because he said the thieves may come back looking for them. Two letters, in Tibetan, were on the floor of the dining chamber, where the fresco was stolen. We had not bothered to read even all the altar letters before. There were other records, copies of letters, in the Qian Long archives. We collected all those involving the amban. When we finally assembled them all and read the ones in Chinese Jiang was transformed. He forgot all his pain, forgot he was dying even. He had a theory that gave him great joy."

"What theory?" Shan asked.

The old man seemed not to hear. "He became sick. The amban. It was a secret, because they thought it would be seen as a sign of weakness. Three letters came, saying the amban's trip home had to be delayed. It was a difficult time for the Qian Long, who had decided to step down from the throne. It was a homage he paid to his grandfather. He said he would not serve on the throne longer than his grandfather, so he would step down after sixty years. It made for great intrigue in the court, for the Qian Long was trying to decide which of the great princes to elevate to the Heavenly Throne. There were spies everywhere, assassinations even. The world was going to change based on one word of the emperor." The old man's voice drifted away as he joyfully gazed at the thangka again.

"For a year the amban and emperor exchanged letters, urgent letters, carried in the imperial post," he said, referring to the highly organized network of riders and way stations established to carry messages throughout the empire. "The amban had all his letters taken to the post in Lhasa, so as not to reveal his location. The emperor urgently wanted the amban back; that we know from the Chinese replies we found in the altar room. The emperor kept a copy of each letter he sent. The emperor said it was vital that the amban return, that there was no need for the treasures, the greatest treasure would be the return of the prince himself. After a few months all the letters switched to Tibetan." He paused and looked at Shan. "You live in Tibet, you said?"

When Shan confirmed that he spoke Tibetan the old man rose and ventured into the shadows, returning with a bundle of ten scrolls, tied with strands of purple silk, their sequence noted by dates on the outside of the scroll.

Shan scanned the Tibetan letters quickly. A copy, from the Qian Long to the amban, describing the Qian Long's pleasure over the new lama adviser the amban had sent to him, saying a new lama temple was to be built in the amban's city of birth. The next was a letter from the amban describing the most joyful development of his life, his donning of a monk's robe. He was living with the artist monks who had been crafting the treasures for the emperor, learning their skills, learning how to impart a deity to a painting. The letter included much of the kind of exchange Yao and Shan had seen in those on Ming's computer discs, though they were more personal, even intimate, in tone. The amban began to describe his decline in health, and reported he was consulting the best of the famed Tibetan healers. The emperor confirmed he understood that the second half of the thangka would tell where to find the treasure, then complained of intrigue in the court, and how difficult it was to find the right heir to the throne. The amban wished him serenity and expressed confidence in his uncle's wisdom. The amban's health grew worse. The emperor offered to send doctors, to send an army to retrieve him if necessary. The amban declined, and said he was feeling much better.

Shan opened the next to the last scroll quickly. It was a long letter, from the emperor, in which the Qian Long expounded his criteria for a good emperor, and his concerns that the empire had become too complacent, too materialistic during his reign, not focused enough on the most important things. When he reached the last paragraph Shan gasped.

"What is it?" Yao demanded.

Shan read the passage again to be certain he understood. "The emperor apologizes for doing this in a letter but circumstances require it. The Qian Long is asking the Stone Dragon Lama, his nephew, to become his successor."

The old man gave a gleeful cry and clapped his hands. "You were right, Jiang!" he exclaimed.

Shan slowly unwrapped the last of the scrolls, the amban's reply. He examined it a long time, then studied his companions. "He announces he is too ill to travel. He declines the offer."

"Impossible!" Yao gasped.

"But true," Shan declared. He saw the inquiry in their eyes but said no more.

After a moment Shan realized that all of them were staring into the candle flame.

"Have you found the Tibetan home of the prince?" the old man finally asked.

"We found his monastery."

"Then take these there, where they will be safer," he said, and handed Shan the bundle of scrolls.

As Yao stood he reached into his pocket and handed the old man several currency notes. "For Professor Jiang," he said.

The janitor looked at the money. "I could light incense at the temple," he said, gratitude heavy in his voice.

Yao handed him more money. "Light incense for a year," he said, and quickly turned back into the dark corridor.

Shan and Yao were nearly outside, approaching the gate of wisteria when the old man caught up with them. He handed Shan one more scroll, a thin one that bore the marks of another letter. "The last one," he said. "The last time the emperor spoke to the amban. The most powerful secret of all perhaps." Shan placed it inside his shirt without reading it.

Yao followed Shan to the little garden behind the Qian Long's cottage, the quiet place Shan had visited so often in his Beijing life. They sat in silence as if neither wanted to be the first to speak, until a policeman escorted Corbett into the garden and Yao quietly explained what they had learned.

When Corbett gave a small exclamation of victory Yao held up a hand. "It doesn't mean anything," the inspector said. "The word of an unrehabilitated class enemy. I could never use it at a trial."

"What it means," Corbett said, "is that we have no more doubt, that we know we are right and they are evil." Shan looked up. The American was speaking like Lokesh. "That makes all the difference." Corbett pulled a paper from his jacket pocket. "And now it's on," he said, and glanced at Yao. "You told him?" When Yao nodded Corbett explained the arrangements to Shan. They would buy Shan some clothes, and depart that night on a nonstop flight to Seattle, with Shan technically in Corbett's custody.

Shan lifted a wisteria flower with a finger and stared at it. "Do I have a choice?"

"I guess," Corbett said hesitantly.

"Then I choose to go, but I have conditions. First I take the torn thangka with me."

"What's the point?" Yao asked. "We still haven't solved its puzzle."

"Maybe I have," Shan replied, and said no more.

The two men stared at him in silence, and first Yao, then Corbett, nodded.

"Second, Inspector Yao tells us where he went this morning."

Yao frowned. "I told you. My office."

"No. You had a Public Security escort. Not your office. Not visiting family."

Yao winced, and looked into his hands. "I have no family but a niece. It was the Ministry of Justice."

"The Ministry or the Minister?" Shan asked.

"The Minister demanded to see me. There have been calls for me to be removed. From the Minister of Culture and two others who are his friends."

"Why?"

"Officially, no reason. He is not going to remove me. Unofficially, because they had calls themselves. From Mr. Dolan, in America."

Shan studied Yao. "But the Minister of Justice doesn't like the Minister of Culture," he ventured.

"He suspects deliberate inattention to socialist priorities." It was one of the political codes for corruption.

"Because of evidence you sent to him, previously," Shan suggested.

Yao exchanged a long somber stare with Shan. They both knew it was how Shan had been destroyed and sent to the gulag.

"You never told us the reason for the audits of Ming's museum," Shan observed.

It was Yao's turn to study a flower. After a moment he looked up, and spoke toward a sparrow on the opposite side of the courtyard. "I had promised to take my niece to one of those roasted duck restaurants for her birthday. A loud party jumped ahead of us in line, flashing business cards, handing out money. Several women. An American and a young Chinese in a suit, both wearing sunglasses. The American stopped and put his palm on my niece's cheek, said she should join them. Before I left I found out who they were. Dolan and Ming. The next day I ordered the audit. I have the authority." He looked back at Shan. "He put his hand on her cheek," he repeated in a brittle voice.

"Holy Christ," Corbett muttered. It had all started because of a chance encounter at a restaurant.

"What is the status of the audit?" Shan asked.

"The thermal imaging equipment has just arrived, on loan from England. We're looking for an operator."

"Where are the artifacts that are to be tested?"

"Still locked in their exhibits."

"My third condition is that you get one of them."

A sly smile rose on Yao's face and he nodded. "Is that all?"

"No. You must go back to Lhadrung."

"I was planning to. When it's over there will be things to be cleaned up there."

"Tonight," Shan said. "Either you go back or I go back. When you get there find the informer, Tashi. Tell him you were able to locate the letter Ming said the police lost. The one Ming said the emperor wrote about Lhadrung. Tell him it, too, is being authenticated."

Yao smiled again. "But why so urgent, why tonight? Your friends Lokesh and Liya are safe."

"It isn't his friends," Corbett said. "He's afraid they will send Ko back." Corbett caught Shan's eye, but Shan looked away, toward the ground. "He's still trying to become a father."

CHAPTER SIXTEEN

Every mile, every minute moving in the opposite direction of Tibet, tugged at something inside Shan. The news he was going to Beijing had been wrenching enough. The news that he was going to America had numbed him. He felt adrift. Several times on the plane he woke with a start, not from a dream exactly, for he had no image in his mind, only a nightmarish sensation, a terrible dread he would never see Gendun and Lokesh again, nor even Ko, despite Yao's promise to return that night.

They landed in a steady rain, at an airport surrounded by highways and warehouses. Corbett, staying only a few inches from Shan's side, led him to two young, well-scrubbed men in business suits who greeted Corbett with cool deference, acknowledging Shan with small frowns, then led them past a long line at the immigration stations into an office where several men and women monitored video surveillance screens. Corbett motioned Shan into a chair while he spoke on the telephone in a low voice for nearly ten minutes, then conversed just as quietly with a dour woman in a uniform who repeatedly gestured with a clipboard toward Shan. The official, clearly unhappy with Corbett's explanation for Shan's presence, finally scribbled on a form on her clipboard, ripped the paper from the board, and handed it to Corbett as she marched away.

They drove through the rain in silence; the two young FBI agents in the front of the large blue sedan; Corbett slumped against one rear window, asleep, Shan staring out the other window.

"Why the long face?" the man at the wheel asked Shan abruptly. He had been introduced as Bailey, though his features had Chinese aspects. "I thought everyone in China dreamed of coming to America. You look like you've been given the death sentence and the last good lawyer just died." His partner laughed, and looked at Shan expectantly. When Shan did not reply, Bailey shot him an irritated glance. "Dammit, Corbett told us you speak English," Bailey said in Mandarin.

"Coming like a prisoner is not in anyone's dreams," Shan replied in the same language. He remembered something Corbett had said in the mountains, to explain his presence in Tibet, that the Bureau had needed someone who spoke Mandarin. But this junior officer, working for Corbett, spoke the language.

Bailey laughed and translated for his colleague. "Does this look like a prison?" he asked in English as he eased the car to a stop in front of a small two-story cottage. The wooden shingles on its walls were grey, its windows and front porch trimmed in white. It had a weathered, disheveled appearance. Vines with purple flowers were growing around the pillars of the porch and overtaking its floor, a line of dense bushes along the front walk dangled long offshoots over the sidewalk.

"Neighbors can't believe I work for the Bureau," Corbett declared. He was standing by the car with his suitcase and Shan's drawstring bag. "They prefer to have all their cops look like young Marines and all cop houses like military barracks." The car pulled away from the curb.

As the American unlocked the door and gestured Shan inside, Shan realized how little he really knew about the man's personal life. "Do you have family?" Shan asked as he examined a cluster of framed photographs on a table by the door. A boy with freckles, on a tricycle. An angry-looking little girl holding a large boot. The photos were faded, the glass in one frame cracked.

"None active," Corbett muttered, and turned away. "Listen quick before I collapse from exhaustion. Here's the tour," he said, and began pointing, to the right, to the shadows beyond, then the left. "Living room, then the kitchen. Downstairs bath." He grabbed his suitcase and kept speaking as he climbed the stairs. "Guest room is first door on the right. Then the bath, then my room."

For a moment Shan stared in wonder. "You have two bathrooms?" His own apartment in Beijing, no bigger than the living room of Corbett' s house, had been prized because it had been only thirty feet from the communal toilets. Bathing had been down the street at a municipal showerhouse.

Corbett didn't reply. "I'm dead. Talk in the morning. Sheets on your bed are clean enough. Sleep well. Tomorrow you make new American friends," he added before disappearing into his room, in a tone that almost sounded bitter.

But Shan did not sleep well. He sat on the bed for several minutes, staring at it, trying to remember when he had last slept on a real bed, with bed linens, then took the extra blanket folded at the bottom of the bed and lay on the floor between the bed and the window, tossing and turning, dozing for a few minutes at a time, each time waking, sometimes gripped in the awful, surreal fear that came with nightmares, though never remembering what he had dreamt. Wrapping the blanket around him, he found his way downstairs in the dark, moving silently through the rooms, feeling like a trespasser, wondering how one person could use so much space, discovering a porch off the kitchen, without walls but with a partial roof that kept the rain off half the porch. It was elevated, above a garage that opened from the rear of the house, so that Shan found himself among the tops of conifer trees, looking downhill toward a large body of water, perhaps half a mile away. It had the feel of being in a mountain cave overlooking a lake, though what he at first took to be stars reflecting off the water he soon realized were the lights of houses on the far side of the water. Rain came and went in rapid cycles, strong showers one minute, fading to mist the next.

On the kitchen table he found a short narrow glass holding dozens of toothpicks. He counted out sixty-four of the little sticks, saw a candle in a tin holder, and gently lifted it from the sill. It was attached to an electric cord. He turned the little round switch in the wire and the candle flickered. He studied it in confusion, watching the little filament that jumped back and forth to simulate a flame. Like many things American, it made little sense to him. If someone wanted a candle, they should have a candle, which would be much less expensive than a dim electric lamp made to look like a candle. His father had promised Shan a trip to America, and had begun teaching him things about the country. Sometimes, his father had once told him, Americans did things just to show they could be done.

Shan set the electric candle back on the sill then stepped back outside. He sat cross-legged upon the planks, under the flickering candlelight in the window above him. Emotion kept swirling around the calm place he sought. Despair, exhaustion, helplessness. He was a frail boat cut from its anchor. He forced himself to sit without moving for a long time, his eyes on the water at first, then vaguely on the distance beyond, blinking only when the rain started again, closing his eyes until it stopped, then gazing at the dim, grey horizon once more.

When he was aware again, the clouds were much higher, most of the lights on the far shore extinguished. He stared at the little sticks in his hand, gradually remembering where he was. Then he tossed the sticks on the planks in front of him and divided them into three random groups, picked up the first group and began counting it, using the centuries-old method to build the tetragrams that in the Tao tradition were used to invoke verses of the Tao te Ching. It was never as random as it seemed, his grandfather had always told Shan, for the sticks, like the thrower, obeyed a certain destiny. After several minutes he had built a tetragram of two lines of two segments over a line of three segments, and a bottom line of two segments. It indicated chapter forty-four in the charts that he had committed to memory as a boy. He whispered the words toward the water:

The stronger the attachments
The greater the cost

The words left him feeling empty. He gazed into the cool, dark mist. In the distance there were sometimes engines and horns, then the call of gulls.

Eventually he became aware of stirring in the kitchen. Rain still fell but the sky over the lake had become a brighter grey, with pink in the clouds. The door cracked open a moment and an acrid, nutty aroma wafted toward him. Coffee, Shan realized. Corbett emerged with two steaming mugs. To his relief the mug extended to him contained strong black tea.

"You never used your bed," Corbett said, staring out over the water.

"I used one of your blankets on the floor."

"Dammit, Shan, it's no sin to be comfortable." Corbett's voice was strangely tentative.

"I like this porch," Shan said, uncertain why his own tone sounded apologetic.

"It belonged to my great-aunt. The house I mean, and a cottage on one of the islands north of here, way up by Canada, a little place on the water, full of flowers this time of year. She died a year after my divorce and left them to me. Otherwise I'd be in some one-room apartment, which was all I had left when my wife . . ." He turned away, looking back toward the water. "Dawa and Lokesh and I passed a lake in the night on the way back to Zhoka. A little one, high in the mountains, with the moon reflecting off it. It reminded me of here somehow. Lokesh said we had to stop and offer prayers to the water deities. Now whenever I look at the bay I'll probably wonder about its deities."

Corbett's mood lightened as he drove Shan through town, speaking of the wet, hilly city, passing beneath a strange giant tower with a saucer top he called the Needle, along the waterfront, then into the parking lot of an old granite building that had the appearance of a fortress. Shan silently followed him up the stairs and through a security station, unable to focus on their task because of the alien sights that greeted him at every step. A woman's naked leg had been painted down the length of a city bus, with some words about love he did not understand. A huge sculpture of a purple fish hung over a door. An elevated train on a single rail passed above a man sleeping, almost naked, in a metal shopping cart. The somber men in uniforms at the security gate had skin the color of rich chocolate.

Corbett kept speaking to Shan as they entered the FBI offices on the fourth floor, talking more quietly than usual, about the city and its weather, about the ubiquitous ferries, about the mountains nearby, until Shan realized Corbett wanted an excuse not to look about the office, not to look back at the staff who looked up from their cubicles as he and Shan entered a large central chamber crammed with desks, each holding a computer workstation. Some of those at the computers looked up and did not take their eyes from Corbett as he led Shan through the room, others glanced and turned away with something like a wince.

Corbett deposited Shan in a small conference room without windows, with nothing but a large table with a plastic top, plastic chairs with thin, lumpy upholstery, and a small, battered wooden stand bearing a telephone and a phone book, whose pages were all yellow. After a few minutes alone Shan lifted the heavy book and set it before him, opening it randomly. PET ODOR PROBLEM? asked the first entry he read. LET US EXECUTE YOUR AFFAIR, the next said. He read it several times, not understanding. He leaned over the book, intrigued, confused, leafing through the pages. They were all about economic activity, though he understood fewer than half the categories. He was trying to decipher a huge ad that read ACRES OF RVs when Corbett walked in with his two assistants and a third, sour-looking man who nodded coolly at Shan. A red tie hung over his plump belly. He carried a thin file which he dropped onto the table.

"Mr. Yun—" the man with the red tie began.

"Shan," Corbett corrected him. "His family name is the first name."

The man did not acknowledge Corbett, but started over. "Mr. Shan, I fear that Agent Corbett acted precipitously, in bringing you from China on American taxpayer money. I was on vacation and could not be consulted. The way I understand things is that he expects to resolve the theft of artifacts from our Mr. Dolan by finding some old plaster painting. He says you and he are certain that the Dolan artifacts were shipped to China, though I can't see why they need more Chinese art in China." He paused, as if expecting laughter.

"Tibetan," Corbett muttered. "They were Tibetan."

The man ignored him. "He seems to think you are some kind of magician. Chinese supercop, I guess," he said, examining Shan with a skeptical air.

Shan forced himself not to glance at Corbett. He had not told his superior any of the details of their investigation, had not presented Shan as a witness. "Precipitously?" Shan asked in a slow voice. "I do not understand this word."

The senior agent cut his eyes impatiently at Corbett and sighed. "No doubt you wanted to see America. I accept that you are one of the leading investigators in your country." The man paused as he looked at Shan's cheap clothing and scarred, rough hands. "I'm sure," he continued in a more tentative voice, "we can find some souvenirs. We have paperweights and pins for important visitors. Somebody can arrange a tour of our crime lab perhaps, have you meet the Chinese consul. This is an American crime. Thank you for your interest."

Again Shan had to struggle not to look at Corbett.

"Are you aware that another murder connected to the Dolan theft was committed in China?" Shan asked in an earnest tone. "Three days ago."

"Another?" the man threw an angry glance at Corbett. "There was not a first one. If a Chinese killed a Chinese, that's not for the FBI."

"British. She was one of the thieves at the Dolan mansion."

"You don't know that."

"She admitted it," Shan said.

"Killed by an accomplice then."

"No doubt," Shan agreed.

"Good work," the senior agent said. "Dolan will be pleased." He threw another frown at Corbett. "I had to hear this from the Chinese?"

"So you would feel good about spending all that taxpayer money," Corbett shot back.

"It was a crime on Chinese soil," Shan said.

"Right," the man replied, confusion crossing his face for the first time. He pulled his eyes from Shan then pushed the file across the table to Corbett. "While you were gone the boys came up with this, an art dealer who did work for Dolan. I agree. He's the best candidate for the inside connection." The stout man nodded at Shan and left the room. He had never sat, never introduced himself to Shan.

Bailey, the agent with Chinese features, gaped at Shan with a wide grin and jabbed a finger toward Corbett. "Somebody's been hosed," he said in a loud whisper, and his young partner laughed.

Corbett glanced at the file then pushed it toward Shan, with something like mischief in his eyes. The label said Adrian Croft.

"It's been three days since I told you it was Croft's office on the phone giving instructions to kill Elizabeth McDowell. I don't need to look at the file," he said to Bailey. "Just talk to me."

Bailey eased the file away from Shan, opened it, began holding up papers. "He's listed on two of Ming's expeditions, both in Inner Mongolia," he explained, holding up a fax document, then lifting another memo below. "Croft Antiquities was paid as a consultant, big bucks, on several museum projects funded by Dolan, and on the construction of Dolan's private exhibition space. McDowell was working for the company as a consultant. Did all the appraisals on his collections. The office where that call was made is half a mile from here. The firm is an expert on Asian art, and how to sell it."

"Do you have a list of all those who were on Ming's expeditions?" Shan asked.

"Sure," Bailey replied. "They market them to rich tourists."

Shan quickly scanned the papers Bailey handed him. "Dolan's name appears on none of these." He looked at Corbett.

"But we know he was on those trips," Corbett told his assistant. "We saw the photos." He glanced back at Shan's grin and grimaced. "Son of a bitch." His assistants hung their heads as if embarrassed. "Social security," Corbett said. "Customs Bureau. Immigration Service. Internal Revenue. Go."

Corbett watched as the two men hurried out of the room, then slowly rose, gathered the file, and gestured for Shan to follow. As they left he paused to lean over the desk of the silver-haired receptionist. "If he asks, we've gone to meet the Chinese consul. And the mayor. Key to the city and all that."

They drove under a grey sky to the far side of the water Shan had seen from Corbett's house. Lake Union, Corbett called it. As they drove slowly along the western shore, Shan asked Corbett to pause a moment for him to watch a plane with pontoons underneath ascend from the water.

"Where do they go?" Shan asked.

"Islands. Away," Corbett said, and watched with Shan as the plane disappeared into the low clouds.

They passed a large brick building perhaps eight stories high that had the appearance of an old warehouse but which housed offices. Corbett pointed to a corner window on the top floor, overlooking the water. "Croft Antiquities," he said, then pulled into a parking lot and found a space facing the building.

After a quarter hour they walked across the road and followed a car into the garage beneath the building. The parking slots were painted with the names of people or businesses. Croft Antiquities had three spaces, two with the company name, one labeled Adrian Croft.

"Security cameras," Corbett observed, pointing to long black boxes mounted near the top of several concrete pillars. "Some quality time for the boys," he added, then, seeing the inquiry in Shan's eyes, explained. "We'll get the surveillance tapes. See who's been parking in this ghost's personal space. Then there's always the office manager to interview if we can find her."

"You know her?"

"Picture in the file. She's part Chinese."

They sat in a small café on the ground floor, drinking tea. Shan tried to watch the front door but found himself staring at the seaplanes that kept disappearing into the clouds. To away. He would like to be in some place away, where people did not lie or steal or kill, or pretend to be ghosts. Gendun had wanted him to go away, to his retreat cave. But a few hours on the Dalai Lama's birthday had changed everything.

Corbett, too, seemed to be struggling not to watch the planes.

"You said your aunt gave you a house, on an island."

"A little cottage. Its walls are almost entirely covered in flowering vines. You can look out over the ocean and see whales sometimes."

"She was the one who taught you to paint?"

Corbett grew very quiet. "That's a long way from here. This is America. This is what I do in America. Not what I am now," he said, and Shan realized he really wasn't speaking of his aunt, but of Bumpari village. "Liya and I spoke, before I left the village. She said something very wise. She said she thought being an investigator was the opposite of being an artist."

"Maybe she was saying that some mysteries require an artist, not an investigator. That an artist has different ways to get to the truth."

"Up there in the mountains with you I learned that the facts are only part of the truth, not the most important part." Corbett looked into his cup. "I never really thanked her. Liya. You'll have to do it for me."

"Maybe you'll see her again."

"Me? Not a chance. If you didn't notice this morning I am heading for the junkpile. After this I'll be assigned to helping old ladies find their teeth." He suddenly turned his head down, into his cup. "It's her. Croft's manager."

Shan studied the slight, stylish Asian woman a moment then rose before Corbett could stop him. He waited by the counter that held napkins and sugars until she was seated at a table, then quickly stepped to her side and dropped into the chair across from her.

"My name is Shan," he said in a low voice as he fumbled with the top button of his shirt. "You work for that antique place upstairs." He pulled out the gau that never left his neck and held it for her to see.

"Do you have any notion what that is?" the woman asked. Her eyes showed impatience, but also amusement.

"It's very old. It's very valuable. I know where more are."

She stared at the prayer box with interest and extended a finger toward it, but stopped short of touching it.

"We aren't buying any," she declared impatiently. "You should go. This is not the way we do business. I could call the security guard."

"Take me to your showroom. Let me see what you're buying. I can find many such things. Tibetan. Chinese."

She took a bite of her salad, chewed, and aimed the fork at him. "We are a private house. No showroom. We procure what is requested. No requests for fourteenth-century prayer boxes," she said, nodding toward his gau. "That was three or four years ago." She jabbed the fork toward the door. Shan sighed, rose, and stepped out of the café.

Corbett joined Shan ten minutes later by his car, studying the top-floor windows as Shan explained what she had said, then spoke to Bailey on a cell phone, explaining the urgent task they had with the building security tapes.

They drove again, in a slow, steady rain, Corbett in a brooding silence, until he parked in a huge parking lot, containing more automobiles than Shan had ever seen in one place, and guided Shan toward a cavernous, sprawling building so large Shan could not see the other end through the greyness.

He paused in silent wonder as they walked through the double set of elegant glass doors. Trees and flowers grew beside a pool with a waterfall. The floors were marble. An ironwork stairway gracefully curved around the waterfall, toward a ceiling of arched glass.

"There's a place we can get coffee, a quiet place to talk."

Shan still stood, studying the strange building and the dozens of people who were wandering in and out of the open doorways off the huge main hall. There were shops, he realized, dozens of shops, two floors of shops. When he looked toward Corbett the American was already ten feet in front of him. Shan followed slowly, puzzling over everything in his path. Adolescents walked by, engaged in casual conversation, seemingly relaxed despite the brass rings and balls that for some reason pierced their faces. He looked away, his face flushing, as he saw several women standing in a window clothed only in underwear. He saw more, nearly identical women in another window adorned in sweaters and realized they were remarkably lifelike mannequins. One of the sweaters was marked at a few cents less than three hundred dollars, more than most Tibetans made in a year.

"Why did you bring me here?" Shan asked, as Corbett led him into a coffee shop and ordered drinks for both of them. "This place of merchants."

"I thought you'd want to see America," Corbett said with an odd, awkward grin, gesturing to a table, then sobered. "And this is where Abigail worked, before getting the governess job. People here knew her, told me stories about her, made her real for me."

So Corbett was looking for what? Shan wondered. Not clues, for he had already covered this ground. It was as if he were paying homage to her, perhaps apologizing to the girl in his own way for not being able to bring her killer to justice.

"I thought it was too great a coincidence. The nanny of the family dies the same night the artifacts are stolen. But Punji didn't do it. I believe what she said." Corbett seemed to have grown comfortable using McDowell's nickname, as if he had grown closer to her since her death. "She and Lodi carried away the artifacts but didn't know anything about the girl. What if it was just a coincidence? What if I have been wrong?"

"It's why you went to Tibet, isn't it?" Shan asked as a waitress delivered two steaming mugs. "Because of the girl, not because of the theft."

Corbett thought a long time about his answer. "I could have sent the boys to follow the artifacts. But every night I kept seeing the girl's face, as she floated in the water. Like she was looking right at me. Like she was trying to say something to me but her mouth wouldn't work anymore." He sipped from his mug. "It's why I went. It isn't why I stayed."

The cell phone in Corbett's pocket rang. He grabbed it and listened intently, pushing the phone tightly against his ear, making small sounds of affirmation before he hung up. He looked down into his mug before speaking. "The tapes were there, with a machine available to screen through them at high speed. The guard on duty helped them. I thought it would take most of a day." He spoke into the mug, in a low, despairing tone.

"You knew who it was already. We both knew," Shan said. "It could only be one person."

"Might as well be God. He's untouchable. I'll never be allowed near him without direct evidence, and he's way too smart for that."

"Lokesh would say that if Dolan did such a thing, if he killed the girl and arranged the thefts, then he will inevitably be touched by the sin."

"So I'm supposed to wait for him to be reincarnated as a beetle and step on him. I prefer my justice in this lifetime." Corbett looked up from his mug. "You don't understand the type. If Dolan doesn't like the way his garbage is picked up he calls the mayor."

"I know exactly the type."

"Right. I forgot. You opposed them and you lost. All those years in the gulag."

"I prefer to think of it as a stalemate. I'm still alive."

Corbett studied Shan intensely, as if he had never seen him before, as if Shan had just made a proposal, then a grin cracked his face, followed a moment later by a deep laugh. "Fine. We brought a surprise for Mr. Croft. Let's find a way to deliver it." He stood, left several bills on the table, and headed for the car.

Shan began to marvel at the rain itself. Beijing was a dry place, most of Tibet a near desert. He had not experienced so much rain since he was a boy, living near the sea. There were many qualities of American rain, and many types of rain clouds. One moment they were in a driving rain, like a storm, the next in a shower, the next in a drizzle that was little more than a thick fog. Once the water came down so violently, in such a sudden wind, that it struck at the car horizontally. Corbett never seemed to notice the rain, but drove at a steady speed, out of the city, into hills with huge houses bounded by high walls and metal gates. He slowed as they passed a long rambling brick structure built into the side of the hill, enclosed by a five-foot-high brick wall. The main structure was nearly two hundred feet long, and surrounded by other buildings, a long garage with eight doors, a greenhouse, and small structures Shan could not identify.

"It looks like a hospital," he ventured. "Perhaps a small college."

"The scene of the crime." Corbett's voice was tight. He did not seem inclined to conversation. He drove a hundred and fifty yards past the gate and pulled to the shoulder of the road where the compound's wall turned into the thick forest, pointing to a large tree growing close to the wall, twenty yards from the corner. "The girl's friends said she sometimes climbed the tree to get over the wall when was she was in a hurry, lean her bike there and go over. I interviewed Dolan's two kids, before my boss intervened. They confirmed it, that she would climb the wall without tripping the alarms. It was their little secret."

"But why would she go back that night?"

"To turn off a kiln. She and the kids made clay pots that day in the studio building, near the back of the compound. The boy said they had forgot to take the pots out of the kiln, that he was sure they would be ruined. But someone had taken them out, turned off the kiln and taken the pots out. She had a class down the road at the local college. She came back here, climbed the tree to turn off the kiln. Then she saw something she wasn't supposed to see." He began driving again, the road approaching the open water again.

"There is no proof," Shan said.

"There is proof against it. The next time I went to the house to look at the scene of the robbery, Mr. Dolan himself sought me out and said he had turned off the kiln."

Shan considered the words. "You mean his children had told him about speaking with you?"

"He had been away, he hadn't seen his kids. Somebody leaked my interview report to him. He came to me when I was studying the grounds to say he had turned off the kiln, then he walked away, wouldn't let me ask any other questions. He said the insurance investigators already had all they needed, that the FBI need not trouble itself further. He had no problem with us, until I raised the issue of Abigail."

Corbett pulled the car onto a narrow track that led to a gravel parking lot overlooking the bay. The wind was lashing the water, creating whitecaps. Corbett pointed to the narrow iron bridge that towered a hundred feet over a small inlet, then silently got out of the car. Shan followed, raising his collar against the raw wind.

"Abigail is spotted at the house, an unexpected witness to the crime. Afterwards he offers to drive her home. Late for riding a bike on the winding roads. They put the bike in the car. When they reach the bridge they stop for a moment. Here, because there are no houses, no one can see. Admiring moonlight on the water perhaps. Maybe he says he thought he saw a whale. Who knows. They get to the edge, he pushes her over. She's small, not very heavy. Then he drives five miles to the bridge near her house, throws the bike over, where it is found by divers two weeks later. Thing is, it was low tide. No water under this bridge then, just rocks. She didn't die from the fall but her back was broken," Corbett added in a tight voice. "She drowned."

Shan stared at the dark, swirling water, fighting a sudden horror within. The girl had landed on the rocks, helpless, in the night, broken, unable to move as the tide had slowly risen over her and carried her out into the bay.

They spoke no more, not even when they returned to the house. Corbett left some food on the table and went up the stairs. Standing by the bridge he had sounded so certain of the girl's murder, but they both knew there was no evidence. It was indeed as if the girl had spoken to him that awful day on the water.

Suddenly hungry, Shan examined the food. A cucumber, a head of lettuce, a loaf of brown bread, a box of instant rice, a banana, a tomato, a jar of mustard, and several cans of vegetables he did not recognize. He sliced the cucumber into long wedges and took it with the banana to the soft chair near the entry, turned out all the lights, and ate. He leaned back in the deep chair, listening to the noises that came from outside, his eyes closed. When he opened them the house was dark, and a blanket had been thrown over him. Hours had passed. It was nearly midnight. He started toward the stairs, then stopped and stepped to the back porch again. The rain on the leaves was like a whisper. In a bucket by the door a cricket suddenly chirped. Strangely, the sound seemed to push the sadness from his heart. For the first time in years he remembered walking with his father through a bamboo grove in a soft rain, his father calling to birds, a cricket laughing. He stood without moving a long time, afraid of stirring away his father.

Finally he returned to the kitchen and began to search, opening drawers and cabinets. At the back of the counter he noticed a white plastic box with a cord, its small cursive label identifying it as a can opener. He paused, trying to imagine how it worked, or why it was necessary. Soon he found a piece of white paper, a heavy black marker, matches, and the stub of a wax candle. He took them out-side and sat against the wall, under the overhang of the roof, lit the candle, and wrote in bold, flowing ideograms.

In a bucket a cricket sang, he wrote, *cutting through my sorrow. I am awestruck. Thank you, father, for teaching me to how to listen.* He folded the paper, wrote his father's name on it, scribbled, in English, *Seattle,* on the upper corner, then lit it with the candle, dropping it into an empty clay pot. He watched the ashes drift into the mist, his postcard from America.

Much later he found his way to the stairs, and was about to step into his bed-room, when he saw that the door at the end of the hall, beyond Corbett's room, lay slightly ajar. He approached with a pang of guilt and pushed the door open. There were unfamiliar scents. He turned on the light. An easel lay at the center, with an unfinished watercolor. A sketch of the intended picture lay on a table beside the easel. It was of a windblown stone building on a mountain, with a string of prayer flags flapping over it. Corbett had been painting.

CHAPTER SEVENTEEN

Shan was sitting on the front steps, studying the flowers, watching the inhabitants of the street, when he heard Corbett come down and move toward the kitchen. He had been sitting there since before dawn, unable to sleep, watching, often not completely understanding what he saw. A white truck with a bloated cargo bay drove slowly out of the mist, men in coveralls emptying plastic barrels of trash into it. Several people sped by in very small shorts and caps, running in the rain. He did not understand where they ran to, or what they might do when they arrived. A truck passed by with a huge, mysterious message painted on it, Positively Overnight.

His mind kept drifting toward another dawn, thousands of miles away, where Surya and his new companions collected human waste, where hermits in Yerpa recited mantras in a chamber filled with butter lamps, where Ko probably slept in manacles, dreaming nightmares of men with skeleton hands. He became aware of Corbett speaking on the telephone, saying Bailey's name frequently, emotion rising and falling in his voice like a tide. Shan entered the house quietly and was sitting in the big chair again when Corbett, still speaking on the phone, handed him a banana.

Five minutes later Corbett hung up the phone and stepped to the door, gesturing for Shan to follow. They climbed into the car and drove, over a bridge, down a sharply winding road through a forest of huge evergreen trees.

"Bailey says the insurance company is about to write a check to Dolan," Corbett reported in a dull voice. "Don't push him. He stayed up all night," Corbett warned as they pulled into a gravel lane.

They arrived at an old house in the process of being rehabilitated, newly painted boards on one wall, what looked like black paper on another. Bailey stood in a separate building, a shed that had been converted into a small gargage, the bay door open. On a long table in the center of the garage were arranged a paperback book, ruined by water, some dirty clothing, several folded papers, a broken necklace, a small pair of shoes, and a bicycle, its frame and front wheel bent. At the end of the table were lenses, small bottles of chemicals, and several delicate brushes.

"Not a damned thing," Bailey said without a greeting. "Lost count of the number of times I've examined each thing. Last night before dark I went down below the first bridge, hoping for some sign she had been there. Nothing. Tide's done its work. It's been weeks now."

Shan stepped closer to the table. A piece of seaweed, dried and shriveled, clung to one of the shoes.

"Police report still says she came onto the bridge too fast," Bailey stated, "hit a wet patch, slammed into the low wall, and the force took her and the bike over."

Corbett picked up the necklace, silver with a small locket, opened to reveal a photo of an old woman. He held the necklace toward Shan. "But this was found in the seaweed on the opposite side of the bridge. Their report can't explain that. Because it came off before she was thrown off the first bridge. Maybe there was a brief struggle. He tossed it off the back of the second bridge when he disposed of the bike."

Shan surveyed the table, then the garage. "The police work is completed?" The evidence should have been in an official lab.

"Case closed," Corbett said. "Accidental death. All done. This was all being sent back to her parents."

"Yesterday we checked every storage rental operation in the region for anything rented to Dolan or McDowell or Lodi. Nothing. We called the antique dealers again. Not one of the Dolan items has surfaced in the Northwest. It's a dead end, boss," Bailey said. "And I'm beat," he added, then handed Corbett a piece of paper with a drawing on it and stepped toward the house. Corbett waved at his back.

They drove again, for ten minutes, and got out in a cemetery, Corbett studying Bailey's drawing as they walked down the rows of wet square stones and dripping conifers.

"Do they stay here?" Shan asked. Some of the graves looked very old.

Corbett gave him a weary, puzzled glance, and Shan realized he thought Shan was making a bad joke. But in the cities of China no one but the very wealthy or famous stayed in graves. If a family could afford a burial at all, the body was interred only for four or five years, to allow for mourning, then exhumed and cremated to make way for the newly dead.

It took nearly fifteen minutes to find the grave, a surprisingly large stone with extravagant carvings of birds and flowers along its edges, Abigail Morgan's name carved in ornate letters. "Dolan insisted on paying for it," Corbett muttered as he extracted something from his pocket and placed it on the stone.

Shan gazed at it, disbelieving at first, searching Corbett's solemn face, then stepping closer. It was a tsa-tsa, one of the clay images of Tara the protectress, the kind the American had seen left on the altar below Lodi's effigy.

As Corbett stood by the grave with a mix of sorrow and anger on his face, Shan surveyed the landscape and began to collect rocks. He had built a cairn several layers high at the foot of the grave before Corbett noticed and began to help. When they had laid the top stone, nearly two feet high, Shan turned to Corbett. "Do you have a clean handkerchief?" When the American nodded and extended the cloth, he took a pen from Corbett and inscribed the mani mantra on it ten times, then anchored it under the top stone. "Everytime it flaps in the wind," he explained, "it recites the prayer."

Corbett seemed about to respond when his cell phone rang. He hesitated, then with a reluctant expression withdrew it from his pocket.

"Corbett," he snapped, and then, "yes sir."

Corbett listened for a long time, his eyes smoldering. "I forgot all about her, sir," he said at last. "You ordered that file closed, I recall." He listened again. "Right," he said. "A new case. Art theft in Boise. We're on it." He returned the phone to his pocket. "Whenever you're ready, Inspector Shan," he said with a dangerous grin.

There was no security guard at the front gate, only a video camera and a speaker in a small box inside a brick pillar. Shan sat at the wheel, having changed places with Corbett fifty yards down the road, and spoke quietly into the box as Corbett turned his face away from the camera. They waited a minute, then two, but the heavy iron gate suddenly creaked and began to slide sideways on a track in the pavement.

If Shan had not previously seen his photograph he would have never picked Dolan out of the group of men standing at the oversize front window. The billionaire was a short, ill-proportioned man whose tanned athletic face did not seem to belong on his stocky body. He was younger than Shan expected, his trimmed brown hair showing only a few strands of grey. Shan had also expected him to be impatient, even irritable, but as soon as he dismissed the men with him Dolan sank into one of the leather chairs and offered a gracious smile. "You must imagine my surprise to hear my old friend Director Ming had sent a present," Dolan said, exaggerating his words with lifted brows. "How intriguing. How is the good director?"

"Busy," Corbett said.

Dolan's eyes were grey, flecked with a darker color, like dirty ice. They studied Corbett a moment, then aimed at Shan. "You must be the Chinese cop. *Nei hou tongzhi,*" he said in Mandarin. How are you, comrade.

Shan did not reply, but reached into the paper sack and produced a small brown box, placing it on the low table in front of Dolan. Dolan studied it for a moment without moving, then looked back at Corbett. "I haven't had a chance to call your bosses yet, Agent Corbett. I will. I told you the FBI was through here."

Corbett returned his steady gaze. "But this isn't business. I'm under orders to escort our Chinese visitor. Oh, my boss did say something about looking into Adrian Croft. Know him?"

When Dolan curled his lips, his face strangely reminded Shan of Colonel Tan's. "There is no Mr. Croft, Corbett. But, of course, you know that by now. A convenient fiction," he added in a flat voice. "My security people recommended it. Nothing illegal in taking precautions." He leaned forward and placed his hands around the box. "This is addressed to Adrian Croft," he observed, a hint of impatience on his face for the first time.

"Director Ming," Corbett lied. "I guess he was just taking precautions."

Dolan opened the box with one eye on Shan and Corbett, obviously suspicious, but just as obviously unable to control his curiosity. When he pulled away the top and the packing material he paused, his brow furrowing. His face went blank for a moment, then he withdrew the beautiful little figure, the four-hundred-year-old saint with the sword in one hand, a lotus in the other, the original of which had been destroyed by Lu and Khan. He sighed, and studied his visitors in silence.

"No doubt your insurers will be glad to hear the news," Corbett said.

"I don't know what you're talking about," Dolan shot back. "If you would study the list of stolen items you would know this was not among them."

Corbett picked up a small pillow adorned with needlework flowers and stared at it. "In my long experience with art thefts, we have learned to verify everything. People with large collections can forget, or have incomplete records. Your wife was showing off your collection last year, Mr. Dolan. I have magazine photos with this piece on your shelves. With, in fact, another dozen or so items not on your own inventory. Museum-quality pieces," he added pointedly.

"I sold them."

"Good. Then there will be records of the transactions. The insurance company will ask. We sent them photographs so they would have complete information."

When Dolan's eyes flared it wasn't just anger Shan saw, but something wild, almost savage. "I'll ruin you, Corbett. You're in direct violation of orders."

"I have photos of the same pieces in the museum collection, published the same month as the magazine that showed them here. Even affidavits from the artists in Tibet who made the forgeries for you and Ming," he lied.

Dolan clenched his fists.

"Enough," Corbett said, "to keep me from being ruined. Enough for the insurance company to reopen their investigation. Insurance fraud is a serious crime."

"It had nothing to do with the insurance," Dolan growled.

"It would be kind of demeaning, for all of us," Corbett agreed. "but I guess insurance fraud is better than nothing."

"Do you know how many lawyers I have? I don't trouble myself with obsessive bureaucrats." Dolan rose, stepped to a corner cabinet, and produced a bottle of whiskey. "Where is Ming?" he asked in a steadier voice as he poured himself a glass.

"In Lhadrung," Shan said. "Being interviewed on television, taking congratulatory phone calls from Beijing. He discovered the long-lost tomb of the amban."

The news seemed to amuse Dolan. "A new exhibit for my new museum wing in Beijing," Dolan observed with an icy smile, and drained his glass. "Thank you for transporting his gift." He set his glass down and gestured toward the door. "I am a busy man."

"There was one other thing from Lhadrung," Shan said as he rose, just loud enough for Dolan to hear. "An old thangka."

Dolan froze, then poured himself another whiskey and returned to the low table, sitting, picking up the little deity. "I have learned a lot about beauty by collecting so many years," he said to the little statue. "It's all about rarity. If you have the only one of something in the world, it is beautiful no matter what it is. It's true," he said in an insistent tone, as if he didn't expect them to understand it. "Take a Rembrandt, or a Tang dynasty vase. If everyone had one it would not be beautiful, it would be a spoon, a bottle, just more household junk."

"That makes me sad," Shan said.

Dolan glared at him, as if Shan had insulted him. "What thangka?" he asked abruptly.

Shan slowly pulled the cotton pouch from the sack, extracted the painting, and unfurled the torn thangka on the table.

For a moment Dolan seemed unaware of anything in the room except the old ragged fragment. He approached it, bent at the knees to examine it. An intense excitement lit his eyes.

"In my library," he said with a gesture to the adjoining room. "There is a better table for this." He picked up the thangka and in another moment had it laid out on a broad, dark wooden table in the center of a chamber filled with bookshelves. He pushed a gooseneck lamp over the painting, and paused.

"I should arrange coffee," he said, and stepped away, returning in less than a minute. "These things surface sometimes," he observed in a quick, dismissive voice. "The flotsam of the ages. It looks genuine, looks somewhat old. But ruined. Of no real value. There are historians who use such fragments for research. I could give you a hundred dollars for your trouble and see it gets in the right hands."

As he spoke a woman in a grey and white uniform arrived, holding a tray with cups of coffee and a plate of sweet biscuits. Dolan let her pour the coffee, then, just as he extended one toward Shan, a series of small explosions came from the back of the house. The woman gasped and ran out of the room. Dolan lowered his cup and followed her.

"Gunshots!" Corbett cried. Shan darted out of the room a step behind Corbett.

They ran through a huge kitchen through a rear door to find Dolan on the lawn, shouting at a man who held a shotgun in his hand. It was squirrels, Dolan said moments later as they reached him. The gardener had decided to take action against the squirrels who kept stealing the nuts from some exotic tree.

When they returned to the library, the thangka appeared undisturbed. The maid was cleaning the carpet where the coffee had spilled. A man with a brown beard, wearing a blue sports jacket, stood at a door at the back of the room and nodded at Dolan.

"A hundred dollars," Dolan said, "Like I said, I could give you a hundred dollars for your trouble, and see that this fragment gets to some scholar."

Shan began rolling up the painting. "I know scholars in Tibet."

Dolan grabbed Shan's arm and Shan looked up into his eyes, which burned with the wild expression again. "Using monks won't stop me. I thought we proved that," he said with a growl.

"Stop you from what?" Shan asked.

"Pushing the right buttons," he said, then turned and left the room.

"A distraction," Corbett said as they climbed into the car. "The shots had to be a distraction," Corbett said. "But for what? He didn't take the thangka."

Shan's eyes stayed on the house. His skin crawled. He felt unclean somehow. "Dolan had it photographed," Shan said. "That's why he wanted it on that table, under that bright lamp. Probably that man in the blue jacket."

They parked on the side of the road near the gate and waited forty-five minutes before another vehicle emerged. The man in the blue jacket was at the wheel. Corbett leapt out and flashed his identification, conferring briefly with the man before hopping back in beside Shan. "There's a coffee shop down the road. We will meet him there."

The little café had been a gasoline station, its pumps still in the islands, draped with vines. The stranger looked up nervously as Shan and Corbett sat at his table.

"I need to know what Dolan had you do in the library," Corbett demanded abruptly.

But the man denied setting foot in the room. "I was checking in with Dolan about our project." He paused, studying Corbett, then looking out the window. He shrugged. "Someone passed me in the corridor when I was going to the library. A kid in white coveralls, one of the ones who does art restoration for him. I didn't see what he did."

Corbett fixed him with an accusing stare. "Did he have a camera?"

The man nodded then produced a business card. Corbett glanced at it, handed it to Shan. It stated he was manager for a mechanical engineering firm. "We work on remodeling projects for Mr. Dolan."

"What sort of projects?" Shan asked.

The man winced. "He's very particular about secrecy. There's provisions in all his contracts."

Corbett extracted the little leather folder containing his official identification and laid it on the table in front of him. "I can be particular, too. What sort of remodeling?"

The man shot a nervous glance around the little café. "Look, he is always changing things around. He has a whole wing that's a personal museum. We helped build it. He's changing it, that's all. Better security, things like that. Everyone knows about the big theft there."

Corbett gave a frustrated sigh and returned the folder to his pocket. "I want the names of those art restorers."

"I don't know them."

Corbett shifted in his seat as if about to rise.

"What sort of changes in the museum?" Shan asked.

"A dining room in the center, surrounded by another heavy security wall, with a little kitchen station outside it, a dumbwaiter connecting to the basement below. A dressing room where waitresses can put on Chinese robes. A climate-controlled closet to store the robes. A bedchamber, fitted with Chinese antiques. He likes taking friends into the museum, likes to live with his art, but he worries a lot about security now. Who could blame him."

"What sort of dining room?" Shan asked.

The man looked at him. "I never saw your identification. Why would the FBI want to know about Dolan's dining room?"

"What sort of dining room?" Corbett asked.

The man frowned, then pulled a napkin from a dispenser and drew a quick diagram, a large rectangle. "The main gallery," he explained, then drew two concentric rectangles in the center. "The security wall, and the dining room. The dining room has two doors," he said, drawing short diagonal lines, one in the center of one of the short ends of the rectangle, another near the opposite end of one of the long walls. "The whole room is twenty feet long, fourteen wide. Lots of unpainted woodwork, mahogany and cedar. No wires."

"You mean hidden wiring," Corbett said.

"I mean no electricity at all, not inside the dining chamber. Dolan is a perfectionist about atmosphere, about authenticity. He'll use candles I guess, maybe old oil lamps."

When Shan reached out and put a finger on the table his hand trembled for a moment. He asked for the man's pencil and drew quickly, explaining as he worked. "A built-in cabinet for displaying ceramics at this end," he said, drawing a box shape across the end without the door. He drew an arc over one end. "A curved ceiling, to be painted like the sky." He drew a small circle at the edges of each door. "Four narrow pillars, enameled red."

The man shot a resentful glance at Shan. "What kind of game is this? If you already know, what's the point of asking? Yeah, sure. But remember I didn't tell you if Dolan asks. And how the hell did you—"

The man didn't finish the sentence, for he stopped in confusion, looking at the intense, excited way Corbett clenched Shan's shoulder, then grabbed the napkin. Dolan was building a replica of the Qian Long's dining chamber.

Five minutes later Corbett pulled the car over at the overlook where he had shown Shan the high, treacherous bridge, where the girl had died. The American walked to the edge of the cliff before speaking. "The bastard killed her because he wanted some plaster painting that nobody else in the world would have. He probably plans to put on a dragon robe and sit on some throne in there, gloating over his empire. And if I breathe a word of this officially, the painting will disappear for years."

"Surely the FBI won't—"

Corbett ignored him. "But we know that he and Ming arranged the thefts and he knows we know. Yao can keep up the pressure over there. I can provide enough evidence to make the insurance company hold back the check and start a fraud investigation. Wear him down."

Shan didn't believe it, doubted that Corbett himself believed it. "I need that piece of paper that lets me fly back," he said to the American.

"No way. I need you here."

"You don't understand. I need to be there when he arrives."

Corbett turned to face Shan. "Who arrives? Where?"

Shan returned his steady gaze. "I need to warn the hill people, get Dawa and Lokesh and Liya to a safe place. Dolan is going to Lhadrung."

"Impossible."

"I'm sorry," Shan said.

"Sorry?"

"He already has his fresco, hidden somewhere. What he wants more than anything now is the amban's treasure. A man like that moves from one obsession to the next. It has driven everything he has done since Lu and Khan discovered that secret compartment in the emperor's cottage. Because only one person in the world can have the Qian Long treasure. It's so secret, so old, so linked to the emperors. Never in his life could he hope to find something that would match it."

"He doesn't know where it is."

"He does now. I told him. He knows the fact that I brought the thangka from Lhadrung means the amban never left his gompa. Because the torn thangka did not leave. He might have guessed but Lu and Khan don't know exactly where to look, don't know for certain that it really is in Zhoka. Dolan didn't know for sure where to look, that was why he was supporting Ming and his field surveys, even the surveys in the northern provinces. Nowhere did the amban ever mention his gompa, for fear of compromising its secrets. But when Dolan translates the marks in his photographs, the ones on the back of the thangka he will know."

"What marks? You never showed us marks on the back."

"Handprints. Inside them were very faint lines done in charcoal, for a map that had been abandoned, the map that was supposed to tie to the other half of the thangka, to complete the amban's puzzle. But his sickness changed everything. He let himself be taken north to stage his assassination, to avoid any search by troops in Lhadrung, but then he returned home to Zhoka. He never sent the treasure, because he died. There are tiny words in Tibetan written along one of the thumbprints, so small they are almost lost with the cracks in the cloth. He apologizes to the emperor, and says the abbot has gone to Zhoka to reside with the treasures of heaven."

Corbett stared in disbelief, then turned back to the black water below. "You knew it, dammit," he said in a hollow voice. "It's why you came so easily with me, to lay the trap."

"You know Dolan will never find justice in America."

"You son of a bitch. You planned it." His confusion seemed to give way to anger for a moment, then was overwhelmed with a hollow laugh. Silence returned, and they watched the tide ripping through the narrow channel.

"If there is no chance of justice for him in America, there's an even slimmer chance in China," Corbett said at last.

"He's not going to China," Shan replied. "He is going to Tibet."

Corbett looked at Shan as if wondering if he had heard right, then he bent, picked a small pink flower growing near his feet, and tossed it over the edge into the water.

Four hours later, sitting beside Corbett, Shan watched out the window, yawning, as their plane lifted into the low clouds. During his entire time in America he had slept perhaps six hours, and he had never seen the sun.

Chapter Eighteen

Entering Lhadrung Valley at the end of night, after sleeping nearly the entire journey back, felt to Shan like entering a bayal, one of the hidden lands. Dawn wrapped the valley in a pink and golden glow, the lights of the distant town glittered like jewels, the shadowed mountains seemed like sentinels keeping the rest of the world at bay. Shan longed to stop, to fix the image in his mind, for soon the sun would be glaring down and he would not be in a secret land of saints but in the dry, dusty valley, facing tyrants and thieves and murderers, gazing into the haggard expressions of the Tibetans.

But something about the town had changed. As they reached the outskirts the boys who played in the empty riverbed were wearing crisp white tee shirts and played with a new soccer ball. By the shops on the first block a smiling teenager jogged, holding a small silver plane over his head. In the square in front of the government center a group of women were admiring shiny new keychains each of them held in her fingers, and an old man watched a boy playing with a toy helicopter that rose under its own power on a wire tether.

As Shan saw a familiar face, he motioned for Corbett to park the car, and jumped out.

"Tashi," Shan said, putting a hand on the informer's shoulder. "What happened?" The informer did not acknowledge Shan until he had asked his question twice.

"That famous American," Tashi said in a disbelieving tone, "he stood on the steps with his hand on Mao's head and gave a speech about how great the people of Lhadrung were, then passed out gifts from bags. His Chinese driver told me that at the airport the American bought everything they had in the gift store. Everything on the shelves, they just dumped it all into bags. He had his own jet plane."

Shan stared, not wanting to believe the informer. Dolan had beaten them to Tibet.

"The American said he was Saint Nicholas, but no one knew what he was talking about. He's crazy. The soldiers came to push him off the steps, and he gave them gifts, too. When he had no more gifts he passed out American currency." Tashi pulled an American dollar bill from his pocket and waved it like a little flag.

"What are you doing here?" Shan asked as he surveyed the square. The informer could be watching for Surya, for purbas, perhaps seeking news of hidden artifacts.

"What are *you* doing here?" Tashi asked Shan in a reluctant tone, glancing toward the upper floors of the government center. He could, Shan realized, be looking for Shan himself.

"The prisoners?" Shan asked.

"Still at work by the cliffs in the lower valley. People say the Mountain Buddha is moving in the hills. A toolshed by the school was broken into. Ropes were stolen," Tashi reported in a puzzled voice. "Ming paid a young herder for information about places a large statue could be kept." When he looked up at Shan the informer's eyes seemed hollow. "I'm scared."

Shan stared at the informer so long Tashi turned away, looking at the ground. "Tashi," Shan said, "I am going to give something to you, too, something perhaps no one has given to you in many years." Tashi looked up. "There is never anything of you in what you say. You are only a conduit. But you can change that, starting now. Because I am going to give you trust. I am going to speak to you of things and then I am going to ask you to tell a lie, to help the Tibetans in the mountains."

Tashi looked forlornly at Shan but said nothing. Shan continued, speaking for five minutes in a hushed, hurried voice. When Shan had finished Tashi broke away from Shan's stare and gazed at the dollar bill. He pointed to the pyramid on the note. "Look at that. Why would the Americans have a temple on their money?"

"The American who gave you that had Punji McDowell killed."

Tashi put his head closer to the bill as he replied, covering his lips, as if now trying to conceal their conversation. "Rumors of her death have not been officially accepted." He cast a meaningful glance at Shan.

It was a warning. Yao had reported the events at Zhoka to Beijing, yet the authorities had not allowed the report to be officially filed.

"My grandfather used to tell me about foreign princes who came to Tibet, for a bride, for a special lama, for a special charm." Tashi spoke to the long-haired man on the front of the bill now. "They would bring destruction wherever they traveled, but they would always leave when they found what they wanted."

"How is your mother, Tashi?" Shan asked.

The informer sighed heavily, and leaned toward the man on the bill, whispering to him. "He carries a small gun, a pistol in a strap around his ankle. The driver saw it, when he was making things ready in their car."

Two new vehicles were at the compound when they arrived half an hour later, shiny white Land Cruisers, the kind available for hire at the Lhasa airport. Shan followed Corbett through the gate slowly, surprised at the nervousness he felt about entering. Yao was inside, Corbett had explained, and they would need to discuss what had happened in Seattle. But Shan stopped in the shadows of the wall, studying the inner yard.

The purging of the altar figures seemed to be in the final stages. Only three of Ming's staff were visible, languidly prying apart small statues with pliers and steel prybars, sitting near a small stack of artifacts on the plank table. A fire was burning in the barrel again at the far side of the yard, a single soldier sat on a bench nearby. Twenty feet from the barrel four Tibetan men labored at a pile of the shards that were not combustible, sorting pieces of metal into barrels to be shipped for recycling, throwing ceramic pieces into a pile near the wall where a man with a sledgehammer was smashing them.

Shan froze, still in the shadows, understanding now the reason for his sudden nervousness. He could not see Ko. Then the figure with the sledgehammer turned and Shan saw his face. His son was smashing the ceramic artifacts. But there was no sneer on his countenance, no derision in his eyes for the Tibetans. He worked with a sober, almost angry expression, working the sledge with an easy, experienced rhythm. The rhythm of a prison laborer.

As Corbett appeared in the sunlight in front of the building the soldier stood, straightened his uniform. The action caught Ko's eye, and he lowered the hammer, turning to gaze at the American. He took a step forward, peering into the shadows where Shan stood. As Shan stepped into the open yard Ko met his gaze a moment, showing no emotion, no greeting, then lowered his eyes and swung the hammer again.

When Shan approached, Ko shifted the hammer behind him, as if somehow embarrassed by it.

"Yao said you went to the other side of the world. To America," Ko said, looking at the shards at his feet.

"For a short time."

"Why would you come back?" Ko asked, disbelief in his tone.

Shan took another step forward, so that he was but an arm's reach away.

"It rained a lot." Shan reached into his pocket and extracted a roll of hard candy and a chocolate bar. He could not understand why he had such difficulty speaking. "I brought these for you, from the United States."

Ko stared at the candy, emotion suddenly coloring his face. "I thought they were taking me back. But then Yao came and stopped them." Ko picked at a callus on his palm. "Once on National Day," he said abruptly, "family visitors were allowed into our camp. Some of them gave candy to their husbands or sons or fathers." He looked up and slowly lifted the candy from Shan's hand. "Candy is a good gift for a prisoner." He shrugged, pushing the long hair from his face.

They stared at the shards beneath Ko's feet. Shan struggled for words, any words. He was having a conversation with his son. "Are you well, Xiao Ko?" he asked clumsily, and chastised himself for using the familiar form of address, which his son hated.

He took a halfstep toward his son and shards broke under his foot. He had broken the head off a little clay Buddha.

"One of those Tibetans told me that after the prayers are taken out of these things, that they become only objects again," Ko said, "that it doesn't matter what happens to them." Shan looked at his son in surprise, and Ko grimaced, as though regretting his words.

Shan bent and fixed the head back on the little Buddha and leaned the little figure at the base of the wall. As he did so, Ko swung the hammer again. "It's just a bunch of clay," his son said. "Dirty old clay. When I'm done I'm supposed to dump all the pieces in the parking lot and rake them into the gravel."

"We're going back into the mountains, Ko," Shan said. "I want you to come with us."

His son looked at Shan uncertainly. "Not inside the mountain," he said, worry in his voice.

"Probably," Shan admitted. "You have to tell me you won't try to escape. No soldiers. Just Yao and Corbett and me."

Ko put both hands on the hammer handle, twisting them. "Do you remember her face when she was in that man's arms, Khan's arms? Looking at us like a child, not understanding she was being killed, not knowing enough to struggle. It wasn't her anymore, it was just something that had been her. Every time I try to sleep I see her face like that, alive but dead. Will he be there? The Mongolian?"

When Shan nodded, Ko clenched his jaw and nodded. He looked back at the wall, then dropped the hammer and picked up a large flat rock, which he leaned in front of the little broken Buddha. He was protecting it. "I am a prisoner," he said, looking at his hands now, as if not understanding what they had just done. "Why should I promise not to escape?"

"Being a prisoner is just something other people do to you," Shan said. "Being a thief or a liar, or becoming a fugitive, that is something you do to yourself."

Ko slowly stood and searched his father's face a moment, then looked away again. "They have many cars in America, I hear. Fast cars. Did you see fast cars?"

Shan was not sure he understood. "I saw fast cars. I drank coffee. They drink much coffee there."

Ko nodded solemnly then lifted the hammer to his shoulder again. "I have never drunk coffee," he said in a distant tone.

"I saw planes bigger than an army barracks," Shan said. "There was a little white box that opened cans by electricity."

A tiny smile flickered on Ko's face a moment, then, with the look of a weary old man, he began pounding the shards again.

As Shan turned, Ko spoke to his back, in a small anguished voice. "I gave him a piece of gold, one of those little statues, gave it to that Khan," he said. "Just before he killed her I gave him gold. He laughed when he took it and said I was just like him."

Shan turned to look at his son but Ko would speak no more, would not bring his head up from his work. He kept smashing the shards, not looking anywhere but the ground in front of him.

Inside, Shan found Corbett sitting with Yao at the conference table, explaining what had happened in Seattle.

"Dolan called Ming from his plane," he heard Yao say as he sat beside them. "By the time Dolan got here Ming had more equipment organized. He sent half his workers home, most of the others deep into the mountains to get them out of the way. A truck came from Lhasa with small machines in boxes. By the time Dolan arrived there was an official greeting party, an agenda. You would have thought the Party Secretary was coming."

"Agenda?" Shan asked.

Yao grimaced and handed each of them a sheet of paper, with words in English and Chinese. *Arrival at the Museum Compound,* it said first, then *Welcoming Ceremony in Town,* followed by speeches and a presentation by Dolan.

"Presentation of what?" Corbett asked.

"He gave a check to Punji McDowell's clinic. Ten thousand American. He said he was very sorry to hear that Miss McDowell was missing in the mountains, that he knew her and had long admired her work."

Yao sighed. "When they arrived back here there was a helicopter waiting. They were in the mountains before dusk yesterday."

"All we can do is be driven into the foothills," Shan said. "With packs, it will be another few hours to Zhoka."

Yao nodded. "I've done what I could to prepare, without being conspicuous."

"I want Ko to go with us," Shan said.

"It's too dangerous," Yao protested.

"He won't do anything to hurt us," Shan insisted.

"Lu and that Khan are up there. They know we were eyewitnesses to McDowell's murder. You, Corbett, me. And Ko."

"But you filed a report," Shan ventured, wary, remembering what the informer had told him. "You explained everything. Corbett can testify that the phone call by Lu was to Dolan, that Dolan told Lu to kill her."

"We don't know that for certain," Yao said in a tentative tone, as if experimenting with a new version of his report. He sighed and stared into his hands. "I have heard nothing since my report was filed. Ming is nervous about Dolan being here. Dolan called people in Beijing. Ming heard from the Minister himself. Afterwards he was on the phone with Public Security, saying they had to find Surya. Then when Dolan arrived and Ming showed what he had found in the valley tomb Dolan was furious. I couldn't hear everything. They were in the meeting room, behind a closed door. I think Dolan was upset Ming told people about what he had found, that the newspapers knew about the old robe and that jade dragon."

"Because he wanted them for himself," Corbett said in a bitter voice.

Shan had only half heard Yao's description of the argument. "Surya. Did they find Surya?"

"I think soldiers are still searching."

Thirty minutes later Shan was watching the cluster of nightsoil sheds from across the street. Half a dozen of the haulers had returned from their morning circuits and were unloading huge clay jars into rusty metal tanks on wheels, which would be driven to the fields south of the town. A woman in tattered clothes approached, walking along the rutted road, holding the hand of a small boy, three or four years old. When she reached the sheds the boy started pulling away, hand to his nose, but she scooped him into her arms and, with nervous glances toward the men at the tanks, stepped into the cluster of sheds. Shan followed, feeling the harsh stares of the men unloading the jars. When he reached the little courtyard in the center of the buildings no one could be seen. There was something new since his last visit, a hint of incense that mingled with the fetid odor wafting from the jars. He stepped into the stone-walled stable, pausing, unable to see into the dim interior. There were sounds of soft voices, and the incense hung more heavily in the air, but bundles of straw and a heap of broken clay jars were all that he could see in the dim light cast from the door.

Suddenly someone clenched his arm from the side. "What is your need?" a stern voice asked. He twisted about to see one of the older soil carriers, a man with a wrinkled face and cracked spectacles.

"I came because of the holy man," Shan said after a moment. The man's grip tightened.

"He was the one who gave him the brush that day," a woman's voice said from the darkness, and the man released Shan. He sensed motion in the shadows, and the darkness in front of him seemed to open. It was a heavy felt blanket hung from wall to wall, obscuring the back half of the stable, which was filled with Tibetans of all ages, some seated on pallets of straw, some on the dirt floor. A cone of incense burned on an upturned bucket to the left, a small makeshift altar with seven cracked porcelain bowls stood at the far wall. Between the incense and the altar was Surya, painting. The stable wall had been plastered once and now the plaster was nearly covered with Surya's vivid images.

"See, it's the white Tara," he heard a woman whisper. It was the woman he had seen with the boy. She was pointing at the central figure on the mural, whose delicate face held a third eye in her forehead. "It's been many years since Tara visited Lhadrung," the woman whispered, excitement in her voice. The boy's eyes were wide with wonder.

"You know him from another town?" the old man asked Shan over his shoulder.

"Another town?"

"They say he just does this, all over Tibet, that he goes from town to town, hauling night soil and carrying deities. It is the way some of the old saints lived, someone said."

Shan turned to study the old man's inquiring face, then looked at Surya and slowly nodded. "Like a saint."

"He sat there every night for a week, staring at his brush and the wall, never speaking, leaving each morning with us to haul the soil, barely eating, just coming back to stare as if the wall had something alive in it. My wife says she thinks the wall must be left from the old gompa that was in Lhadrung. People had left him some money when he was begging. One day he came back with some paints and began. He talked a little more after the painting started, like something had been released inside. He said it just needed to be done, that he was just giving color to the deities that resided here. He carries night soil from dawn to noon. He said if he did not carry night soil he would not know how to paint."

An old woman pushed past them and bent at Surya's side. "My wife makes him eat twice a day. Otherwise I think he would forget to eat at all." The woman took the brush from Surya's hand and helped him to his feet. As he let her lead him away the other Tibetans leaned closer to the painting, and Shan heard a mantra start, the invocation for Mother Tara.

Shan found Surya in the courtyard, eating a bowl of tsampa. He was chewing absently, looking toward the sky with a distant expression, when Shan sat beside him, and he took a long time to notice his visitor.

"I know you," he said in a raspy voice, and Shan's heart leapt. "You brought me a brush, a very good one. How did you know?"

"Surya, it's me, Shan."

The absent expression returned to the old man's eyes.

"Surya, you must listen carefully. I know now what happened on the festival day at Zhoka. I saw the man who is paying the thieves. I went inside the underground palace, I was on the ledge above the little chapel where you found the body. You discovered the looters, and they made you angry. You knew they were up above, on that ledge, trying to chip through a tunnel, trying to cheat their way inside. When you saw that they had stolen a fresco your anger made you take the old ladder that led up to the ledge. You took it and threw it in the water, so it went into the chasm. And when you came back you found that man dead, in a pool of blood. You thought you had killed him, that he had tried to step down onto the ladder but it was gone and he had fallen to his death with the chisel, which pierced his body. But you didn't. He was attacked on the ledge above, with a chisel, because he was trying to stop those who were breaking into the mandala temple." Shan still saw Dolan's wild eyes, when he had refused to leave the thankga with the American. Using monks doesn't stop us. We proved that, it didn't stop us from pushing the right buttons. No doubt Dolan had ordered Lodi killed, from Seattle, just as he had ordered McDowell killed, by pushing the buttons of his phone.

"Then he was thrown down, left there to die. You had nothing to do with it." Surya's expression did not change.

"You're listening," Shan said. "Something in you is listening, I know that. You didn't kill a man, you can go back, you can put your robe back on."

The old Tibetan looked into his hands a long time, then gazed with sympathy into Shan's face. "You have a kind face," he said. "I am sorry for your friend who moved that ladder." He sighed. "But you know souls aren't killed by physical action. A soul isn't burned away by the killing itself, but it can be by the fire of hate that precedes it, even by discovering a long life has been wasted."

Abruptly Shan recalled the words Brother Bertram had written. Death is how deities are renewed. As he gazed into the old man's face he realized at last that it wasn't his old friend who sat there, that Surya had indeed gone away, that the fire that had raged through the old Tibetan's spirit had burnt away much of the memories, the humor, the lightness that had made up Surya, leaving a strange innocent reverence, leaving a deity that was Surya and not Surya, a new artist who had to paint different gods, in a different way. And that, Gendun would say, was miracle enough.

He stood and took a step away before trying one more time to reach the old man's memories. "There is a great struggle for the riches of Zhoka," Shan said. "People have come from far away to oppose the lamas for it."

"Such people only fight themselves," the old Tibetan said. "It is just the way of things for them. Everyone has a different path to the center of their universe." He set down his bowl and rose. "The nature of earth taming is not in the earth, but in the people," he said, and paused, questions rising on his face as though he were surprised by his own words. Then, after a moment, he shrugged and stepped back into the stable.

Shan watched the empty doorway, considering the strange words. They had the sound of prophecy.

The haulers had stopped working and were gathered behind one of the rusty tanks, exchanging worried glances when Shan left the courtyard. Colonel Tan was in the street, standing by his car. Tan said nothing as Shan approached, but opened the door for Shan to climb into the front seat. There was no sign of his driver or usual escort, and Tan drove himself, speeding out of town, past the army barracks, never speaking, not even looking at Shan, until they reached the hill above the 404th People's Construction Brigade. He pulled the car to the side of the road and climbed out, immediately lighting a cigarette.

The big supply tent that had been erected for Ming's field teams was gone. In its place were two dozen smaller tents, the mobile camp of an army unit. Tan had ordered new troops to the prison. He had brought Shan here as a warning, to remind him of the power he still wielded.

"Do you have any idea who this man is?" Tan said with a strange, almost contemplative tone. "The American who went into the mountains with Ming?"

"He is a criminal."

"No," Tan said flatly. "He is one of the richest men in the world. He has been a great benefactor to the Chinese people. He has dined with the Chairman of the Party, has the Chairman's personal phone number to use whenever he wants. He can speak to the President of the United States." Tan paused to inhale on his cigarette again, then shrugged. "It is not possible to define him as a criminal. I received two calls from different generals about him, one in Beijing."

Shan studied Tan. "I thought you brought me here to warn me."

"What the hell do you think I am doing?"

"It sounds more like you are trying to protect me."

Tan turned his back to Shan and kicked a stone into the air, then walked away several paces.

"He had the British woman, McDowell, killed," Shan said to his back. "The one who helped hungry children."

When Tan turned back toward Shan he was pulling a piece of paper from his pocket. "Your Inspector Yao has been recalled. He is to return immediately to Beijing for reassignment." He showed Shan the facsimile addressed to Yao, bearing the elegant legend of the Council of Ministers at the top.

"Yao knows this?"

"I went to give it to him at the compound. I left it in an envelope in his bedchamber."

Shan studied Tan. "You mean you don't officially know. You didn't officially tell him."

Tan's head moved slightly up and down in a nod, his mouth curled downward in a frown. He turned to face the prison. "A recalled investigator. An American without authority to act in China. And you. There's no chance you can stop them."

Shan had to clench his jaw not to show his surprise. Tan was secretly telling Shan he would not prevent Shan and his friends from returning to the mountains.

"I have a helicopter coming out of repairs. It needs a test flight, that's how it will be recorded. It can take you and the others to Zhoka. Or a mile away if you prefer. But that's all I can do."

"My son. I want my son to go with us."

"He's a prisoner. The paperwork is on my desk, for his transport back to his coal mine. I've already held it up too long." Tan studied Shan's face a moment. "You don't have enough pain in your life? You have to go out of your way to find more? If he runs, then there will be new charges against you, for aiding an escape. Five years at least."

"I would have thought ten."

As Tan lit another cigarette a perverse pleasure entered his eyes, as if he were grateful to be badgered by Shan. "If Ming calls for the army to help, or that American Dolan, my troops will go to assist." He let the smoke drift out of his open mouth as he studied Shan. "I just want them out of my county."

They landed a mile south of Zhoka, and headed north in silence, Ko hanging back as if reluctant to reenter the ruins. A chill wind, strange for midsummer, had begun to blow behind them, so loud they could not hear each other speak. It seemed to be blowing them toward Zhoka, as if the old earth temple was summoning them. They were less than half a mile away, on the high ridge that first brought them into sight of the ruins, when Corbett lifted his hand in warning. A figure was jogging up the slope toward them, a sturdy Tibetan with a shambling gait, as if his foot hurt. As he approached he slowed, staring at them in confusion, then stopped and took off his cap, wringing it in his hands. It was Jara.

"We thought you had gone," he said in an apologetic tone. "They are ordering all the herders and farmers in the hills to help," he explained as Shan and his friends approached. "That man Ming and the rich American. Someone saw you and they sent me to bring you. They thought you were Tibetans."

Shan surveyed the ridge. "Saw us how? From where?" They had only just come into sight of the ruins.

"A man they call Khan, he's in that old stone tower with binoculars. He called them on a radio."

Any chance of surprise was lost. Corbett frowned in disappointment. Yao wore a satisfied expression, as if he welcomed the news. Ko just stared at the ruins with a cold, determined glint.

"Who else is here?" Shan asked.

"Six herders. The old lama. My niece and Lokesh. Dawa insisted I bring her back to the chorten. Liya was there but ran away last night. After that the American had that man Khan watch, with a rifle."

"Gendun?" Shan asked. "Gendun is with Dolan?" He began running down the slope.

The central courtyard had been turned into an operations base, with a large blue nylon tent at one wall, piles of boxes, and a cooking station in front of the chorten. Dawa, squatting by the cooking fire, gave an excited cry of greeting and ran to leap into Corbett's arms.

Dolan was standing with his back to them, at the far wall, studying the glowing screen of a small, sophisticated piece of machinery. A thin metal band over his head held a small cup to one ear and suspended a microphone near his mouth. He was speaking urgently into the microphone, a finger tracing a pattern of lines on the screen.

Gendun sat against the wall, using his finger to draw in the dirt. Lokesh, squatting next to Gendun, straightened as he saw Shan, a look of alarm on his face. Gendun greeted Shan with a weary nod and returned to his drawing. Ko paused, staring warily at the lama, and Shan remembered that the two had met before, in the dark, when Ko had thought Gendun a ghost.

A shrill whistle blew. Dolan was summoning everyone. He kept blowing the whistle, waving those in the courtyard toward him. Shan recalled the reports of Dolan's early experiences in China, as the sponsor and sometimes manager of archaeological digs.

"We have discovered a chamber," the American called out in Chinese. "Precisely in the center of the gompa, under the rubble, right where our theory suggested." There was a smug sense of victory in his voice. "Ming!" he shouted. "We can be in by sunset! Get these people moving to—" He stopped midsentence as he saw Shan and Corbett. He flung his headset onto the table and marched toward them.

"You must be suicidal Agent Corbett," he barked as he approached. "This will be entertaining, watching an FBI agent ruin his career."

When his eyes shifted to Shan his face filled with a cold anger. "And you must think you're very clever, Comrade Shan. It changes nothing," he said dismissively. "All you did is guarantee that I find the amban's treasure."

"It changes everything. You're here now," Shan said with a gesture encompassing the ruins. "It is a dangerous place to misunderstand, and you have always misunderstood it." He realized Dolan was looking over his shoulder, but pointing at him, and suddenly Shan felt hands on his shoulders. It was Lu, patting him down. When Lu was done Corbett raised his arms, inviting Lu to do the same for him.

"As long as you're here," Dolan said, after Lu confirmed they carried no weapons, "you will join our little project. We are about to open the vault."

"It's an old monastery," Shan said. "A place of reverence. Many people died here."

"No doubt," Dolan said with a cool smile, and motioned Gendun to rise. "Everyone helps move the rubble!" he barked. When the lama seemed not to notice he nudged Gendun's legs with his boot. Gendun smiled as if just seeing him, and slowly rose.

Ming was piling equipment onto a canvas sheet near the center of the ruins, small metal canisters attached by long wires to another sophisticated instrument panel from which a small antenna projected.

"Ground sensing radar," Dolan explained, "borrowed from the Ministry of Petroleum. It confirmed a chamber under that central pile of rubble," he said, pointing to a mound of rocks nearly twenty feet high. A square, ten feet to the side, had been marked on the mound with orange spray paint. "We're going to open it, extract what's inside, and leave. Cooperate and we'll just tie you up when we fly out. I'll be on the way home before you make it to Lhadrung. Everyone lives. You get your ruins back."

There was a murmur at the rear of the group. Gendun was speaking.

"What did the old man say?" Dolan demanded.

Lokesh stepped forward. "He said perhaps you should take this." He offered the American a little tsa-tsa, an image of the future Buddha. "He said you will need it." Dolan accepted the little figure with a frown. "He said," Lokesh explained in a matter-of-fact tone, "if you don't understand what's there it will go very badly for what's left of the deity that dwells within you. A very powerful thing is buried."

Dolan's eyes flashed with anger again. He threw the little tsa-tsa against a rock, shattering it. "Tell him I understand exactly what is there. There's nothing like it in all the world, and it's mine. It will be mine forever," he said in a taunting voice. "And tell him, of all the people in the world, I know about power," he added with a sneer.

"I am sorry," Lokesh said with a sigh.

Dolan muttered under his breath and pushed the nearest man toward the rubble. It was Ko, who paused only for a quick, inquiring glance at Lokesh before pulling the first rock away. Had his son understood, Shan wondered, had he known that Lokesh had not been apologizing, but saying he was sorry for Dolan?

Jara joined Ko, followed by the other herders, wearing curious, expectant expressions as they studied the wealthy American. Only Gendun lingered, his eyes sad, settling to the ground in the shadow of a wall as he gazed upon the orange square in the rubble.

As Shan approached and squatted beside him Gendun began drawing in the soil again. It was another of the ancient symbols, Shan thought at first, but then he saw the block shapes and gaps like gates or arches between the blocks. He was sketching buildings, the buildings that had stood before the ruin, the way they had appeared from where Gendun now sat. Two long graceful buildings, walls canted slightly inward at the top in the traditional Tibetan fashion, stood over the east and west stairways to the underground temple. Between them was an unusual structure, one that probably dated to the days when gompas also served as fortresses, a tall tower, twice as high as the other buildings, that would have allowed those at the top to survey the surrounding lands from the center of the walled gompa, and from which sacred banners or giant thangka would have been suspended on festival days. A tower whose first purpose may have been to guard over the sacred treasure chamber which must have been directly below it.

Dolan watched with cool amusement as Lokesh wrote a prayer on a piece of paper and directed the Tibetans to stack the rocks they removed into a cairn over the prayer. The old Tibetan's action seemed to energize the herders, who worked quietly to excavate a hole in the center of the orange square. Dolan did not seem to notice when Jara handed Gendun the pieces of tsa-tsa broken by the American to bury with the prayer.

They worked an hour, then two, exposing a hole in the center nearly five feet deep, building their cairn higher and higher. They exposed long fragments of wooden beams, then heavy slabs of stone Dolan declared to be the roof supports for the vault. Shan kept looking back toward the drawing Gendun had made in the earth.

Ming seemed to no longer share Dolan's enthusiasm. He shot nervous glances toward Yao and Corbett, and leaned into Lu's ear repeatedly, Lu always shaking his head as if disagreeing. Shan carried rocks with the others, and was standing in the rubble, waiting for Jara to hand him a rock to carry, when he saw that Gendun had disappeared. He visualized the sketch the old lama had made in the soil. The old tower must have been erected on a base of solid rock, and the treasure room would have been built beneath that base, far below the solid surface. But Dolan's equipment had shown a chamber inside the rubble.

The American magnate seemed to have worked himself into a strange euphoria, driving his workers on with a glint in his eyes, encouraging them not with sharp words but with what sounded like bribes. "Twenty dollars to each of you if we finish with daylight left," he announced after another half hour of excavating. An hour later he raised the payment to fifty dollars, never joining the work himself but seeming to work almost as hard, blowing his whistle, cajoling the Tibetans, telling them of the new shoes they could buy, the new hats, the new sheep, sometimes standing expectantly by the instruments again, sometimes consulting Ming, who seemed to watch his American partner with growing unease. Partner no more, Shan realized. Dolan had taken over, Dolan and the two men who worked for him had killed both of Ming's allies, and Dolan had seemed to have dropped any pretense he might share the treasure with Ming.

When Shan saw Lokesh standing over Gendun's drawing, he lowered the rock he carried onto the cairn and joined him. "There must have been a chamber in the bottom of the tower," Shan explained. "A storage room perhaps, or a passage to a stairway. He's wasting his time."

Lokesh nodded his agreement. "I have met Americans before but never one like this. I think he was never taught how to seek." It was a rare condemnation from Lokesh, or perhaps not so much a condemnation as a sad reflection on the state of Dolan's spirit. "He seeks so zealously yet there is no substance in what he seeks."

With two hours of light left they struck an opening under the rubble, a small hole that led into black shadow below. Dolan climbed onto the rocks and probed it with a pole, confirming there was a floor, or something firm to stand on, six feet below. As half the crew moved more rocks, Dolan ordered the others to bring large metal cases like suitcases from under a canvas in the courtyard. They were carrying cases, special cases for shipping fragile, expensive objects. Dolan had decided the emperor's treasure was at last within his reach.

Gendun was suddenly at Shan's side. In his hands he held several neatly folded robes, and Shan realized he must have gone below to retrieve them from the living chambers on the third level of the temple. "Why would you—" he began to ask, but saw that the lama had settled onto a flat rock and was already deep in his beads, reciting a sad, weary mantra.

To his alarm he saw Lokesh was standing beside Dolan. "This is not the way," Shan heard Lokesh say in a loud voice as he moved toward them. "You must find something of your deity first."

Without warning Dolan turned and slapped Lokesh hard on the cheek. "You insult me, old man," the American growled. "I am tired of all of you acting so damned superior. Keep it up and I'll teach you who I am."

Lokesh did not touch his cheek, did not seem to notice the blow. "Sit with us," Lokesh said in a worried voice. "We can go to a quiet place and speak of things."

Before Shan reached them Dolan had motioned Lu over, and the short Han began pulling Lokesh away. But now the American was looking at Lokesh not with anger, but with a passing curiosity.

Dolan insisted on going into the chamber first, dropping into it with a small lamp fixed to a band around his head, a rope tied to his waist. The American surveyed the group with a victorious gleam, casting a taunting smile at Corbett and Yao, who stood in the shadows. Shan watched uneasily as Ko stealthily moved beyond the Tibetans, edging closer to Dolan, studying Dolan with what seemed to be an intense fascination. Dolan disappeared into the hole and Ming began handing him equipment, two of the metal cases, a camera, more lights. They spoke, though Shan could not hear the words, and then Ming stood, making a show of removing a small radio from a pack on his belt, as if to remind everyone of his ability to summon soldiers in helicopters.

Suddenly there was a loud, terrified groan from somewhere, then an abject cry. As Ming bent over the hole the rope, coiled at his side, began sliding into the hole. There were sounds like sobbing, and as Ming lunged to grab the end of the rope his weight brought down the end of the chamber. The small mound of rubble shifted, rocks moved, dust rose, and from somewhere timbers creaked. As the dust cleared Ming was standing at the edge of a new, bigger hole, partially filled with rubble.

Everyone leapt forward, digging, pulling away the rocks and jagged pieces of timber that had been exposed by the latest collapse, Ming and Lu desperately calling out Dolan's name. In twenty minutes they had enough cleared away for Khan to fit back inside the original opening. He followed the rope and returned a minute later, Dolan on his back.

The American wasn't unconscious, did not appear physically hurt, but his eyes had a strange glaze in them. He sat on the rocks, his face drained of color, rubbing his arms as if he were cold, his eyes vacant, not reacting when Ming and Lu offered him water. Finally he stood, stepped to Ming, and shoved him to the ground. He jumped on him, pummeling his face and chest with his fists as Lu struggled to pull him away. Ming did not resist, not even when his nose began bleeding, but gazed in horror at the American.

The violence seemed to revive Dolan, who shrugged off Lu, and stood, ignoring Ming, looking at Lokesh now. "You knew, you son of a bitch!" Dolan shouted at the old Tibetan, and charged toward him as if to attack him. Shan jumped in front of Lokesh, Corbett a step behind him.

Lokesh did not retreat, did not react to the American's strange burst of temper. "I only knew that what you need would not be found here," he said in a calm voice. "I told you that."

Dolan grabbed the army radio, switched it on, then halted, looking at the Tibetans, who had fallen back to the shadows of the walls, staring in fear at Dolan, then at the slope above. Several Tibetans were running up the ridge, fleeing the wild American. He seemed about to speak into the device, then cursed, lowered it, and with a venomous expression marched back to the camp in the courtyard.

By the time Shan and Lokesh reached the entrance to the chamber Lu had tied the rope to a standing pillar twenty feet away and Ming was being lowered inside. Without a word Lokesh lowered himself onto the rocks, his legs into the hole, and dropped down as soon as Ming stepped away. When Shan followed a moment later he assumed the sound behind him was Corbett, but it was Ko who stepped to his side in the shadows, holding one of the electric lamps.

They seemed to be inside a frame of heavy timbers, a chamber perhaps twelve feet to a side, with a wooden floor whose shattered planks jutted upward at wild angles. Behind them was a short, intact wall of planks, all uniformly broken along the bottom. Ming was only a step ahead of them, navigating around the planks and other debris, nervously sweeping his light about the chamber, aiming high, mostly at the ceiling beams, because, Shan suspected, he was worried they might collapse. Suddenly Ming moaned and stepped backward. Lokesh pushed past him, paused, and reached back to touch Ko's arm. "You must bring Gendun Rinpoche," he said softly, and moved aside for Shan. Ko, his face drained of color, backed away.

Dust had long ago settled over the two dead men who sat against the wall in front of them, though not so much as to obscure their features, preserved by the dry, cold air, nor so thick as to cover the short grey hair on their scalps, or the gold fringe on the collar of the maroon robe worn by the man on the left. The man beside him wore a robe, too, and with his colorless, desiccated face he might have looked like another Tibetan monk, except for the grey handlebar moustache under his nose and the unusual raiment he wore over his robe. As Shan squatted and touched the dust-encrusted fabric, enough dust fell away for him to see it was a red tunic, a gold brocaded tunic, the dress uniform of a British soldier from another century. It was a uniform Shan had seen before, in the photograph at the cottage. Brother Bertram, once Major McDowell, seemed to be staring at his legs, which were obviously broken, and the dark stain beneath them, which probably indicated that the shattered bone had cut into blood vessels.

As Lokesh knelt by the bodies, Shan looked again at the shattered timbers along the walls, which seemed crushed from a great pressure, not broken or burned by explosion. "It was the top of the tower," Shan said as the realization hit him. "The tower was hit by a bomb at the bottom and collapsed. The top chamber slid downward, crushing the timbers." He looked toward the jagged upturned timbers at the far side of the room, where they had entered. "That's not a wall of timber, it was a veranda, a balcony that was sheared upward as the chamber fell."

"But why were they here?" Lokesh wondered. "Not in the temple?" He gently prodded at a grey blanket on the major's lap. Dust fell away, and vivid colors were revealed, diagonal stripes of red and white and blue.

"Because they were trying to stop the bombers," Shan said. "There was a place above the major's bed where something large had hung. This flag. When he learned what was happening, he grabbed his tunic and the flag, trying to make the pilots see a British soldier, a British flag, thinking it might stop them."

"And the abbot," a voice rasped behind them. Gendun had arrived. "It is the blessed abbot with him." Gendun touched the gold fringe of the robe, a symbol of high rank in the old gompa. "The last of the Stone Dragons." Shan turned. There was no sadness in Gendun's voice. The old lama was smiling radiantly as he stepped forward and reverently grasped the abbot's mummified hand. In his arm were tucked the robes from the temple. Lokesh took them and laid one over the legs of each of the dead men.

As Shan helped Lokesh, he saw Ko, standing five feet away, his light out, staring at the bodies. "They were both still alive when the rubble trapped them," Shan explained, "both suffering mortal wounds." He pointed to the odd angle of the abbot's left arm and the dark stain beside it on his robe. It had probably been a piece of shrapnel that broke the arm, and pierced his body. "They sat together in the dark, trapped, knowing they were dying, knowing their gompa was destroyed."

"No," Gendun disagreed, in a whisper. "Knowing that their gompa could never be destroyed." He settled onto the floor in front of the mummified bodies and began a mantra that had a tone not of mourning, but of greeting.

"They should have had rifles," Ko said. "You can shoot down a plane with rifles, if you know what you're doing." He ventured closer. There was something in his face that looked revulsed, yet something else that seemed to compel him to keep looking at the remains of the two old men, who looked as serene in their painful deaths as no doubt they had been in life.

When Shan looked up Ming was gone. Gendun was lost in his mantra.

"We'll need a lantern, full of fuel," Shan said. Lokesh nodded. Gendun would probably not move for hours.

"Why doesn't he just bring in the soldiers?" Ko suddenly asked. "He could rip everything apart. He can do whatever he wants."

"No," Shan said. "He can't. He wants to steal the treasure. He wants no one to know about it, no one to even know of its existence."

"We know," Ko said.

"He thinks we are powerless. He thinks he has neutralized us."

"And if he can't find the treasure he'll leave?" Ko asked.

"He knows it is here. He won't leave. He is certain he will find it. He is certain at least one of us knows, and that will guarantee he finds it."

"Gendun? Only Gendun knows, right? Dolan wouldn't . . . Gendun can be hidden. There's more of us than them." Ko, Shan realized, was asking Shan what they should do.

"Gendun won't hide, won't do anything because of fear. And Dolan doesn't know how to act without using fear," Shan said, gazing at the dead men. He felt not frightened, but strangely empowered by them, as if their tomb had been opened for a reason, to pass something on to the living.

When they returned to the camp Ming had fled.

"He called a helicopter to meet him at the old stone tower," Jara explained. "That man Lu went with him, too. They flew away just minutes ago." Dolan and Ming had argued while Dolan had been drinking from a bottle of whiskey, Jara reported. Tashi the informer had arrived in a helicopter delivering equipment, then when Dolan had gone into the tent with the whiskey Ming, Tashi, and Lu spoke quietly and began packing. "They took the radios, all the radios."

Dolan still seethed with anger, but not at Ming. His furor seemed directed to the two dead monks he had found, as if they had cheated or mocked him somehow. If he seemed determined to find the treasure before, now he seemed fanatic, obsessed beyond words with finding the amban's treasure. He ordered the remaining hill people to leave, handing each of them some American currency as they departed. Khan stayed closer now, brandishing his rifle, holding it at the ready as he walked a circuit around the ruins.

"I don't understand," Ko said as they ate fried rice prepared by Lokesh. "There are two policemen, one from America, one from Beijing. How can Dolan act like this?"

Corbett stared into the fire. "He called me over while you were hauling rocks. He reminded me he had filed complaints about me, saying I was on some kind of vendetta, that I seemed on the verge of some sort of mental breakdown. He said no matter what I said, what I reported, he would have at least four witnesses ready to say the opposite, he would have phones ringing off the hook in Washington. He said if I helped him he would guarantee I would be the next regional chief of the Bureau. I expect he already knows Yao understands the same applies to him in Beijing."

"They only have the one rifle," Ko said in an insistent voice. "I could stop that Khan, jump him with a shovel." He surveyed his companions in silence a moment. "You have no plan," he said in a voice full of accusation. "Why did we come? I thought you were going to stop them. Instead you carry rocks for them."

Corbett and Yao did not react. Shan gazed at his son with a plaintive expression but could think of no words that Ko would hear.

"We saw Khan kill McDowell. We have the right to kill him."

"No," Shan said. "No one has the right to kill."

Ko gave a snort of disgust, threw what remained of his meal on the ground, and disappeared into the shadows.

"Every emotion Ko has," Lokesh observed in a matter-of-fact tone, "has a fire in it." Before Shan could react the old Tibetan reached behind a stone and produced a handful of twigs. "Juniper," he whispered, and Shan realized that Lokesh, at least, had a plan. "I hid it, on the festival day, just in case." As he dropped the twigs into the flames he saw the query on Corbett's face. "Their smoke will attract the deities," he assured the American.

But as the twigs burned it was Dolan who appeared, staring at them with a dark expression, swaying for a moment, apparently feeling the effects of his whiskey. "We have one day," he announced. "I have to get back to board meetings in the States." The anger had left his voice, replaced by something cold and venomous. Ming had abandoned him, and the dead monks seemed to have defied him somehow. He was clearly not used to being defied. "You are going to take me to the top chamber, to the amban's treasure, tomorrow. You will help me pack everything we find, load it, then I will let you get on with your miserable lives."

No one responded. Dolan kept glancing toward the open hole where Gendun spoke with the dead. "You will forget everything. Nothing here can be so important to you," he said in an oddly plaintive tone. He reached into his pocket and produced a checkbook, began writing. "I am not an evil man, I am just a very busy man." He tore off a check. "One hundred thousand dollars," he announced, and dropped it at Shan's feet. Shan did not look at it. Dolan wrote again. "Another hundred thousand," he said, and dropped the second check onto Corbett's lap. Corbett ignored it. "Dammit. You people have nothing to gain and everything to lose. This is just business." He wrote a third time and dropped a check in front of Yao. "Made out to cash. Use it any way you want."

Corbett slowly picked up the check on his lap. "Fine. I'll help," the FBI agent said. "But for a hundred thousand dollars I want you to say you killed the girl in Seattle." He dropped the check into the fire. The action seemed to upset Dolan, who dropped to his knees and for a moment seemed about to reach into the coals to extract the smoldering check. "We're alone," continued Corbett. "No tape recorders. No witnesses who could be relied upon back home. Only us. You've already said our testimony will mean nothing. I just paid you a hundred thousand dollars. Just business."

When Dolan looked up to return Corbett's stare, his eyes seemed dull, almost confused. "I just want to get what's mine and leave. I can make you rich," he added in a hollow voice. "That's all anybody wants." As he spoke Lokesh rose and approached the brazier. His proximity seemed to disturb Dolan, who looked at Khan, standing fifty feet away with the rifle.

"We are finishing that cairn," Lokesh said to Dolan, "to honor the abbot and that British monk. Each of us will put on one more stone and offer a prayer."

They all stood. Dolan said nothing as they began to move toward the cairn, did not react when Ko slipped out of the darkness to pick up the two remaining checks where they had fallen.

Lokesh had found a prayer scarf somewhere, probably one of those that sometimes blew around the rubble, and laid a corner under the top of the stones. No one spoke as they laid on the stones, Ko lifting a large flat one for the cap. Without speaking they formed a half circle around the cairn, facing the open chamber where the dead lay. The stars were coming out and the single butter lamp by the cairn sputtered in the sand and seemed about to go out.

Suddenly Dolan appeared out of the shadows, a flat rock in his hands. He placed it on the cairn. "I didn't mean to disturb them," he said in an uncertain voice. "I wouldn't have . . ." he began again, and stopped. "Ming should have told me," he said, and awkwardly bent to pick up another rock. "What went on fifty years ago between China and Tibet, that has nothing to do with me, you know." He spoke quickly, gripping the rock tightly, using two hands as if the small stone had grown immensely heavy. He looked up, suddenly angry again. "Let it be a lesson!" he growled. "Tomorrow's the last day," he added in warning, and marched away.

"He has become," Corbett said, "the scariest person I have ever known."

"His deity is gasping," Lokesh observed in a heavy voice.

They wrapped themselves in blankets for the night, Khan standing watch with the rifle, Ko appearing and settling into a corner of the crumbling walls. Shan dropped into a troubled sleep and awoke abruptly, from a terrible nightmare, though he could remember nothing but a great sense of loss. It had been about Ko, something terrible happening to Ko, because Shan and the others had failed to act. He rose and, finding Khan asleep at his post, wandered into the moonlit ruins. He found himself in the foregate, sitting on the broad lintel stone Gendun had used on the festival day. He did not know how much time passed, an hour or more, when suddenly a voice spoke at his side.

"Why did you bring him? He's going to get himself killed. He acts like he wants to get himself killed." It was Yao.

The words did not hurt as much as Shan might have expected, because the thought had already occurred to him. "When this is over they will take him away," Shan said. "Dolan and Ming know he is a witness. He will be buried in the gulag so deep no one will ever find him. You know what they do when they want prisoners to disappear, if they don't execute them. They'll change his name, give him a new tattoo, a new background, destroy his old file. I'll have no way of ever finding him. I'll never see him again." The last words came out in such a rush of emotion Shan bent and buried his head between his hands.

"When this is over Dolan and Ming will be in prison."

"No," Shan said, lifting his head to gaze at the stars. "All we can hope for is to keep them from the treasure, keep them from hurting the lamas. Get them out of Lhadrung," he added, realizing as he spoke them that the words echoed those of Colonel Tan.

"Things can be different," Yao said. "I mean for you and Ko."

"I can't see how."

"When I get back to Beijing I'm going to see people I know. Judges. I can convince them. People who disappeared can also be brought back to life. I can bring you back to life, get you a fresh start in Beijing. You're one of the best investigators I know. I can get you work, maybe create a new job in my office for you. Once that happens we can find Ko, together."

"You're going to have enough problems in Beijing without me."

Yao gazed at Shan in silence, then seemed to force a grin. "What, that recall? It happens every year or so. Not the first time. I'll go home, have a few candid exchanges of views, and all will be forgotten."

"Not the recall. The fact that you ignored it."

The inspector's silence lasted longer this time. "I don't let criminals go free. That's not what I do."

"Go home," Shan said. "Let me find a way."

"And steal all my glory?"

"No," Shan said, and looked away. "Because I don't want you to become like me." He spoke to the darkness.

Yao didn't speak for a long time. "You and I, if we had met in Beijing, we would have become good friends."

Shan pointed to a shooting star.

"Two things I promise you," Yao said in a determined voice. "I will get Ming. And I will rehabilitate you. It's how you can save Ko. We can save Ko."

In the stillness that followed Shan replayed the conversation in his mind. Yao wanted to take Shan back, to start over in Beijing. He remembered he was supposed to be on a retreat, because he had cried out in delirium he wanted to go home. Strangely, he wondered where the cave was that Gendun had selected for him. He needed a month of silence, needed time alone to settle the unfamiliar emotions that had been surging through him since the festival day.

He did not know how long had passed when he turned to find Yao gone. He felt in his pocket and found a box of stick matches, which he put in front of him on a rock. He tore the top edge off the airline ticket envelope in his pocket, the only paper he could find, and pulled a pencil stub from his pocket. *Father,* he wrote in the moonlight, *My fear for my son wakes me up, shaking. I used to laugh when I was a son*. He stared at the words, blinking, awash in memories of his joyful youth, then lifted the pencil once more. *Show me a way to make them take me, instead of him,* he finished, then folded the paper. He made a little fire of the matchsticks and set the message on it, watching the ashes float skyward, sending his message to the heavens. Suddenly he smelled ginger and somebody was sitting beside him. But when he dared to look, no one was there.

CHAPTER NINETEEN

The last day arrived in a tempest, one of the rare midsummer storms that broke across the Himalayas into Tibet. Wind tugged at the flaps of the tent Dolan had erected, rain put out the cooking fire before breakfast could be prepared, and thunder shook the frail, crumbling walls around them. Gendun had disappeared without a trace, and Lokesh was standing in the rain when Shan found him in the foregate, looking into the sky. "It won't be much different below," the old Tibetan said to Shan, awe in his voice. "The earth is speaking today."

Dolan raged like a storm himself, full of fury, with no sign of the strange hesitation that he had shown the night before, no sign of what Lokesh had called the gasping of his deity. Ko, too, seemed like a changed person, his own brooding uncertainty replaced with a fawning attention to Dolan. Shan heard him explain to the American that they could escape the storm by going below, that he knew the way to the third level even if the others would not tell Dolan, that he would show Dolan little treasures in the chapels along the way.

"He has the checks," Corbett muttered. "Two hundred thousand dollars. He figures maybe he has a way out after all."

The checks. Shan had forgotten how Ko had retrieved the checks from the ground after the others had left them there.

Shan watched his son in dismayed confusion as they descended into the underground palace, leaving Lokesh in prayer by the cairn. Ko would not return his gaze, and seemed eager to keep Dolan or Khan between him and Shan and the others, even joked with Khan about the little golden Buddha Ko had stolen and given him. By the time they had climbed out of the tunnel chipped into the first level Ko had convinced Dolan to send Khan with the others to the third level while Ko showed Dolan the chapel treasures. Dolan readily agreed, letting Ko lead, holding a light while the American carried a sack into which he began stuffing altar pieces even as the others watched. Yao and Shan exchanged a weary glance.

No one spoke as they climbed first the stair of pegs then the narrow passage up to the mask room. As they reached the third level Shan silently led the group to the amban's quarters and lit several butter lamps. He was examining the old paintings on the walls when a low, haunting moan rose from outside the door. Warning them not to leave the chamber, Khan stepped into the corridor. Through the darkness a moment later came a groan. Corbett leapt out the door and seconds later reappeared, holding Khan's feet. The man was unconscious. Ko, holding his arms, cast a victorious glance at his father, then set Khan into the chair. As Yao began tying him to the chair with his own bootlaces, Ko retrieved the rifle from the hallway, handing it to Corbett.

"Where is Dolan?" Yao asked.

"He carried a load outside," Ko said in a hurried voice. "We must leave before he gets back."

"Where is Dolan?" Shan repeated.

"He's not a problem for us now."

Shan searched his son's turbulent face. "You left him in the maze," he said with sudden realization. "You took the light and you left him in the blackness."

"He isn't so smart for being so rich. He let me hold the only light. I didn't hit him hard, just enough to knock him down."

"You planned it," Corbett said. "It's why you told him about the chapels, why you befriended him this morning."

Ko did not seem to hear. He just stared at his father with challenge in his eyes. "You wanted justice. This is justice. I told him her body was in there with him, in one of the chapels. McDowell's."

"He could die in there," Shan said.

"He killed Punji," Ko shot back. "When it was over he was probably going to kill all of us. But then I saw how scared he was when he found those dead monks. That's when I saw what should happen to him. We should go now. Into the mountains. Back to Lhadrung if that's what you want. Leave him to rot."

Khan began to stir. He struggled against his bindings, emitted a loud roar, like a caged beast. Corbett knocked the butt of the gun against his head and the man slumped forward, unconscious again. Corbett looked at the gun and shrugged. "Sorry," he said, as if the weapon had moved on its own, then leaned the rifle against the shelves.

Shan and Yao turned back to their examination of the room, looking at the peche, studying paintings again, trying to understand the last puzzle of the mandala palace.

"We have to go," Ko urged again after several minutes.

"We have to understand," Shan said.

"Then I'll leave alone," Ko said, challenge back in his voice.

Before Shan could reply, Lokesh tumbled into the room, propelled toward the bed by a violent shove from the back. Behind him entered Dolan, a pistol in one hand, a butter lamp in the other.

As Corbett took a step toward the rifle, the pistol cracked twice. Two feet past Corbett's head, near the shelves, wooden splinters exploded into the air. "Keep going. Give me a reason," Dolan snarled. His face seemed to have lost all its color, a trickle of blood ran down one cheek. His eyes appeared to have sunk. He appeared to have aged several years. As Shan picked up one of the splinters and stepped to the shelves Dolan advanced toward Ko, who had retreated to the shadows along the wall, and slammed the pistol against his temple, knocking him to his knees.

"You didn't know the old man was coming inside with a light to find his friends, you little bastard! You were going to leave me there!" Dolan's voice still held an edge of the horror he must have felt in the darkness, thinking he was entombed in the ancient temple.

"You needed to go on retreat," Ko growled, holding his head, still kneeling.

Shan looked at his son in surprise, and took a step closer to him. Dolan warned him away with a gesture of the gun.

"That's what you think, isn't it, that my money makes me shallow, that all your mumbo jumbo about souls somehow makes you all superior." An unsettling wildness was in Dolan's eyes now. The darkness had touched him, perhaps exactly as Ko had intended. "You know nothing! I've won awards, humanitarian awards, all over the world. I earn my treasures."

"No," a slow, steady voice said. Lokesh had stood, and was staring at Dolan with an intense, accusing look. "Maybe once you understood such things, maybe once you loved them. But now you only love the owning."

"You old fool," Dolan spat back, "what do you know about the world? You people sit around and stare at your navels while people like me are shaping the world."

"You need to go back, and find what you lost," Lokesh said.

The words seemed to stab Dolan. He twisted about, grimacing, but he seemed unable to break away from Lokesh's gaze. Khan began to stir. He looked up with a gloating expression. "My hands," he growled. "Untie me and I'll teach them a lesson."

Dolan ignored him, kept staring at Lokesh. "You don't think I understand things. Think I don't have a conscience?" He took a step toward Khan. "I'll show you conscience! You want justice for Punji's killer?" With one swift movement he raised the pistol, pointed it at Khan's head, and fired.

321

No one moved. Dolan's face was like that of the wild-eyed demons on the ancient thangkas. "There! That's what Chinese do to killers, right? A bullet in the head." Khan slumped forward, his head on the table, a pool of blood spreading around it.

"Your deity is leaving you," Lokesh said. He had not taken his eyes off the American. "You can catch it only by stopping now. You have to let go, you have to start over."

Dolan seemed struck again by the old Tibetan's words. He looked at the gun in his hands, then Khan. "I don't even know how to use one of these things," he said in a small confused voice. "It just went off. You saw, it just went off."

"You're mad, Dolan," Corbett said. "Certifiable. You should be spending your money on doctors." He took a step toward the shelves, where the rifle leaned.

Lokesh stepped to the dead man, placed a hand on his back as if to comfort him, then began untying his bindings. Shan stepped to his side to help. The small-caliber bullet had left a neat circle near the center of Khan's forehead.

"That girl in Seattle," Shan said. "It wasn't you either, was it?"

Dolan waved the gun, settling its barrel on Corbett. He tilted the weapon upward as if pretending to shoot, then walked away, to stand in front of the portrait of the Qian Long emperor. "That was my car," he said in an absent voice, speaking to the emperor. "I was just watching when she was knocked unconscious."

"And you were just watching when you threw her over the side, when you dropped her bike off the second bridge?" Corbett asked. He glanced at the rifle, still leaning on the shelves.

"Little Miss Perfect," Dolan said in a voice like a stretched wire. "I could have given her so much. But she said she wasn't going to be one of my concubines. She scratched me when I tried. I would have fired her but she would have sued me, the bitch."

A deep, sad sigh wracked Corbett. "She saw you that night, when you turned off the alarms and let Lodi and Punji in."

Dolan still faced the Qian Long. "She didn't think I knew about her secret way over the wall. She always avoided me. Shared secrets with my kids. So perfect she had to come back to turn off the damned kiln." He slowly turned. "I want him to come home with me," he said.

Shan took a step forward, not understanding, but sensing that Ko was about to lunge at Dolan.

"Look at their eyes. They were great men. They understood such things, the weight of power. Take him, too," Dolan said with a motion toward the portrait of the emperor's nephew. "Roll them up," he ordered, gesturing with the gun toward Ko.

"I am not one of your slaves," Ko shot back.

"Yes you are. And after we find the treasure I have a plan for you. I am going to take you into that maze and shoot you in both legs, then leave you in the dark. The army will take your friends away and you'll die alone, after a few days." Dolan's smile seemed chiseled out of ice. "If it had been the emperor you just tried to kill you would have been condemned to the death by a thousand slices. How lucky for you."

"They don't know where the treasure is," Ko snapped. "This is as far as you go."

Dolan pulled the trigger again, then a second time. Ko jerked back, wincing, holding his hand. One of the bullets had gone through his hand. Blood began seeping through his fingers. But he stepped forward, closer, as if daring Dolan to shoot again.

"You know nothing about emperors," Dolan hissed.

Yao pulled out a handkerchief and pressed it to Ko's wound.

Shan stepped in front of the gun.

"I am going to kill him," Dolan said in a voice like ice. "Try to stop me and I'll just do it quicker, shoot him right now. You can decide, Shan, what do you want? Let me kill him slow in the dark, or quick in front of his father?"

When Ko looked into Shan's eyes there was no pleading on his countenance, only defiance.

Shan turned his back on his son, stepping in front of him. "I will take you to the amban's treasure," Shan said.

The chamber grew silent as death again.

"Dammit no!" Ko spat.

"You will take me there, you will help me load it, and get it back to Lhadrung," Dolan demanded, his empty eyes beginning to fill with a cruel, excited fire.

"I will." The words came from his own tongue but the voice seemed far away to Shan.

"You don't know the way!" Ko shouted to Shan's back.

"I know it now. Mr. Dolan showed it to me."

"I hate you!" Ko moaned.

Shan closed his eyes a moment, but did not turn, because of what he would see in his son's eyes. "But only if you promise not to hurt the boy," he said to Dolan.

"Get me the treasure and I will not hurt him."

"You will let him go back to his prison. No new charges."

"No new charges," Dolan agreed with an cold, victorious grin. "But afterwards you will surrender yourself to that Colonel as the killer of Khan. You will sign a statement that you tied him up and shot him in cold blood in revenge for his killing Lodi and Punji."

Shan lowered his eyes and nodded. He did not know how long he had stared at the floor, only became aware that everyone was gazing at him. He stepped toward the corridor. "Did you see the rays of light?" he asked. He could no longer look into Dolan's face. "There are segments of rainbows over the doors on this level, only this level, pointing upward, making a circle of rainbow segments, the bases of many rainbows. It is said that when holy men die their bodies dissolve into light, that their essence ascends to the sky in a rainbow. To heaven. Above."

"We already know there's another level," Dolan snapped.

"Over every door there is a segment," Shan continued, "except one, the entrance to the abbot's chamber next door. Because the abbot was the senior monk, the one to whom the rainbows led, who lived at the gate of heaven." Everyone but Lokesh followed. The old Tibetan lingered by the body of Khan, now laid on the floor below the shelves. He was gently cleaning the man's head, looking into his scalp, whispering the death rites. To the Tibetans one of the greatest things to be feared in death was a wound that might block the top of the head, where the soul exited.

"We go to the center of the universe," Shan said to Lokesh.

Lokesh raised a hand as though to acknowledge Shan, but did not look away from the dead man.

Dolan took a step toward Lokesh and seemed about to bark an order, then hesitated as he stared at the dead man. For a moment his eyes filled with the wild confusion he had shown when coming out of the maze. "He's gone, you fool. There's nothing left," Dolan said in an oddly plaintive tone.

"No," Lokesh said. "In some, there is more to work with in death than in life," he said in a pointed voice.

Dolan raised his pistol, but in a halfhearted, uncertain way, as if to argue with Lokesh.

Shan approached slowly, his eyes on the end of the pistol. When Shan touched the cold steel of the gun Dolan jerked, as if Shan had touched Dolan's skin. "When a killer dies," Shan said, "what's left is in danger of never finding the beauty."

For a moment Dolan searched Shan's face, as if about to ask Shan to explain, but said nothing. He let Shan push the gun down and followed Shan out of the room.

Moments later Shan stood in the center of the next room, the abbot's quarters, studying the chamber in silence. Khan and Lu had been at work. The walls had been stripped of their paintings. Four of the seven ritual bowls had been removed from the simple altar that was built into the wall, dropped onto the floor in front of it. Shan lifted one of the bowls, examining it before replacing it on the altar. "The bowls," he said quietly, studying the wall. "Khan and Lu thought they might be valuable, I think, and set them down when they saw they were not made of precious metal. They are heavy, have the heft of solid gold, but they are not gold, they are lead. Those three," he pointed to the bowls remaining on the altar, "still hold the remains of the traditional herbal offerings. The other four would have held water, which long ago evaporated." He surveyed the confused faces of his companions. "I need your water bottles."

Corbett and Yao looked at Dolan as they reached into their small packs and produced two bottles. The new Dolan who had come out of the labyrinth had become even more frightening than before. He sat on the bed, his eyes sometimes glazing over, holding his arms around his chest and swaying forward and backward. Shan saw the glance exchanged between Corbett and Yao and, alarmed that they might try to rush Dolan, touched Corbett and pointed to the empty bowls.

"Here you attain heaven by paying homage to the deity," Shan explained.

"Fuck you," Dolan said. He rose, leveling the pistol at Shan. "I pay homage to no one. You have no idea of my power."

"Nothing like the power," Shan said, "of an old Tibetan trying to help the soul of a Chinese killer."

Dolan's lip curled in a silent snarl.

"If you want to go up, to the center, you must place an offering on the altar," Shan continued. "Each of you."

Dolan's countenance did not change but he did what Shan asked, filling a bowl with water.

As Ko set the fourth bowl on the altar a muffled thud could be heard, as if somewhere nearby blocks of wood had shifted, tapping each other.

"We tested many of the walls before," Shan said, "But we had no time to check every surface, every section. When Dolan fired the shot that hit the shelves in the other room I thought it hit a book cover." He held up the splinter he had retrieved. "But this is from the wall. The bullet hit the wall behind. The wall is made of wood, painted to look like stone." He stepped to the wall by the abbot's bed, in a place he judged opposite where the bullet had struck in the other chamber. The surface was painted with a protector demon reaching toward the sky. He studied it, then laid his hands over the outstretched hands of the demon and pressed. The wooden wall moved inward, revealing a small chamber like a closet. At its rear was a crude ladder stair, made out of rough hand-hewn timber. It was the kind of stair he had seen in impoverished temples, used to reach elevated shrines. The kind that might have been used hundreds of years before when Tibetan temples were first being built.

Dolan was suddenly reluctant to ascend. He said nothing when Shan began to climb, and stood silently as Corbett, Yao, and Ko followed to the top of the old ten-foot ladder, joining Shan in a short corridor lined with fragrant wood that led to a low doorway beside which was a shelf holding over a dozen bronze butter lamps. Before he realized what he was doing Shan extinguished the electric lamp in his hand, put it on the shelf, and lit a butter lamp. Without asking why the others did the same.

They hesitated, looking at each other, then Shan gestured for Ko to lead the way. As they walked down the corridor a noise like the rustle of wind grew louder, the air colder. The side walls fell away and Ko stopped and looked at his feet. The floor, too, had fallen away. He was standing on a single beam. The beam was gold, ornately worked with figures of deer, birds, and flowers. Tethered to the beam was a yak hair rope that extended in a graceful arc into the shadows beyond. Ko extended his lamp to the side. Black water rushed underneath the beam.

"The moat," Shan said. "The symbolic ocean that surrounds Mount Meru at the center of the universe. After the oceans came golden mountains."

As Ko ventured across the beam, Dolan appeared behind them, holding another of the butter lamps. It was the hollow, angry Dolan, still holding the gun. A hungry smile grew on his face as he saw the gold beam, the symbolic drawbridge.

Past the bridge, on pedestals carved from the living rock, were seven mythical mountains, gleaming, sculpted in gold, appearing to be modeled after the peaks of the Himalayas, the first over two feet high, the others descending until the seventh was less than ten inches. Dolan pushed at several of the mountains, tried to lift the smallest, as if assessing them for shipment.

Suddenly they were in a round chamber, no more than twenty feet in diameter, under a high central dome that seemed to have been painted black, like an endless sky. A band of silver encircled the dome just above their heads, worked with images of sacred emblems, with a section of a different material marking each of the cardinal directions: gold on the north, clear crystal in the east, sapphire in the south, rubies in the west, according to the Meru tradition. The chamber's floor was surrounded by the rushing water, giving it the appearance of being suspended in a sea.

Four elegant curving altar tables were spread in a circle around the edge of the floor, with gaps like gates between them under the marks of the four directions, each altar nearly covered with renderings of deities in gold, silver, lapis, or precious jewels. As Shan walked along the richly laden altars the sound of rushing water grew stronger. When he reached the mark of the north he extended his lamp over the moat and discovered a treacherous churning of water, a violent whirlpool perhaps three feet in diameter, marking where the water drained. It was the head of the waterfall, he realized, the source of the water that swept into the chasm below Zhoka.

He turned to see the others entranced by the contents of the altar tables. Yao stood in front of the most elegant statue of the Historical Buddha Shan had even seen, a two-foot-high image cast in gold, with eyes subtly set in lapis, a face so real, so detailed, it seemed to be a life mask.

"The mandala machine," Yao whispered, "just as the amban described." He pushed a lever on a domed device of silver and gold, watching the top lift like the petals of a lotus as four concentric rings rose up in a miniature of the Zhoka palace. "They are all here, as described in the amban's letter." Beside the mandala device were two richly colored thangkas unfurled nearly horizontally on low wooden frames, then a carving of the protector deity Jambhala in jet black stone, kneeling as if about to leap, holding a huge ruby in the shape of a treasure vase, an intricate silver statue of the Future Buddha; and behind them a stately Buddha on a golden throne, the throne not the traditional one of lotus flowers but the dragon throne of the Ching empire.

Dolan was making a strange sound that one moment seemed like a prayer, the next a groan. Beyond him Corbett stood staring into the whirlpool.

Dolan picked up the black statue, which had been described in the amban's letters, staring at it, and set it by the entry to the chamber. His face had become grey again, and confusion passed over his countenance as he looked from the statue back to the empty place on the altar where it had sat. He rearranged the figures that had flanked it as though to hide its disappearance.

Shan was convinced he could persuade this Dolan, the uncertain Dolan, to leave; persuade him to reconsider, to at least buy time, let them attend to the dead monks who haunted him before stealing from them. But it seemed impossible to predict when the angry, violent Dolan would emerge, the one who killed people one moment and forgot it the next. Something was stirring inside Dolan which Dolan himself seemed unable to recognize.

But as the doubting Dolan stared at the altars, Corbett suddenly towered over him. "I can't let you do this anymore, Dolan," the FBI agent declared.

The defiance revived the angry Dolan. His face went hard again, and the pistol rose in his hand.

" little Italian shooter of yours has a clip of eight shots," Corbett said.
ot three left. There's four of us."

I kill one or two, that will stop the rest," Dolan sneered.

Corbett shook his head. "Here's how it happens. I charge you, maybe knock
the gun away. Maybe you pump a round into me, maybe not. But I'm a big guy
and you're a lousy shot. It'll take more than one to put me down, long enough
for the others to get the gun away. Without a gun you're just another two-bit
looter."

"But no matter what else, it leaves you dead." Dolan seemed to welcome the
new game Corbett was playing.

Corbett shrugged. "I've been thinking about that. These people here, the
people to whom Zhoka really belongs, they're more important than you'll ever
be. I have no one back home. If I die, then I know that people like Lokesh will
sit with me and say the right words. You know what this place has taught me
most of all? No matter how people like you screw up the world, the true things
stay true. There's always another chance."

Dolan's hand with the gun trembled. He pressed his free hand around it,
steadying it, then suddenly aimed it at Shan. "I don't have to kill you to stop you
and Yao. I will shoot Shan if you come closer. He's the one who caused all this.
He's the one who tricked me into coming here. I didn't think it would be like . . .
I should have stayed home and sent others. The rest of you can leave, but he has
to die, no matter what else, he is going to die. He's like one of those damned
protector demons, who think they will frighten you away. They think Dolan
kills. They think Dolan doesn't love the beautiful things."

Shan did not move. Dolan's eyes flared, he took a step toward Shan and pulled
the hammer back on the gun. "You think Dolan is a lousy shot? Watch this."

A shape streaked across Shan's vision, an arm shoving him aside as the gun
fired. Shan watched, confused, his ears ringing with the explosion of the bullet,
while Yao, as if in slow motion, twisted with a shudder, a hand on his belly, and
fell to his knees. Dolan stepped backward, shock in his eyes, mouth open as if to
protest something. Then, still as if in slow motion, Ko launched himself through
the air. Ko hit Dolan hard, wrapping his arms around him, trapping the hand
with the gun against his body, pushing him back, off balance, back one step then
two, under the golden mark of the north. And then they vanished.

"No!" Shan cried. In an instant he was at the edge of the floor, over the
water. Ko had taken the American directly into the whirlpool. They were gone.

He turned to see Corbett kneeling beside Yao, who was leaning against one
of the altars, speaking to them. Yao's hand was on his abdomen. Blood was
seeping through his fingers.

"Go!" Yao shouted. He was on the floor, leaning against one of the ⸝
"Ko may be hanging on below! Both of you! Run!"

Shan hesitated, looking at Yao's wound. His shirt was drenched in blood.

"It's nothing!" Yao snapped. "Go!"

Three minutes later Shan and Corbett reached the side of the underground stream, below the waterfall, sweeping their lights from side to side, studying the banks as they jogged along its course toward the outfall. At the end, where the stream cascaded into the chasm, the last iron bar, the corroded one to which Corbett had clung to two weeks earlier, was broken, twisted outward as if a great weight had hung from it. As Shan stared at the broken bar a terrible emptiness welled within.

"He probably hit his head," Corbett said in a mournful voice. "I doubt he felt anything." Shan knew he wasn't speaking of Dolan.

"Go help Yao," Shan said. "Get him to the surface." When he turned back after watching Corbett run up the tunnel a low moan rose from his throat and he dropped to his knees.

After a long time he stood, still numb, and began walking back toward the temple. There was no sign of Corbett and Yao. When he climbed through the narrow tunnel chipped in the rock he paused, then found himself walking away from the peg stairs to the next level, into the first corridor of chapels they had visited.

At first when he reached the north gate, the chamber they swam into, it seemed empty. But when he swept the room a second time with his light there was a pile of rags on the far side, hanging over the water. He approached slowly, as if in a dream, until suddenly something seized his consciousness and he was awake, running. "Ko!" he shouted.

His son was lying with an arm in the frigid water, breathing but apparently unconscious. Shan rolled him over, pulling his head onto his lap, stroking his son's hair, rubbing warmth back into his hands.

"He was carried away by that stream," a weak voice said. "I was caught under the falls. He struggled, pushed me into the falls, than he was swept away by it, and I was sinking. I kept falling, deeper. I am sorry. I still had two of those little gold statues. Then Lokesh was with me and he said those words again. You have to let it all go to start over. So I emptied my pockets, let the gold keep falling, and I began to rise." Ko rushed the last words out, and began coughing.

A quarter hour later they were ascending through the temple, Ko wrapped in Shan's jacket. Shan kept expecting to meet Corbett and Yao, kept listening for signs they were descending, but only silence came from above. "They've all gone outside," Shan explained when he saw that Lokesh had left the Stone Dragon's chamber, Khan's body still on the floor.

But when he finally set foot on the golden beam he paused. There was a new quality to the silence. Then he heard the words and a sickening paralysis overtook him once more. He managed two steps before he had to lean on one of the golden mountains for support. Lokesh was reciting the death rites.

Corbett looked up from where they sat with Yao as Shan stumbled into the chamber. "He wanted you to go," Lokesh said in an apologetic voice. "He didn't want you to see how bad it was. He had to write a letter." The old Tibetan pointed to a folded paper tucked in Corbett's pocket.

Ko appeared and, emitting a groan, knelt at Yao's side.

"The bullet hit an artery in his abdomen," Corbett explained. "He was almost gone when I returned. He knew there was no chance, he said, when he felt how hard his belly was, because it was filling with blood."

"The letter?" Shan asked.

"It's for Colonel Tan and the Council of Ministers," Corbett explained.

Ko rose and, inexplicably, began wiping the dust from all the statues.

A silent sob wracked Shan, then he settled onto the floor, numbly straightening Yao's clothing, mouthing the death rites with Lokesh as his son cleaned the deities who resided in the center of the universe.

CHAPTER TWENTY

The silence just after death is a sound unto itself, like an empty scream, a deep wrenching rumble that reaches not the ears but the essence behind the ears. Shan took Yao's hand, still warm, and pressed it between his own.

Lokesh paused to sip from a water bottle offered by Corbett and saw the pain in Shan's face. "He'll have no trouble here," he said in a calm, assuring whisper.

"Here?" Shan asked in a breaking voice.

"Zhoka. Even for a soul as meager as that American's, there might be a chance, because it was released among all the beautiful ghosts who dwell here."

Shan offered a small, sad smile. "That letter, what did he . . .?" he asked Corbett. His question was interrupted by a desperate cry from below.

Ko darted out of the chamber and returned seconds later. "It's Jara!" he reported. "He says soldiers are invading Zhoka!"

The herder stood at the foot of the stairs in the third level, agony in his eyes. "They landed in helicopters by the old stone tower," he reported, "many soldiers, all running this way."

"We must meet them," Shan said wearily. "Or else they will keep searching until they find the temple."

"We have to bring Yao," Corbett said in a grim tone. "Or they will search for him."

Even with Jara's help it was difficult work carrying Yao's body back through the temple, sealing the secret doors as they descended, but after a quarter hour Shan and Corbett were climbing the stairway to the surface.

They were almost into the sunlight when several voices simultaneously demanded that they halt. Green uniformed soldiers sprang from the shadows of the side walls, guns leveled at them. A minute later they were standing in front of Colonel Tan, who was leaning against the chorten, a cigarette in his mouth, anger in his eyes.

He pulled a folded paper from his pocket and tossed it at Shan. It was one of

Ming's draft memoranda to Beijing. *Prison Insurrection in Lhadrung,* read the heading. He seemed not to notice the grim expressions worn by Corbett and Shan. "It says it happens today."

"There was a terrible tragedy, Colonel," Corbett interjected. "Yao was killed by looters. Dolan fell to his death trying to resist them."

Shan stared at Corbett, struggling not to show his surprise.

Tan studied each of them in silence. "You're lying."

Corbett extracted Yao's letter and handed it to Tan. "Inspector Yao explained it all before he died. He was . . . he was a hero."

Tan stared at Shan without opening the letter. The colonel's gaze drifted past him and Shan watched as his anger changed, not extinguishing, but growing somehow weary. He straightened, then stepped past Shan to the wall nearest the chorten, to a white patch under a protecting shelf of stone, a patch of white flour left from the festival. Tan touched the patch, put his finger to his mouth, and turned back to Shan with an accusing glare. "If Ming's right, if this is all some scheme to help prisoners escape, it will be the end of you."

"The end of both of us, Colonel," Shan countered. "Why would you come here if you were worried about the prisoners?"

"Because Ming said so." Tan grimaced, as though regretting his words. "Because he said Tibetans are moving a large golden Buddha, the Mountain Buddha, as a means of inciting insurrection, that the prisoners are planning to escape so they can take it across the border as a gift to the Dalai Lama, enlisting local citizens as they go. He's says it's all been a conspiracy by outsiders for political destabilization of the county." His hand tightened around the letter as he stared at it with an uncertain expression, then he looked back at Corbett. "No doubt the bodies are missing," he growled.

"Only one," Corbett said.

They went down the stairs, slowly, soldiers deploying ahead as if wary of ambush. At the base of the stairs Lokesh and Ko sat with Yao's body, which was propped against the wall. Tan squatted and grabbed one of Yao's arms as if to shake him, as if to call their bluff. He instantly dropped it and recoiled from the now cool flesh. A low groan escaped his lips.

"They never understand in Beijing." It sounded as if he were apologizing to Yao. Then, abruptly, all business again, he stood and demanded to see where Dolan had fallen.

They walked slowly down the tunnel, past the waterfall, in complete silence, Tan's aides looking uneasily at the wall paintings, Tan pausing more than once to gaze at the demons, looking as if he wanted to ask questions, but each time moving on.

"Was he still alive when he was washed out of the mountain?" Tan asked as they stood at the outfall, looking at the twisted, broken iron bars.

"We don't know," Shan said. "Probably."

"We'll need his body. His heirs will need to be certain." He stepped closer to the outfall. "It's too dangerous for a helicopter down there."

"The gorge opens into the valley five miles from here," Shan explained.

"I'll send a squad."

"There're two bodies," Shan said. "Others should go, to say things."

Tan frowned. "You mean the McDowell woman. You mean Tibetans should go to say prayers for an American and a Briton? Ridiculous."

"To say prayers for two people who died in a Tibetan monastery. Take Lokesh."

"And me," Ko said, stepping forward. "I am going."

"You need a doctor," Shan protested. Ko's wounded hand still dripped blood.

Tan frowned again. "You are a prisoner. You go where I say."

Ko seemed to shrink. Shan watched his son look into the swirling black water as he replied in a slow voice. "I am a prisoner. I go where you say."

Tan began snapping orders to the aide who stood behind him. "Manacles," he added when he was finished. The officer extracted a pair of handcuffs from his belt and stepped toward Ko.

"Not him," Tan said, and pointed to Ko. "I order you to go with the recovery squad up the gorge, to help the old Tibetan keep up with my men. Tomorrow Public Security officers come to take you back to your coal mine."

He took the manacles and fastened one end around Shan's wrist. "This one goes with me," he said, "to stop the prisoner uprising." Tan closed the other end of the manacles around his own wrist.

Ko paused as the officer herded him up the tunnel, pulling some papers from his pocket and, without looking at his father, pushed them into Shan's pocket. Shan glanced down at Dolan's checks. Ko's last hope of freedom. He held Ko for a second with his free hand, then pulled something from his own pocket for Ko, who glanced at it then quickly covered it, pushing it inside his shirt. It was the sketch of Punji McDowell Shan had taken at Bumpari.

Half an hour later Shan stood with the colonel, surveying the 404 work site with a puzzled expression. The prisoners were back in the lower valley, clearing and leveling fields at the base of the high cliffs.

"I thought you would have kept them in camp," Shan observed. As he studied the landscape something tugged at his memory.

"We are not going to be cowed by rumors," Tan said, and lit a cigarette. "They were already at work when I discovered Ming's report." Shan followed his gaze toward a silver car parked between two army trucks. Ming's car.

"You mean he didn't tell you himself."

"Apparently he was not planning to share his insights with me."

As if, Shan knew, Ming was hoping the escape would be successful. Ming's desperation had not affected his political prowess. Tan would be discredited. Ming would deflect any investigation into his own activity, and his political acumen proven to Beijing. If the golden Buddha were located by Ming without witnesses, it would make him a rich man. And if the golden Buddha were revealed publicly Ming could simply seize it for his museum amid national headlines. The political gold Ming was harvesting in Lhadrung was worth more than the amban's treasure to him.

Tan did not object when Shan moved toward Ming's car. The doors were locked but in the backseat was a cardboard box, with several hammers and chisels inside. A hundred feet down the road was a small sturdy truck with three men sitting in the back, waiting. Ming had planned for every contingency.

The prisoners labored in the field at the base of the high cliff, carrying rocks, breaking the earth, pushing barrows of dirt to fill in low swales. But the only guards were the handful of soldiers who maintained the two-hundred-yard zone between the prisoners' field and the Tibetan farmers scattered over the adjoining plots. He followed Tan, still chained to him, along the back of the work site, toward the grey trucks that would take the prisoners back to the barracks at the end of the day. Tan seemed careful not only to avoid any opportunity for Shan to reach speaking distance from any prisoner, but even to make eye contact. He pulled Shan along at a near trot, studying the landscape with a predator's eyes.

"Perhaps it is indeed only a rumor," Shan suggested in a weak voice as they reached the trucks.

"Every house, every camp in the hills is abandoned," Tan announced in a terse voice. "Herds have been left in canyons, guarded only by dogs. We can find no trace of the people." When he stared at Shan his eyes held a cold fury, but also something else, something that almost looked like pain. "Don't make me do this," he said. "If you want to stop it, do it now."

Shan did not reply.

Tan studied Shan in silence, clenching his jaw repeatedly, then pulled back the canvas cover on the truck behind them. Half a dozen soldiers sat inside, alert, an unsettling hunger in their eyes. In front of them was a machine gun mounted on a tripod.

"There're two more squads," Tan explained. "Hidden in the rocks and the thicket at the base of the cliff. Procedures are dictated." He gestured toward an aide standing in the shadows nearby. "Lieutenant. The protocol."

The young officer stepped forward and straightened. "If there is sign of mutiny among the prison population one warning will be given, sir, and those who cooperate will be allowed to escape the fire by lying on the ground below the bullets."

It wasn't possible, Shan told himself. Surely they had not struggled so long to find the truth about Zhoka and the robberies, paying such a terrible price already, only to be led to this catastrophe. Surely Liya and the hill people would never be so foolish as to try, Tan would never be so foolish as to respond with such violence. But Shan looked into Tan's eyes and knew otherwise. There was no cruelty left in Tan's eyes, only a hint of sadness. He wouldn't order the guns to fire because of cruelness. He would do so because of policy, because of standing orders that gave him no discretion on how to quell prison revolts.

Shan studied the scene again, desperate to understand, hating himself for telling Tashi to tell Ming the Mountain Buddha was moving, that Dolan was trying to find it. All Shan had wanted was to separate Ming from Dolan. But now Ming's greed could destroy the 404th prison brigade. Ming was going to stage an uprising, or cause an uprising. If he had been satisfied with a false tomb surely a false uprising would be adequate for his purposes. "The man named Lu left with Ming from the mountains," Shan said.

"He's not been seen." Tan blew two streams of smoke from his nostrils. "We have no reason to look for him. You have yet to prove any of them to be criminals."

"Yao proved it."

"Yao's report disappeared in Beijing."

As they spoke, the museum director appeared at the edge of the field, wearing an army jacket over his white shirt. Someone walked beside him, draped in a long army coat, moving with small, uncertain steps, a broad-brimmed hat on his head. The figure was too tall for Lu, but Ming seemed to know him well, pausing with a hand on his shoulder, leaning toward the man to speak in his ear. Ming, too, was uncertain, Shan sensed, he only knew that the treasure was close now.

Tan's impatience was becoming obvious. He lit another cigarette, then a third, one-handed, tapping the pack, extracting a cigarette with his lips, pulling Shan along the perimeter, pointing when he saw movement in the rocks at the edge of the cliff, cursing when he saw first a scurrying pika, then a large ground bird.

As Shan's gaze moved back toward Ming the coat suddenly fell from the shoulder of Ming's companion, though the man kept moving as if not noticing it was gone.

Shan's arm shot forward of its own will, only to be abruptly stopped by the manacle. It was Surya. Ming had brought Surya to the prison brigade. It could be his way of inviting an incident, for eventually Surya would not be able to hold back, would be drawn to the old lama prisoners, and when it happened he would be deaf to the protests of the guards, would break the security line without regard to his own safety. Or it could be Ming's way of assuring that Shan would not interfere.

"Ming acts like a damned political officer," Tan groused. "Strutting along—" Tan stopped midsentence. There was a new sound. The distant bellowing of an animal, Shan thought at first, but then, after faltering, the sound became stronger, steady, a strange grinding vibration in the air. Most of the prisoners halted, staring with wonder at the cliff, where the sound seemed to originate, its power amplified by the rock face.

"Dungchen!" Shan heard Ming exclaim from nearly forty paces away.

Smiles appeared on the worn faces of the old men in rags, who had all ceased work now, dropping their tools and barrows. It was one of the long telescoping horns that he had last heard at Bumpari village, one of the horns that summoned the faithful, a sound most of the prisoners had not heard for decades.

"Dungchen!" Ming repeated loudly, as if hoping to incite the prisoners.

Tan's aides began scanning the wall with binoculars. There was no visible sign of the horn, but the top of the cliff held many clefts, covered in shadow, where the horn could be hidden.

Whistles began to blow. Half the guards along the perimeter began moving among the prisoners, yelling at them, cursing, lifting their batons in threat.

But the more the horn blew, the less the prisoners seemed to notice the guards.

"Buddha's breath!" one of the old men called, and Shan remembered how the phrase had been used in the prison tales, to describe the deep resonation of the horns. But to Shan it sounded like a booming throat chant, as if the mountain itself was throat chanting, rattling its soul. As if the Mountain Buddha were coming.

"Back thirty paces," a dry voice commanded.

Shan was not even sure Tan had spoken the order, not certain it hadn't been imagined somehow. But as he watched, one of Tan's aides ran among the guards, who slowly, reluctantly, retreated along the perimeter. Tan slowly moved along the field's edge, his face dark, sometimes pulling Shan, until they were in front of the trucks again. Shan watched the colonel, and saw that through his thinning veil of anger, a strange, remote curiosity had entered his countenance.

The sound continued for over five minutes, the guards scowling, the prisoners slowly gathering in the center of the field, the old ones still smiling, the younger ones circling about their old companions, as if to protect them. Beyond the work site the farmers began to pause in their labors, looking toward the cliff.

Suddenly the top of the high rock wall began to shift. A prisoner called out in joy. An officer called out in alarm—but even he did not move, transfixed like everyone else at the sight. A Buddha had materialized on the wall. It was one of the huge ancient banner paintings, fifty feet wide and twice as long. Without a doubt it was a work of Zhoka, for the image had all the features of the living god paintings, the huge serene smiling face looking out over the valley like a blessing, one hand holding a begging bowl, one in the earth witness mudra. The hair was blue, with a green halo around it, the eyes alive, the skin glowing with a bright gold paint. Shan knew then that he had read about the painting in Brother Bertram's journal. He recalled the pulleys and rotten yak ropes on the underground ledge, the long cavity that must have been used to store the painting, the bones arranged by Lodi to point out the location to Liya, the ox-like herder's report of people carrying things away from Zhoka the night after Lodi's death. It was the festival banner, unrolled from the top of the gompa's central tower on special days. The Mountain Buddha.

Prisoners began dropping to the ground into the lotus position, some offering loud prayers of gratitude, some standing as if paralyzed with joy, tears streaming down their smiling faces. Shan became vaguely aware of the sound of an engine being started, and turned in time to see Ming speeding away.

The guards had their batons out now, most looking expectantly at Tan, several watching Surya, who was wandering, face uplifted to the Mountain Buddha, toward the prisoners. His aides darted to Tan's side, one pointing back toward the valley. The farmers were running across the fields, hoes and rakes in hand. Children were streaming out of the few houses that could be seen, all converging toward the Buddha banner.

One aide gestured Tan toward the side of the truck. When Tan looked at the officer but ignored his obvious request to move, Shan realized the colonel had assumed a position directly in front of the gun mounted in the truck. Tan raised his head and gazed at the banner in silence.

"A monk!" an aide gasped, pointing to the top of the cliff above the banner, where a maroon-robed figure had appeared. Even from the distance, there was no mistaking the figure. From the start this had been what Gendun had meant when he said he would liberate the prisoners.

"Hard to tell at such a distance," Tan said after gazing at Gendun. "I think it's a goat."

As the aide raised binoculars to his eyes, a second, older officer pushed them down. "The colonel said it was a goat," the older man reminded the first.

"We can summon a helicopter," the first aide said. "Sever the lines with bullets, land troops on the top."

Shan realized Tan's eyes were on him. The colonel looked at him with the same impassive gaze he had held on the Buddha. For a moment he seemed to search Shan's eyes, then he sighed, and turned to his aide.

"No helicopters are available," he told his officers. "This," he said, gesturing toward the giant banner painting, "is an exercise arranged by Director Ming. They are cleaning an old artifact in the wind. Tell the men they have responded well to my training exercise." His face hardened, and he snapped several orders. The hidden soldiers jogged out of the rocks and thicket, boarding the truck with the other soldiers in combat gear, which then roared to life and headed north, leaving only the older aide and the prison guards.

"The prisoners have worked exceptionally hard this week," Tan said in a gruff voice. "They will no longer be productive in their work for the people unless they take an hour's break. I order them to stand down." He did not release Shan from the manacles, but handed him his binoculars. In the lenses Shan could clearly see the features of the lama on top of the cliff. Beside Gendun was Fiona, in her festival dress, her arm around Dawa. Jara, too, was there, and perhaps thirty other hill people. From somewhere behind Shan, from among the farmers, a bell began ringing.

It was a strangely quiet celebration, all the prisoners eventually sitting on the ground, some chanting mantras, the farmers gathered at the line of guards, children pointing to the huge Buddha, many of the older Tibetans embracing, some dropping into the posture of prayer. Surya walked among them, pausing to kneel among the children. Even from the distance Shan could see his smile. More and more Tibetans were arriving, some on foot, some galloping up on horseback.

Several of the farmers began tossing apples to the prisoners, over the heads of the guards, who looked at Tan uncertainly but did nothing to stop them. It became a strange ethereal kind of picnic, some of the prisoners taking up song. Tan seemed determined not to let Shan get closer to the prisoners, but did not object when Shan lifted the binoculars to study them. He spotted faces he knew, and longed to go to them, would have gladly suffered the batons of the guards to hear some of the old lamas say his name again, but Tan would not remove the manacle, and kept Shan in the shadows, where the prisoners would not see him.

Tan smoked, one cigarette after another, silently studying the prisoners, watching Gendun, not objecting when a Tibetan woman ventured close, nervously glancing at Shan, then offering them both apples from a pocket in her apron. Tan stared at her uncertainly, accepting the apple, his mouth opening and closing several times as if he could not find words. "Thank you," he called at last, to her back, so softly she probably didn't hear.

Tan tossed aside his cigarette, then they ate their apples slowly. When he was finished eating Tan signaled the officer, who blew his whistle. The prisoners began to rise. The banner began to roll back up on its ropes.

"I should have had him followed," Tan said as they stepped back to his car. "Ming." He offered no apology as he released the manacles from Shan's wrist. "He's safe by now, out of Lhadrung. People will protect him."

Shan looked across the valley. "No," he said. "Ming's not gone. He doesn't know Dolan is dead."

"Meaning what?"

"Meaning he thinks he is still in a race with Dolan, to take as much of their bounty from Lhadrung as possible. He's worried Dolan will get more than he does. He wants to leave Lhadrung, but his greed will be greater than his fear."

"Meaning what?" Tan asked again, as he settled into the backseat, his aide at the wheel.

Shan slid in beside him. "Meaning I have to go to the town square."

A quarter hour later, Shan climbed out in the alley beside the government center. Tashi was in the shadows at the back of the square. "I need to know what Ming did, when you told him those words, and returned in the helicopter." Shan said.

"Like you said, I told him Dolan knew about the Mountain Buddha and was planning to take it back with him, that he had changed his mind and wanted everything back. Ming asked where he could get a truck and some strong men. Then he got in his car, with that Lu, and drove south."

"South? There is nothing south."

"South," Tashi repeated.

Shan gazed down the street that led south in silence, then jogged back to Tan's waiting car. He explained what he and Yao had discovered about Ming's use of forgeries as they drove, speaking until the aide eased the car to a stop in the shadow of the wall around the abandoned brick factory.

They stayed in the shadows, crouching as they ran past the silver car, silently entering the open door. Lu was busy at a crate as they entered the loading dock of the main building, pasting a label over another label. "You can't just—" he snarled as he looked up, reaching for the pistol in his belt.

There was no sound, no warning. Tan's hand flew up, slamming the back of his own pistol against the side of Lu's head. Lu collapsed onto the crate. Inside the cavernous main hall of the building Ming had his back to them, standing with a clipboard in front of over twenty crates, some open, showing shredded paper as packing material, while a small black box played Western rock music.

Tan turned off the music. "Croft Arts and Crafts," he read loudly from the freshly pasted label on the nearest create. "Shanghai."

Ming spun about, eyes flaring.

"No doubt a contractor for the museum," Tan said.

"Of course. Restoration specialists," Ming said uneasily, searching the shadows behind Tan.

Tan shrugged. "Shouldn't be hard to verify."

"You have no authority," Ming spat.

"Perhaps you forget that this county is under martial law. You may be surprised at how much authority that gives me. I can send you to reeducation camp for a year or two without having to consult with anyone."

"Authority perhaps, in this forgotten backwater. Real power, no. Try it and I'll ruin you. People in Beijing will learn about it."

"By the time they do I will have had time to verify things."

"Things?"

"The statement by Mr. Dolan that you switched priceless artifacts in the museum for forgeries," Tan lied. "Your business arrangements with William Lodi. What do you suppose the Chairman will do when he hears you stole the Qian Long frescoes, then lied to him about a letter implicating Lhadrung? He'll have to make an example out of you. The fresco was in the public eye. You were a trusted public servant. The Chairman was embarrassed diplomatically."

Ming glanced at the door.

Tan looked at his watch. "If you hurry you can catch the evening flight to Beijing."

Ming took a step forward, stopped, obviously confused.

"You're free to go," Tan said. "But you'll only get this offer once. Tell me where the Qian Long fresco is, and I guarantee you will not be executed. Prison, for many years. But no bullet in the head."

Ming returned Tan's stare, then looked at his clipboard as if returning to his business. "I never killed anyone," he said in a distant voice. "No one was supposed to die. That was Dolan. It was all Dolan."

Shan stepped to a long, narrow crate. Inside, a slab of plaster was wra⸢pp⸣ bubble wrap, supported by wooden slats. He pulled at the plastic, revealing richly painted chain of lotus flowers along the top of a thick piece of plaster infused with horse hairs. The fresco taken from Zhoka.

"I'm not going to surrender to that bastard Yao," Ming said.

"You don't have to. Just know that it was Yao and Shan who stopped you."

Ming's hollow gaze settled on Shan a moment. "You're just one of the home-less convicts," he said. "Nobody."

"What did you do with Surya at the gompa, Ming?" Shan demanded. "After you told him you were an abbot you did something else. You crushed him. You made him think his life was a waste."

Ming fixed Shan with a thin smile. "I had my computer with me. The old fool had never seen one. I told him I could create wonderful works with the motion of a finger. I opened the computer and called up the program I have that reproduces famous paintings, creating a painting with each tap of my finger. He was terrified. He cried. But when I left the old fool kissed my hand."

And that night, Shan knew, was when Surya had destroyed his own art, had decided his life had been a sham. Because an arrogant stranger from Beijing had tricked him with a computer.

Ming turned back to Tan. "Dolan's insane, you know. People ignore it, because he's so rich. Like some of the old emperors." He stepped to the crate with the fresco, fingering a long piece of tape that extended from the top, then abruptly stepped to the crate with the papers, extracted a clean sheet, and began writing. "The emperor's fresco is in a shipping container full of computers. Agent Corbett will have to help. It was scheduled to arrive in Oregon yesterday."

Chapter Twenty-one

The guest compound was overflowing with strangers by the time Shan and the colonel arrived. Two ambulance trucks were parked by the gate, one with its lights flashing, a dozen utility vehicles nearby. Reporters had arrived from Lhasa, an officer reported to Tan, the U.S. embassy had called with inquiries about Dolan's accident, and three generals had left messages.

Dolan's body lay wrapped in canvas on a table by the fountain. Several men were photographing it as one of Ming's assistants was being interviewed in front of a television camera with the table in the background.

Tan escorted Shan to a shed on the far side of the compound, where a soldier stood guard. "Public Security comes for him tomorrow," the colonel reminded Shan. "We'll have to take him to the brig," he added, referring to the military jail at the army base near the 404th camp. They had already deposited Ming and Lu there, under heavy guard, after taking their complete statements. "This afternoon." The colonel fixed Shan with a steady, impassive gaze. "They say he wasn't any trouble," he added, then wheeled about and marched away. Tan was saying this was the end, that Shan would have to say good-bye to his son now.

Shan stared at the closed door a long time, trying to find words. The guard finally muttered something, then turned and shoved the door open. Ko sat on the dirt floor, his hand freshly bandaged, his outstretched legs straddling a familiar bag.

Ko looked up, his face empty. "Lokesh said you would need this," he said, and pushed the bag toward Shan. It was his retreat bag. They stared at it in silence for what seemed like a long time.

"When we were in the gorge," Ko suddenly said, "wrapping her body in the shroud, Lokesh told me something. He said don't mourn her death, mourn that she had only just begun to know herself. He said of all the mysteries in life, the greatest is that of finding our own deities."

Shan saw that his son was holding something in his good hand, a long canister of lacquered bamboo. "I had wrapped it in the blanket," he said as he lowered himself to the ground. "But I never thought it would . . ." He didn't finish the sentence. Ko leaned over and dropped the canister in front of him. "They have been in our family for five generations," Shan said. "You are the sixth." He pushed the canister back to his son.

Ko stared at it a long time before taking the canister in his hand again. He held it differently this time, more gingerly, even awkwardly, bracing it with his bandaged hand as he turned it, studying the faded ideograms on it before he opened the top and looked inside.

"There are sixty-four of them," Shan said, as Ko pulled the lacquered sticks from inside.

"Prayer sticks, Lokesh called them. Like beads, I guess."

"They were your great-grandfather's, his father's before. You use them to find verses."

"Verses?" Ko asked.

For a moment time stopped. Shan forgot the guard outside, forgot that a squad would soon come to take Ko away, perhaps forever. His son was asking about the Taoist verses.

"Is it funny?" he heard Ko ask, and Shan realized he was grinning. Shan shook his head, still smiling, unable to speak.

Ko gazed at the sticks. "Show me, father," he asked in a near whisper.

Shan tossed the sticks, dividing them into piles, letting Ko count as he explained the ages-old process. He repeated several verses, Ko joining him as he grasped their rhythm, his gaze always on the sticks. Finally his son slowly replaced the sticks in the canister, staring at it with something Shan had never seen on his face. Calmness. "I am the sixth," he said. "The son of the master criminal Shan Tao Yun," he added with a tiny grin. He closed the canister and handed it back to Shan. "They'll take it from me. They will destroy it, or sell it. Keep it for me."

Shan nodded solemnly, then reached into his pocket and handed him a shiny, bluish pebble. "Lokesh spent most of his life in prison," he explained. "When he was released a few months before me, he gave this to me, said he had had it all those years, that it was a protector charm of great power." Ko accepted the pebble from Shan. "He said rubbing it kept him connected with the rest of the world, the important things in the world."

Ko pushed the stone deep into his pocket. "Once or twice a year they let mail inside," he said. "Sometimes they let us send letters."

Shan struggled to keep his own voice calm. "I'll send letters. I'll try to find an address where you can write me."

The door opened and two soldiers entered, one holding a pair of heavy leg manacles. Ko stood as the chains were fastened to his ankles. "We made justice," he said in a voice suddenly proud. "When no one else could." The soldiers pulled him toward the door.

"Stay alive!" Shan said in a hoarse voice. "You know how to stay alive."

Ko replied with a defiant grin as the soldiers led him away.

Shan stayed in the shed for several minutes, staring at the canister in his hand, then packing it into the bag for his retreat.

"Someone came from the hills about the McDowell woman's body," Tan said, when Shan found him outside the gate. The ambulance with the flashing lights was gone. Dolan's body was gone. "She asked if she could use a phone to call England."

When the helicopter landed at the old stone tower the next morning, Lokesh and Jara were waiting with a heavy blanket to transport Punji McDowell's remains. They nodded silently to Shan and Liya as they climbed out, and looked with surprise as Corbett followed, picking up a corner of the blanket. Shan had gone to the little conference room the afternoon before to find Liya on the phone, tears streaming down her cheeks, trying to speak with Punji's mother in broken English. He had taken the phone from her and sat, translating between the two women for half an hour. Corbett had used the same phone an hour later, Shan at his side, as he spoke first with Bailey, then several others in America, arguing with some, then, after confirming that the emperor's fresco had been recovered, agreeing to sign a statement attesting to Dolan's heroic accidental death.

Over fifty Tibetans stood in solemn silence as they entered the courtyard with the white chorten shrine. Shan saw faces he had seen at the village, most of the Yerpa monks, many of the hill people who had gathered for the festival at the chorten, even half a dozen of the ragyapa, the old blind woman among them.

The monks took over as Shan and his friends set Punji McDowell's body by the large pyre of stacked timbers from the ruins, arranging her body by that of Brother Bertram. Another shroud lay beside that of the abbot. On the outside of his folded letter Yao had scribbled a last wish. Let me stay at Zhoka, he had asked.

Butter offerings in the shape of the sacred symbols were set around the pyre, and as Gendun began a mantra which the other Tibetans quickly joined, the monks lit these first. It did not take long for the brittle wood to ignite, and soon the flames became so hot no one could stand closer than thirty feet. The flames leapt high, and the wind died, so that the smoke rose straight into the cloudless sky.

"I don't understand," Corbett said after they had watched in silence for a quarter hour. "I thought the dead were all taken to the birds."

"Not in the old times," Shan said. "For saints and great teachers, this was the tradition." There had been another body that no one had spoken about, except a quiet whisper from Liya. Khan had been taken to the charnel ground.

It was over in less than an hour, the pyre reduced to ashes. Liya called for everyone to join her in the foregate yard, where food had been set out on blankets. Shan saw a familiar face nearby.

"Give you joy," Shan said in English. Fiona was roasting crabapples on a little brazier.

"Give you joy," Fiona replied. "My niece has been with the monks," she added in Tibetan.

Her great-niece, Shan thought, as he turned and saw Dawa standing by Gendun. But there was a stranger with Dawa, a sturdy woman to whose arm the girl clung, and beside the woman was a man whose clear, honest face looked weary from travel. Dawa's parents had arrived.

"They are going to stay," Fiona said. "They are going to help me rebuild the kiln. We are going to make pots and tsa-tsa, like the old days, tsa-tsa for everyone in the hills."

Corbett was soon surrounded by the Bumpari villagers, who brought him food and tea. Those who could speak Chinese explained how they had cleaned one of the cottages for him to live in. When they announced it, Shan saw no surprise in the American's eyes, and heard neither protest nor acceptance.

Shan left them speaking in sad, yet somehow excited tones, to sit alone near the chasm edge.

"I can still show you where that cave is," a familiar voice said behind him.

Shan patted the stone at his side for Lokesh to join him. "I need a retreat," he agreed. "But I left my bag in town. You could draw me a map."

"I will be here when you are ready. I will take you. There is a place I want to show you on the way, where cracks in the mountain form the signs of the mani mantra. There are berries ripening on the south slopes." Lokesh seemed to follow Shan's gaze toward the distant mountains and, as usual, seemed to read his mind, or at least his heart. "You found him, Xiao Shan, and he found you. This is not the end. This is a beginning."

"He asked me about the prayer sticks," Shan said. "I showed him how to use them."

Lokesh's eyes lit with great satisfaction but he did not speak. They sat in silence, watching a bird drift in the updraft below them, then, just as Shan's father had done so many times when Shan was a boy, Lokesh found his hand and squeezed it, hard, just once, then dropped it and rose. "The American said he had a message for all of us from Inspector Yao."

The group with Corbett had grown quiet. Even from the distance Shan could hear Corbett speaking of Yao and how he had stopped the looters, how the Chinese inspector had saved Zhoka.

"He speaks of the looters," Shan said to Lokesh. "But no one asks about the treasure the looters sought."

"I told our friend Corbett that Gendun still has not spoken to all the deities down there," Lokesh explained. "It will take many more weeks. Even then," he said, pausing to search for words. "Even then not everyone will be ready to go below. We know it is not for everyone."

Corbett was holding a small piece of paper in both hands as Shan stepped closer. It was one of Dolan's checks, which Shan had turned over to the American. "A hundred thousand American," Corbett said. "Before he died Mr. Dolan told Inspector Yao that he wanted this to go to Punji McDowell's children's clinic." It was one of the reasons Corbett had argued on the phone the night before. He would not agree to sign the statement on Dolan's death unless he had assurance that the check would be honored, based on the written words of the dying inspector. It was not part of Dolan's legacy, but of Yao's. Yao had signed his letter attesting that Dolan had given him two checks, made to cash, one to be used for the clinic, one to go to the parents of the woman who had died in Seattle.

But Corbett had a legacy of his own. He pointed to two large crates and a suitcase, carried down from the stone tower by Jara and his family after being unloaded from the helicopter. Jara handed Corbett the suitcase, bound with tape. Shan and Corbett had retrieved them that morning, but not from Ming's warehouse. They had been addressed to McDowell at the Children's Clinic, on the opposite side of the old brick factory. Tan had asked no questions when they had set them beside McDowell's body, had even helped to put them in the helicopter.

When Corbett pulled the tape from the suitcase revealing objects wrapped in newspapers and plastic wrap the Tibetans crowded around, sitting again as he lifted the first and unwrapped it. The priceless little fifteenth-century Buddha, set on a throne of gems, glowed in the bright light. He held it high for a moment, then set it in the hands of Fiona. "Who else had a deity taken by the godkillers?" he asked as he unwrapped a statue of Tara that had once sat in Ming's museum, then in Dolan's collection.

Shan had expected to find the suitcase with the artifacts brought by Lodi on the plane from Seattle, but the crates had seemed too conspicuous to ignore when they had found them flanking the suitcase. McDowell had sent the other artifacts taken from Dolan to the clinic. And now Corbett, who had told his superior by phone the day before that for the first time he had failed to recover stolen art, was distributing Dolan's entire collection to the people of the hills.

Shan watched as the suitcase was emptied and the first crate opened, then moved toward the shadows where a young woman in dark clothing sat watching the others. The smile with which Liya greeted Shan seemed forced. "Gendun says they will hold another festival here, when the mourning is over," he announced.

Liya seemed not to hear. "There is no path left for us," she said. "With Lodi and Punji both gone Bumpari will surely die."

"Zhoka is alive again," Shan said. "Bumpari can do what it always did, make art for the monastery."

"I found a note Punji had written to Lodi. She was going to go to Dharmsala, to tell the entire story to those with the Dalai Lama. She said that would ensure the protection of Bumpari. Now there is no one to go, no way to explain ourselves."

"I know someone. She is the new leader of Bumpari."

"I have nothing to interest the people across the border."

"You could take a story about how the Chinese empire was almost ruled by the Stone Dragon Lama, about how the destiny of the entire empire was almost changed here. That's why all of this happened."

"What are you talking about? It was just because of that treasure."

"The treasure was here because of the amban. The amban was here because of the art, because he wanted to honor the emperor with the works of Zhoka." When Shan saw the question still on Liya's face, he settled onto a rock beside her and began the story. After several minutes he realized a dozen Tibetans had gathered round. After ten minutes everyone in the foregate was listening.

When he had finished, still seeing doubt on some of their faces, he pulled a pouch from around his neck and withdrew the small silk scrolls he had carried there since leaving Beijing. "These are the final two letters between the amban and the emperor, after the amban received news of the Qian Long's offer to make him the imperial heir. The amban knew he was too ill to accept, too ill even to leave Zhoka. It is written in Tibetan, just a short note, for so much had already been said." Shan glanced up at the expectant faces and began to read:

My Cherished Uncle, there could be no honor in all the wide universe so great, no praise I could receive that would strike me so deeply. You ask me to decide quickly, but the decision has been made by time and the frailty of my body, which I must soon leave. I have often watched the wind blow the blossoms from the tree but have never seen them blow them back on. The honor I can return is the truth, and the truth is I know no matter how high the rank you might have bestowed there would have never been serenity greater than that I have found as the Stone Dragon Lama here in the mandala inside the mountains, where wisdom and beauty are one. The monastery I have been given is empire enough. Had we met again my uncle I would have given you the chance to reconsider, for I would be a ruler who yearned for compassion over power, and kindness over gold. I am a better Chinese as a Tibetan than ever I was as a Chinese.

Shan kept staring at the two-hundred-year-old letter after he had finished, unaware at first of the silence around him. When he lowered it he saw wonder in Liya's eyes, and in all those who surrounded him. "The emperor replied," he added, showing the second scroll. "Only a few lines." He raised it and read:

Noble nephew, in my heart I have crowned you my emperor. I am only ruler of this meager empire, dealing with the events of my short time here. But you deal with worlds beyond, and reach beyond time. Please keep the treasures in Tibet. May the gods be victorious.

"I brought them to leave in the temple here," Shan said, and looked at Liya as he spoke. "But now I think you should take them to the Dalai Lama." He handed the letters to Liya. "For his birthday, from the people of Zhoka." Gendun was grinning like a young boy.

It was late afternoon when Shan and Corbett climbed back to the stone tower to wait for the helicopter, Corbett clutching a rectangular package given to him by Liya.

"I've been thinking," the American said. "You should go back with me. I can arrange it. That house of mine on the island. You can live there. There's kayaks. We can kayak around all the islands. We can go fishing together. You can make a new life. You're owed a new life."

Shan's surprise and gratitude came out in a small grin. But after a moment he turned back toward the ruins. "I have a new life," he said.

"Everyone loves America," Corbett said, with a strange sound of defeat. "Everyone wants to live there."

"It's not my country," Shan said.

"Your country turned its back on you."

"That was just my government."

They sat in silence.

"That shining place," Shan said slowly. "What you called the shopping center. You said you took me there so I could see America. When I first stepped inside I thought it was a church. Then I saw the people there. I don't know, I have no words. It made me sad somehow. I'm sorry." But Shan did remember words, words that Lokesh had used after visiting a city. He said everyone seemed so thin, so transparent, they were so far stretched from their deities.

Silence returned. Corbett picked up a stone and threw it in a long arc over the ridge, then turned as the sound of the helicopter rose behind them.

"What's a kayak?" Shan asked as they stepped away from the tower.

They did not speak, only looked out the windows as they flew back to the guest house.

"I have more to write up," the American said, and stepped away in the direction of the conference room. Shan, feeling exhausted, collapsed onto the bed that had been assigned to Yao. When he awoke in the middle of the night, light still leaked around the conference room door. He entered to find Corbett asleep at the table, head on his folded arms. There was no evidence the American had been writing. He had been drawing, with pencils, pictures of Yao and the lamas. Several completed drawings were scattered across the table, several incomplete ones lay crumpled underfoot. Shan straightened one from the floor, an image of Yao with a little Buddha in his hand, that had been nearly completed before being discarded. Shan flattened out the wrinkles as best as he could, folded it, and put it in his pocket.

In the early morning Shan was sitting by a tree as Corbett emerged, bag in hand, dressed for travel.

Corbett saw the bag by Shan's side, and gestured to a car. "Where can I take you?"

"Town."

"Last night I thought about things. That little cottage on the island," Corbett said. "I'm going to open it up, live there for a while. Paint."

"You don't have to go back so soon."

"This isn't over until I give the check to the girl's parents. And I told Bailey to hold the emperor's fresco. I want to see it before it goes back."

Minutes later, as Shan climbed out, he saw the package Liya had given Corbett sitting on the American's bag. "What was it?"

"Haven't worked up the nerve yet." Corbett reached for Liya's gift. It was wrapped in several layers of heavy felt, and when the last fell away Corbett's breath rushed out. "Lama's pajamas," he whispered.

It was the framed limerick, the one the major had left in his cottage on the wall, written on army letterhead. There was a note on the back. A grin grew on the American's face as he read it, then he handed it to Shan. *The tale of the tall American dancing with the old blind woman in the moonlight will live in our hearts all our lives,* it said. *Already the children have seen a rainbow extending in the direction of America and asked if you were at the other end. When you find the right rainbow, there will be a house for you in Bumpari.*

"Will you return?" Shan handed it back and shut the car door.

Corbett put the car into gear. "All it takes is the right rainbow." He reached through the open window and grabbed Shan's hand a moment, then sped away.

Most of the night soil collectors had already left on their morning rounds, but in the old stable two women were refilling butter lamps in front of the secret painting.

"Do you expect him back soon?" Shan asked.

The nearest woman straightened and slowly shook her head. "Never. He is gone from us."

"Gone?"

"Yesterday, after the Mountain Buddha appeared," she said. "He began gathering his brushes and paints. He said he had to go, he had to go find another town where he was needed. I gave him a sack with some food and he just walked away, singing an old pilgrim's song."

Without thinking about it Shan helped the women fill the remaining lamps, then studied Surya's painting again in silence. It was how some of the saints had lived, the old man had said on his prior visit, traveling from town to town, illuminating deities. When Shan finally emerged from the compound, holding his retreat bag, a familiar car was waiting.

Tan, at the wheel, stretched across the seat and opened the door for him. Shan climbed in, clutching his bag to his chest. "Public Security came early this morning," the colonel said in a tight voice. "They're gone now. Ming, too. There will be one of those secret trials they provide for senior Party members."

Shan assumed Tan needed help with the statement he would be expected to make at Ming's trial. Yet they did not turn at the gate for the army base but continued onto a gravel road Shan knew all too well. He pressed the bag tighter to his chest and looked at the distant mountains.

"There were powder marks on Dolan's hand," Tan said as the prison compound came into view. "He had shot a gun just before he died."

"Looters," Shan said. "You read Yao's letter. He struggled with the looters, got a gun away from them."

"We both know it was a lie. Would it be so bad if one of the wealthiest capitalists in the world were shown to be a murderer and thief, a common criminal?"

Shan studied Tan's face a moment, weighing his words. He had learned in Tibet not only that justice was an elusive thing, but that it was one of the essential things, one of the true things, Lokesh would say, for which words were never sufficient. It was constructed partly of truth, partly of the spiritual. And for someone like Tan it was always at least partly political. "If it were so, an army of investigators would descend on Lhadrung from Beijing and America, then journalists and diplomats and television news teams from all over the world, hordes of them, nothing like the handful that came yesterday. Lhadrung would be under a microscope. Perhaps it would be a great opportunity for you," Shan ventured.

Tan sighed and stopped the car short of the gate, near where the supply tent had been pitched. He stared at the mountains a long time, letting the smoke drift out of his mouth. "Opportunity," he said slowly, "interests me no more." He shrugged. "I'll have to alert the adjoining counties since the looters have obviously abandoned Lhadrung."

He stepped out of the car. Shan followed. The field where the extra troops had camped was empty. As Tan lit another cigarette, Shan turned toward the wire, fifty feet away. It was the prisoners' rest day, and a few of the old men could be seen at the far side of the prison grounds sitting in a circle.

"I am going back into the mountains," he said with an uneasy feeling. Tan, pacing along the side of the car, appeared not to hear. A sentry stationed outside the gate seemed to recognize Shan and muttered something to the guard inside the entrance, who began watching Shan warily.

Finally the colonel returned to the driver's door, and seemed about to climb back in when three men emerged from the administration building, two guards and a gaunt youth, manacled, his freshly shaven head down, wearing newly issued prison greys. Shan watched in silence as the guards pulled the new prisoner toward the inner wire.

"I can't change what he did, the sentence he received," Tan said. "But I told them the 404th is harsher than any coal mine, that I deserved to keep him for all the trouble he caused me."

The prisoner was pushed toward the wire, spreading his arms to grip the fence, staring at the thin, bent figures inside. He did not move as the guards unlocked his manacles and opened the gate, did not react as they pulled him from the fence and led him through the razor-wire-lined passageway into the prison. But then he slowly raised his head as if sensing onlookers, and turned toward Shan. It was Ko.

As his gaze locked with that of his father, he froze, then was shoved forward by the guards. When he passed the razor wire, into the dead zone, he stopped and stared again at Shan, who took several steps forward, toward the wire, into the dead zone on the outside of the wire. He heard the protests of the guards, a sharp reprimand from Tan that quieted them.

Ko's mouth curled up into his defiant grin. He raised his injured hand, wrapped in a now-bloody bandage, and lifted it over his head toward Shan. Shan silently raised his own hand, and for a moment they stared at each other, both grinning, until a guard's baton found Ko's shoulder. His son dropped to his knees as the second guard's boot pushed him forward. They lifted him by the waist of his pants, carried him out of the dead zone, dropped him facefirst into the dirt, then left.

A terrible silence descended over the camp, punctuated by the sound of the gate closing, its bolt loudly clicking into place. Then a thin old Tibetan clad in prison rags hobbled from behind one of the barracks and knelt at Ko's side. In the still air Shan heard a sound, not distinct words but a tone of comfort, as the aged lama reached out and rested a hand on his son's back.

GLOSSARY OF FOREIGN LANGUAGE TERMS

Terms that are used only once and defined in adjoining text are not included in this glossary.

aku. Tibetan. Uncle.

amban. Chinese. The representative of the Manchu imperial government (Ching dynasty) in Lhasa. The office was created in 1727 and abolished by the Thirteenth Dalai Lama in 1913.

Bardo. Tibetan. A term used for the Bardo death rites, specifically referring to the intermediate stage between death and rebirth.

bayal. Tibetan. Traditionally, a "hidden land," a place where deities and other sacred beings reside.

chorten. Tibetan. The Tibetan word for stupa, a traditional Buddhist shrine including a conspicuous dome shape and spire, usually used as a reliquary.

dorje. Tibetan. From the Sanskrit *vajre,* a scepter-shaped ritual instrument that symbolizes the power of compassion, said to be "unbreakable as diamond" and as "powerful as a thunderbolt."

dronma. Tibetan. A small wooden churn used for making buttered tea.

dungchen. Tibetan. A long, deep-sounding ceremonial trumpet, usually made of telescoping sections.

durtro. Tibetan. A charnel ground, where Tibetan dead are dismembered in preparation for feeding to vultures.

dzi. Tibetan. An agate bead, typically banded or etched, worn as a protective charm.

gau. Tibetan. A "portable shrine." Typically a small hinged box carried around the neck into which a prayer and often other sacred material have been inserted.

gompa. Tibetan. A monastery, literally a "place of meditation."

gonkang. Tibetan. A protector deity shrine, often found in monastries, frequently in the lower levels of temple buildings.

goserpa. Tibetan. Literally "yellow head," one of the terms used to refer to any foreigner.

kangling. Tibetan. A ceremonial trumpet traditionally made of a human thigh bone.

khata. Tibetan. A prayer or greeting scarf, usually made of white cotton or silk.

kora. Tibetan. A pilgrim's circuit, a circumambulation around a holy site.

lama. Tibetan. The Tibetan translation of the Sanskrit *guru.* Traditionally used for a fully ordained senior monk who has become a master teacher.

lao gai. Chinese. Literally "reform through labor," referring to a hard labor prison camp.

lha gyal lo. Tibetan. A traditional Tibetan phrase of celebration or rejoicing, literally "victory to the gods."

mala. Tibetan. A Buddhist rosary, consisting of 108 beads, used to mark mantra recitation and other devotional practices.

mandala. Literally, a Sanskrit word for "circle" (Tibetan *kyilkhor*). A circular representation of the world of a meditational deity, with the particular deity at the center, traditionally made with colored sands, although its symmetrical, symbolic arrangement may also take a three-dimensional form in some temples.

mani stone. Tibetan. A stone inscribed, by paint or carving, with a Buddhist prayer, typically invoking the mani mantra, *Om mani padme hum.*

Manjushri. Sanskrit. An important member of the Tibetan pantheon, the deity of wisdom, often depicted holding a sword to cut through obscuring thoughts.

Milarepa. Tibetan. The great poet saint of Tibet who lived from 1040 to 1123.

mudra. Tibetan. A symbolic gesture made by arranging the hands and fingers in prescribed patterns to represent a specific prayer, offering, or state of mind.

nei lou. Chinese. State secret, literally "for government use only."

peche. Tibetan. A traditional Tibetan book, typically unbound in long, narrow leaves which are wrapped in cloth, often tied between carved wooden end pieces. Traditionally a peche contained the printed text of prayers and religious teachings; since they contained sacred words they were not permitted to touch the ground.

ragyapa. Tibetan. Corpse cutters, the people who perform the dismemberment of bodies that is part of the Tibetan sky burial tradition.

Rinpoche. Tibetan. A term of respect in addressing a revered teacher, literally "blessed" or "jewel."

samkang. Tibetan. A brazier, often found in monasteries, used for burning fragrant woods.

Tara. Tibetan. A female meditational deity, revered for her compassion and considered a special protectress of the Tibetan people. Tara has many forms, the two primary ones being the Green Tara and the White Tara. She is sometimes referred to as the mother of Buddhas.

tsampa. Tibetan. Roasted barley flour, a traditional staple food of Tibet.

thangka. Tibetan. A painting on cloth, typically of a religious nature and often considered sacred, traditionally painted as a portable scroll on fine cotton and sewn into a brocade frame.

tsa-tsa. Tibetan. A small image stamped in clay (often mixed with sacred substances), typically representing a religious figure.

Yama. Tibetan. Lord of Death.

Author's Note

In early 1904 one of the strangest expeditions in history began climbing over the Himalayas through Sikkim's Jelap La Pass into the unknown lands of Tibet. Acting on vague reports that Russia might be establishing a presence in the country, the British government dispatched fifteen hundred fighting men supported by nearly ten thousand porters and thousands of mules, horses, camels, buffaloes, yaks and even, as Peter Fleming reminds us in his captivating book *Bayonets to Lhasa,* two zebra-mule hybrids, all under the direction of Colonel Francis Younghusband. While this armed invasion of what was essentially a demilitarized country may not have been a high point in the foreign policy of Great Britain, the human dimensions of the campaign and its aftermath were remarkable. Colonel Younghusband's soldiers came equipped for battle, pestilence, severe cold, and treacherous mountains, prepared for everything but the society they encountered. British soldiers equipped with state-of-the-art Maxim machine guns faced Tibetans armed with matchlocks, swords, and paper protective charms. British officers squared off against lamas brandishing yak hair fly whisks and prayer beads. Neither side had rules of engagement for such encounters. Good-natured Tibetans handed the British traditional greeting scarves even as the troops advanced on Lhasa's ragtag army. The British leaders were perplexed when their counterparts sometimes offered them Buddhist prayers; the Tibetans were equally confused when the British began opening field hospitals to treat the Tibetan wounded.

The expedition did eventually reach its destination of Lhasa, negotiated the trade treaty that was its primary purpose, then quickly withdrew into the footnotes of history. But for a few souls on both sides the campaign left an indelible mark. The expedition opened a window for the first time on the outside world for the people of the high plains beyond the Himalayas, and a handful of Tibetans began attending school in India and England. Any lingering animosity was soon replaced with trust, which grew so strong that when in 1910 China made an early attempt to seize control of Lhasa, the Dalai Lama took sanctuary in British India. Colonel Younghusband soon resigned his commission, turning to a spiritual existence which led him to found the World Congress of Faiths, and he later wrote that the most spiritual moments of his long life had been in Tibet. He devoted himself to trying to build bridges between the religions of the world, especially those of the East and West. When he died in England in 1942 an image of Lhasa was carved on his tombstone and a clay sculpture of Buddha placed on his coffin. Many of the small cadre of British military and foreign service officers who took up residence in Tibet seemed to fall under the spell of the country, likewise turning to scholarly and philosophical pursuits. One, David McDonald, eventually stayed two decades in the service of the British and Tibetan governments, chronicling how Tibet changed his life in his *Twenty Years in Tibet*. Another field officer, Austin Waddell, who first entered Tibet in disguise on early intelligence gathering missions, devoted himself to the study of Tibet's complex Buddhist traditions, becoming the foremost Western authority on Tibetan culture and religion of his time.

While the Younghusband expedition represented the first significant incursion of Westerners into remote Tibet, Europeans had long been a part, albeit an obscure one, of the imperial court in Beijing. Jesuit priests had a presence in Beijing even before the Manchus arrived there to establish the Ching dynasty in the mid-seventeenth century. The beloved Qian Long emperor's passion for the arts did not exclude representative works of the West. A small but flourishing colony of European painters was supported by the Qian Long in the eighteenth century, the most prominent member of which was Giuseppe Castiglione, and by the time he began planning his retirement cottage, it was no surprise that the emperor called upon Castiglione and his Chinese protégées to assist in its adornment. That cottage, known as Juanqin Zhai, the Lodge for Weary Diligence, still stands in the Forbidden City, the building and its peculiarly Western murals having sat almost undisturbed for two centuries. The Qian Long's inclusion of lamas and elements of Tibetan culture within his court is also well documented, and he took many steps to assure that Buddhism, and Buddhist artists, flourished during his long reign.

The emperor was one of many who have, through the ages, been intrigued by Tibetan art. At first glance Tibetan thangkas may seem simplistic, stiff, even crude representations of obtuse religious subjects. But, like most good art, the more you study them the more they draw you into their complex world, in which every color, every image—from carefully arranged human hands to uplifted lotus petals—has a symbolic meaning. Their creation was a selfless, worshipful act—the names of those who created many of the finest pieces are lost to us because they did not sign their works—and no painting was complete until it had been consecrated to install its deity. The stark beauty of these godly residences is only underscored by the fact that the mortals who made them had available only the natural materials of their high mountain world, deriving their pigments from local plants and minerals. For those who would learn more about the intriguing world of Tibetan art, a number of excellent books are available. Three of the most comprehensive and helpful are *Sacred Visions* by Steven Kossak and Jane Casey Singer, and two volumes sharing the title *Art of Tibet,* one by Robert Fisher, the other by Pratapaditya Pal.

A sad consequence of the West's awakening to such art has been the looting of temples. While only a small part of Tibet's treasures survived the wholesale destruction of the Cultural Revolution in the 1960s, those that did survive were often in remote, unprotected temples, caves, and ruins. Thieves, some highly sophisticated in technique, have plundered more than a few in recent years, including the famed Nyetang shrine south of Lhasa, the extraordinary collection housed in the small museum in Tsetang, and ancient artwork from the thousand-year-old temple of Toling in far western Tibet. Centuries-old statues in shrines on the pilgrim's route around sacred Mount Kailash were bypassed by the Cultural Revolution but did not survive a ring of thieves who raided the shrines ten years ago. Time too is taking its toll on surviving treasures. Pamela Logan's *Tibetan Rescue* captures the challenges of one international effort to save the crumbling frescoes of the remote Pewar Monastery.

Tibet's earth-taming temples, of which Zhoka is a fictional example, were the depositories of some of the land's most significant early art. While such temples may not figure prominently in contemporary Buddhist teaching, during the extraordinary years when early Buddhists were embracing the animists who traditionally inhabited Tibet, such temples were the most important structures in the country. Their construction involved marvels of engineering and art. Like a Tibetan thangka, there was no aspect of their creation that was not symbolic or carefully planned to address the deities they evoked. Traditionalist Tibetans will still point out that before the earth-taming temples were built, Tibet was a land plagued by earthquakes.

———

Finally, as I will never hesitate to point out, although the characters and places in my novels are fictional, the struggle of the Tibetan people to maintain their faith, culture, and integrity unfortunately is not. The lands of traditional Tibet may be inhabited by deities, but they are also populated by thousands of silent heroes, who can teach us much about bravery and endurance on the raw edge of life, living for the things that are most important. *Lha gyal lo.*

Eliot Pattison